Gertrude Sparrow Simpson, W. Sparrow Simpson

The Life and Legend of S. Vedast

Gertrude Sparrow Simpson, W. Sparrow Simpson

The Life and Legend of S. Vedast

ISBN/EAN: 9783337393533

Printed in Europe, USA, Canada, Australia, Japan

Cover: Foto ©Raphael Reischuk / pixelio.de

More available books at **www.hansebooks.com**

THE
LIFE AND LEGEND
OF
S. VEDAST

BY

GERTRUDE SPARROW SIMPSON

AND

W. SPARROW SIMPSON, D.D., F.S.A.

Sub-Dean and Librarian of S. Paul's Cathedral
One of the Hon. Librarians of His Grace the Archbishop of Canterbury
Rector of S. Vedast, Foster Lane, London

LONDON

1896

TO THE MEMORY OF

S. VEDAST

IN THIS YEAR OF GRACE

MDCCCXCVI

IN WHICH WILL BE CELEBRATED THE
FOURTEENTH CENTENARY OF THE BAPTISM OF

CLOVIS

IN RHEIMS CATHEDRAL
WE DEDICATE
THESE OUR IMPERFECT LABOURS

W. S. S.
G. S. S.

CONTENTS

ILLUSTRATIONS IN THE PRESENT VOLUME

PREFACE

THE dedication to S. Vedast of a Church in England is so rare and unusual that, as Rector of S. Vedast, Foster Lane, in the City of London, I feel that no apology can be necessary for the interest which I have taken in the history of the Patron Saint.

When I became Rector, in 1882, a great many friends, parishioners and others, asked for information about the Saint. The period at which he lived (if indeed he was not altogether a mythical personage), the country in which he laboured, the office which he held, were entirely unknown. So I thought it desirable to deliver, in the Choir Vestry attached to the Church, a lecture on the *Life and Legend of S. Vedast*. This was subsequently read before the British Archaeological Association and was printed in the Journal of their Proceedings: a little later, with some enlargement, it appeared in a separate form, privately printed, for circulation amongst my friends, in 1887.

A visit to Arras in the autumn of 1894, led to the printing of two fasciculi, *Carmina Vedastina*, a collection of Vedastine Hymns and Poems; and *Tragico-Comoedia de Sancto Vedasto*, a Latin play in which the history of the Saint is told in a very quaint manner. And now I complete the task which I had set myself, in the issue of the present volume, the joint work of my daughter and myself.

We have tried to present, in a brief form, a sketch of the Life and Labours of S. Vedast. Part of the work has consisted of translation and adaption. There has been no attempt at originality. The great sources of information, such as the *Acta Sanctorum* of the Bollandists, the useful and more portable book *Les Petits Bollandistes*, and a considerable number of other publications, have been carefully read and laid under contribution. Copious quotations have been made, it is hoped that they have in every case been acknowledged. An Appendix has been added containing notes on various subjects which could not be conveniently dealt with in the Life itself: some of these illustrate points of archaeological interest only.

Numerous legendary stories are related in the course of this memoir. I have repeated some of them just as they were told in mediaeval times; and some of them will be read much as fairy-tales are read. I refer, especially, to such stories as that of the bleating gloves (in Appendix No. V.). The day has gone by when they can be taken as veritable histories: perhaps they were never intended to be so taken.

The Bishop of Oxford remarks, in his *Memorials of the Life of S. Dunstan*, that "among the original sources of mediaeval history no insignificant place belongs to the *Acta Sanctorum*. The value of the results which flow from the study of these monuments of devotion is not to be estimated by their direct bearing on narrative history any more than by the bulk of the volumes that contain them." He proceeds to say that "a very large proportion of the men whose lives have been thus written owed the distinction to their services done to mankind. Even the saint whose reputation is due apparently to the reported performance of posthumous miracles, must be presumed to have been such a person as would be likely to perform such acts. The ecclesiastical beatification is in a vast majority of cases the result rather than the cause of popular devotion. Many of the early biographies are thus connected directly with history, because they profess to be the private memorials of the lives of those who are the more prominent actors on the historical stage. These books, are always interesting, and sometimes most valuable."

In a Life of S. Vedast written for English readers there is a serious risk lest it should be thought that because miraculous incidents are mingled with the history of the Saint, the Saint himself should be deemed a mythical person. The writers of the biographies of mediaeval saints did not, however, hesitate to embroider upon their simple narratives such florid ornaments as seemed suitable to the occasion: and these must not be taken to weaken the solid basis of historical truth which underlies the story.

It must not be supposed that I hold myself responsible for the historic truth of the legends now to be related. It is observable that they are, for the most part, omitted in a modern *Vie de S. Vaast* intended evidently for devotional reading. But the Saint himself is a very real personage, and the conversion of Clovis, in which he played a prominent part, is an event of the very highest importance in the history of the evangelisation of France.

Of some of the miracles ascribed to S. Vedast, it will suffice to say that they are common to almost every mediaeval hagiology. The devotees of particular saints seem to have thought that they did them great injustice unless they attributed to their special heroes miracles like those of the Redeemer and of the Apostolic band. And hence the scanty story of their lives is eked out and amplified by a profusion of these legends, some almost too puerile to bear repetition.

We smile at many of these legends, and we wonder at the credulity of those who believed them, yet it is not so very long ago since, amongst ourselves, meteors, comets, parhelia, and even the aurora borealis, were thought to presage plague, pestilence, war, and bloodshed; and even in our own time, in remote country villages, poor old women have been half-murdered on the supposition that they were witches,—a supposition resting on no better foundation than the admitted fact that the unhappy victims were old and wrinkled.

Nor can it be forgotten that on March 16, 1895, a peasant woman named Bridget Cleary was roasted to death by her husband Michael Cleary, in the presence of her own father and of some neighbours.[1] They thought, it is said, that the woman herself had been stolen away by fairies, and that the living body which they were burning was a sort of phantasm.[2]

This is not the place in which to enter upon a general discussion of Ecclesiastical Miracles: but it may be well to bear in mind the careful and judicious words in which the Bishop of Stepney concludes the tenth Chapter of his Memoir on Venerable Bede. "On a review of Bede's writings as a whole," he writes,[3] "we may fairly say that the miraculous influence claimed for illustrious missionaries was confined to the first and second generation of Christian teachers in the land. To say that even in the first and second generation there was no such influence at work, would be to say more than we are entitled to say. In the earliest years of a mission, as the experience of times later than those of Bede has shown, there are occasions on which it is very difficult to say whether the Divine power which the Christian believes to be really working has wrought openly, whether the Lord has, in fact, in the sight of men confirmed the words of His Apostles with signs following."

Those are weighty sentences in which Cardinal Newman sums up the substance of his Essay.[4] These are "the conclusions to which the remarks which follow will be found to tend. They are such as these: that Ecclesiastical Miracles, that is, miracles posterior to the Apostolical Age, are on the whole different in object, character, and evidence, from those of Scripture on the whole, so that the one series or family ought never to be confounded with the other; yet that the former are not therefore at once to be rejected; that there was no Age of Miracles, after which miracles ceased; that there have been at all

[1] The scene of this atrocity was Ballyvadlea, near Clonmel in Ireland: the husband was tried at Clonmel assizes in 1895.

[2] See *Notes and Queries*. 8th series, viii, 94.

[3] *The Fathers for English Readers. The Venerable Bede. p.* 171.

[4] *Two Essays on Biblical and on Ecclesiastical Miracles*, 10th edition, pp. 99, 100.

times true miracles and false miracles, true accounts and false accounts; that no authoritative guide is supplied to us for drawing the line between the two; that some of the miracles reported were true miracles; that we cannot be certain how many were not true; and that under these circumstances, the decision in particular cases is left to each individual, according to his own opportunities of judging."

The Rev. J. B. Mackinlay, O.S.B., in his recently published *History of the Life and Times of Saint Edmund, King and Martyr*,[1] has some interesting remarks on the same subject. Whilst relating the miracles popularly ascribed to his hero, he says, "It is not intended to write a vindication of them here. Their possibility to the Creator and Ruler of the universe cannot be a subject of discussion among His children and believers. Whether He uses supernatural, or unfathomed natural forces to bring about those extraordinary results which we call miraculous is of little moment. God can manifest divine power in whichever way He wills. That He has done so times without number is beyond reasonable dispute. The history of the patriarchs and prophets in the old dispensation, and of the apostles and saints in the new, affords overwhelming evidence of the facts. Indeed not only His own glory, the honour of His servants and the spread of His Kingdom demand it, but the soul of man unconsciously looks for these displays of God's existence and provident watchfulness over the interests of His creatures. The invisible world surrounds man so closely that it would be the strangest of phenomena if it did not sometimes visibly affect his material being. Apart from these general principles a wide field is still left open for the discussion of evidence for and against any miracle in particular. To be accepted each must rest on testimony which no historian can reject or impartial judge refuse. Some of S. Edmund's miracles hardly deserve the name: his clients saw in them the supernatural, where others would see only the natural; but all of them are interesting pictures of the customs and habits of thought of the times."

[1] Octavo, London and Leamington, 1893, p. 271.

A very copious, and, it must be confessed, a very varied Appendix has been added to the *Life and Legend.*

By far the most important Article is an English translation of the earliest extant Life of S. Vedast, the work of an anonymous author, written probably towards the close of the sixth century. It has been thought desirable to present an almost verbal rendering of this ancient biography, that the English reader may lose as little as may be of the archaic flavour of the work. Here it stands in its simple dignity, the earliest attempt at a memoir of the Saint. The greater part of its substance will be found in the *Life and Legend*, but this has not seemed any sufficient reason for excluding a work of such venerable antiquity.

Article II., on the Birthplace of S. Vedast, may perhaps be held to determine the vexed question as to the country honoured by his birth. At any rate it exhibits the opinion of some of the most earnest French scholars who have discussed the question in recent times.

Article III., on the River Crinchon, a little stream mentioned not infrequently in the history, may be of slight interest to those who care for the topography of Arras, but will certainly be "caviare to the general."

In Article IV., as in other Articles, the writers have been led to wander into the pleasant bye-paths of Archaeology.

Article V., on the Miracles ascribed to S. Vedast, will be found to contain an enumeration of nearly all the wonders ascribed to him in the *Acta Sanctorum*, together with some very quaint and curious stories collected from other sources.

Article VI., "S. Vedast in Art," almost demands the aid of copious illustrations, of which a great number are lying on the writers' study table, but which certain inexorable considerations prevent our offering to the public. The list of Books given in Article XIV. will show where many of these illustrations may be found.

Article VII, S. Vedast in the ancient English Liturgies, has cost some little labour, and yet will be read by very few persons. Still, it seemed worth while to gather into a brief space some of the early Offices of the *culte* of S. Vaast in our own country.

Article VIII., on the Churches dedicated to S. Vedast, is, so far as the English Churches are concerned, a humble attempt, and not a very successful one, to examine into the interesting question of the origin and ancient history of these three churches, in London, in Norwich, and at Tathwell, of which churches only two are in existence to-day. We have been able to carry back the history of the London Church beyond the earliest date which Newcourt had supplied, and to show that it certainly existed as early as 1240 A.D. In the case of the Norwich Church, now no longer standing, a higher antiquity is claimed. Its local champion will be satisfied with nothing less than the period of Edward the Confessor, and it must be admitted that his arguments are cogent. Tathwell Church, too, is evidently of venerable antiquity.

Article IX. is a discussion of the remarkable name by which the London Church is described in official documents, "S. Vedast *alias* Foster." The opinions of various writers are cited, and the conclusion arrived at, that Foster is nothing more than a corruption of Vedast, seems to rest upon a basis which cannot be shaken.

Article X., on a Labyrinth in the pavement of the ancient Cathedral of Arras, has nothing whatever to do with the history of S. Vedast, and yet we believe that its insertion will be pardoned, because the subject of these Labyrinths (for there were many in various French Cathedrals, though the spirit of "making all things new" has caused most of them to be destroyed) is really very curious, and somewhat unfamiliar to English Antiquaries.

Of Article XII., a Note on the Library at Arras, it can only be said that a volume would be needed to do justice to the magnificent collection of manuscripts therein contained.

The few remaining Articles require no special notice here: save that Article XV. is the fullest list of Rectors of S. Vedast, Foster Lane, that has yet been printed.

The task of preparation and compilation of these

Essays has been a most delightful one: a great relief and relaxation after more serious labours. No one can know better than its Authors the manifold omissions and imperfections of the little book; but, still, it is an honest attempt to rescue from oblivion, here in the Parish which bears his name, the memory of our Patron Saint.

It is a most agreeable duty to express our grateful thanks to those who have assisted us in our labours.

First and especially to Mr. Sidney Young, F.S.A., who, during a visit to Arras, collected and presented to me an important series of books relating to S. Vedast and to the City of Arras; to Father Ethelbert Horne, who obtained for me a transcript of a prose from the Arras Missal of 1491, of which there is a copy in the Library at Douai, and has given me much valuable information as to the association of S. Vedast with Douai and with Downside; to the Rev. W. Hudson, Vicar of S. Peter Permountergate, Norwich, for important communications relating to the Church of S. Vedast which formerly existed in that City; to M. Wicquot, librarian of the Bibliothèque de la Ville d'Arras, not only for his courtesy during my stay at Arras, but for an interesting note about S. Vedast which he was so good as to transcribe for me; to the Rev. Geo. Hennessy, for the list of rectors of S. Vedast Foster Lane, printed in Article XV.; to Mons. Lavoine, for the admirable tracings from manuscripts at Arras, which have supplied three of the illustrations; and to many other kindly correspondents.

Easter, 1896.

THE LIFE AND LEGEND OF S. VEDAST

CHAPTER I.

INTRODUCTORY.

DEAN MILMAN observes, in his *History of Latin Christianity*,[1] that "no record whatever, not even a legend, remains, of the manner in which the two great branches of the Gothic race, the Visigoths in France, and the Ostrogoths in Pannonia, the Suevians in Spain, the Gepidae, the Vandals, the mingled hosts which formed the army of Odoacer, the first King of Italy, and at length the fierce Lombards, were converted to Christianity." He has been speaking in the previous paragraph of the inestimable gift which Ulphilas, the Apostle of their race, had conferred upon the Teutonic Christians, by translating the Holy Scriptures into their own language. "The Faith," he continues, "appears to steal from nation to nation, and wins King after King."

He proceeds to say that "The first conversion of a Teutonic nation to the faith, of which any long and particular account survives, was that of the Franks, by Catholic prelates, into stern proselytes to the Catholic faith. The conversion of the Franks was the most important event in its remote as well as its immediate consequences in European history. It had great influence on the formation of the Frankish monarchy.

[1] Vol. i., p. 347, edit. 1872.

The adoption of the Catholic form of faith, by arraying on the side of the Franks all the Catholic prelates and their followers, led to their preponderance over the Visigothic and Burgundian Kings, to their descent into Italy under Pepin and his son, and to their intimate connexion with the Papal see; and thus paved the way for the Western empire of Charlemagne."[1] The conversion of Clovis issued in results of profound importance to mankind.

It is in this great event that S. Vedast appears upon the scene.

The northern part of Gaul exhibited at this time the spectacle of a general disorder.[2] The Western Empire assailed on every side, encroached upon and dismembered, had fallen into decay. The Romans could no longer conceal from themselves their decadence and their ruin, and the Gauls as well as the Germans were making renewed efforts to regain a portion at least of their old independence. The Gallo-Romans of the towns of Arras, Cambrai, and Thérouanne, who had survived the havoc wrought by the barbarian hordes, were intermingled with their conquerors. In the country of the Atrebates, as indeed everywhere else, Roman institutions had disappeared. The barbarous chiefs, to whom the title of Kings was given, ruled over conquerors and conquered alike. There was no longer any security for person or for property. Force usurped the place of law; ambition and revenge spent their fury upon their victims; and the country, already utterly neglected, was soon completely devastated and ruined by the incessant raids of the intruders.

But after the first crisis, when the terrible convulsions which often accompany the birth of a new empire were passed, a fresh era began for the Gauls. Clovis,[3]

[1] Milman, *Latin Christianity*, i. 349.

[2] This paragraph and that which follows, are taken in substance from MM. de Cardevacque and Terninck's *L'Abbaye de Saint Vaast*, i. 3, 4.

[3] His name appears under several different forms: Clovis, Cludoecus, Clodoveus, Chlodovecus, Hlodoveus. In modern French the equivalent is Louis.

["Karlus

was born in the year 466, and when hardly fifteen years of age, succeeded his father Childeric, one of the Kings of the Salian Franks, in 481. His kingdom was composed of the district of Tournai and of the country of Liège: it extended to Artois and Soissons. But so small a state did not satisfy the ambition of the Prince, and hardly was he proclaimed King of the Salic Franks before Clovis attacked and defeated the Roman General Syagrius, near Soissons, and took possession of that place. Soon after, he received the submission of Rheims, Troyes, Sens, Auxerre, and many other cities.

The Franks, the most barbarous of the Teutonic tribes, had settled in a Christian country, a country already illustrious for the virtues of Remigius, the bishop who presided over the cathedral city of Rheims.[1]

A singular incident which led to the election of Remigius, or S. Remi as he is called in France, to this high office, is too picturesque to be omitted. He was in the great church at Rheims when the clergy and people were assembled to choose a bishop, and a ray of sunlight shining through a small clerestory window fell upon his head. "In the dark church, the irradiated handsome face of the young noble shone out on the people as though marked by God for their future pastor,"[2] and he was chosen by acclamation to be Archbishop of Rheims. His after-life fully justified the popular choice. An eloquent preacher, a man of saintly life, stately in manner, majestic in stature, he gained a power over his people which proved of the highest value for the consolidation of the true religion.

Clovis was a pagan, and a man of war from his youth; he was at this time only the chief of some 4,000 Frankish

"Karlus Imperator constituit Hlodoveum filium suum simul imperare cum eo." *Lambeciani Annales Francorum.* Col. 109.

"Hlodoveum. Ita ibi scriptum est. Qui quidem locus valde est notabilis, quoniam eo probari potest, unum atque idem esse nomen Ludovici et Clodovaei." Muratorius: *Rerum Italicarum Scriptores.* (Folio, Milan, 1726. Vol. ii. Pars Altera).

[1] *Dictionary of Ecclesiastical Biography*, art. "Clovis."

[2] Baring Gould, *Lives of the Saints.* S. Remigius. Oct. 1.

warriors, but full of adventurous daring and unmeasured ambition.

Some parts of the Teutonic character, says Dean Milman,[1] seemed to harmonise with Christianity. There was a depth, a seriousness, and a tendency to the mysterious which would prepare them to receive the Gospel. The Germans had the conception of an illimitable Deity, towards whom they looked with solemn and reverential awe. It was to them a degradation to represent those vast unseen powers under a human form. Their religion was in some points a nature-worship. Woden—he is also called Odin—was to them the all-mighty, all-permeating spirit, the mind, the all-wise, the god of speech and of knowledge. He was also the god of battles and of victory. Fierce, relentless, he was propitiated by human victims. At a later period S. Boniface charges some of his Christian converts with the sale of captives to the pagans for sacrifice.

The solemn groves, dark dwelling-places of the gods, the sacred trees, the strange, uncouth symbols of the Deity, survived the introduction of Christianity. It was the crowning triumph of many a Christian missionary to hew down some stately tree, venerated for ages as the special abiding-place of Deity, whilst the new converts stood around in horror, fearing lest, after all, the sleeping divinity might arise and slay the sacrilegious priest who dared to lift unhallowed hand against his sanctuary.

The heathen priests were greatly venerated throughout Germany. They presided over the sacred ceremonies of sacrifice and worship. They administered justice, branding cowardice, inflicting punishment, which the free German spirit would endure only from those who bore a divine commission.

In Christianity they found a powerful priesthood—a hierarchy of bishops, priests, and deacons, from whom they were to learn that, with the one great sacrifice upon the Cross, all human sacrifice was at an end. They were to see a purity and nobility of life of which they had never

[1] Milman, *Latin Christianity*, i, 329-334, Book II, ch. ii.

dreamed—a strength and force of moral influence entirely new. The cross of Christ glittered on the standards of the legions. "The walled cities with their towers, temples, basilicas, forums, aqueducts, baths, and churches, now aspiring to grandeur, if not magnificence," amazed the Teutonic conquerors and filled their minds with awe at the superior intellectual power even of those whom they had subdued. The mysterious sanctity which surrounded the Christian's God, hallowed the Christian bishop. It was the time for great Christian virtues. Never would Christianity appear more sincere, more devout, more commanding, or more amiable. The courage of the Christian martyrs, the fortitude even of Christian women, astonished the barbarous conquerors, and compelled their respect.

"The Teutons had always paid the highest respect to their females, a feeling which cannot exist without high notions of personal purity, by which it is generated, and in its turn tends to generate. This masculine modesty of the German character had already excited the admiration of Tacitus; marriages were held absolutely sacred, and producing the most perfect unity; adulteries rare, and visited with public and ignominious punishment."[1]

The Christian teachers often exhorted their feebler followers to imitate these virtues of the Teutons. "Amongst the chaste barbarians," says Salvian, "we alone are unchaste: the very barbarians are shocked at our impurities. *We* cherish, *they* execrate, incontinence; we shrink from, they are enamoured of, purity; fornication, which with them is a crime and a disgrace, with us is a glory."[2] Even if we make, as no doubt we must, a large allowance for the rhetorical exigencies of this weighty passage, it cannot be denied that it supplies strong evidence of the manliness and self-restraint of the conquering people.

A very different view of the question is, however, taken by Professor Kurtz.[3] "Much of what has been

[1] Milman, *Latin Christianity*, i. 362.

[2] Milman, *Latin Christianity*, i. 363.

[3] *History of the Christian Church to the Reformation*, edited by Dr. Edersheim, second edition, i. 286, 287.

vaunted about the special pre-disposition of the Germans towards Christianity" he considers to be "either exaggerated or based upon misapprehension. Admitting that in German mythology many deep thoughts, concealed under the garb of poetic legends, bear evidence of the high religious aspirations, the intellectual endowments, and the remarkable spiritual anticipations of the Germanic race, it will scarcely be maintained that these characteristics apply to it in greater measure than to the myths, speculations, or mysteries of ancient Greece. The pre-disposition should rather be traced to the peculiar character of German national life." He proceeds to specify the devotedness and attachment of vassals towards their lord; the native readiness to combat and to persevere in their struggles for their rightful ruler; their intense love of freedom; and the spirituality of those religious rites which pre-disposed them to the worship of God.

Kurtz further points out that, in general, "heathenism can only thrive on its own native soil." Transplanted into Europe, it had lost whatever elements of life it possessed: and wherever Christianity had entered, the full development of heathenism became impossible. "Besides, in many instances, the alliance of heathen rulers with Christian princesses led to the conversion of the former, and with them of all their subjects. Such influences were peculiarly characteristic of the Saxon tribes, who alone assigned so high a place to woman."[1]

Christianity had not, as yet, softened the savage manners of the northern tribes, and Clovis, though endowed with many brilliant qualities, sorely needed the influence of the true faith. His alliance with a Christian princess was the first great step towards his conversion. Clotilda, the daughter of Chilperic (of whom Gregory of Tours says that he was "the Nero and Herod of this age"), had been early left an orphan, her parents

[1] Kurtz cites the evidence of Tacitus: Inesse quin etiam sanctum aliquid et providum putant, nec aut consilia earum adspernantur, aut responsa negligunt.

having been murdered by her uncle, Gundebald, the Burgundian king.

This Gundebald came of a fierce, wild race. "Gundicar, King of the Burgundians, left four sons. The fate of the family was more like that of a polygamous Eastern prince, where the sons of different mothers, bred up without brotherly intercourse in the seraglio, own no proximity of blood. Gundebald, the elder son, first slew his brother Chilperic, tied a stone round the neck of Chilperic's wife and cast her into the Rhone, beheaded his two sons and threw their bodies into a well. The daughters, of whom Clotilda was one, he preserved alive. Godemar, his next brother, he besieged in his castle, set it on fire, and burned him alive. Godesil, the third brother, shared the same fate." [1]

Gundebald, it should be added, remained obstinately Arian; but Clotilda, his niece, through what influence is unknown, embraced the true orthodox faith, and though the daughter of an alien was a fervid and devoted Catholic.

About the year 492 or 493, as Gregory of Tours relates, the envoys of Clovis paid frequent visits to Burgundy. Here they heard tidings of Clotilda, of her beauty, of her piety, of her tragic history: and bringing their news to Clovis, were sent back again to ask her hand in marriage on their King's behalf. Gundebald dared not refuse.[2]

[1] Milman, *Latin Christianity*, i. 350, 351.

[2] This chapter is in the main based upon Milman's *History of Latin Christianity* read side by side with the chief ancient authority, Gregory of Tours.

CHAPTER II.

THE MARRIAGE OF CLOVIS AND CLOTILDA.[1]

THE brief and simple narrative of the marriage of Clovis has been expanded by the authors of *Les Petits Bollandistes*[2] into a charming and romantic story. It is here translated and compressed. As for its fidelity to historic fact, it is enough to say, that as the masters of classical antiquity are permitted to place in the mouths of their heroes elaborate speeches, which show evident traces of the historian's hand, so, no doubt, the hagiologist may fairly claim a similar licence. To the very name of Clotilda the writers give a pleasant significance. "Clotilde," they say, "signifie, en langue germaine, vaillante consellière ou bonté illustre"; whilst Clovis signifies "célèbre guerrier."

Gundebald, the uncle of Clotilda, murdered Chilperic her father, about the year 477: and the two young princesses, Clotilda and Chrone, fell into his hands. Chrone the eldest entered a convent where she took the veil, assuming the name of Mucuruna.[3] Clotilda, who was still very young, was shut up in a castle belonging to her uncle, her father's murderer, at Montmorot near Lons-le-

[1] The name of Clotilda, like that of her husband, appears in different forms: Crotechildis, Chrotildis, etc. Fredegarius, or his continuator, calls her Baldechildis or Balthildis (See Migne, *Patrologia*, Vol. 71, § 663). It is added in a note "Visitur etiam nunc ibi [in monasterio Calae] ejus sepulchrum in crypta subterranea."

[2] *Les Petits Bollandistes*. June 3.

[3] This unusual name is found in Gregory of Tours.

Saunier. The ruins of the donjon keep in which she was imprisoned are still existing.

Gundebald feared that the interest which attached to the fate of the innocent orphan, might arouse against him the hatred of the partisans of Chilperic. He treated her, however, with kindness, and the young princess became famous for her wisdom and her beauty. Although brought up in an Arian court, she remained faithful to the Catholic religion. Her gentleness, her piety, her love for the poor, made her blest by all around, especially by those to whom it was her custom to give alms.

Clovis, who was then reigning over France, heard the report of the many virtues of Clotilda, and desired to have her for his wife. From a political point of view this marriage did not offer the advantages which are usually sought in royal alliances. Clotilda could only bring to her new husband virtue, with no other treasures. Despoiled of all personal fortune by the murderer of her parents, kept in a semi-captivity which rendered her invisible even to the foreign Ambassadors sent to the court of the Burgundians, the King must seek her for herself alone, with no after thought of increased territory or of ambition.

The Catholics throughout France were in favour of the marriage, ardently trusting that it would lead to the conversion of the king, and that the orphan, when she became Queen of the Franks, might one day win them to the faith. It is natural to believe that the counsel of S. Remi, in whom the King had complete confidence, was friendly to Clotilda.

Clovis sent frequent embassies to the Burgundians, says Frédégaire, in the hope that his envoys might meet Clotilda. They were not, however, permitted even to see her. Clovis then had recourse to a stratagem which a noble Gallo-Roman, Aurelian, willingly undertook to carry to a favourable issue.

Aurelian disguised himself in the rags of a beggar, with a wallet on his shoulder, and set out alone for the city of Geneva where Gundebald was then residing. He carried the royal signet which Clovis had confided to his care. One Sunday, after Mass, Clotilda advancing, as was her wont, under the porch of the Church, was occupied in distributing her alms to the poor assembled there. Amongst them were Romans despoiled of their goods, Gauls ruined by exactions, fugitives from the countries devastated by the Franks, women, old men, and children, whom the wide-spread reputation of Clotilda's beneficence had attracted from all countries. The young Roman, who maintained, under the beggar's dress, an air of dignity, attracted her attention by the whiteness of his hands, by the perfume of his hair, and yet more by the mingled courtesy and audacity with which he drew aside her veil, in order to gaze steadfastly upon her countenance whilst kneeling before the Princess. He held out his hand to receive her gifts. Surprised, she asked the motive of his disguise and of his boldness.

"Most illustrious Clotilda," he replied, "I am Aurelian, son of a Senator of that name, of a consular family. King Clovis holds my family and myself in high favour. Since he has honoured me with the title of his guest, he has raised me to the rank of his lords, and at this moment I am accomplishing a mission which is one of the highest proofs of his confidence. 'Aurelian, son of a Senator,' he said to me, 'I have determined to seat upon the throne beside me, a princess of the same religion as thy people, a princess who is esteemed lovely above all the women of Gaul. Go, succeed in seeing her, without the knowledge of her uncle Gundebald, and if I am not deceived, if you find that she is worthy of the commendation which the world has bestowed upon her, give her my ring.' Noble princess," added Aurelian, "my expectations are surpassed." At the same time he gave her the royal signet which was to be the authentic proof of his mission.

Clotilda received the gift with joy, and said to the envoy, "A Christian is not allowed to marry a heathen. If, however, it is the will of God, if it will help me to lead the King of the Franks to know Him, I shall gladly do His bidding. Receive, I pray you, as a recompense of your service this sum of money.[1] Here is my ring.

[1] Cent solidi.

Carry it quickly to your master, and tell him from me that if he desires to become my husband, he must immediately send ambassadors to Gundebald my uncle, to ask my hand."

Aurelian promptly returned and recounted to Clovis the incidents of his journey. He was at once sent back, no longer as a beggar, but now as an Ambassador to Gundebald, to demand in the name of the King of the Franks the immediate surrender of his betrothed wife, whom the Burgundian was unjustly detaining. The exchange of the two rings between the King and the Princess, had given to Clotilda the title of betrothed. She was aware of this, and had consequently taken care to place the ring of Clovis, secretly and unknown to her uncle, amongst the other jewels of the royal treasury.

Aurelian, admitted to an audience of Gundebald, discovered that he was ignorant of all that had passed, but without hesitation said to him: "The King of the Franks sends me to claim his affianced bride whom you detain at your court." "Who is this affianced bride," replied Gundebald? "The affianced bride of Clovis my master," said Aurelian, "is your niece Clotilda. The King of the Franks has exchanged rings with her. Appoint then, yourself, the day when my master shall receive his bride."

Gundebald, greatly amazed, sought counsel from the nobles of his court. They all feared lest a refusal on his part should draw upon the Burgundian provinces the arms of Clovis; and they counselled the King on this wise: "Let the maiden be interrogated. Let us hear from her whether it is true that she has actually received the ring from Clovis, and has consented to be his spouse. Should the fact be as asserted, and if she has really exchanged pledges of betrothal, she must be surrendered without delay to the ambassador of the French King, rather than that we should be exposed to a disastrous war."

Clotilda was sent for. She affirmed that she had indeed actually received the ring of Clovis, she showed it to her uncle, and added that she would willingly become the wife of the brave monarch. Aurelian was summoned. He hastened to offer to Gundebald "un sou et un denier," the customary pledge amongst the French of a marriage contract.[1] It was agreed that Clotilda should forthwith set out on her journey to the King, and that they should return together for the solemn celebration of their nuptials at Châlons-sur-Saône, where Gundebald would make ready for their reception. The ambassadors received Clotilda from the hands of the King of Burgundy, and placed her in a covered chariot (*basterne*) drawn by oxen. But Clotilda, fearing the return of Aredius, a Counsellor of the King, who would certainly be hostile to her marriage and whose arrival was immediately expected, objected to this slow method of conveyance. "If you wish to place me safely in your master's hands," said she, "it is not in a *basterne* that we must travel. Give me a good horse, and let us hasten to leave the territory of the Burgundians, otherwise Aredius will pursue us and we shall be hindered on our way." The Franks asked nothing better, and the young maiden mounted on a swift courser, hastened on her journey.

Her expectations were fulfilled, for Aredius, who had landed at Marseilles, hastened immediately to the court of Gundebald, and received from him an account of the events which had occurred during his absence. "Let me tell you," said the Prince, "that I have contracted an alliance with the Franks, and that I have given my niece Clotilda in marriage to their King." "An alliance," replied the Burgundian Minister, "say rather that you have made the beginning of an interminable war. Have you forgotten, that your brother Chilperic, the father of Clotilda, fell by your sword, that her mother perished beneath the waters of the Rhone, and that her two brothers were slain by your command? Believe me, if she ever has the power, she will avenge their death. Send soldiers in pursuit, that they may bring her back by force. It will be an easier

[1] President Fauchet says that perhaps the offering of thirteen pence now made at the wedding mass, is a survival of this custom.

task to deal with Clovis once for all, than to cope with a lasting enmity between the Franks and the Burgundians under the influence of the new Queen." Gundebald approved this counsel, and at once sent a company of soldiers to bring Clotilda back, together with the treasures which had been given to her.

But it was too late. Clotilda and her escort had already reached the frontiers. Hearing of the pursuit by Gundebald's soldiers, she sent at once to Clovis, who awaited her arrival at Villery in the territory of Troyes, asking for instructions as to her procedure, and suggesting his armed intervention to defend her against the violence of her uncle. Clovis ordered the soldiers of her escort to burn and plunder the Burgundian towns in their immediate vicinity. They at once carried out his orders, and amidst the general confusion Clotilda safely reached Villery.

The marriage of the first Christian Queen of France took place at Soissons, in the year 493, amidst surroundings of great splendour.

Clotilda caused an oratory to be constructed in the royal palace, in which she was accustomed to spend much time in the exercises of devotion. Her large charity to the poor knew no bounds. She honoured her royal husband, studied to soften his warlike disposition, conforming herself to his mode of life in things that were indifferent,[1] gradually gaining that strong moral influence which was to issue in his conversion to the faith.

[1] Alban Butler, *Lives of the Saints*.

CHAPTER III.

CLOVIS AND CLOTILDA.

Clovis was soon to reap the benefit of his alliance with Clotilda. His gentle wife, with all a woman's ready wit and earnest piety, took the opportunity afforded by the birth of her first-born son, when her husband's heart might fairly be supposed to be softened, to endeavour to wean him from his idolatry. Gregory of Tours recounts, in a very dramatic manner, the story of her urgent pleadings with her husband :

"The gods whom you honour," she boldly said, "are nothing in the world. They can do nothing for themselves, nothing for others, for they are made of stone, of metal, or of wood. The names which you have given them are the names of men, and not of gods. Who is Saturn, who escaped and fled lest he should be driven from the throne by his own son ? Who is Jupiter ? . . . What is there that Mercury and Mars have ever done ? They were magicians, rather than deities. He who should receive honour is the great God who formed out of nothing the heavens and the earth, the sea and all that therein is; who made the sun to give its light, and adorned the heaven with stars ; who filled the sea with fishes, the earth with animals, the air with birds ; at whose command the earth brought forth fruit, by whose hand the human race was created, and by whose bounty it is sustained." [1]

The historian, it will be observed, does not hesitate to

[1] Gregory of Tours.

use the names of Roman deities, and to make Clotilda speak as if she were of the Latin race. He composes very elaborate speeches, and puts them into the mouths of the several actors in the scene.

Clovis listened to her gentle pleading, and although he was not convinced by his wife's appeals, he yielded so far as to permit the baptism of the child. The little one was named Ingomir. Unhappily the child died soon after the sacred rite, passing away whilst still wearing the white baptismal robe.[1] The King did not hesitate to ascribe its death to the resentment of his offended deities. "Had the child," he said, "been dedicated to my gods, it would have lived: baptised in the name of the God whom you worship, it could but die." His pious wife, however, did but reply: "I thank God, the omnipotent Creator of all, Who hath not deemed me unworthy, and has deigned to receive into His kingdom my first-born child. My heart cannot retain its sorrow now; for I know that children who die whilst vested in the chrisom will live for ever in God's presence."

Clotilda's influence with Clovis must have been very powerful, for when a second son was born she prevailed so far that this also was baptised. The name given to the babe was Chlodomir. Once more the mother's faith was called upon to endure a severe trial, for the child fell sick, and her husband hastened to remind her of its brother's death, and to predict a fatal issue in this case also. But Clotilda's prayers were heard, and by God's mercy the child was restored to health.[2]

It was not, however, to the God of the babes and sucklings that the King's proud head should bow; but, rather, to the God of Hosts. The Franks and the Alemanni fought at Tolbiac (now called Zulpich, a small town seven leagues from Cologne), and the tide of battle turned against the arms of Clovis. The day was nearly lost, when Aurelian approaching the King, besought him

[1] "In ipsis albis obiit."—Gregory of Tours.

[2] *Liber S. Gregorii Toronis Episcopi: Corpus Francicae Historiae* (Folio, Hanoviae, 1613.)

to call upon the Lord of heaven, of whom Clotilda his Queen had so often spoken.

Moved even to tears, as Gregory of Tours declares, Clovis raised his eyes to heaven and cried: "O Jesu Christ, whom Clotilda my Queen proclaims to be the Son of the living God, who givest help in time of trouble, who givest victory to those who trust in Thee, I devoutly pray Thine aid. Grant me the victory over mine enemies, and I will believe in Thee and be baptised in Thy name. I have invoked my gods, and they have turned a deaf ear to my petition. They are powerless to help. I call upon Thee, the true Lord and God; I desire to believe in Thee. Deliver me, I pray Thee, from mine enemies." And at his prayer, the tide of battle turned. The King of the Alemanni was slain, and his people, in danger of total destruction, hailed Clovis as their sovereign.

Clotilda without delay sent to Remigius, the Bishop of Rheims, the good news of the vow and of the answered prayer. Her ceaseless preaching of Christ by her lips and in her life was now to have its reward, and the words of S. Paul were to be fulfilled: the unbelieving husband is sanctified by the believing wife.

The Bishop at once called upon Clovis to fulfil his vow, but the King hesitated. "Gladly would I hear thee, blessed father," said he; "one thought alone hinders me; the people whom I lead are not prepared to renounce their gods. I will go to them, and speak according to thy word." His warriors heard him eagerly. "The mortal gods," they cried, "we cast behind us, O glorious King. The true immortal God, whom Remigius preaches, Him we are prepared to follow."

Our own English history can supply a story not dissimilar, for here also a royal princess has exercised a marvellous power in the planting of the religion of Jesus.

"Tradition records the gentle and lovable virtues of Queen Bertha, and her judicious zeal for the conversion of her husband and his subjects. It is believed to have been from her that Gregory received his information as to the desire of the English to be converted, with which he had enlisted the interest of Brunehaut and her sons.

The great-granddaughter of S. Clotilda seemed thus destined to be herself the S. Clotilda of England. She has left a brief illumination on those distant and dark horizons, over which she rises like a star, the herald of the sun of truth." [1]

The delightful story of Ethelbert's conversion cannot here be told. Suffice it to say that the deep faith of his wife Bertha, who was the daughter of Caribert, King of the Franks of Paris, and grandson of Clovis, greatly strengthened the hands of S. Augustine, and conduced to the re-conquest of England for the faith of Christ.

[1] Montalembert, *Monks of the West*, iii., 343.

CHAPTER IV.

THE CONVERSION OF CLOVIS.[1]

MM. DE CARDEVACQUE and Terninck are of opinion that the Christian Faith had cast its first beams of light upon the Atrebates about the year 270, A.D.

In *Gallia Christiana*, however, the early Christianising of Arras is dismissed in a single sentence: "non proferant monumenta." From the same source is taken this brief but pleasant description of the country of the Atrebates. "It rejoices in the salubrity of its atmosphere and the fertility of its soil; it abounds in all the necessaries of life, wine only excepted; its produce is so plentiful that it sends annually large quantities of corn to distant regions." The people of the country even founded a colony in Britain at Callevam Atrebatum, that is to say, at Silchester.

It is more pleasant to believe, with the authors of *L'Abbaye de Saint-Vaast*, that in spite of the opposition of emperors and heathen priests, in spite of the revolt of human passions, the holy word had triumphed, and the ancient city of the Atrebates[2] was Christian by the fourth century. Those who accept this view affirm that Arras, in very early times, became the seat of a Bishopric, and received as its first pastor Saint

[1] The early part of this Chapter is a translation, somewhat condensed, of MM. de Cardevacque and Terninck's memoir of S. Vedast in their work *L'Abbaye de Saint Vaast*. Vol. i., pp. 6-10.

[2] The name Atrebates is still preserved in the names Arras and Artois.

Diogenes. This Prelate laboured so earnestly for the conversion of the people, that within a brief space of time he had built several churches; of these the first and most important was that of Arras, which he dedicated to Notre Dame.[1] After an episcopate of about eighteen years, he was martyred in his church by the Vandals, who were ravaging the cities of the province of Artois, and who had pillaged and burned the City of Arras, reducing the Cathedral Church to ruins.

In those ruins lay entombed the Christianity which Saint Diogenes had preached, and whose truth he had generously attested by shedding his own blood: so that, after a time scarcely any vestige of it remained, the few surviving inhabitants who had escaped the sword and the flame relapsed insensibly into idolatry, having now no one to instruct them.

Always calm in the midst of so many calamities and disorders, the priest, holding the Cross between the oppressed and the oppressor, exercised the sole moral authority in the midst of the overthrow of society; but frequently blood flowed in the Churches, the ministers of religion were slaughtered at the foot of the Altar, and the Bishops in their apostolic zeal were only too often martyrs. It was necessary then to curb, in the name of the faith alone, the fierce passions of the conquerors, and to supply strength to the conquered. The barbarians desired to annihilate the last traces of Christianity. God in His great wisdom, however, ordained that the Franks, who by their occupation of the country could have re-established idolatry there, should on the contrary be the means of its overthrow.

Even before the reign of Clovis, a large number of the Franks had embraced Christianity. There needs no better proof of this fact, than the election to the Frankish throne of Egidius, a Christian prince, as the successor of Childeric the First, who was driven out by reason of his licentious conduct.

[1] "Diogenes ecclesiam construi curavit, eamque Deiparae Virgini nuncupavit." *L'Abbaye de Saint Vaast*, i., 6.

The city of Arras remained without a Bishop until the time of S. Vaast,[1] the celebrated Apostle who was chosen by one of the greatest saints of the French Church to establish the Christian Faith in that country. But his mission was difficult and very perilous, for he had to struggle both against the votaries of the ancient Druids, and against the violence of the Germans protected by Chararic and Ragnacaire.

The birthplace of the pious Bishop, who prepared Clovis to receive baptism, and who evangelised an important part of Gaul, is not certainly known. According to some authors, he was born in the province of Aquitaine, famous for so many holy confessors.[2] Others have maintained that Vedast[3] was kinsman to S. Firmin, Bishop of Verdun; but this assertion is incapable of proof, and we believe that the biographers have only spoken of the spiritual relations between two men who emulated each other in zeal, in charity, and in devotion.

The *Vie de Saint Vaast* printed at Arras in 1887, states that the saint was born between the years 445 and 450 A.D.; that he lived, as a poor man, in the vicinity of Toul, and that he selected this particular district because he had heard from the Bishop of Verdun, his uncle, that it was a stronghold of paganism.[4] M. Taillar, in his history of the Abbey of S. Vaast says, that the Saint went to the borders of the Meuse, preaching the Christian faith at the peril of his life; that he was ordained priest about the year 486, and continued to labour in this district for some ten years: "the ancient Celto-Belgians, the degene-

[1] Fuit civitas Atrabates sine principe sacerdotii usque ad tempus Sancti Vedasti. Balderic. *Chronicon Cameracense et Atrebatense.* Cap. vi.

[2] See Note ii., in the Appendix, *On the birthplace of S. Vedast.*

[3] The primitive name of our Saint Vedast has formerly been abbreviated to VEAST. It is so spelt in a MS. in the Library at Arras. It is only in later times that it has been disfigured into VAAST. (Note in *L'Abbaye de Saint Vaast*, p. 7.)

[4] The Bollandists, and later, Ghesquière, who devoted all his learning to the Saints of Belgium and the north of France, have left no document which might elucidate this question. They lean, however, to the opinion which has just been expressed.

rate Romans, worshippers of Jupiter and Venus, the German tribes, fierce and fanatical idolaters, promising a rich harvest for his zeal." [1]

Admitted to the holy order of the priesthood, and earnestly desiring a life of solitude, Vedast retired to the banks of the Meuse in the diocese of Toul. There he lived, in solitude, until the Bishop of that place enrolled him amongst his clergy. From time to time he emerged from his hermitage to preach, and by his earnest exhortations to lead to the true God many who did not know Him: and soon his virtue, his gentleness, his charity, and his ceaseless self-devotion, acquired for him a popularity far beyond anything which he had hitherto experienced.

But God, who knew his fervid faith, reserved for him a yet higher office. Clotilda, Queen of France, had retained the Christian faith in all its purity, and her influence had induced her husband to abandon his idols, and to adore the Crucified. After the battle of Tolbiac, Vedast was chosen to instruct him. His preparation for baptism was mainly due to the teaching of Vedast, aided by the influence of the pious Clotilda and of S. Remi, Archbishop of Rheims, whom the Queen had summoned to her assistance, for she greatly feared lest, whilst abandoning idolatry, Clovis might fall into the errors of Arianism, having heard that he had talked much with Thierry, King of Italy, who was an Arian, as was also Lantechild, sister of Clovis.[2]

Something beyond the example of the most exalted virtue, and the teaching of the priests, was needed to touch the proud heart of this haughty and barbarous monarch: miracles were needed. God who desired the conversion of the nation, manifested His power by supernatural deeds, which produced a profound impression.

Clovis, accompanied by his court, was returning victorious from his battle with the Germans, and passing by the town of Tours, he encountered Vedast and besought him

[1] *Vie de S. Vaast.* Ch. iii.
[2] *Vie de S. Vaast.* Ch. v.

to go with him to Rheims in order to give him full instruction upon Christian Baptism, which he desired to receive at the hands of S. Remi. When they reached the bank of the river Aisne, near the village of Rilly,[1] a blind man who had for years stationed himself on the bridge lifted up his voice, and besought the Saint to give him sight. Vedast, whilst with characteristic modesty he shrank from so unusual a petition, trusted that God would manifest His power so that by a miracle the yet ignorant warriors who formed the King's escort might be converted. Offering a fervent prayer to heaven, he laid his right hand on the suppliant's eyes, and making the sign of the Cross said, "Lord Jesus, Thou who art the true Light, Who didst open the eyes of the man who was born blind, open also the eyes of this man, that the people may understand that Thou art the only God who workest miracles in heaven and earth." Immediately the blind man received sight,[2] and following the holy Priest, gave glory to God. Later on a Chapel was erected on the spot where this miracle had taken place.

Clovis, greatly impressed by what he had witnessed, and confirmed in his faith, became still more desirous to be baptised. He hastened on his journey, with S. Vedast as his companion, and in due time arrived at Rheims, where all was prepared for the solemn ceremony.

[1] The *Vie de S. Vaast* says, "at Vongise, a hamlet on the river bank." Ch. vi.

[2] The organs of vision were destroyed: "ses yeux étaient absolument éteints." *ibid.*

CHAPTER V.

THE BAPTISM OF CLOVIS.

THE night before the baptism of Clovis, S. Remi visited him in his palace, and conducting him with the Queen and a great number of princes and officers to the Chapel of S. Peter, gave them a discourse on the unity of God, the vanity of idols, the incarnation of the Eternal Word, the redemption of the human race, the last judgment, the hell of the impious, and the paradise of the just. Then the chapel was filled with light and with a wondrous fragrance, and a heavenly voice was heard, saying, "Peace be with you. Fear nothing. Continue ye in My love." The countenance of S. Remi shone in the glittering radiance; the King, the Queen, and all the Court prostrated themselves at his feet. He raised them up, and predicted to them the future greatness of the Kings of France if they would remain faithful to God.[1]

The next day Clovis went to the Church of Notre Dame, where the baptismal ceremony was performed with the utmost splendour; no accessories were wanting which might impress the minds of the pagan warriors in attendance upon their King. "The procession moves from the palace; the clergy lead the way, bearing the Holy Gospels, the cross, and the banners, singing hymns and canticles; then comes the Bishop leading the King by the hand; after him, the Queen; lastly, the people. On the road it is said that the King inquired of the Bishop if *that* were the kingdom of Heaven promised to

[1] *Les Petits Bollandistes.* October 1. S. Remi. pp. 590, 591.

him. 'No,' said the prelate, 'but it is the entrance to the road that leads to it.'[1]

"The church was hung with embroidered tapestry and white curtains; odours of incense, like airs of Paradise, were diffused around; the building blazed with countless lights. When the new Constantine knelt in the font to be cleansed from the leprosy of his heathenism, 'Gentle Sicambrian,' said the Bishop, 'bow thy neck! Burn what thou hast adored; adore that which thou hast burned.'"[2] The holy Bishop signified by these words the heathen idols which Clovis had adored, and the Christian churches which he had destroyed.[3] The King replied distinctly, according to the teaching of S. Vedast, his instructor, "I adore the true God, Who is the Father, the Son, and the Holy Ghost."

The time arrived when the baptismal water should be consecrated. But just at the critical moment it was found that there was no hallowed oil. The clerk who bore the unguentarium could not penetrate the dense crowd. S. Remi, in this emergency, raised his eyes to heaven, and prayed that God would supply that which was wanting. At the same moment, a dove whiter than snow descended from on high, carrying in its beak a phial full of celestial unguent, prepared by the ministry of angels, which it bore to the hands of the prelate. He received with amazement and with thanksgiving the heaven-sent gift, and pouring part of it into the font, anointed the head of the King. At the same time, the dove flew away and disappeared; but the phial remained. It is that which is called to-day the Sainte Ampoule.

Cardinal Baronius says that in addition to the baptismal unction, S. Remi conferred upon the King the royal unction, which has ever since been administered to the Kings of France in the august ceremony of their

[1] Baring Gould, *Lives of the Saints.* S. Remigius.

[2] Mitis depone colla, Sicamber: adora quod incendisti, incende quod adorasti. (Gregory of Tours).

[3] Milman, *Latin Christianity*, vol. i., pp. 352, 353.

consecration. For this purpose the holy oil of the Sainte Ampoule has been employed, for it was preserved intact until the days of the French Revolution.[1]

A very similar account is given in the life of S. Clotilda:[2] but, as a few picturesque details are added, it may be well to insert them here.

Clovis, having recited the Apostles' Creed, passed with the Bishop into the Jordan, for so they called the sanctuary of circular form, in the midst of which was a large font of porphyry filled with consecrated water. Looking toward the East, the figure of the true Light, then to the West, the symbol of darkness, S. Remi poured upon the forehead of Clovis the water of baptism. At that moment a dove descending from heaven bearing in its beak a little ampulla,[3] entered the baptistery by one of the open windows.

S. Remi took the ampulla, and poured upon the head of Clovis some drops of the sacred oil which it contained. After the holy rite Clovis came forth from the baptistery clothed in the white robe of a neophyte, and approaching the prisoners of Tolbiac took off their fetters. The King of France commenced his new life by an act of mercy. "O Clovis," sang the bards, "no earthly power is equal to thine: for the aureole of the Christian shines on thy forehead:[4] one of thy hands holds a spear, and the other rests upon the Cross."

The font of red marble in which Clovis was baptised is preserved in the great Library at Paris;[5] and Rheims, the church of his baptism, became the place where, in after times, the Kings of France were wont to be crowned.

The exact date of the Baptism of Clovis is Christmas

[1] *Les Petits Bollandistes.* Oct. 1, p. 591.

[2] *Les Petits Bollandistes.* June 3. S. Clotilde.

[3] The same ampulla, say some, has ever since been used at the Coronation of the Kings of France. See Note xi. in the Appendix.

[4] L'auréole du Chrétien rayonne sur ton front.

[5] The font is engraved in MM. Bordier et Charton's *Histoire de France*, vol. i., p. 126, "Cuve en marbre rouge, que l'on suppose avoir servi au Baptême de Clovis, conservée à la grande Bibliothèque de Paris."

Day, A.D. 496.[1] The fourteenth centenary of that event will be celebrated with great magnificence at Rheims on Christmas Day of the present year 1896.

The three thousand men who were about to be baptised together with their leader, cried aloud, "We abhor the mortal gods, and we are ready to serve the immortal God." The same day were also baptised the sisters of the King; Albofleda,[2] who had been a heathen; and Lantechild, who had been an Arian.

Upon the subject of these "wholesale conversions" accomplished by Christian princes, Professor Kurtz observes[3] that whole heathen tribes were baptised without having received any adequate previous instruction. "At the same time," he adds, with great candour, "it must be admitted that only in this manner considerable and rapid results could have been obtained; nay, that in the infant state of the German races, something may be said in favour of this practice."

"According to the measure of his knowledge, Clovis was sincere and earnest in his profession of Christianity. Not that he had undergone any change of heart: he had made a compact with the God of the Christians, and he was prepared faithfully to observe its terms. It affords sad proof of the low state of religion at the time, that the grossest faithlessness, treason, and assassination, stained the life of Clovis after his baptism. The conversion of Clovis, however, sealed the doom of the barbarous and fanatical Arianism of the German tribes."[4]

It seems very strange that a whole tribe should, on the instant, change its faith at the word of command, following its chief into a new religion just as it would have done into a new field of battle. But due allowance must be made for the habit of obedience to a ruler, and for the powerful ascendancy which such a warrior as Clovis would have gained over his subjects. With scanty

[1] See the *Dictionary of Ecclesiastical Biography*.

[2] Quae non post multum tempus migravit ad Dominum. *Gregory of Tours*.

[3] *History of the Christian Church*, i., 287.

[4] Kurtz. *History*, i., 294.

instruction, and with little moral change, they would follow his example. And yet it cannot be denied that very important results flowed from these conversions, if such they may be called.

It cannot be correct to say that Clovis had undergone no change of heart. The mere fact of his submission to Christian baptism appears to be proof to the contrary. The acts of a newly-converted heathen at the close of the fifth century, are not to be judged by the standard of full Christian life in the nineteenth.

A characteristic incident has been recorded, arising out of one of the interviews between Clovis and Remigius, in which the true spirit of the barbarous warrior-king breaks out. During one of their conferences the Bishop dwelt upon the cruelty of the Jews to the crucified Redeemer. Clovis was moved as he heard the story of the Passion; moved, but not to tenderness. "Had I and my faithful Franks been there," said he, "I would have avenged His wrongs."[1] The good Prelate's words had touched the King; but the hands which had so successfully wielded the sword, only longed to strike the blow.[2] Well; there had been, in the bygone days, others (better instructed than he) who said, "Wilt Thou that we command fire to come down from Heaven and consume them?" not knowing what spirit they were of. It was not very wonderful if a new convert (and such a convert) had yet much to learn.

At that time Clovis, the Frank, was the only Catholic Sovereign in Christendom; so that the importance of his conversion can hardly be exaggerated. It is not necessary to enter into his subsequent history. It will suffice to say that he remained a Christian to his life's end; that in the early part of the year 511 he summoned a council of thirty-two bishops to Orleans; and that before the close of the year he died, and was buried

[1] Si ego ibidem cum Francis meis fuissem, injurias ejus vindicassem. See Fredegarius, *Epitom.* Ch. xxi., tom. ii., p. 400.

[2] "It was a prophecy of the sword of Charles Martel, of Charlemagne, of Godfrey of Bouillon." *Vie de S. Vaast*, Ch. vii.

in Paris, in the Church of the Apostles, afterwards called S. Geneviève, which he and his wife Clotilda had built.[1]

Alcuin, in an eloquent passage, compares the work of S. Vedast and of S. Remi in the conversion of Clovis. The one led the King onward to the fountain of life; the other laved him in the fountain of eternal salvation. The one ministered to him the doctrine of the Faith; the other gave him the water of baptism. The two together gave unto the King Eternal, the Earthly King as an acceptable offering. These are the two olive branches,[2] these the two brilliant lamps, by whose instrumentality the King, instructed in the way of God, and rescued from the fetters of the Evil One, by the mercy of God entered the gate of everlasting life, being called out of darkness into marvellous light.[3]

"Avitus, Bishop of Vienne, addressed a letter to Clovis, in which he augurs, from the faith of Clovis, the victory of the Catholic faith. Even the heterodox Byzantine emperor is to tremble on his throne; Catholic Greece is to exult at the dawning of this new light in the West."[4]

How grand a spectacle, says Avitus, to behold a throng of sacred ministers assisting at the baptism of a great King; to see that head, feared by the nations, bow itself before the servants of God; that hair, nourished beneath the martial helmet, receive by the holy unction the helmet of salvation; that warrior, quitting for the time his cuirass and clothing himself in a white robe, the symbol of innocence and purity.[5]

The ceremony ended, Pope Anastasius wrote a congratulatory letter to Clovis; and he, in turn, presented the Pope with a crown of gold. The event ranks in importance next to the conversion of Constantine.

After the death of Clovis (in 511 A.D.) Clotilda lived principally at Tours, paying rare visits to Paris. Her

[1] *Dictionary of Ecclesiastical Biography.*
[2] The reference is to Zechariah iv., 2, 11.
[3] *Acta Sanctorum.* Feb. 6, p. 804, col. 2.
[4] Milman, *Latin Christianity*, i., 353. Avitus, *Epist.*, 41.
[5] *Vie de S. Vaast*, Ch. vii.

daughter was married to Amalaric, the Visigothic King of Spain. After the death of her son Chlodomir, she gave shelter to his children, until they were craftily abstracted from her care, and two of them murdered by their uncles. She was the real or reputed foundress of several religious houses, notably of S. Mary of Andelys, near Rouen, to which girls were sent for education from England during Bede's time.[1] The original foundation was destroyed by the Normans. Clotilda, however, remained the patron saint of the place, and miracles were worked there in her name down to the Revolution, and have re-commenced since. She died at Tours in 545, and was buried at Paris beside her husband in the Church of the Apostles, afterwards S. Geneviève.[2]

Clovis had several sons. Theodoric or Thierry, the eldest son, was illegitimate. The sons of Clotilda were Ingomir, who died soon after baptism; Chlodomir, Clotaire, Childebert, and Lothaire. She had also a daughter who bore her mother's name.

[1] *Historia Ecclesiastica*, iii., 8.

[2] *Dictionary of Ecclesiastical Biography*, art. "Clotilda," by T. R. Buchanan, Fellow of All Souls', Oxford.

CHAPTER VI.

THE LABOURS OF S. VEDAST.[1]

After the Baptism of Clovis, some writers affirm, that S. Vedast returned at once to his beloved solitude: but others, with greater probability, that he remained at Rheims; Clovis having specially recommended him to the favourable notice of S. Remi.[2] Here he became a most successful preacher to the poor, as he had been to the King; and here he remained some four or five years.

His biographer delights to dwell upon his austerities, his constancy in prayer, his deep devotion, his chastity, his frequent fasts, his zeal in consoling the afflicted whose needs he freely supplied, preaching to them patience, and counselling them to have recourse to prayer, the consolation of all that are in trouble. He set before them the kingdom of heaven, in which the highest place is reserved for those who have meekly endured the trials of this lower world. With entire trust in God's provi-

[1] This Chapter is mainly a translation and adaptation of MM. de Cardevacque and Terninck's memoir of S. Vedast in *L'Abbaye de Saint Vaast.* (Vol. i., pp. 10-20), and of the *Vie de S. Vaast* printed at Arras in 1877.

[2] Baptizatus itaque rex cum optimatibus suis ad sceptra regni regreditur: Vero S. Vedastus cum B. Remigio per aliquod temporis detinetur. Balderic, Lib. i., Cap. vii.

Remis aliquandiu commoratus Vedastus, sanctissimi Praesulis amorem haud aegre sibi conciliavit. *Breviarium Atrebatense.* Feb. 6. Lectio. v.

"Omnibus omnia factus, fuit congressu facilis, vultu hilaris, sermone jucundus, in pauperes effusus, divitibus affabilis": so says the Arras Breviary. *Breviarium Abrebatense.* Lectio. v.

dence, he never disquieted himself about his material wants, and his house was open to the poor, as readily as to the Frankish chiefs who came to learn of him. God commended His servant, and gave His benediction to his apostolical labours.

Careless about worldly matters, he did not always provide for the needs of the coming day, as the following incident will show. A Frankish nobleman came to visit him at Rheims, and as their religious conversation was prolonged until the evening, Vedast invited his guest to partake of supper. But it had not occurred to him that there was no wine, until the truth became manifest upon their sitting down to table. Then wishing to show to this man, who was yet undecided, the mighty power of God, he raised his eyes to heaven and commanded his servant to go to the wine-skin and to bring to table that which he found there. His faith was not in vain, for the wine was so abundant that there was enough not only for the guest but for all the people who accompanied him. The saint enjoined silence upon his servant, but the witnesses of the miracle spread the news abroad.[1]

Vedast, during his stay at Rheims,[2] had been appointed Archdeacon, and he is thus designated in a Catalogue of the officers of this Church compiled by a Benedictine. After that of the Bishop this office was the most important: the Archdeacons, who are called the Eyes of the Bishop, were charged with the duty of visiting the Parishes of the Diocese. They were to ascertain that the ornaments and furniture of the Altar were in good condition, that documents relating to the property of the Church were carefully preserved, that the rights and privileges of the Church were maintained, and that alms

[1] Siccum vas dederat nectaris undas.
(*Carmina Vedastina*, Hymn No. 1).
Vase nam sicco dederat amico
Gaudia vitis.
(ib. Hymn No. 8).

[2] All authors agree in saying that after his conversion, Clovis had recommended Vedast in the most urgent manner to the Metropolitan of Rheims.

were given to the poor. To them belonged the institution of Abbots and other ecclesiastical Dignitaries, the examination of candidates for Holy Orders, the determination of questions relating to the Festivals of the year and the Divine Office, and also the visitation of the prisons at certain solemn seasons. Some authors do not hesitate to give to these important officials the title of Chorepiscopus. Whether or no S. Vedast had received this office, it is certain that S. Remi called him his Vicar.[1]

The zeal of S. Remi was not confined to the limits of his diocese. Amongst the Franks there were still many idolaters: these had retired to Ragnacaire, who was then in the neighbourhood of Cambrai, and near to Chararic, lord of Thérouanne, two princes who were yet heathens. Remi, who regarded himself as charged with a divine mission for the conversion of all the Belgae, sent to them missionaries, who, under the protection of Clovis, might labour for their instruction. S. Vaast preached the Gospel at Arras, Anthimond at Thérouanne.

Vedast did not refuse this heavy task laid upon him. He would have preferred to live in solitude, but God who had already chosen him to instruct the powerful King, and to convert a great nation, reserved for him also the duty of preaching the faith to the tribes which were yet heathens and barbarians. His words soon caused the knowledge of God to spread far and wide; the fruits of his labours have endured for twelve centuries, and have supplied an impregnable rampart for the Catholic faith which drew from that district some of its most zealous and devoted defenders.

S. Vedast was then consecrated Bishop of Arras, of which honour he proved himself worthy by his zeal and virtue.

Hincmar[2] says that S. Denis had already defined the limits of the Sees of Arras and Cambrai. This

[1] "Vicariae sollicitudinis co-operarius." Balderic, Lib. i., Cap. viii.

[2] Balderic (Chantre de Térouane au XIe siècle), *Chronicon Cameracense Atrebatense.* Lib. i. Cap. v., quoting Hincmar, Epist. vi. Cap. xviii.

district, once partly Christianised, had lapsed into heathenism, the pagans endeavouring to exterminate the believers. Arras was a mass of ruins spiritual and temporal.[1]

S. Vedast arrives at Arras entering the city by the Gate of the Vine

"Creditur illa fuisse dedit cui vinea nomen,"

afterwards called Porte des Clarisses, near the convent of the nuns of S. Clare.[2] Here he found two men, a blind man and a lame, who asked in plaintive tones for alms. The Holy Bishop replied to them, after the manner of the Apostles, "Silver and Gold have I none, but such as I have give I unto thee." And immediately he besought the Lord with tears to succour these afflicted people, as much for the sake of the bystanders, as for their own. Then, he made over them the sign of the Cross, and both were immediately healed.

After this he entered the City, searching eagerly for some remains of the Church which S. Diogenes had erected. He found only ruins.[3] Attila had left there traces of his presence. He had overturned the temples, massacred the ministers of religion, and killed or dispersed their followers, and the few who had returned to their country were so poor, so destitute, that none had been bold enough to rebuild the sacred structure. Whilst contemplating the ruins, the Saint uttered his lamentations: "These calamities," he cried, addressing himself to heaven, "have fallen upon us because we and our fathers have offended Thee. Our unrighteousness and our iniquity have drawn down upon us Thine anger. But now, O Lord, remember Thy mercy, and forget the sins of Thy poor servants." Whilst the Apostle, kneeling,

[1] *Vie de S. Vaast.* Ch. ix.

[2] *Vie de S. Vaast.* Ch. x.

[3] Tandem inter fragmenta murorum diligentius contemplatus, invenit aram Sanctae Dei Genitricis Mariae, quam licet inter stragem murorum tamen inlaesam adhuc servari divinitus non ambigit." Balderic. *Chron. Cam.* Lib. i. Cap. vii.

was praying for the City still in heathen bondage, a bear[1] came forth from the melancholy ruins. Vaast, full of faith in God, was not afraid; he commanded the animal in the name of heaven to go back to the woods and never to recross the river Scarpe.[2]

Père l'Hermite is of opinion that the first Cathedral of Arras was built under Constantine the Great about the year 320, was destroyed by the Vandals in 406, and rebuilt by the liberality of Clovis.

S. Vaast discovered the ruins of several ancient oratories, open to the four winds, the resort of robbers: these sacred places he restored to their original use. He soon surrounded himself with fellow helpers; he founded schools, trained candidates for the ministry, ordained Deacons and Priests.[3] He became the founder of Christianity in the northern provinces.

He restored to its due dignity the Altar, which he found intact amidst the ruins. The Apostle did not content himself with raising the material temple. His zeal knew no abatement in its energy. In the words of a Prose for S. Vedast's Day:

Nil dura corda civium,
Horrens nil movet civitas.[4]

The Temples of the Holy Ghost were in a yet more deplorable condition. The once faithful people had lost even the very semblance of the faith. To the darkness

[1] A huge bear, "d'effroyable grandeur." *Vie de S. Vaast.* Ch. xi.
Ursus immani latitabat antro.
(*Carmina Vedastina.* Hymn No. 15).

[2] From Alcuin's *Life of S. Vedast.* Many mediaeval paintings represent the scene: in others Vedast is accompanied by his bear. The bear was at that time common in this district. Venantius Fortunatus, a poet of the sixth century, includes amongst the savage creatures of the country, the bear, the elk, the wild ox, the stag, and the wild ass (*Fortunatus Ad Gogonem. Carm. Trist.* Lib. vii. Cap. 4). Saint Ghislain found a bear and her cubs in a forest, in the seventh century (*Acta Sanct. Belg.*). Charlemagne hunted the bear in this country.

[3] Ita ut Christo innumeros acquisierit ethnicos, et pluribus in locis Ecclesias erexerit, in quibus Diaconos constituit et Presbyteros. *Brev. Atreb.* Feb. 6. Lectio. vi.

[4] (*Carmina Vedastina.* Hymn No. 20.)

of profound ignorance had succeeded the still grosser darkness of idolatry. Vedast, like S. Paul, knew how to be all things to all men: respectful to the aged, genial to the young, fatherly with the children, he won all hearts. He neglected no opportunity of witnessing to the power of God. Rich and poor alike fell under his influence. A Frankish nobleman, Ocinus by name, invited him one day to dine with him, to meet the King Clotaire who had just succeeded Clovis (511 A.D.). S. Vedast on entering the apartment observed several cups filled with beer (*cerevisia*), which, having been offered to idols, were now to supply the wants of the guests. He made the sign of the Cross over the vessels, which immediately burst asunder[1] in the presence of the King and his nobles. To his amazed audience, the Bishop explained that the devil, subtle in deceiving men, had been concealed within the vessels, and unable to bear the sacred sign had been compelled to flee. He also spoke of the vanity of heathen superstitions, and greatly impressed his audience by his appeal.

During many years S. Vaast's eloquent and persuasive voice was heard amongst the Atrebates, and the people who inhabited the district near Cambrai. In all parts of his vast diocese the praises of God were sung: the holy days were strictly observed, and prayer ascended to heaven like pure incense. In the countries so long troubled by dissensions, by war, and by internal discords, moderation and peace now reigned. S. Vaast found in the midst of his people many sweet consolations; very few of the inhabitants remaining insensible to his voice. He neglected nothing to insure success, neither intercourse with the most powerful men of the age, nor charity with regard to the poor, nor multiplied preachings. He had organised an earnest body of men, who feared neither fatigue nor privation; who under his vigilant eye were trained to virtue by prayer, meditation, and study; and, who after the example of their Bishop, showed

[1] Fugit ursus, perfringuntur
Ocini fideliae.
(*Carmina Vedastina.* Hymn No. 27.)

themselves ready to carry the faith to the farthest limits of this vast diocese.

The city of the Atrebates, which had then attained to very great importance, and was considered to be one of the foremost cities of Gaul, did not extend eastward beyond the Crinchon[1] which skirted its ramparts: but westward it extended to the springs of Beaudimont, some say, even as far as to the hamlet of Wagnonlieu. The Romans, in order to command the city, had raised upon the other side of the stream, a powerful fortress, which they called *Castrum Nobiliacum* (Château Noble): it was useful not only as a shelter for the legions, but probably also as a shelter for the Roman camp followers, who planted in these conquered regions colonies which tended to the fusion of the two peoples. This camp, or castle, was of great extent, as it comprised all the land now surrounded on one side by the Rue S. Aubert, between La Salle des Concerts and the Rue des Agaches: on the other side by this street and that of the Teinturiers; on a third side by the Rue de l'Abbaye, Rue des Trois Visages, and Rue de l'Ancienne Comédie; and finally by the Rue des Bouchers and des Petites Vierges, as far as the Rue Neuve des Récolets. But when the Franks had routed the Romans, and the latter overpowered by numbers had retired into Artois, the fortress was dismantled; and there remained only extensive ruins, witnesses for many years of the foreign dominion, and trophies of the Frankish valour.

In the midst of his exhausting labours S. Vaast desired to find a site for an Oratory and a cell, where he might the more readily devote himself to prayer and to meditation. He found this solitude in the midst of the vast ruins of the Castrum Nobiliacum, and thither he often resorted with some favourite disciples.

S. Vaast built his Oratory in the place where in later times a Church bearing his name was to be erected. He loved to spend long days in retirement, to

[1] See Note iii., On the River Crinchon, in the Appendix.

commune with the young Levites[1] whom he was preparing for the service of the Lord, and to resume the studies which were too often interrupted by the cares and troubles of his laborious life, consecrated to holy living. It is said that he formed the nucleus of a community, but this is not confirmed by any contemporary writer. He had, however, in his Cathedral, Canons distinguished by their learning, the purity of their lives, their devotion to the poor, fellow-helpers with whom he loved to surround himself. The Oratory near the Crinchon was a place of retreat and repose for the Bishop, and of preparation for his disciples.

S. Vaast found also in the affection of S. Remi great encouragement and real sympathy. This holy prelate laboured without ceasing to destroy idolatry and heresy, and he stirred up the zeal of those whom he selected as the companions of his toils. Arianism was unable to penetrate into Artois, and idolatry received a severe check.

S. Vaast founded the Churches of Douai, La Bassée, and Armentières. At S. Remi's request, as has been already said, he undertook the charge of the Diocese of Cambrai (510, A.D.) in addition to that of Arras.[2] In the following year he represented S. Remi at the Council of Orleans, increasing infirmities preventing the attendance of the Archbishop.[3]

S. Remi died on January 13, 530 A.D., at the advanced age of ninety-seven years.[4] His well-spent life had been of the highest value to the good cause. He had founded

[1] Instituit sacerdotes,
Et Levitas et pastores,
Totem gentem renovat.
(*Carmina Vedastina.* Hymn No. 31.)

[2] The union of the Sees of Arras and Cambrai lasted until the end of the eleventh century, when the dioceses were separated. The Chapter of Arras consisted of a Provost, a Dean, two Archdeacons, a Treasurer, a Penitentiary, forty Canons, and fifty-two Chaplains. There are about 400 parishes in the diocese, and twelve rural Deans. *Gallia Christiana.* iii. 319.

[3] *Vie de Saint Vaast.* Ch. xiii.

[4] "Venerabilis memoriae praesul, plenus aetate, plenus etiam virtutum munere." *Chronicon S. Vedasti.*

Churches, enriched Monasteries, converted Arians, brought idolaters to the knowledge of the truth. In his last testament, he speaks of S. Vaast as "my most dearly beloved brother." To the Church of Arras he bequeaths the villages of Souchez and Ourton, and in addition twenty sous d'or.[1] S. Vaast was one of the signatories of the document: his name immediately follows that of S. Remi, and this is the formula which he employs: "Those whom my father Remi has cursed, I also curse; those whom he has blessed, I also bless. I was present at the reading of this document, and I append my signature thereunto."[2]

At the death of the Archbishop of Rheims all eyes were turned to S. Vaast as his successor. He, however, declining the higher dignity for himself, recommended to the suffrages of the Clergy and of the faithful laity the Priest Romanus, and after having installed him in his metropolitan throne Vedast returned to Arras. He enlarged the area of his preaching: he went beyond the limits of Artois in his labours to exterminate idolatry, and to establish new Churches; and according to tradition he preached the Christian faith to the people of Beuvry, of Béthune, and of Estaires, the ancient *Minoriacum*. He had to contend against the violence of Ragnacaire, but finally succeeded in extending the domain of the faith to the banks of the Escaut. Vedast was accompanied by deacons whom he had diligently prepared. They had studied under him in the same place, in which, in later days, the city of Arras grew.

The districts in which he travelled still bear traces of his visits: the road of S. Vaast, the way of S. Vaast, the Mount of S. Vaast, the Fountain of S. Vaast, still bear his name. He is the patron of many Churches in

[1] Ecclesiae Atrebatensi, cui, Domino annuente, Vedastum fratrem meum carissimum episcopum consecravi, ex dono jam dicti principis villas duas in alimoniis clericorum deputavi, Orcos videlicet et Sabucetum quibus etiam pro memoria nominis mei solidos viginti dari jubeo. Flodoard. *Hist. de l'Eglise de Reims.* Tom. i.

[2] "Vedastus Episcopus. Cui pater meus Remigius maledixit, maledixi; et cui benedixit, benedixi; interfui quoque et subscripsi."

Arras and Cambrai, on the banks of the Manche, and in parts of Belgium, where his name occurs more frequently than that of any Saint save the B.V. Mary or S. Martin. He rebuilt the Churches which had been destroyed, created parishes, reformed the gross habits of the nobles of the country who were greatly given to excess, and proved himself a victorious champion against idolatry.[1]

> Concio Pontificis multos, sanctissima vita
> Traxit ab idolis ad baptisteria plures.
>
> Ant. Meierus. Lib. ii.

An anonymous biographer is so bold as to ask, "Did S. Vaast ever pass over the British Channel to evangelise England? We do not dare to say so, as history is silent. But we may suspect it, for his zeal made him capable of so doing: and his name is honoured, especially at Salisbury, where it is found in the martyrology under the form of Zawter or Foster."[2] The suggestion of a missionary visit to England on the part of S. Vedast, is, however, entirely destitute of even a particle of evidence.

CHAPTER VII.

THE DEATH AND BURIAL OF S. VEDAST.

As the life of S. Vedast had been marked by apostolic labours, so his death had its attendant marvels. Worn by the weight of an episcopate of forty years, rich in virtues and in generous deeds, the end was drawing on apace. "One cold winter's night, when the hoar frost covered the earth, and the stars were glittering in the sky, a luminous cloud appeared to flow from the house where the Prelate dwelt, and to rise up even to Heaven.[1] The prodigy lasted for two hours, and being seen by the whole city, plunged it in the deepest perplexity. The pious servant of God understood that he had not long to remain on earth. He summoned to his side the priests who had been his faithful companions, and those for whom he had a fatherly affection, and conversed with them in a firm voice, and with heartfelt eloquence, enhanced by the conviction of an approaching separation. Strengthened by the *Viaticum*, and already parted from the world, he spoke in tones which drew tears from all his hearers. Thus he calmly ended his days, and slept peacefully in the Lord, on the 6th of February, A.D. 540.[2] It is said that at the moment when his soul rose to Heaven, a sound as of a choir of angels

[1] Cum mox iturum ad proemia
Ignis columna proderet.
(*Carmina Vedastina.* Hymn No. 6.)
See also Hymn No. 7.

[2] The date here given is accepted by the Bollandists, by Arnould Raissius, by Surius, and by the authors of *Gallia Christiana*.

filled the room, testifying that Vedast was already the possessor of eternal bliss.[1]

Priests and deacons hastened from divers parts of the dioceses over which S. Vedast had presided to render the last offices to the Apostle of the Atrebates. Multitudes also of the faithful laity thronged into the city to pray beside the body of the saint still lying in the chamber in which he had died, his calm, peaceful features reflecting the serenity of his soul.

When the hour had come for his burial, it was resolved by common consent to place his body in the Church of Notre Dame, which he had built and enriched. But with all their efforts the bearers were unable to move the corpse. The clergy understood that only a miracle could thus arrest their purpose, and sought for the cause of this strange intervention. Amongst the priests who had lived in the greatest intimacy with S. Vedast was Scopilio, arch-presbyter of the place, a pupil of the saint, and a man of pure and honourable life. He was asked whether the dead Bishop had expressed any desire with regard to the place of his interment. Scopilio replied that he had often heard him say that no one ought to be buried within the precincts of the city, for he said that a city should be the place for the living and not for the dead. His modesty had led him to select as the place of his sepulture the oratory built by the banks of the Crinchon. All who were present protested against this humble burial place, saying that the virtues of S. Vaast were too eminent to permit them to entomb his body in a place which was not accessible to all the world. The banks of the Crinchon were, at that time, very marshy, and difficult therefore of access. The assembled company knelt down, and in the midst of their tears and lamentations, Scopilio cried: "Alas, O blessed Father, what course do you desire that we should take, for the day is now far spent, and night is approaching. The multitude which has gathered to the funeral rites must soon return home. Permit, I pray, that your

[1] *Les Petits Bollandistes*. Feb. 6.

body should be laid in the place prepared by the loving care of your children." Immediately the bearers were able without any difficulty to raise the bier, and they went on their way, chanting as they went "Ambula, Sancte, viam quam elegisti." The body of Saint Vedast was deposited with honour near the place where he had sat in his episcopal throne during public ceremonies.[1] As for the inhabitants of Arras, they were filled with joy at a miracle which enabled them to preserve his holy relics. They recognised herein a palladium for the safety of their city, assured that the remembrance of the Bishop would keep them in the right way to which he had directed them. It was said that angel voices joined with the singers in the choir in the psalms and hymns recited at the obsequies.

Some years later a fire broke out in Arras which threatened to destroy a great part of the city. The flames were already surrounding the humble dwelling in which S. Vaast had died: when a woman named Abite, (or Habita) renowned for her piety and the innocence of her life, invoked the name of the Bishop; and, so the legend says, she saw him appear above the lowly cabin and draw away the flames from it. Not only the cell of S. Vedast, but even the bed on which he had breathed his last, were spared.

It is scarcely necessary to prolong the account of the legends which now gather thickly round the history.

It will suffice, in this place, to relate one other story told in the *Vie de S. Vaast.*[2]

S. Aubert, whilst in charge of the Dioceses of Cambrai and Arras, frequently visited the Canons of Notre Dame-en-Cité for religious refreshment. Whilst walking one night on the ramparts of the city,[3] for his limbs were stiffened with cold, the thought came into his mind

[1] Near the High Altar, on the south side. *Vie de S. Vaast.* "Haud procul ab altari, verso ad australem plagam sepulchro, quiescebat." Balderic, cap. xix.

[2] *Vie de S. Vaast*, Ch. xix.

[3] In 667, A.D., according to *L'Abbaye de S. Vaast*, i., 24.

that for more than a century[1] the body of S. Vaast had lain in a very humble grave. Seven Bishops of the Diocese had successively ascended the episcopal throne of Arras, and, one after another, had passed away. Suddenly, on the other side of the Crinchon, he saw a brilliant light, and gazing still more earnestly beheld a shining figure tracing with a golden wand the plan of a basilica. He invited S. Omer, then Bishop of Thérouanne, to consider with him whether it might not be expedient that the body of S. Vaast should be translated[2] to the spot indicated by the heavenly visitant. Although aged, infirm, and blind, S. Omer hastened to Arras. He agreed with S. Aubert's interpretation of the prodigy, and decided that the translation of the body of S. Vaast should be accomplished.

The day for the ceremony arrived. Crowds of people of every rank were present—the clergy, the nobles, the faithful of both sexes. The grave was opened, the remains were placed in a shrine which had been previously prepared; a procession passed through the city. Thousands of tapers and torches were kindled, sacred hymns were sung, the streets were decked with richest ornaments, processional crosses and banners headed the assemblage. The cortège crossed the river Crinchon and reached the confines of that part of the city which was then called Le Vieux Bourg.[3]

Here the sight of S. Omer was suddenly restored that he might behold the relics of the Catechist of Clovis, the Apostle of Artois.[4] But he then besought the Lord that, having seen this great sight, he might once more become blind, and so be spared the pain of beholding the wickedness around him. A strange petition: but the legend goes on to say that it was granted.

[1] Some say 118 years, others 128.

[2] Quem B. Autbertus, designato sibi ab angelo aedificandi oratorii loco, et fundata ecclesia, adhibito secum B. Audomaro, Terwanensis urbis Episcopo, transtulit. Balderic, Lib. i., cap. xix.

[3] In 667, A.D., *L'Abbaye de S. Vaast*, i., 25; 658, A.D., *Gallia Christiana*, iii., 6.

[4] Balderic, Lib. i., cap. xix.

The Feast of the Translation of S. Vaast is still solemnised in the Diocese of Arras, and special offices are found in the Breviary and Missal.

When the Normans invaded Artois, the Religious of the Abbey of S. Vaast sought shelter at Beauvais, and carried thither the body of the saint. Later on, Dodillon,[1] provost of the abbey, was raised to the Bishopric of Cambrai. At his urgent desire Honoré, Bishop of Beauvais, consented to restore the relics, which, after having rested for twelve years at Beauvais, were now carried back to Arras by the brothers of the monastery. Bishop Dodillon delivered an éloge in the presence of a great multitude of people.[2]

The Feast of the Relation of the Relics is observed on July 15 in every year at Arras.

[1] *Gallia Christiana* makes no mention of this name: according to this authority Autbertus was succeeded by Vindicianus in 669.

Regendae ecclesiae curam Dodilo suscipiens, Anno Domini DCCCLXXXVII et XVI Kalendas Aprilis, episcopus ordinatur.

Balderic. Lib. i. Cap. lx.

[2] *Vie de S. Vaast*, Ch. xix.

APPENDIX

OF SHORT PAPERS ON VARIOUS QUESTIONS CONNECTED WITH ARRAS, OR WITH THE LIFE AND LEGEND OF S. VEDAST.

APPENDIX

I.

Earliest Extant Life of S. Vedast.

Prefatory Note.

The original Latin text of this brief life of S. Vedast, now for the first time translated into English, was printed by Canon Van Drival[1] from a manuscript of the fourteenth century at Arras. In his memoir on the birthplace of S. Vaast he remarks that Canon Arbellot is of opinion that the author of this ancient Life had certainly visited Courbefy, as his description of it is that of an eyewitness. "This high mountain, which is nearly equidistant from Limoges and Périgueux, on which are still to be seen the ruins of a city or *castrum;* these magnificent fortifications which the writer describes, and which answer so well to the double enceinte of the deep fosses which protect the citadel; all this description shows clearly that he had visited the place. May one hazard a conjecture? We suspect that the author of this life is Saint Géry (*Gaugericus*) the successor of Saint Vedast in the See of Cambrai: who, in making a pilgrimage to the tomb of S. Front, and in going to visit the domains which the Church of Cambrai possessed in Périgord, the result of a legacy from his predecessor, may have visited in passing, the birthplace of S. Vaast."

S. Vedast's immediate successor at Cambrai was Dominic, at whose death S. Vedulfus was elected, and he in turn was succeeded by Gaugericus who died in 619 A.D. If S. Géry is indeed the author of the Life it

[1] *Mémoires de l'Académie des Sciences, Lettres et Arts d'Arras.* 2 Série. Tome xvii. pp. 209-216. (8vo. Arras, 1886).

may be regarded as a work of the close of the sixth century.

In the great *Acta Sanctorum* (Feb. 6, pp. 801-803) this Life is printed under the title of *Vita Brevior ex MSS. Vedastinis et Andrea Chesnaeo*, and in the margin it is said to be the work of an anonymous author. The Bollandist version contains virtually the same matter as the text printed by Canon Van Drival, but the matter is differently arranged, and there are many various readings or emendations of the text. This is especially noticeable in the Prologue, where the author has essayed to write in a style far above his capacity, with the result of becoming almost unintelligible. In the Bollandist recension, attempts appear to have been made to render the construction a little more consistent with the usage of the Latin tongue: but it still remains, so far as the opening sentences are concerned, very intractable.

Our own countryman, Alcuin, found the style of this Life so rough and harsh, as indeed it is, that he composed a far more elegant biography of the Saint, founded, however, it may be believed, on this earlier document. In his skilful hands the Life is extended to twice the length of the original.

In the translation here given an attempt has been made, by a rendering so close as to be almost word for word in many places, to give some idea of the abrupt, crude, style of the original text. There has been no endeavour to produce a smooth version, on the contrary such an endeavour has been firmly repressed, that the earliest extant Life of the Saint might be offered to the English reader in as close a resemblance to the work of the author as the difference of language and of idiom would permit.

HERE BEGINNETH THE LIFE OF THE HOLY AND MOST BLESSED VEDAST, BISHOP AND CONFESSOR.

I.

THE glory of holy Bishops, by a special right and after a wise investigation, is ever to be handed down to memory, either by imitating their example, or in a written chronicle, that, being represented in a right clear light they may strive to recall the minds of the feeble to the imitation of their own way of life, so as to rejoice not only that the rewards gained for themselves have been won in abundance, but are united also with the profit of others.

And the Eternal Creator of the universe will be a just Judge; so that He who has bestowed upon them [the Bishops] encouragements for increasing their store of religion, will not refuse that there should be afforded to the imitators additional means of accomplishing [their task]. Nor ought anyone to grudge that in some things, which seem to men of small moment, tokens of divine power should thus co-operate; seeing that ofttimes, in great and trivial things alike, the righteous Judge both succours in thought, and affords help in so succouring, that men may grow strong in greater things.[1]

Therefore we deem it right to transmit to posterity the memory of that venerable man, Vedast, Bishop of the City Arras. Whence he derived his birth, in what

[1] Probably the writer's meaning is, that God "puts into our minds good desires" (succours in thought), and in so helping lends aid "to bring the same to good effect."

manner he spent the course of his holy life, how that life was ended, all this we now endeavour to relate in detail.

II.

THERE is a mountain in Aquitaine which separates Périgord from Limousin, being about equidistant from each city. This mountain covers a large space of ground, extending far and wide, its summit piercing the clouds when they are low. Upon its top, in ancient days long since gone by, there stood either a city or a camp, it is not certain which it was; the ruins and the heaps of fallen material sufficiently indicate the vast size and the strength of the fortifications. The name of the mountain, now as then, is Leucus; the castrum itself takes its name from the mount; and the people of the district, the greater part of Aquitaine down to the sea, are called Leuci. Both the evidence of common and continuous report, and of written documents, support the assertion that these names are still in use. S. Vedast, then, sprang from the Leuci, beyond all doubt from noble parents, of a free born race, so famous and illustrious, in the affluence of its estates and the abundance of its riches, that nothing was lacking to it of this world's glory. The boy, with hearty goodwill, devoted himself to study; all things which pertain to a liberal education, these he eagerly acquired, the grace of God assisting him. In all his studies there was no waste of opportunity, but step by step, aspiring after the highest things, he applied himself to the knowledge of the true God and of the things which pertain unto Him, so that he might apprehend God, and His will, and His commandments, sure of the reward laid up for him in heaven. At length this most blessed one, just on the verge of manhood, left his parents, despising the wealth and glory of his family: and so lightly esteeming their very great possessions, that as if they were utterly insignificant, he left his country. At last, as a solitary, unworldly, he approached the boundary of the district towards the Alemanni. There he passed from place to place, living as a poor man, as an exile, for the love of life eternal.

III.

When Clovis, the illustrious King of the Franks, a man of consummate energy, expert in affairs, reigned over the Franks, it came to pass that, at a certain time, amidst the heat of battle, he set forth to fight against the Alemanni, a fierce nation. And when the troops had come together on either side, in order that he might not be exposed to his enemy, he desired to cross the river Rhine. In the rear and on both sides the squadrons[1] of the enemy were standing, and both Franks and Alemanni were longing for the encounter. When the fight began, so violent a terror seized the heart of Clovis, that he weighed in his mind with terrible anxiety the prospect of a fatal issue of the battle. And when he perceived that his men were being overwhelmed with utter destruction, he at length, supported in his mind by divine aid, raised his eyes to heaven, and said: "O only God of power and majesty, whom Clotilda my wife[2] confesses, and whom with humble prayers night and day she does not cease to supplicate, grant me this day victory over mine enemies, and I will thenceforth accept and adore Thee with a believing heart." And when with these and such like prayers he had earnestly besought the Author of all things, the enemy fled, leaving the victory in the hands of Clovis. Then the conqueror received the submission of the Alemanni and their King, and hastening back in triumph to his country came to the city of Toul.

IV.

And when an earnest desire possessed the King, that he

[1] Cunei hostium: the wedge-shaped bodies of men.

[2] Conlateranea.

should quickly receive the grace of Baptism, he sought instruction from the blessed Vedast, whom he had taken as his companion in his journey, so that he might live in the practice of religion. Travelling on together, they came on a certain day into the district of Vongise, which is called Grandpont, near the village of Reilly[1] on the river Axona.[2] Here was a blind man, who for many years had been bereft of sight. He besought the blessed Vedast that of his great piety he would seek divine aid, that at his word, the light so long wanting might be granted to him. Vedast, fully trusting in the mercy of God, raising his right hand made the sign of the Cross upon the eyes of the blind man, who forthwith received sight. And on that spot a Church[3] erected by Christian men may now be seen, where, in the honour of S. Vedast, many wonderful deeds have been done.

And thence Vedast led the King to the city of Rheims, to Bishop Remi, who at that time presided over the Cathedral Church. Here Clovis sojourned for a season, and professing the faith of the Holy Trinity, received the grace of Baptism: departing thence, he returned as victor to his own country, having commended the said Vedast to the favourable notice of S. Remi.

V.

VEDAST remained for a season with Bishop Remi, and dwelt in the aforesaid city of Rheims. It came to pass, at a certain time, that one of the nobles visited him in his cell. Vedast was gentle in spirit, and kindly in speech. He knew how to give aid to the wretched, to comfort the sorrowing by his words, to bring the careless to the rules of sobriety, and he earnestly desired to teach the laws of religion, and to exemplify them both by his words and by his life. When, as we have said, this illustrious person came to him, Vedast, after he had made

[1] Riguliacum. [2] The river Aisne.

[3] Basilica.

an end of speaking the words of salvation, desired his servant to bring quickly a cup of wine for his guest. The servant said, that in the vase from which he was accustomed to drink, not a single drop of wine remained, which, when he heard, the Saint sighed, looked up to heaven, and lifted up his soul to God, praying that of His merciful clemency, He would send him aid. Immediately, He who at Cana of Galilee had changed water into the flavour of wine, in the same manner, gave help at this time of need. And immediately when his prayer was ended, Vedast urgently commanded his servant to hasten quickly to the vase, and bring that which God had given. At once the obedient servant quickly came, and found the vase from which he had been accustomed to drink full of wine to the brim. Filled with joy, he bears the gift which had been sought, and joyfully proclaims its overflowing abundance. Vedast hearing his words, fearing lest the divine favour vouchsafed should injure his own humility, ordered his servant not to gossip about it to anyone out of doors,[1] but rather to endeavour to lead a higher life and learn to maintain silence.

VI.

And when in the aforesaid city of Rheims there were noised abroad great reports about Vedast, the blessed Remi desired to exalt him to honour and designed to make him Bishop of Arras, where, little by little, by teaching and admonishing the nation of the Franks, he might bring them to the grace of Baptism. Having undertaken the burden of the Episcopal office, Vedast came to the city of Arras; and when he was about to enter the gates of the city, he encountered a blind man and a lame who asked for alms. And when he, after the manner of the Apostles, replied that he had neither silver nor gold, they besought him yet more earnestly, and still importuned him for money. To them, urgently imploring help, he said "Instead of the gift of gold and silver, if your faith

[1] Jubet ut nulli hoc in propatulo jactitando denuntiet.

will associate itself with my desire, the wealth of divine gifts shall be bestowed." They replied, that they were ready to do as he bade them. "If your faith," he continued, "keeps pace with my words, the right hand of the Almighty shall restore to both of you your former health." And immediately, placing his hands upon the eyes of the one, and stroking the weak limbs of the other, making also the sign of the Cross, he lifted up his eyes to heaven, and accomplished that which he sought. Then immediately the blind received his sight, and the lame walked, each returning to his home with joy.

VII.

THEN it came to pass that he would enter into a church: but finding it neglected, and by the carelessness of the heathen citizens forgotten, filled with a dense mass of briars, polluted by the dung of the beasts which had been stabled there, he gave up his heart to grief, and bowed his head in sadness. Nor truly were there any habitations of men in the city, which had been destroyed by Attila, King of the Huns, and still remained in utter squalor. Here was the dwelling place of a bear, which with a sorrowful heart he sent forth outside the wall of the city, and commanded that it should not pass the river Crinchon,[1] which flows there. It never did return.

Vedast was then in possession of the royal palace. He was unable to induce the men of the Franks, as a nation, to leave their profane errors, but only little by little could he convert them; and those who, by his sweet words submitted themselves to religion, he received into the bosom of the Church.

VIII.

IT came to pass afterwards, when Clovis was dead, that Clotaire his son, occupying his father's throne, ruled over

[1] Crientium fluviolum.

the Franks: and as he ruled the kingdom worthily, a certain Frank, Hocinus by name, invited the King Clotaire to dinner[1] and invited also the venerable Bishop Vedast amongst the courtiers of the King. But he, not because by consenting he would show favour to their gluttony, but that he might instruct in wholesome doctrine the crowd gathered together at the feast, and by the authority of the King might bring many to Holy Baptism, was present. And when, surprised at being invited to the feast, he entered the house, he perceived certain vessels filled with beer[2] which were standing there according to the heathen custom. He enquired why these vessels were standing in the midst of the house, and was answered, that some were for the Christians, and that others according to the heathen ritual had been offered in sacrifice. When he learnt this, he signed the vessels with the sign of the Cross, and calling with faith on the name of the Omnipotent God, with the aid of divine help, pronounced a benediction. And when he pronounced the benediction, and made the sign of the Cross over the vessels which had been set apart for the heathen rites, the bands round the vessels burst asunder, and the liquor which they contained, flowed out upon the pavement. Thereupon the King, together with the crowd of nobles, astonished at the miracle, enquired what was the reason why these things were done, and ordered that the cause should be stated openly. To whom the venerated man Vedast said, "O King, the glory of thy Franks, thou canst discern how great is the cunning and fraud of the devil to deceive the souls of men. For the demons desired, by the use of this liquor, to cause the hearts of the faithful to wander out of the right way into the paths of death. But now, the craft of the devil being routed and put to flight by the power of God, it is necessary that all should learn, that they ought to turn to the wholesome medicines of the faith of Christ, and earnestly to cast aside heathen superstitions." This act was profitable to the salvation of many of those who were

[1] Ad prandium. [2] Cervisia.

present: for many of them came to the grace of Baptism, and bowed their heads to the true religion.

IX.

He governed the aforesaid Church for a long space of time, about forty years; and then, his earthly course being ended, it pleased the Lord to take him from the cares of this life to the Celestial Kingdom: he was seized with a fever, and he announced that his end was near. For, as he lay in a certain little cell in the same city, a column of fire came down from heaven, and rested upon the roof of the cell, and for a long period of the night, upwards of two hours, remained immoveable. When the venerable man heard of it, he told the bystanders that he was about to depart, and bidding them all farewell, after some words of admonition, surrendered his soul to his Creator on the 8th of the Ides of February,[1] making a happy departure out of this life, and leaving to the survivors a deep love for him. Many at this hour heard choirs singing in heaven. When all men were aware of the death of the blessed one, the clergy and people, not only of that city, but also Bishops and priests from neighbouring cities, gave to this servant of God Vedast the burial of a bishop, of which indeed he was worthy.

X.

The blessed body was laid in the middle of the house, as is the custom; but when all those who held the bier on which that same holy body lay, endeavoured to move it from its place, they were unable to do so. Enquiry was made of a venerable man named Scupilio, archpresbyter of that place, whom the blessed Bishop himself had brought up, as to the cause of this unexpected difficulty: he said that he did not know. But he added

[1] That is, February 6.

"This one thing I know, that when he was in the body, I often heard him say, that no dead person ought to lie within the walls of a city. For the Bishop himself, whilst he was alive, had made arrangements to rest in an Oratory which he had built of wooden planks on the banks of the river Crinchon. But, nevertheless, neither the place selected, nor the monument seems to be prepared." Whilst they were discussing amongst themselves what they ought to do concerning him, the venerable man Scupilio, filled with grief of heart, moved to tears, falling on his knees by the body of the blessed Vedast, began to speak, saying: "Woe is me, most blessed Father, what do you wish me to do? For the day is now already waning towards evening, and all those who have assembled together hasten to return to their own homes. Permit then that we bear you to the place which we have prepared for you." When he had so said, taking up the bier on which lay the mass[1] of the body of the saint, they raised it on their shoulders, no one perceiving any weight; and bearing him with a great company of singers, they sang, saying: "Ambula, Sancte, viam quam elegisti: festina ad locum qui tibi praeparatus est."[2] They delivered him up to burial, at the right wing of the Altar,[3] in the church in which he had fulfilled his episcopal office, meet resting place for the servant of God.

XI.

AND now some time had passed, and the very house in which the holy man Vedast had ended his days took fire, and great part of the house was consumed: when suddenly it seemed that one of the most faithful handmaids, Habitta by name, visibly discerned the blessed Vedast drawing away from the little cell in which the

[1] In quo gleba corporis Sancti jacebat.

[2] Walk, O Saint, in the way thou hast chosen:
Hasten to the place prepared for thee.

[3] Ad dextrum cornu Altaris.

couch had been upon which he died, and it was not consumed: the cell, together with the couch, alone remained unhurt. This the Creator of all things did not suffer to be burnt, in order that by the favour of His bounty He might leave to the survivors a memorial of the virtue of the Saint; our Lord Jesus Christ manifesting His power, to whom is glory and dominion for ever and ever. Amen.

THE LIFE OF SAINT VEDAST IS ENDED.

II.

The Birthplace of S. Vedast.

M. l'Abbé Dehaisnes has edited a chronicle of the monastery of S. Vaast, which states that the tomb of the father and mother of the Saint exists in Aquitaine; and that local tradition asserts that Courbefy was the birthplace of S. Vaast. The Château of Courbefy, which had long been a retreat for robbers, was destroyed in 1660 by the inhabitants of Limoges: but extensive ruins still remain.[1]

Bernard Guido,[2] Bishop of Lodève, a writer of the early part of the fourteenth century, says, "S. Vedastus, qui fertur oriundus de Castro, quod dicitur Curvifunium in monte situm, apud Atrebatum, ubi quadraginta annis fuit dignus episcopus, requiescit."

In the *Mémoires de l'Académie des Sciences, Lettres et Arts d'Arras* (1873, pp. 251-260), is an important paper entitled *Le Lieu de Naissance de Saint Vaast: Dissertation Historique par* M. l'Abbé Van Drival, Chanoine d'Arras, from which the following details are taken.

The *Vita Brevior* states that Saint Vedast was born in Aquitaine, on a mountain named Leucus, and that his parents were noble and wealthy. The Saint, longing for a solitary life, quitted his parents and his home, and went to dwell at a place where now stands the city of Toul. Hence it has been sometimes said that he was born at Toul. Leuci is, however, the

[1] *Vie de S. Vaast.* Arras, 1877. Ch. i.

[2] Bernardi Guidonis apud Labbe. *Nova Bibliotheca MSS.* lib. 1. 636.

historic name of the people of the country of Toul. May there not then be some confusion between the name of his birthplace, and the name of the country in which he resided?

A MS. of the eleventh century, at Douai (No. 753), affirms that S. Vaast was born at Périgord, from whence he went to Toul.

The Bishop of Limoges stated in 1867, that in a place named Courbefis, on a mountain, were still to be seen the ruins of the castle in which the parents of S. Vedast dwelt.

The village is situated on the extreme limit of Limousin and Périgord. It was many times occupied by the English, says Monstrelet, in the wars of the fourteenth century. At the siege of this castle, *Castrum Lucii de Capreolo*, Richard I, King of England, was wounded and died in 1199. Some English writers call the place *Castrum vice-comitis Lemoviceusis Caluz:* Ralph de Diceto, the famous historian, Dean of S. Paul's (to which dignity he was admitted in 1181), names it *Castellum Chaluz in Lemovico territorio.*

One Lucius Capreolus is said to have founded the Castrum, whose name degenerated little by little into Chalus. From Lucius to Leucus is a very easy step. The conclusion of the whole article is, that S. Vaast was born in Aquitaine, at Courbefis, near Chalus, between Limoges and Périgueux.

Canon Van Drival has a second paper on the same subject in the *Memoires de l'Académie d'Arras* of 1886 (pp. 193-203). He attacks the argument of M. l'Abbé Pergot, who endeavours to assign the birthplace of S. Vedast to the Diocese of Périgueux: and maintains the conclusion arrived at in his first paper.

III.

The River Crinchon.

"Le Crinchon, Crientionis fluviolum, est une petite rivière qui traverse Arras: elle baignait les murs de l'abbaye de S. Vaast."[1]

The monastery of Arras had its first foundations in the little cell constructed of wooden planks beside the Crinchon,[2] "in cellula ligneis tabulis compacta ad Crientionem rivulum."

In a Plan of Arras in the twelfth century,[3] the Crinchon seems to have two streams: one flowing northward past the Abbey Gardens, where it is crossed by the Pons S. Vedasti, turns to the east, and finally passes through the city walls at their extreme N.E. angle. The other branch makes with the former an island on which stands the Church of S. Aubert; whilst yet another branch flows northward, and then turning eastward joins what may perhaps be called the main stream. Two Churches closely adjoin the Abbey, S. Petrus in Castro and S. Maria in Castro. The Abbey Church itself is in the Castrum.

There is a very valuable *Plan de l'Ancienne Abbaye de S. Vaast au XVI siècle*,[4] in which also the Crin-

[1] *Chronique d'Arras et de Cambrai par Balderic.* Notes par le docteur Le Glay. ii. 419.

[2] *Gallia Christiana.* iii. 3.

[3] Guiman. *Cartulaire de l'Abbaye de S. Vaast* (edited by Canon Van Drival in 1875).

[4] Terninck. *Recherches sur les Monuments et les Objets d'Art relatifs a l'Abbaye de Saint Vaast.* 4to. Arras, 1869.

chon may be traced, flowing to the west of the Abbey Gardens, crossed by several bridges, turning northward, and then westward not far from the N.W. angle of the present Cathedral.

I did not see any trace of the rivulet during my visit to Arras in 1894, nor could I find it in two modern plans of the city. I can only suppose that like the river Fleet in the City of London it has retired from public observation to fulfil a useful, though less picturesque, purpose.

The Plan just mentioned is of the highest interest. It shows in strongly marked lines the arrangements of the Abbey and its buildings in the sixteenth century, and in faint colours the arrangements of to-day. From this it is seen that the existing Cathedral is not built upon the site of the old Abbey Church, but considerably to the north of it.

An enlarged copy of a portion of this plan is shown by Mons. Henri Loriquet,[1] part of the Crinchon seems to run beneath the Hospital of the Abbey.

It was on the right bank of the Crinchon, outside the walls of Arras, that S. Vedast built the simple Oratory to which in his later life he delighted to retire for prayer and meditation.

> Ipse suburbanam cellam sibi legerat, amnis
> Qua strepit exiguus: structo rudiore sacello.
> Hic sibi restituit vitam sine teste priorem,[2]

as Antoine Meyer sings.

This Oratory is not to be confused with the Cathedral. The Cathedral belongs to the early part of S. Vaast's mission, to the period in which he discovered the Altar of the B. V. Mary in the midst of the ruins.[3] The Oratory belongs to the later years of his episcopate. It was a retreat on special occasions, and it became, long afterwards, the famous Abbey of S. Vaast.

The district in which the Cathedral is situate is still

[1] *La Place Saint-Vaast et la Croix dite de S. Bernard.* 8vo., Arras, 1884.

[2] Antoine Meyer, *Ursus*, quoted in *Vie de S. Vaast*, Ch. xvi.

[3] See *supra*. p. 34.

called by the older people *Le Cloître*, because the Clergy serving the Cathedral dwelt in houses surrounding the sacred edifice, living apart, but having their meals in common in a large hall called *La Synagogue*.

The Oratory, which appears to have been constructed after S. Vedast had been forty years bishop, was built in the form of a little cloister outside the city in a place called Neuilly near the Crinchon.

To the original cell, which was of the simplest and poorest, S Vedast added a more commodious dwelling in which he received those who desired to converse with him on serious subjects. Amongst his visitors, perhaps the most famous was S. Dominic, his successor in the See of Arras.[1]

IV.

S. Vedast's Bear.

The Bear is the constant companion of S. Vedast. It is found everywhere. The Lectern in the Choir of the Cathedral, upon which the music books are placed, is supported by two bears surrounded by their cubs. It attends the patron saint in paintings and in sculpture. It is found on seals and medals, in the poems of the monks, in the popular saying of Artois which evidently springs from a Vedastine source: "You want a servant? A defender? Take my bear."[1]

In the gardens of the Collège Anglais at Douai is a statue of S. Vaast, vested in cope and mitre; by his side, on the left, is a bear which the Saint holds by a chain. The statue, which is about five feet high, stood at one time over the entrance gateway of the old Abbey or Priory of S. Vaast; and, when the buildings of the Abbey were destroyed, the figure was purchased by the College.[2]

On a tapestry preserved at Lille, there are two panels representing scenes in the history of S. Vaast. In the first, the Saint is endeavouring to tame a bear, the same beyond doubt which appeared to him amongst the ruins of the ancient Cathedral. The scene is laid in the midst of a garden, between a gateway and a tower; rabbits are disporting themselves. Below is written,

Vast en Arras eustung . . . rumeur
Ou jadis fust apparence d'Esglise
Duquel saillit ung ours . . . fureur
Qui obeit à Saint Vast sans faintise.

[2] C. le Gentil. *Le Vieil Arras.* 8vo., Arras, 1877. *p.* 259.
[1] From a letter addressed to me by the Prior of the College.

The tapestry belongs to an earlier period than the reign of Louis XI.[1]

The incident in the Saint's life commemorated by these representations has been already told in its proper place.[2]

S. Vaast was visiting the ruins of an ancient Church at Arras, overgrown with brushwood, almost concealed in a dense thicket when a huge bear, *un ours colossal*, broke out from its lair; "the bristling hair, the fiery eyes, and the fierce growls of the wild creature, terrified the Bishop's companions. S. Vaast, by a simple gesture, caused the bear to cease from growling, and to flee with lowered head to the vast forests which surrounded the city."

In later days, the monks of the Abbey, desiring to perpetuate the memory of their Saint's conquest of the ferocious beast, were wont to keep a living bear in a large cage adjacent to the Church, exhibiting it to all visitors. Gérard Robert, the chronicler, relates in a very naïve manner the visit which Louis XI made to the imprisoned creature on the 29th January, 1463. The narrator's words are worth preserving here.

"Il voult veoir l'ours de l'église; auquel ours nostre sire le roy fit plusieurs esbatements luy même d'un baston, par dehors le logis dudit ours, et fit nostre dit sire le roy mettre ung chien avec ledit ours; mais ledit chien n'osa oncques remeuvoir d'un onguelet; et quand le roy vit ce, dit: On fache que mon chien n'ait nul mal, à un nommé Jehan Haret dit Coquillart, varlet des œuvres de ladite église, et garde dudit ours. Il entra dedans en donnant à manger à l'ours et en tant le chien sali hors du logis, et le roy donna audit Haret ung éscu d'or."[3]

I am indebted to Mons. Wicquot, the courteous Librarian of the Bibliothèque de la Ville d'Arras for the following very interesting communication.

[1] Terninck. *Arras.* (4to., Arras, 1879). p. 239.

[2] See *supra.* p. 34.

[3] *L'Abbaye de S. Vaast:* De Cardevacque et Terninck, iii., 120, 121.

"Extrait de la chanson de geste de Ciperis de Vignevaux.[1]

"Le Comte de Flandres fut enseveli dans Arras, et, pour remplir ses dernières intentions, Thierri son gendre fonda plus tard dans cette ville l'Abbaye de Saint Wast.

> Ainsi li ot convent Thierri, je vous affie,
> Et Saint Vast en fonda celle noble Abbaye,
> Et là fist grans vertus le noble fruit de vie;
> Car un beste mue leur fist grant courtoisie,
> A la pierre poser et le machonnerie.
> Seigneurs, ce fut uns ours, escripture l'affie.
> Et en la remembrance de ceste œuvre prisie
> En y a tousjours ung et plus en l'Abbaye,
> Que les seigneurs nourrissent dedans l'enfremerie.

"Alcuin qui a composé la vie de Saint Wast, raconte autrement la légende de cet ours. Le Saint l'aurait rencontré sur l'emplacement de l'église qu'il se proposait d'ériger; il lui aurait alors ordonné de ne pas sortir des forêts voisines, et surtout de ne jamais franchir les rives du fleuve. L'ours se serait empressé d'obéir, et, depuis ce temps, on n'en aurait plus jamais vu dans ces parages: *Nec unquam postea illis visus est in partibus.*"

The story may be carried a little farther.

S. Vaast had gone to construct an Oratory on the other side of the Crinchon, in a place called Neuilly (according to a MS. preserved in the Bishop's Palace), and he found there once more his bear, which, like a faithful guardian attached itself to his person ready to devour anyone who might offend him.

> Non illic aberat fera, non innoxius ursus
> Ille idem, templi qui excesserat ante ruinis.
> Haerebat lateri custos, semperque paratus
> Ceu canis ulcisci, si vis illata fuisset.

[1] *Histoire littéraire de la France*, i., xxvie, p. 35. Cipéris or Chilperic was the illegitimate son of Philip (son of Clotaire), and Clarisse, daughter or sister of Marcus, Duke of Orleans. Vignevaux, the place in which Cipéris was born, was a forest in Normandy. The Poem is of the fourteenth century: the first verse here cited is numbered 6584. ibid, p. 19.

says Meyer:[1] and that is the reason why S. Vaast is represented accompanied by his bear, and why a living bear was always kept by the monks.

> Hinc est quod statuam Divi, pictamque figuram
> Effigies ursi comitatur more recepto,
> Et quod Coenobium vivus non deserit ursus.

For the same reason, Toussaint Sailly,[2] another monk of S. Vaast's wrote in honour of this legendary bear.

> Hujus adhuc ursi manet aeternumque manebit
> Gloria, dum vivet tuus ursus, Meiere, musa
> Dum mea, dum Divi stabit domus alta Vedasti.

The bear is now extinct in France. But in 1884 and 1885, no less a sum than 180,000 francs was paid for the slaughter of wolves: the premium paid in 1894, however, had fallen to 25,000 francs. "The presence of wolves is rarely reported now in fifty-five departments," and the extinction of wolves in France is proceeding rapidly.[3]

[1] *Ursus*, Manuscrit de la Bibliothèque d'Arras.

[2] *Vedastias*, Manuscrit de la Bibliothèque d'Arras: quoted in *Le Vieil Arras*, par C. Le Gentil. Arras, 1877. p. 260.

[3] *The Times* newspaper of August 17, 1895.

V.

Miracles ascribed to S. Vedast.

In the earliest Life of S. Vedast,[1] the unknown author relates comparatively few miracles. He limits himself, indeed, to these: the blind man at the bridge over the river Axona, the wine poured from the empty vase, the healing of the blind man and the lame, the taming of the savage bear, the breaking of the beer vessels at the feast in the house of Ocinus (or Hozinus), the column of light seen over the house in which S. Vedast was breathing out his life, the immovability of the dead body until the intervention of Scopilio (or Scobilio), and the preservation from fire of the house in which S. Vaast had died.

Later on, Alcuin supplies a Memoir of the Saint, *Alia Acta ab Alcuino emendata*. (*Acta Sanctorum*, pp. 803-8.) He relates all the miracles recorded by the earlier biographer. He adds a general allusion to the miracles wrought by the merits of the Saint during the 160 years which had elapsed since his decease, but he says of these "nullo sunt stylo memoriae tradita." As an illustration of the vision seen by S. Aubert of the heavenly visitant tracing with a wand the plan of a basilica, he cites the Antiphon then in use:

"Hic est Beatus Vedastus, cui Templum fieri ab Angelis jussum est hominibus."

In his *Adhortatio* (*Acta Sanctorum*, pp. 808-9), he asks: "Vel quid non potest pietatis precibus impetrare in caelis, qui tantis in mundo claruit in miraculis?"

[1] See Appendix. Article i. *Supra* pp. 49-58.

Alcuin, it will be remembered, was a countryman of our own, of noble Northumbrian parentage, born about the year 735, A.D. "He was, he tells us, the hereditary representative of the noble house from which S. Willibrord, the Apostle of the Frisians, sprang."[1] The favourite pupil of Egbert, Archbishop of York, he attained to remarkable eminence. Amongst his scholars were Charlemagne himself with his sons Charles, Pipin, and Louis.

Other biographers of S. Vedast are Haiminus, a Vedastine monk, a disciple of Alcuin. The Bollandists have printed the *Miracula S. Vedasti auctore Haimino Presbytero* and the *Sermo Haimini in Natali S. Vedasti de ii parvulis meritis ejus sanatis.* (*Acta Sanctorum*, p. 810-12).

He is followed by Hubert a disciple of Haiminus (*ibid* 812-13): and then are found a long series of miracles, collected by the monks of Arras in 852, A.D. and 880, A.D. (*ibid* 813-821). To these Bishop Balderic makes a small addition (*ibid* 821); and a writer of the fourteenth century concludes the long enumeration (*ibid* 822-3). The scantiness of the earlier records in the matter of these legends contrasts favourably with the copious abundance of the later biographers.

The great *Acta Sanctorum*[2] supplies a vast number of legendary stories in connection with the life of S. Vedast: I select three of these, which I have translated from the Latin, and now present in a somewhat condensed form.

The first is of considerable interest. The anxiety of the Saint to be called by his proper name is certainly quaint enough.

"It came to pass that a certain Scot visited a monastery in which the venerable body of the most blessed Saint was reverenced day and night. He humbly sought that relics of the Saint might be given to him, pledging himself to build a church in Scotland in honour of

[1] *Dictionary of Ecclesiastical Biography.*

[2] February 6, pp. 804-819.

S. Vedast. The brethren refused his request, seeing that he was a stranger, and judging him to be an impostor. He, however, reverently visited the altar and the tomb of S. Vedast, and collected from the pavement ashes and dust; with these he returned to his home, where by his own gifts and the contributions of the faithful he built a church. This good man had a hive full of bees and honey in front of the doors of S. Vedast's Church: and one night, whilst mortals were calmly sleeping, there came a thief to steal the honey. Hardly had he taken it, before he became fixed immovably to the spot. When the cock crew, the elder brother of the monastery rose to ring the matin bell, and to his amazement he found the thief still rigid. Those who saw the prodigy desired to deliver the culprit to the magistrate. But when the Scot rose from his bed there appeared to him an aged man of most fair countenance, bald-headed, venerable, who said: 'Do not punish the wretched culprit;—Christus illum vinxit, non tu. Et ego absolvo eum in nomine Jesu. Know also that my name is not Badastus, as you call me in your barbarous speech, but Vedastus.' The thief was sent away unharmed. This miracle was related by a Scotch pilgrim, named Echo."[1]

The scene of another curious story is laid at Wlfara, "in comitatu Baduano":

"There were two gossips (*compatres*), neighbours, of whom one stole from the other a little sheep. The poor man who suffered the loss called upon S. Vedast, and sought the punishment of the offender. The priest, in church, enquired who had done the deed, and denounced the sin, threatening on the next day to excommunicate the guilty person. No one, however, confessed the crime. Whereupon, on the next Lord's Day, the Priest spoke to the people upon the matter: the guilty man standing in the midst. Suddenly from his bosom, his gloves (*chirothecae*) gave forth a sort of bleating. And the people praised God and venerated S. Vedast."[2]

[1] *Acta Sanctorum*, p. 815, c. [2] *Ibid*, 822, A.

Here we may profitably hold our hands from detailed narratives: the following abstract of marvels recorded in the *Acta Sanctorum* will suffice.

S. Vedast restores a blind man to sight (805, A); puts a bear to flight (806, E); heals a blind man and a lame man (806, C); breaks, by signing the cross, some vessels "male gentili errore daemoniacis incantationibus infecta" (806, F); a column of fire is seen over his house shortly before his death (807, C); those who sought to bury him within the city were unable to move his body, for he had said that none ought to be buried within the walls, the city was the place of the living not of the dead (807, D); after his death he extinguished a fire which threatened to destroy the house in which he had died, and the couch on which he had breathed his last (807, F).

At his shrine: a dumb and deaf man and two lame men are restored; by invocation of his name a cattle plague was stayed (810, F); a horse was restored to health upon its owner offering up a taper; a linen cloth for the altar had been vowed by a dying woman, her daughter, however, after her decease, brought one of inferior value, which flew away from the altar of its own accord (816, E); insufficient materials brought to repair S. Vedast's Church became adequate, a beam, too short for the required purpose, extending itself to the necessary length (816, F); a falling wall is strengthened (816, F); evil spirits in the form of bats were cast out; a man possessed by evil spirits is cured (819, B); a dry staff becomes a tree, whence a wood springs up (820, A); oil for lamps is miraculously supplied (816, E); two sick children restored to health (811, D); a dying man recalled to life (812, C); a blind woman and palsied man healed (821, B, C.)

To the foregoing details may, with advantage, be added the following short notices of S. Vedast, either from manuscript sources, or from printed works of considerable rarity.

The first of these is found in a MS. of the early part of the fourteenth century, preserved in the British Museum.

It is comprised within a few lines, but brief as it is, it illustrates the never-failing tendency of the hagiologists to ascribe to their heroes miracles closely resembling those of the Redeemer. It is a very brief version of a story already related.

"*De Sancto Vedasto et Amando.*

"Egregia et omni acceptatione digna merita sanctorum Christi presulum Vedasti et Amandi sancta consuevit celebrare ecclesia. Sanctus igitur Vedastus quia sitienti amico vinum de vacuo produxit vasculum diuturnum sanctitatis sue perhibet testimonium. Christus in Chana Galilee vinum de aqua fecerat, Vedastus vero de arido poculo vinum produxerat. Magnum igitur quod Dominus, magnum quod gessit famulus."[1]

The second is taken from the *Legenda Sanctorum*, one of the favourite books of the fifteenth century, if the numerous editions which issued from the press may be taken as a proof of popularity.

This Life is chiefly remarkable for a droll bit of etymology. The name Vedastus, we are gravely told, is derived from *vere dans estus;* or from *Vae distans;* for the excellent reasons which are therein set forth. But it is to be feared that these will not convince the more critical etymologists of to-day.

"Vedastus, quasi vere dans estus, quod vere sibi dedit estus afflictionis et penitentie. Vel quia ve distans, quod ve eternum ab eo distat; nam damnati semper dicent ve, scilicet quia Deum offendi, ve quia dyabolo consensi, ve quia natus fui, ve quia mori non valeo, ve quia tam male torqueor, ve quia numquam liberabor.

"Vedastus a beato Remigio in Trajacensem episcopatum ordinatus fuit. Qui cum ad portam civitatis venisset, et ibidem duos pauperes, unum cecum et alium claudum petentes elemosinam reperisset, dixit eis, Argentum et aurum non est mihi: quod autem habeo vobis do. Et facta oratione utrosque sanavit. Cum autem in quadam ecclesia derelicta, vepribus operta, lupus[2] habitaret, eidem precepit ut inde fugeret, nec ultra illuc redire auderet. Quod et factum est. Denique cum verbo et opere multos convertisset, quadragesimo anno sui episcopatus vidit columnam igneam a celo usque in domum suum descendentem. Qui finem suum adesse considerans post modicum in pace quievit, circa annum Domini quingentesimum. Cum autem corpus ejus transferretur Audomarus pro

[1] British Museum. Bibliothec. Reg., viii, Ch. vii.

[2] The animal is more generally said to be a bear. In the Blythburgh window it appears to be a wolf or a fox.

senio cecus dolens quia corpus episcopi videre non poterat, mox lumen recepit, sed postmodum ad votum suum lumen amisit."[1]

In *Les Annales de Saint Bertin et de Saint Vaast*,[2] a similar derivation is suggested, but this is, perhaps, a more poetical conception: the name of Vedastus is derived from *vere dans thus*.

With regard to the derivation of the name Vedastus here given, Mr. W. de Gray Birch, whose important works on mediaeval Seals are well-known to all students of Sigillography, sends me the following seal inscription, surrounding a figure of the Blessed Virgin with the Holy Child:

PORTA SALUTIS AVE, PER TE PATET EXITUS A VE,
VENIT AB EVA VE, VE QUIA TOLLIS, AVE.

This is the Seal of Arbroath Abbey and is of the thirteenth century.[3] The same legend is found on the Seal of Middleton Abbey, Dorset, surrounding a representation of the Annunciation.

The Seal of Boxgrave Priory, Sussex, bears a similar inscription:

QUI TRANSMISIT AVE BOXGRAVAM LIBERET A VE,
JUDICIUMQUE GRAVE NON SENTIET, IMMO SUAVE.

The third, and most interesting notice, on account of the quaint early English in which it is written, is taken from the *Golden Legend*, printed by Wynkyn de Worde, a book of very high value to the student of mediaeval religious literature.

The *Liber Festivalis* put forth by Caxton[4] was, as he tells us in the introduction, founded upon the *Golden Legend*. It was intended to be used by those parish priests who, by reason of "default of books" and also for "simpleness of cunning," were unable to compose dis-

[1] *Legenda Sanctorum*, or *Lombardica hystoria* (Nuremberg, 1482), fo. xxxiv, xxxv.

[2] *Les Annales*, etc., p. 376.

[3] W. de Gray Birch. *Catalogue of Seals in the British Museum*, iv., 130.

[4] There is a fine copy, with Caxton's well-known monogram, and "Caxton me fieri fecit," in the University Library of Cambridge.

courses of their own. But let Caxton speak for himself; he is well worth hearing:

"¶ The helpe and grace of almyghty god thrugh the besechynge of his blessed moder saynt mari be wyth vs at our begynnyng helpe vs & spede vs here in our lyuyng | and bryng vs vnto the blisse that neuer shall haue endyng Amen".[1]

"Myn owne simple vnderstōdyng I fele well how it fareth by other that ben in the same degree and hauen charge of soules & holden to teche their parishes of all the princypalle festes that come in the yere. shewynge vnto theym what the holy sayntes suffreden & deden for goddys sake & for his loue | soo that they sholden haue the more deuocion in goode saintes | and wyth the better wyll come vnto ye chirche to serue god and pray his holy sayntes of their helpe | But for many excuse hē for defaute of bokis | and also by simplenes of connyng | Therfore in helpe of suche clerkes this treatis is drawen out of legende aurea . that he that lyst to study therin he shall fynde redy therin of al the pryncipalle festis of the yere of eche one a short sermon nedeful for hym to teche | and for other to lerne . and for this tretis speketh of all the hie festis of the yere . I wyll and praye that it be called festiuall | the which begiñith at the first sōday of aduent in worship of god & all his sayntes that ben written therin |

"¶ Incipit liber qui vocatur festialis | ."

If the Rector of S. Vedast in 1527 was an unlearned man, an idea which is not to be entertained for a single moment, he would probably have read to his congregation gathered in S. Vedast's Church upon S. Vedast's Day (February 6) the little sermonette here following.

"¶ Here foloweth ye lyfe of saynt Vedaste.

"Saynt Vedaste was ordeyned bysshop of Arras by ye hande of saynt Remyge. And saynt Vedast was of moche grete holynes & clennes. For whā he came to the gate of Arras he founde there two poore men of whom ye one was lame & ye other blynde. These two poore men demaunded of hym some almes. And saynt Vedast answered to them & said | I have neyther golde ne syluer | but this y^t I haue I gyue to you. Than he made them bothe hole by ye vertue of his prayer. It happed on a tyme he came in to a chirche destroyed | & founde there a wolfe amonge ye busshes | & he commaunded hym y^t he sholde go his waye | anone he obeyed to hym & fledde | so y^t syth y^t tyme he was not seen. At the last whan he had conuerted moche people by his worde and predicacyon to the fayth of God | & also by good ensamples shewed euydently to ye people | in the .xl. yere of his bysshopryche he sawe a doue

[1] Transcribed from a copy in the Bodleian Library. Press-mark, 66, 13.

of fyre y[t] came fro heuen to his hous | and by y[t] he understode wel y[t] he sholde fynysshe & passe out of this worlde | & so he dyd. For he dyed anone after aboute y[e] yere of our lord v. c. l. whan his body shold be translated | Saynt Omer whiche was blynd for age was sory y[t] he myght not se y[e] body of saynt Vedast | & anone our lorde enlumyned hym & rendred to hym his syght and sawe the body of saynt Vedast. But anone after he was blynde agayn as he had bin before. Let us pray to hym &c."[1]

The Priest Haimin, guardian of the Church of S. Vedast relates other wonders which are duly set forth in the Vie de S. Vaast.[2]

A poor man whose eyes had been torn out by the civil authorities, and who from a long incarceration had contracted a nervous malady, sat at the door of the church to beg for the bread which he could no longer obtain by labour. His limbs were crippled, he crawled on hands and knees from place to place. One Christmas night in a dream S. Vaast appears to him: bids him to remain no longer at the church door, but rather to enter and approach as near the sanctuary as he could. He does so, and is cured. The wooden shields with which he had guarded his hands and knees from injury, were hung up at the portals of the church.

A priest named Hubert, a disciple of Haimin, who had charge of a parish in the environs of Arras in the eighth century, relates that one Wednesday, about three o'clock in the afternoon the harvest labourers of his uncle, the priest Imbode, were returning from the fields. As they drew near the house of Dagebert the carpenter, they saw upon the threshold his wife in great distress, beating her breast, tearing her hair, and uttering cries of sorrow. Her husband, she said, was dying, and she feared that he could not have time to receive the last sacraments. Hubert hastens to give him the viaticum. The sick man lies in a deplorable condition, without motion, without speech. Consciousness returns to him—he receives the sacrament—but at once relapses. Presently his wife addresses the almost unconscious sufferer—he revives,

[1] *The Golden Legend*, Wynkyn de Worde, quarto, London, 1527, fol. lxxxxii. b, transcribed from a copy in Sion College Library.

[2] Ch. xviii-xxiii.

and tells her that he has had a blessed vision of S. Vaast. In two days he is restored to health.

Balderic says: that a certain robber[1] cruelly maltreated an enemy, binding his hands behind his back, twisting the cords with great violence. This took place in a church dedicated to S. Vaast in the diocese of Liége. By the intervention of the Saint the sufferer is thrice released from his bonds.

In 875, the fishermen who supplied the Abbey of S. Vaast with fish, had set forth on their expedition in the English Channel. They encountered other fishermen in the service of other monasteries, who endeavoured to anticipate them in casting their nets, and threatened to drive them from the fishing ground. A sudden tempest arose, and drove away the vessels of the hostile sailors. The fishermen of S. Vaast implored the protection of their patron, and the storm ceased, and they obtained a marvellous draught of fishes. Henceforth the mariners of Artois paid a yearly duty of two sous to the religious of S. Vaast for permission to fish in these waters.

During the reign of the weak Emperor Lothaire, the Abbey of S. Vaast fell into the hands of Count Adalard, who enriched himself with the property of the Abbey and seized upon its fair domains. One of its estates he gave to a courtier named Léthard, who tyrannised over the farmers and subjected them to heavy exactions. They, in their trouble, had recourse to S. Vaast—they offered to him a taper of great size—"conferentes cereum mirae magnitudinis." Léthard, with his followers, was about to fall upon them. Suddenly he cries aloud—"Come to my aid. A man armed with a poignard is about to strike me." Grasping his sword, he threatened to attack his own companions. He fell into a sort of madness, without, however, entirely losing his reason. His only daughter whom he greatly loved, died; and was soon followed by his wife—the latter dying in terrible agony, from cancer in the tongue. Léthard himself perished miserably.

[1] Balderic, Lib. i., Cap. ii. "Raptor quidam pessimus."

Amongst the best estates belonging to the Abbey of S. Vaast was that of Demencourt in the suburb of S. Catherine near Arras. It had been rendered highly productive by the toil of the religious, though originally only a marshy land covered with woods and brambles. The Count of Arras, named Theobald, desired to possess himself of this property, and with this view he approached the reigning prince, seeking from him a band of soldiers so that he might take the land by force: the prince was weak enough to consent to this unjust demand. Theobald also enlisted in his scheme his colleague the Count of Rheims. This great abuse of power, this scandalous injustice, was about to be completed. The religious betook themselves to prayer at the tomb of S. Vaast, "suumque patronum, Vedastum, tum multâ precum instantiâ currentes."[1] The guardian of the Cathedral of Rheims, in the middle of the night, heard a plaintive voice calling upon S. Remi. It was the voice of S. Vaast pleading for his children. S. Remi bids him call together his fellow-workers in the evangelisation of the district: S. Omer, S. Audoen, S. Bertin with Vulmaire and the preachers of the maritime parts; Amand, Quentin, Géry, Eloi and Lucien. S. Remi will bring with him, Martin and the Saints of Aquitaine, the healer Médard, Germain; the two shoemakers of Soissons, the brothers Crispin and Crispianus; S. Denis and his companions. They will all come to succour their servants. The guardian or sacristan related the vision to the Bishop; the Bishop told it to the Count of Rheims, who immediately prepared to set out for Arras. The Count burst into boisterous laughter, asserted that the guardian had drunk too deeply and hence had been the sport of a foolish dream. Hardly, however, had the Count reached the door of the Cathedral of S. Remi, than his horse stumbled and he himself fell from the saddle and fractured his leg: he was carried half-dead from loss of blood to his house. Meanwhile, Theobald set forth to meet him, but as he

[1] Guimann, Cartulaire, p. 318.

mounted his horse, a wasp or fly[1] stung its nostrils, the horse reared, the rider was thrown violently upon the ground, fracturing his skull and expiring instantly. From that time the religious of S. Vaast were no more molested in their possession of Demencourt.

The most eager devourer of mediaeval stories cannot desire a fuller banquet than that which has been here provided.

[1] Musca equi nares occupavit, qua sonipes molestia efferatus, levatis in altum calcibus, sessorem suum excutiens miserabili obitu extinxit. Guiman, *Cartulaire*, p. 319.

FIGURE OF S. FOSTER, THAT IS, S. VEDAST, BISHOP OF ARRAS, FROM A WINDOW IN BLYTHBURGH CHURCH, SUFFOLK.

To face page 72.

VI.

S. Vedast in Art.

In Art S. Vedast appears, says Mr. Baring Gould,[1] "with a child at his feet; or, with a wolf from whose mouth he saves a goose, a popular tradition being that he saved a goose belonging to some poor people from a wolf that was running away with it; or with a bear."

In *Das Passional*, 1480, he is depicted with a wolf before him in a thicket; in Cahier (*Les Caractéristiques des Saints dans l'Art Populaire*, 1867) he is represented as curing a blind man.[2]

Mr. Watling, a well-known Suffolk antiquary, has been so good as to send me tracings of a fine figure of S. Vedast from one of the north clerestory windows of the church at Long Melford; and of another very dignified figure from Blythburgh Church, Suffolk, which has supplied the design from which a clerestory window erected in 1886, in the church of S. Vedast, Foster Lane, was taken.[3]

Mr. Watling has also sent me some other very interesting drawings illustrative of my subject.

1. From the beautiful parapet of Blythburgh Church, Suffolk. A seated animal, probably a bear, his paws resting on his knees, holding in his jaws a goose.

2. A spandrel "now over the door of a cottage in Earl Stonham, but formerly in the church." Here a

[1] *Lives of the Saints*, February 6.

[2] F. C. Husenbeth, *Emblems of Saints*, 3rd edition, edited by Dr. Jessop. 8vo. Norwich, 1882.

[3] These figures form illustrations to the present volume.

fox is seen, with a goose held between its jaws, the body of the bird slung over its shoulder. Another bird, apparently an owl, looks on.

3. A spandrel from the roof of the Nave of Earl Stonham Church. The stump of a tree in the centre; on the dexter, a fox with the goose in its mouth; on the sinister, a bird, perhaps a duck, is looking on.

4. A plaque on the mantlepiece of the Hall at Charterhouse, London. Here a fox is seen in the very act of seizing a goose. The fox and goose is, however, so common a subject, that I do not suggest, in this case, any allusion to S. Vedast. In the case of the figure from the parapet at Blythburgh, the existence of the effigy of S. Vedast in the stained glass window leaves little room for doubt that this may fairly be classed amongst the Vedastine emblems.

The Seals of the Abbey, of the Abbots, and of the Cathedral at Arras are frequently adorned with figures of the Patron Saint. These Seals are very fully illustrated in the *Sigillographie de la Ville d'Arras*, by Mons. A. Guesnon[1]; in Mons. Terninck's *Arras: histoire de l'Architecture et des Beaux-Arts;* and in the *Collection des Sceaux* of Mons. Douët d'Arcq.[2] Amongst the finest examples may be mentioned the Seal of Bishop Lambert in 1097; a very fine Seal of the Abbey in 1195, SIGILLUM ECCLESIE SANCTI VEDASTI, a dignified figure of the Saint, seated, his right hand in benediction, whilst his left holds his pastoral staff; the Seal of Abbot Raoul in 1301; of Abbot Martin Asset in 1529, very similar to that of Abbot Caverel, except that the animal, which seems to be a wolf, is sitting on his haunches and looking upwards to Saint Vaast; and the remarkable Seal of the illustrious Abbot Philip de Caverel in 1598. This Seal is an excellent piece of work: in the upper half, S. Vaast standing under a canopy, the bear at his feet, holds his pastoral staff in his right hand and an open book in his

[1] Professeur au Lycée Impérial de France. See especially Plates xvi.-xxi. Published at Arras and at Paris in quarto, 1865.

[2] Sous-Chef de Section aux Archives de l'Empire. Quarto, Paris, 1863.

FIGURE OF S. VEDAST, BISHOP OF ARRAS, FROM A WINDOW IN THE CHURCH OF LONG MELFORD, SUFFOLK.

To face page 80.

left, an angel on either side of the central figure kneels on a fald-stool and swings a censer; in the lower half the Abbot kneels, on the dexter side are the arms of S. Vaast, on the sinister the arms of Philip: Argent, a chevron vert, between three estoiles gules.

Some rude, but early, medals, bearing the Saint's figure, are shown in Mons. Terninck's *Arras*, plates 77 and 78.

In the South Transept of the Cathedral at Arras is a fine picture, SAINT VAAST GUÉRIT UN AVEUGLE. In the foreground is the stately figure of the Saint who lays his right hand on the eyes of a blind man. Beside the Saint are Clovis wearing his crown and royal robes, his wife Clotilda, and some attendants. The principal figures are dignified, and the effect of the entire picture very pleasing.

Mr. Everard Green, *Rouge Dragon*, has kindly informed me that the Arms assigned to S. Vedast are seen everywhere at Downside Priory, in wood, in iron, in stone, and in glass. The blazon is: Or, a cross moline gules.

VII.

S. Vedast in the Ancient English Liturgies.

1. The Benedictional of S. Æthelwold.
2. The Missal of Robert of Jumièges.
3. The Leofric Missal.
4. The Sarum Missal, Breviary, and Martyrology.
5. The York Missal and Breviary.
6. The Hereford Missal.
7. The Office formerly used at Arras.

Liturgical students will probably be interested to note the various forms of devotion to S. Vedast which are found in ancient English service-books. The earliest which has fallen under my notice is that which occurs in the Benedictional of S. Aethelwold, a contemporary of S. Dunstan, and Bishop of Winchester.[1] It is a magnificent volume, in the possession of the Duke of Devonshire, and was edited by Mr. Gage, with facsimiles of the illuminations, in the *Archaeologia* (vol. xxiv, p. 66) of the Society of Antiquaries. The date assigned to the MS. is the tenth century. The text is evidently corrupt, but is here printed exactly as it stands in the *Archaeologia*, without any attempt at conjectural emendation.[2]

No. 1. *Benedictional of S. Aethelwold.*

"*In Natali Sancti Vedasti, Conf.*[2]

"Deus fundator fidei et indultor sacerdotum congregatio plebis

[1] Maskell, *Monumenta Ritualia*, 2nd edit., vol. i, p. 146.

[2] In the *Cod. S. Theoderici*, Op. S. Greg. Mag., tom. iii, fo. 640, occurs "Benedictio in Nat. SS. Remigii, Germani, Vedasti, et Bavonis." It is different from our Benediction. See in Lambecius (403), "Hymnus de Sancto Vedasto."

sanctificatio confessoris qui beatum Vedastum ad hoc armasti virtute ut Tibi militaret in fide concede huic familiae Tuae pro se hunc intercessorem quem dedisti pontificem. Amen.

"Sit apud Te nunc pro nobis assiduus intercessor qui contra hereticos pro Te extitit tunc assertor. Amen.

"Vt Te retribuente populus crescat in numero pro quo sacerdos sudavit in fide. Amen.

"Quod ipse praestare dignetur."

No. 2. *Missal of Robert of Jumièges.*—The second example is taken from the Missal of Robert of Jumièges, Bishop of London 1044-1050, Archbishop of Canterbury 1051-1052, written about the year 1012 A.D., selections from which are printed by the Rev. F. E. Warren in his edition of the Leofric Missal.

"*VIII Id. Feb. Nat. S. Vedasti Confessoris*

"V.D. aeterne Deus. Cujus munere beatus Vedastus, confessor et sacerdos, et bonorum operum incrementis excrevit, et variis virtutum donis exuberavit, et miraculis coruscavit. Qui quod verbis edocuit operum exhibitione complevit, et documento simul et exemplo subditis ad caelestia regna pergendi ducatum praebuit. Unde Tuam clementiam petimus, ut ejus qui Tibi placuit exemplis ad bene agendum informemur, meritis muniamur, intercessionibus adjuvemur; Qualiter ad caeleste regnum, illo interveniente, Te opitulante, pervenire mereamur. Per Christum.[1]

"*Kal. Oct. Nat. SS. Remigii, Germani, Vedasti, Bavonis.*

"V.D. aeterne Deus. Qui sanctorum Tuorum Germani, Remigii, Vedasti, et Bavonis hodierna geminasti nobis in confessione laetitiam. Qui pariter sacerdotes aegregii quod praedicaverunt ore operibus compleverunt, et pervenerunt ad gloriam sempiternam. Per Christum Dominum nostrum."[2]

No. 3. *The Leofric Missal.*—The notice in the Leofric Missal (used in the Cathedral of Exeter during the Episcopate of its first Bishop 1050-1072) is brief enough, consisting only of a single clause in the Litany, "Sancte Vedaste, ora." But brief as the notice is, it is worthy of remark, for, as the learned Editor points out, "Vedastus is the only name in the Litany which is written in rustic capitals, and ornamented with patches of red and green paint. This exceptional treatment of the name points to the volume having been written in a locality

[1] *Leofric Missal*, p. 288. V.D.—*vere dignum.*

[2] *Ibid.*, p. 289.

where S. Vedast was held in special honour; that is to say, probably in the dioceses of Arras or Cambray, dioceses which were held together from the time of S. Vedast, their first Bishop, till A.D. 1095."[1] It is somewhat remarkable that the name of S. Vedast, though so conspicuously treated here, does not occur at all in the calendar prefixed to the Sacramentary.

The three following examples, Nos. 4, 5, and 6, are taken from a group of English Missals; those, namely, for Sarum, York, and Hereford.

No. 4. *The Sarum Missal.*

"*Sanctorum Vedasti et Amandi Episcoporum. Ad Missam.*

"*Officium.* Sacerdotes ejus induant salutare: et sancti ejus exsultatione exsultabunt.

"*Psalmus.* Memento Domine David: et omnis mansuetudinis ejus.

"*Oratio.* Adesto, Domine.[2]

"*Epistola.* Plures facti sunt.

"*Gradale.* Sacerdotes (*as above*).

"*V.* Illuc producam cornu David: paravi lucernam Christo Meo Alleluya. *V.* Fulgebunt justi: et tanquam scintillae in arundineto discurrent in aeternum.

"*Evangelium.* Sint lumbi.

"*Offertorium.* Exsultabunt sancti in gloria: laetabuntur in cubilibus suis: exsultationes Dei in faucibus eorum.

"*Secreta.* Hostias laudis, Domine, Tuis altaribus adhibemus, quas eorum Tibi patrociniis commendandas suppliciter exoramus; in quorum veneratione pietati Tuae haec sacrificia offerimus. Per.

"*Communio.* Ego vos elegi de mundo ut eatis et fructum afferatis: et fructus vester maneat.

"*Postcommunio.* Sumentes, Domine, divina mysteria, quaesumus, ut (sanctorum confessorum Tuorum atque pontificum Vedasti et Amandi precibus) sanctificationem nobis jugiter operentur. Per Dominum."[3]

[1] *The Leofric Missal.* Edited by F. E. Warren, B.D., F.S.A. 4to. Oxford, Clarendon Press, 1883. Introd. p. xli; p. 210.

[2] As in Hereford Use, but reading "confessorum tuorum atque pontificum."

[3] *Missale ad Usum Insignis et Praeclarae Ecclesiae Sarum.* (Burntisland.) The Officium, Psalmus, Epistola, Gradale, Evangelium, Offertorium, are those for the Mass, "In Natali Plurimorum Confessorum." Coll. 709, 715*, 716*. (Epistle, Hebrews vii, 23-27; Gospel, S. Luke xii., 35-40.)

No. 4A. *The Sarum Breviary.*—The Sarum Breviary (I quote from the valuable edition lately issued from the Cambridge University Press) gives the Feast of SS. Vedastus and Amandus in the calendar as a feast of nine lections; but the editions of 1519 and 1526 read here, as the Editors are careful to point out, "iii lectiones," and three lessons only are found in the text.[1] The third of these lessons, the only one relating to S. Vedast, stands thus:

"*Lectio III.*

"Sanctus vir Dei Vedastus, ubi regem Lodowicum post insperatam victoriam ab Alemannis adeptam fidei doctrina ad sacramenta baptismatis perduxit, a sancto Remigio episcopus ordinatus est: et Attrabatae civitati missus est verbum Dei praedicare, qui in introitu civitatis mox caecum et claudum curavit. Rexit autem sacerdos Dei Ecclesiam Christi divina auxiliante gratia annis circiter quadraginta: sub magna evangelicae praedicationis instantia. Qui cum post multa virtutum insignia diem sui obitus instare divinitus didicit: vocavit filios suos ad se. Et post dulcia monita pietatis paternae (sacro sancto corporis et sanguinis Christi confirmatus viatico) inter manus lachrymantium spiritum emisit: sepultus in ecclesia beatae Dei genitricis in dextra parte altaris ubi quondam pontificalis cathedrae fungebatur officio. In quo loco per aliquod jacuit tempus: quousque Domino revelante ad locum ubi nunc fulget ejus memoria est a viris sanctis Autberto[2] et Audomaro episcopis felici mutatione translatus. Ubi incessanter quotidie divina celebrantur praeconia, et frequenter miraculorum signa: ad laudem Domini nostri Jesu Christi qui vivit et regnat in secula seculorum. Amen."

No. 4B. *The Sarum Martyrology.*—There is a copy of this scarce book in the British Museum.[3] The title is as follows:

¶ The Martiloge in englysshe after the vse of the chirche of Salisbury | & as it is redde in Syon | with addicyons.

The introduction opens thus:

¶ Unto the deuoute reders | Rychard Whytford preest and professed broder of Syon | in our lorde god and moost swete sauyour Jesu Salutacyon.

and is signed by

¶ The sayd wretche of Syon Rychard Whytford.

[1] *Breviarium ad Usum Sarum*, fascic. iii, coll. 161-164.
[2] Auberto, *Leg.*, 1518.
[3] Press mark. C, 25, c.

On folios xv and xvi is the following notice of our Saint:

¶ The vj day of February . . . The feest also of saynt Vedast called comynly in englysshe saynt Sawster | bysshop of traiectens | & of saynt Amand a bysshop also | & both gloryous | and of many myracles.

just before the colophon:

¶ Praye for the wretche of Syon your moost unworthy broder Rychard Whytford.

Then the colophon, followed on the *verso* by Wynkyn de Worde's full-page mark:

¶ Thus endeth the martiloge with the Addicyons. Imprynted at London in Fletestrete at the signe of the sonne | by Wynkyn de Worde. The yere of oure lorde god, M.CCCCC.XXVJ, the xv day of February.

No. 5. *The York Missal.*

"*Sanctorum Confessorum Vedasti et Amandi* (*VIII Id. Feb.*)
"*Officium*. Sacerdotes ejus induantur.
"*Oratio*. Deus, qui nos sanctorum confessorum.
"*Epistola*. Plures facti sunt sacerdotes.
"*Gradale*. Sacerdotes ejus. Alleluya. *V*. Fulgebunt justi.
"*Evangelium*. Sint lumbi vestri *usque ad* filius hominis veniet.
"*Offertorium*. Exsultabunt.
"*Communio*. Justorum animae."[1]

No. 5A. *The York Breviary*.—The first lection for S. Vedast's Day is as follows:

"Egregia et omni acceptione digna merita sanctorum Christi presulum Vedasti et Amandi; sancta celebrare consuevit ecclesia. Sanctus enim Vedastus: quia sitienti amico vinum de vacuo produxit vasculo: laudabile et diuturnum sanctitatis sue prebet testimonium. Christus igitur in Chana Galilee de aqua vinum fecerat: Vedastus vero ex arido poculo vinum produxerat. Magnum igitur quod Dominus: sed majus est quod gessit servus. Non tamen Vedastum Domino: sed Dominum preponimus Vedasto."[2]

[1] *Missale ad Usum Insignis Ecclesiae Eboracensis*, vol. ii, p. 23. Edited for the Surtees Society by Dr. Henderson, now Dean of Carlisle.

[2] *Breviarium ad Usum insignis Ecclesiae Eboracensis* (Surtees Society), ii, col. 194.

The close resemblance, in some places almost word for word, between this lesson and the short Life of S. Vedast, (printed *supra*, p. 72, from a MS. in the King's Library at the British Museum), cannot fail to attract attention. Is the MS. a portion of a York service-book?

No. 6. *The Hereford Missal.*

"*Sanctorum Vedasti et Amandi, Episcoporum.* (*VIII Id. Feb.*)

"*Officium.* Sacerdotes Dei.

"*Oratio.* Adesto, Domine, populo Tuo cum sanctorum confessorum Tuorum Vedasti et Amandi Tibi patrocinio supplicanti, ut quod propria fiducia non praesumit, intercessorum Tibi placentium meritis consequamur. Per Dominum.

"*Epistola.* Plures facti sunt sacerdotes.

"*Gradale.* Exsultabunt sancti. *V*. Cantate Domino. Alleluya. *V*. Fulgebunt justi.

"*Vel Tractus.* Qui seminant.

"*Evangelium.* Sint lumbi vestri.

"*Offertorium.* Exsultabunt sancti.

"*Secreta.* Propitiare, Domine, supplicationibus nostris, et intercedentibus pro nobis sanctis confessoribus Tuis atque pontificibus Vedasto et Amando, his sacramentis caelestibus servientes, ab omni culpa liberos esse concede, ut purificante nos gratia Tua, eisdem quibus famulamur mysteriis emendemur. Per Dominum.

"*Communio.* Justorum animae.

"*Postcommunio.* Deus, qui nos a delictorum contagiis expias perceptione sacramentorum, praesta ut beatorum confessorum Tuorum et pontificum Vedasti et Amandi meritis a cunctis eruamur adversis, et caelestibus vitae deliciis perfruamur. Per."[1]

No. 7. *Office formerly used at Arras.*—The last example is not taken from an English service book: it is an office formerly in use at Arras, but it has, I am informed, been superseded. It is here printed from the *Acta Sanctorum*.[2]

"Quae hactenus de cultu et veneratione S. Vedasti dicta, concludimus prolatis ex Officio Atrebatensi, Hymno, Antiphona, et Oratione de S. Vedasto; ne quis ea quoque desideret. Evangelium ex communi Evangelistarum legitur ex capite x. S. Lucae, *Designavit Dominus et alios septuaginta duos, &c.*

[1] *Missale ad Usum Percelebris Ecclesiae Herfordensis*, p. 241. Edited by Dr. Henderson. 1874.

[2] *Acta Sanctorum*, February 6, p. 801.

Hymnus.

"Voce jucunda resonemus omnes."[1]

"*Vers.* Confessor sancte, et sacerdos magne.

"*Resp.* Beate Vedaste, intercede pro nobis.

"*Antiphona.* Hic est beatus Vedastus, quem fama celebrior verbum Dei praedicaturum Chlodoveo Regi socium itineris adscivit.

"*Oratio.* Deus, qui nos devota B. Vedasti Confessoris Tui atque Pontificis instantia, ad agnitionem Tui sancti Nominis vocare dignatus es; concede propitius, ut cujus solennia colimus, etiam patrocinia sentiamus. Per Dominum nostrum, etc."

The three Feasts of S. Vedast found in the Arras Missal of to-day are:

February 6. Festum Depositionis S. Vedasti Episcopi et hujus Dioecesis Patroni Secundarii, *solemne majus.*

July 15. Festum Relationis S. Vedasti Episcopi. (Atrebati, *duplex minus.*)

October 1. Festum Translationis S. Vedasti Episcopi (Atrebati, *duplex majus*).

[1] The Hymn is printed *in extenso* in *Carmina Vedastina.* No. 8.

VIII.

Churches dedicated to S. Vedast in England and in France.

Almost every person who visits for the first time the Church of S. Vedast in Foster Lane, asks the question, And who was S. Vedast? This enquiry is usually followed by a second, How did it come to pass that a Church in the very heart of the City of London was dedicated to a Saint whose name is so very unfamiliar to English hagiology?

Sir Walter Besant,[1] for example, asks, "Who brought the fame of Vedast and the history of his miracles to the heart of London City?"

The Bishop of Oxford in his *Memorials of S. Dunstan*,[2] points to "the traditionary connexion of Canterbury with the Flemish Churches," and suggests that "the Church of S. Vedast in the City of London, which was in the patronage of the Prior and Convent (of Canterbury) up to the fourteenth century, was no doubt a result or sign of this connexion." The suggestion is one of great interest.

I am not able to answer Sir Walter Besant's question with any certainty. But, in the lists of Sheriffs of London, I observe that one Ralph d'Arras held office in 1276. Is it possible that some ancestor of the Sheriff may have been founder of the Church, or at any rate a generous benefactor to the fabric? That the Sheriff

[1] Besant, *London*, 1892, p. 63.

[2] "The most ancient MS. of the earliest Life of Dunstan is found in the Library of S. Vedast at Arras." *Memorials*, pp. 26, 121.

came from Arras is certainly a highly suggestive circumstance: and the suggestion now offered may serve as a working theory, at any rate until it is dislodged by one more probable. Ralph was clearly a man in high office; it is likely therefore that he was a wealthy man. The fact of his holding such an office would seem to point to his having been for some time resident in the City, as a mere stranger would hardly have been chosen for a post so influential. If his family had been settled for any length of time in London, what is there more probable than that they should have desired to give to a sanctuary in their parish the name of the Patron Saint of the City from which they themselves had come?

Nor is it to be forgotten that a body of Clergy from Arras was settled in England in the middle of the twelfth century. John Myrc, the author of *Instructions for Parish Priests* (edited by Mr. Edward Peacock for the Early English Text Society in 1868) was "a Canon of Lilleshull in Shropshire, a house founded by Richard de Belmeis (nephew of Richard de Belmeis, the first of that name, Bishop of London) between 1144 and 1148 for a body of Arroasian Canons. They were a branch of the order of Canons Regular of S. Austin, who took their name from the City of Arras, near which their first house, dedicated to S. Nicholas was situated."[1] In Dugdale's *Monasticon Anglicanum* it is said that there were five Houses in England which "observed S. Austin's Rule according to the regulations of S. Nicholas of Arroasia";[2] Harewold or Harwood, in Bedfordshire, Nutley or Noctele in Buckinghamshire, Hertland or Hartland in Devonshire, Brunne in Lincolnshire, and Lilleshull in Shropshire. In the Charter of foundation of Lilleshull the Canons are described as "Canonici de ordine Arroasiae": they had previously been settled in the Abbey of Dorchester in Oxfordshire. Arroasia or Arrowasia[3] is the Latinised name of Arrouaise, an Abbey

[1] *Instructions*, etc. Preface, p. 5.

[2] Vol. vi, p. 38. See also pp. 330, 277, 435, 261, 750.

[3] *Monasticon Anglicanum*, vi, 331, 436.

near Bapaume in the immediate vicinity of Arras; of which an account is given in *Le Vieil Arras* par C. le Gentil, juge au Tribunal Civil d'Arras, and published in that City in 1877.[1] The ancient name of the place appears to have been *Arida Gamantia*.

It will be remembered that the Bishopric of Dorchester was transferred from that place to Lincoln by Bishop Remigius about the year 1086.[2] As there had been Canons from Arrouaise at Dorchester, and as these Canons also had a House at Brunne in the county, is it altogether improbable that their association with Lincolnshire may have brought about the dedication of the Church at Tathwell to the Patron Saint of Arras? This is, however, mere conjecture: the dates of the foundation of Brunne and Tathwell are too uncertain to allow of a more distinct theory.

The habit of the Canons of S. Austin "was a long black cassock with a white rochet over it, and over that a black cloak and hood. The monks were always shaved, but these Canons wore beards and caps on their heads."[3] In Helyot's *Histoire des Ordres Monastiques* (edition, Paris, 1714, Vol ii, p. 104-107) a Chapter is devoted to the Canons Regular of Marbach and Arrouaise, and a plate is given representing a Canon of the former place in his habit.

It is certain that the foundation of the Church of S. Vedast in Foster Lane is of very considerable antiquity. Newcourt, in his *Repertorium*, mentions the name of a Rector who was presented to the living in the commencement of the fourteenth century:

"Walt. de London, pr. 16. kal. Jul. 1308."

The Rev. George Hennessy has greatly enlarged Newcourt's list,[4] and has discovered the names of two Rectors of S. Vedast prior to Walter de London, viz:

John de Ruberge, instituted 12 August, 1291.
John de Sevenoke 1299.

[1] See p. 716-726.
[2] *Monasticon Anglicanum*, vi, 323.
[3] *Monasticon Anglicanum*, vi, 38.
[4] In place of Newcourt's list of 33 Rectors, Mr. Hennessy has a list of 43 names: in addition to 9 others since Newcourt's time.

A series of Deeds preserved in S. Paul's Cathedral carries back the existence of the parish to the middle of the thirteenth century. Here is a list of these documents.

Deed No. 1183 defines a tenement in the parish of S. Leonard as being bounded on the south by the church of S. Vedast and on the west by S. Vedast's Lane. The names of the Mayor and Sheriffs who witness the deed give 1284 as its date.

Deed No. 22 grants a tenement in the parish of S. Vedast before the wall of S. Paul's, *in veteri piscaria* (this deed is not dated).

Deeds Nos. 24, 26-56, and 1732, of the reigns of Edward I, Edward II, and Edward III (1272 to 1377) relate to tenements in the Lane called Old Change in the parish of S. Vedast.

Deeds Nos. 25, 265, 1727-1729, of the reigns of Edward I and Edward II (1272 to 1326) relate to tenements in Goderon Lane, now called Gutter Lane, in the parish of S. Vedast.

Deed No. 1726 is a grant by Henry de Cornhill, Dean of S. Paul's, of a piece of ground in the parish of S. Vedast, at the west end of the great street called Westchepe, opposite the great bell tower, *campanale*, of S. Paul's; dated 1249.[1]

So the Parish of S. Vedast in London was certainly in existence in the year 1249.

The church at Tathwell, in Lincolnshire, which is dedicated to S. Vedast, was also of great age, for although the existing building is only a brick structure about a century old (as I learn from a letter with which I have been favoured by the Rev. W. G. Patchell, the present Vicar), yet the "low tower, much patched with brick, and hidden by plaster and rough cast," contains a well preserved Norman arch between the tower and the nave." No old stained glass remains, nor do any of the well-known symbols of S. Vedast appear in connection with the structure.

The church of S. Vedast at Norwich was certainly an ancient foundation also, for, "according to the *Norwich Annals*, by Bartholomew Cotton, the Grey Friars came to Norwich in 1226, and settled between the churches of S. Vedast and S. Cuthbert in Conisford, in a house

[1] See *Historical Manuscripts Commission.* Report ix, pp, 14b, 24b, 25a.

given to them by John de Hastingford, or Haslingford, who from thence is esteemed their founder."[1] This church was, therefore, standing in 1226. The Rev. W. Hudson, Vicar of the church with which S. Vedast's parish is now united, claims for it a very high antiquity; and gives good reasons for believing that the church was commenced in the reign of King Edward the Confessor. "It is plain," he says, "that the occurrence of a dedication to S. Vedast in Norwich at so early a period is to be traced to foreign influence. The existence of that influence is not difficult to discover, though it may not be possible to determine exactly when it led to the dedication of the church."

In Dugdale's *Monasticon* (iv. 17) is printed a Charter of Henry II. which enumerates "medietatem ecclesiae Sancti Vedasti" amongst the possessions of the monastery at Norwich. The King reigned from 1154 to 1189, but from internal evidence it appears that the Charter can scarcely be later than 1160: so it is quite certain that the church of S. Vedast existed at this early period. (In 26, Henry VIII., the church still appears in a list of the property of the Religious House, though under the curious disguise of Ecclesia Sancti "Devasti.")

The Rev. W. Hudson remarks upon the circumstance, that only half the revenues of S. Vedast were in 1160 in the possession of the monastery; and adds that as late as about the year 1200 the other half was still in private hands, and was then held "in the forms of one-sixth and one-third. It is this sub-division," he remarks, "which makes it not unreasonable to identify the church with that of which Edstan held one-sixth in the Confessor's time. His sixth part might have been incorporated in the half held in 1160 by the Monks." If this identification be correct the foundation of the Norwich church will be carried back to the days of the Confessor.

"There are not wanting indications that in the parish of S. Vedast we may trace something of the most primi-

[1] Tanner, *Notitia Monastica*, Norfolk, li, 14; quoted in Dugdale's *Monasticon*, viii, 1522.

tive history of Norwich. The great river-side meadow of Nether Conisford, which extended inland almost to King Street, was here penetrated in early times, not only by the navigable creek over which this bridge was afterwards built, but also by another similar one lower down the river on the other side of the Prince of Wales' Road, which may have been the 'South Creek.'

"They are both marked in King's Map, and were both covered over about the same time. In the bed of the southern one the remains of an old boat were found not long ago. It was near the head of these two creeks that the church of S. Vedast was established, as is generally supposed, before the time of King Edward the Confessor. We may well imagine that the fishermen who formed the earliest population of Norwich could find no more convenient or secure a spot to settle on, at the very foot of the Castle. Moreover the unusual dedication to S. Vedast, a French bishop, suggests the inquiry, how he came to be commemorated here. The name certainly points to some intercourse with Flanders, where S. Vedast lived and was honoured."

The Rev. William Hudson, Vicar of S. Peter Permountergate, Norwich, in a history of his parish (of which the first part was printed in 1889), supplies so many interesting details about the Parish of S. Vedast, that it is well worth while to insert them here.

"The Parish of S. Vedast," he observes, "is most interesting in its early history. It contained the spot where I have suggested that the ford was most probably situated which gave its name to Conisford, and I believe there are indications that its church was first founded at a very early date indeed. It stood in Rose Lane behind Cook's Hospital, and the churchyard extended from Rose Lane to about the middle of the road where Cathedral Street now crosses the Prince of Wales' Road. It is supposed to be mentioned, though not by name, in the Domesday Book of William the Conqueror, where we are told that in the time of King Edward the Confessor

[1] History of the Parish, etc., pp. 3-6, 23.

a certain Edstan held the sixth part of a church in Norwich. That means that a sixth part of the endowment was in his hands. About fifty years later the sixth part of S. Vedast's Church was transferred to the Almoner of the Cathedral Priory, so it is thought that S. Vedast's was the Church of which Edstan held a portion. The name of the Saint to whom it was dedicated seems to indicate a still earlier foundation. About the time of King Alfred the Great there was considerable intercourse between England and Flanders, and when Alfred left the Danish King Guthrum in peaceable possession of Eastern England on condition of his embracing Christianity, and, not finding scholars in England to instruct him, sent for some to France, a distinguished monk named Grimbald came over from S. Omer, quite close to Arras. He settled at Winchester and set up a school there. It is almost certain that among the books he brought with him was a Life of S. Vedast who was much thought of and whose life had been written by the celebrated scholar Alcuin in the time of Charlemagne. In a Benedictional or service book used at Winchester not long after, the name of S. Vedast is specially mentioned. There is therefore nothing improbable in supposing that some of Grimbald's pupils may have come here from Winchester to assist in the instruction of the Danes, and caused the dedication of a church to S. Vedast, whom their master had taught them to honour. This would make the original foundation of the church about the year A.D. 900.

"Though the Church and Parish of S. Vedast have long ceased to exist, the name of S. Vedast still lingers amongst us; but in a form not easily recognizable. 'S. Faith's Lane' is a corruption of 'S. Vedast's Lane.' The change has come about in the following way: The word 'Vedast' was popularly written 'Vaast,' and pronounced differently according to different dialects. Here in Norwich the people pronounced it almost like 'Vaist.' The lane which was near it (the Street of Nether Conisford) was called by the inhabitants. 'S. Vaist's Lane.' Now, it happened that at Horsham, about six miles from Norwich, a Norman knight had founded a monastery dedicated to S. Faith, a very popular virgin martyr. A village sprang up round it, which also took the name of S. Faith's. Here the founder's family got licence to establish a fair, and for many ages 'S. Faith's Fair' for horses and cattle was one of the great events of the year. So it came to pass that in course of time as 'S. Vaist' became forgotten and 'S. Faith' was a familiar name, the virgin-martyr ousted the bishop from his rightful inheritance; S. Vaist's Lane became S. Faith's Lane; and S. Vaist's Church became S. Faith's Church, the change arising solely from a confusion between two words which sounded very much alike. It is interesting to observe that in London, where a church was also dedicated to S. Vedast, a similar confusion has taken place with a very different result. There the people pronounced 'Vaast' like 'Vorst' and so came at last to confuse it with the word 'Forster'; so we have to this day in London S. Vedast's Church in Foster Lane. It is strange that 'Foster' in London and 'Faith' in Norwich should have grown, by confusion of sounds out of the same word.

"One other existing relic of S. Vedast's Church must not be passed over without notice. In the wall of the house attached to Sillett's Stableyard, at the corner of Cathedral Street and Rose Lane, is a large stone with curious markings on it. I have been told that this stone was built into the Churchyard wall. The supposition is that it had at some time or other been taken from the ruins of the church which stood at the back of the stable-yard." The stone here referred to has been recently removed from the wall, and deposited in the Norwich Museum. It has been examined by the Bishop of Stepney, who considers that the interlaced animals represented upon it are of Danish work; that it came from the north, probably from Whitby, to which district the material of the stone belongs; that it is probably part of a Churchyard Cross; and that its workmanship points to the beginning of the tenth century, probably about 925 A.D.

"S. Vedast's Church stood on the low ground of Sillett's Stableyard. It belonged, like those of S. Peter de Parmentergate and S. John the Evangelist, to the Cathedral Monastery. I have already given some account of its probable origin, and how, in the time of King Edward the Confessor, one of the principal burgesses named Edstan is supposed to have held one-sixth part of its endowment. In the time of King Henry I. the Monastery held half of the endowment. Somewhat later Geoffrey de S. Vedast gave the monks a sixth part which then belonged to him, and so by degrees they got the whole. It was the custom in a large monastic establishment to divide the business of the monastery into separate departments, each presided over by its own officer, and to appropriate different portions of their possessions to the different departments. In this way the endowment of S. Vedast was appropriated to the Almoner of the Monastery, whose duty it was to provide for the charities dispensed by the monks, and the endowment of S. Peter de Parmentergate was appropriated to the Infirmarer, who was expected to provide for the wants of the monks when they were ill. Of course the monks were bound to find priests or chaplains to conduct the services. The Churchyard included a good deal of the ground now occupied by South Cathedral Street, and extended as far as the middle of Prince of Wales' Road."

The Church of S. Vedast was destroyed about the year 1570, being then too dilapidated for use. The churchyard was converted into a garden or orchard-ground, and leased out by the Dean and Chapter of Norwich as "S. Vedast's Churchyard."[1]

Many churches in the French Dioceses of Arras, Cambrai, Tournai, Amiens, Rheims, and Beauvais have S. Vedast for their Patron. His Festival, February 6, is observed in the greater number of the Dioceses of France and Belgium. The grandest church raised in his honour was that of the Monastery which bears his

[1] From a letter from the Rev. W. Hudson.

name at Arras. The *Vie de S. Vaast* from which the following particulars are taken, enumerates the successive buildings which have been here erected:

1. The church constructed by S. Aubert on the plan traced by an angel.[1] This was destroyed by fire in 787 A.D.

2. Abbot Raddefride began to build, Abbot Radon completed a new church, finished in 795 A.D. Alcuin, friend and contemporary of Radon gives many details of this grand work in the Poem commencing:

> "Sed miserante Deo, Raddo venerabilis Abbas
> Construxit melius et renovavit eam."[2]

On Easter Monday, 892 A.D., this church was partially destroyed by fire, and a similar fate befell it towards the close of the tenth century.

3. The church was rebuilt 1020-1031, after some long delay, said to have been occasioned by a prevalent idea that the year 1000 A.D. would be the period of the end of the world. Guimann[3] gives an interesting account of this edifice, and of its treasures: amongst which were two chalices of gold adorned with jewels, presented by Charlemagne, together with the crown of that monarch, and a golden frontal set with jewels for the high altar; five stoles of cloth of gold, with maniples, given by Ermentrude, the wife of Charlemagne; "forcipes Sancti Vedasti," the scissors with which his tonsure had been made, and the saint's pectoral cross of gold on which members of the Abbey took their oaths before entering upon any high office.[4]

4. In 1259 A.D., Abbot Paul laid the foundation of a still more magnificent structure, which existed till the middle of the eighteenth century. This church suffered greatly during the siege of Louis XI, the vaulting of the

[1] See *supra* p. 43.
[2] See *Carmina Vedastina*, p. 43.
[3] Guimann. *Cartulaire*, pp. 105-112.
[4] "Crucicula aurea qua de collo ejus aliquando dependisse dicitur: super quam quia periculosum est jurare, homines Sancti Vedasti jubentur Abbati et ecclesiae securitatem facere." Guimann, p. 108.

roof was pierced, and in 1751 the ruined church was taken down.

5. The erection of the present church was interrupted by the Terror, was resumed during the first Empire, and continued during the reign of the Bourbons. King Charles X came to offer prayers in this church in 1827 during his visit to the North of France. It was consecrated June 6, 1833 by Bishop de la Tour d'Auvergne.[1]

Monsieur Terninck in his *Arras* gives details from which the following chronological table may be constructed. It does not accord very well with those just given.

880. A.D. Cathedral destroyed by the Normans, p. 36.
1030. Cathedral consecrated after rebuilding, p. 47.
1189. Serious Fire, p. 88.
1228. Destroyed by Lightning, p. 104.
1259. Cathedral Rebuilt, p. 104.
1372. Tower struck by Lightning, roof destroyed, p. 114.
1493. Devastated by Germans, p. 138.
1747. Church fell, p. 198.

IX.

S. Vedast *alias* Foster.

In legal documents and in public notices the church in Foster Lane is usually called "S. Vedast *alias* Foster." The *alias* has been a source of great perplexity, for it certainly appears, at first sight, that Vedast and Foster can have but little in common.

So, assuredly, thought James Paterson;[1] for he says, in his *Pietas Londinensis*, published early in the eighteenth century, in a notice of the Church of S. Vedast:

"Now it's a very beautiful church, adorned with a fine altar-piece, communion-table, gallery, painting, and several new monuments; and a stately new tower, ninety foot high, wherein is a peal of six fine bells. It's the last of these that are dedicated to two conjunct saints; at the first it was called *S. Foster's*, in memory of some founder or ancient benefactor; but afterwards it was dedicated to *S. Vedast*, Bishop of *Arras* forty years; he died in 570."

He cuts the Gordian knot by inventing the fable of the "two conjunct saints"; if, at least, I understand him rightly: the earlier S. Foster, and the later S. Vedast,—though he seems to have had some misgiving here, and hints that Foster was a "founder or ancient benefactor."

Newcourt falls into a similar error. He says:

"As to the Parish-Church of S. Vedast, alias *Foster*, it stands on the East-side of *Foster Lane*, near the South-end thereof, sometimes called S. Fosters (tho' by

[1] *Pietas Londinensis*, 8vo., London, 1714.

the way, *Mr. R. Smith*, in his fore-cited manuscript saith, that he finds not in any Author, the Name of S. Foster given to any Saint, therefore rather conceives, that it was first given, either from the Street where situate, or from some eminent Man there dwelling, perhaps (if not the Founder) yet some special Benefactor to this Church or place."[1]

Good old Thomas Fuller had, however, hit the mark some fifty years earlier, for in his *Church History of Great Britain*, published in 1655, we find the following passage, which is, for other reasons, of sufficient interest to be transcribed in full. He is writing about the "Douay Convent in Artois," and he says that John Roberts and Father Augustine "obtained leave of Pope Pius Quintus and the King of Spain to build them a convent in Douay; and though Roberts, coming over into England to procure the Catholics' contribution thereunto, had the hard hap to meet with Tyburn in his way, yet the design proceeded and was perfected. For the lord abbot of S. Vedastus (Anglice, S. Forsters) in Arras, a wealthy man and great favourer of the English, yea, generally good to all poor people, built them a cloister, and fine church adjoining, on his own proper cost; to whom, and his successors, the English monks are bound to pay yearly, on the first of February, a wax candle weighing three score pound, by way of homage and acknowledgment of their Founder."[2]

Now here it will be observed that Fuller says "S. Vedastus, *Anglice*, S. Forsters": in other words that *S. Foster* is the English equivalent of the Latin *Sanctus Vedastus*.

Stow evidently understands this, for he says, in the edition of 1603 (which may be conveniently consulted in the very handy reprint edited by Mr. W. J. Thoms,[3] a little volume which is, for many antiquarian purposes,

[1] Ric. Newcourt, *Repertorium Ecclesiasticum Parochiale Londinense*, 4to., Lond., 1708, vol. i, p. 563.

[2] Fuller's *Church History of Britain*, edited by J. S. Brewer, vol. iii, pp. 501, 502.

[3] Published in 1876, p. 117.

to be preferred to the costly "best edition" edited by Strype[1]):

"Then in the same street on the same north side is the Saddlers' Hall, and then Fauster Lane, so called of S. Fauster's, a fair Church lately new built."

Fuller and Stow were right, for the truth is, as Mr. Baring Gould points out, "the name of S. Vedast has gone through strange transformations. He is called Vaast, Vaat, Wâst, and Wât. In French, Gaston. In English, Foster, a corruption marked by Foster Lane, properly S. Vedast's Lane, in the City of London." In the *Salisbury Martyrology* he appears under the name of S. Sawster.[2]

A correspondence took place in the *Athenaeum* during January, 1885, in which the corruption of Vedast into Foster was discussed at length. The first step, from Vedast to Vast, is not altogether unlike the change from Augustine to Austin, or from Regina to Reine. From Vast to Faste is an easy transition, and this is found in a deed in S. Paul's Cathedral, dated 8 Edward III., where the lane in which S. Vedast's Church stands is called "Seint Fastes lane." Another deed, dated May 1360, styles it "Seyn Fastreslane": from Fastreslane[3] to Foster's lane is a natural change enough. After the great Fire the church was called S. Vedast *alias* Foster, a form of the name which it had never previously borne. The connection between Foster and Vedast was forgotten, and the name of Vedast retained for the church, and that of Foster reserved for the lane in which it stands. The steps in this change are Vedast, Vaast, Vast, pronounced Vaust, Faste, Fastés, Fastres, Faustres, Foster.

The deeds referred to in the last paragraph, as being preserved in S. Paul's Cathedral, are these:[4]

[1] The best edition is the sixth, published in two vols., folio, 1754.

[2] See *supra*, in this appendix, p. 86.

[3] "Faster in Faster lane, diocis Canterbury." See "Ancient List of the Parishes of London" (Stowe, Strype), ii, 124, edit. 1754.

[4] See *Historical Manuscripts Commission*. Report ix, pp. 13b, 49b, 55a.

No. 1128. A grant of a messuage at the corner of "Saint Vastes Lane" opposite to the church of S. John Zachary. A.D. 1271.

A series of deeds of the reigns of Edward I. and Edward III., in which the same lane is called "Seint Fastes Lane," and "Venella Sancti Vedasti."

No. 1780. "Seint Fastes Lane." 8 Edw. III.

Nos. 1958, 1959. Seynt Fastres Lane." A.D. 1360.

There has recently been published in *The Index Library* an alphabetical *Catalogue of Wills in the Prerogative Court of Canterbury*.[1] Here are no less than seventy-three wills of inhabitants of S. Vedast's parish, and the name of the parish appears in these various forms:

S. Vedast	48 times	1400-1554.
S. Vedaste	9 ,,	1538-1557.
S. Faster	4 ,,	1474-1513.
S. Faister	5 ,,	1496-1549.
S. Fauster	once	1503.
S. Fouster	,,	1537.
S. Foster	thrice	1548-1555.
S. Fostar	once	1551.
S. Forster	,,	1502.

Changes no less remarkable have occurred in the now Anglicised name of Fidler. It was originally Vicus de Lupo, then Vis de Loup, Videlou: in this form it came to England, where it was changed to Vidlow, Vidler, and Fidler.[2] The change from V to F is not remarkable; it occurs in the names Vane and Fane, and in the words fox and vixen.[3] At Norwich, by a similar change, S. Vedast's Lane was altered into S. Vaist's, and thence corrupted into S. Faith's Lane.[4]

At Colchester, S. Helen's Lane has been changed to

[1] In two volumes, with a copious index of localities.

[2] Condensed from an excellent letter in the *Athenaeum* of 3 January 1885, by Mr. Henry B. Wheatley.

[3] Rev. O. W. Tancock, Head Master of King Edward's School, Norwich, *Athenaeum*, 10 Jan. 1885.

[4] Rev. W. Hudson in *Original Papers of the Norfolk and Norwich Archaeological Society*, vol. x, Part I, pp. 117-142.

Tennant's lane; and S. Osyth into Toosey; just as in London S. Olave's Street has become Tooley Street; and S. Osyth's lane contracted into Sise lane.

It must be admitted that the Saint's anxiety about the pronunciation of his name was fully justified.

It has been suggested that the English surname Foster is derived from S. Vedast[1]: but probably Mark Antony Lower is right when he says: "*Foster*, a nourisher—one who had the care of the children of great men. We have also *Nurse* as a surname. *Foster*, however, is sometimes a corruption of *Forester*."[2]

In a paper contributed by the Rev. F. W. Weaver to the *Proceedings* of the Somerset Archaeological Society,[3] several other curious corruptions of names are noted: as Agace for S. Agatha, Audrie for S. Etheldreda, Bittle for S. Botolph, Bride for S. Bridget, Leger for S. Leodegar, Loy for S. Eligius, Pallets for S. Hippolytus, Parnell for S. Petronilla: whilst Tosting's Well, Herswell, Rumwell, Luckwell, Skippenham Well, Pedwell, represent the Wells of S. Austin, S. Ursula, S. Rumbold, S. Luke, S. Cyprian, and S. Peter.

The Bishop of Stepney[4] adds some other remarkable examples, such as Price from Ap Rhys, Pritchett from Ap Richard, Forrest from Of Orrest; whilst "in a similar manner Saint Liberius has given birth to Saint Oliver, through the form Santo Liverio; and Saint Odo to San Todo from Sant' Odo."

The subject has attracted a good deal of attention amongst learned French Antiquaries. In the *Mémoires de l'Académie d'Arras*,[5] Monsieur le Chanoine Van Drival, Secrétaire-général, has written an important paper, "Des diverses transformations du nom de S. Vaast."

[1] *Sanctorale Catholicum*, Feb. 6.

[2] *English Surnames*, 4th edition, vol. i, p. 134, and vol. ii, p. 62.

[3] Vol. xxxix. On a Painting of S. Barbara at Cucklington.

[4] *Off the Mill*, p. 237.

[5] *Mémoires*, etc., for 1886, pp. 204-208. Canon Van Drival refers to the correspondence in the *Athenaeum* of January 3, 10, 24; and of February 7, in 1885.

He observes that although the first Rector of S. Vedast, Foster Lane, whose name is recorded was instituted to that church in 1308, the church itself is mentioned in the *actes mortuaires* of a century earlier: and he suggests that at the time of the Norman Conquest, or possibly in the days of Edward the Confessor, a body of Frenchmen passing over into England may have founded the Church.

It has already been pointed out (*supra*, p. 89) that Ralph d'Arras was Sheriff of London in 1276. It may be possible at a later period, when the most ancient documents of the City of London are printed *in extenso*, to trace back the history of the family to an earlier date. For this purpose the names of witnesses to deeds are of great value.

X.

Labyrinth in the Pavement of the Ancient Cathedral at Arras.

In the *Archaeological Journal* (vol. xv. pp. 216-235) is a very interesting and able paper by the Rev. Edward Trollope, F.S.A. (afterwards Bishop of Nottingham) entitled "Notices of Ancient and Mediaeval Labyrinths," illustrated by engravings of no less than fourteen examples. The learned author describes several Labyrinths of very ancient times, in Egypt and in Greece; and passes on to consider their frequent occurrence in churches and cathedrals in Italy and in France, and even in Algeria.

"An octagonal Labyrinth," he says, "thirty-four and a half feet in diameter, composed of yellow and grey quarries, formed part of the pavement of the Nave in Arras Cathedral, until the Revolution." It was almost identical in plan with a Labyrinthine pavement in the parish church of S. Quentin, constructed during the twelfth century, of exactly the same size as that of Arras. "A precisely similar pavement was placed in the centre of Amiens Cathedral in 1288, but of a rather large size measuring forty-two feet across. It was destroyed in 1825, but its central compartment, still preserved in the Amiens Museum, consists of an octagonal grey marble slab, decorated with a brass or latten-cross in the centre, between the limbs of which were ranged small figures of Evrart, Bishop of Amiens, the three architects of the Cathedral, and four angels, cut in white marble, with a legend around the whole octagon referring to the building of the fabric."

LABYRINTH IN THE PAVEMENT OF THE ANCIENT CATHEDRAL AT ARRAS.

Dr. Trollope adds that the signification and use of these curious works varied from time to time. "The church had adopted them as symbolical of herself: and when figures were designed in the centre of their manifold windings, such as those of deceased bishops, architects, or builders, ranged round a cross, instead of the actual words SANCTA ECCLESIA, the same idea doubtless was intended to be conveyed, and the persons so represented were presumed to be resting in the bosom of the Church as in an Ark of Salvation. But afterwards, these Labyrinths were made to serve another purpose, and received an entirely new name. This was when the period of the Crusades was drawing to a close, and when certain spots nearer home than Jerusalem began to be visited by pilgrims, instead of their actually resorting to Palestine: and a pilgrimage to our Lady of Loretto, to S. James of Compostella, or even to the shrine of S. Frideswide at Oxford, to that of S. Thomas of Canterbury or of S. Hugh of Lincoln, began to be looked upon as too great an exertion on the part of the faithful.

"Then Labyrinths became, as it is stated, instruments of performing penance for non-fulfilment of vows of pilgrimage to the Holy Land, and were called *Chemins de Jérusalem*,[1] as being emblematical of the difficulties attending a journey to the real Jerusalem, or of those encountered by the Christian before he can reach the heavenly Jerusalem: whence the centre of these curious designs was not unfrequently called CIEL. And, finally, they were used as a means of penance for sins of omission or commission in general: penitents being ordered to follow out all the sinuous courses of these Labyrinths upon their hands and knees, to repeat so many prayers at fixed stations, and others when they reached the central CIEL, which in several cases took a whole hour to effect; whence these works, as stated by

[1] A drawing, made during the last century, representing a Labyrinth in the Abbey Church of S. Bertin at S. Omer, has this inscription: "Entré du Chemin de Jérusalem autrefois marqué sur le carreau de l'Eglise de S. Bertin."

M. Wallet,[1] were not unfrequently termed *La lieue.*"

In the Nave of Chartres Cathedral, a large circular Labyrinth exists; it is figured in the *Archaeological Journal*, and is thirty feet in diameter, its path being 668 feet in length. At Sens, there was a similar work, the lines being filled in with lead: it is said to have required 2,000 steps in order to reach the centre.

The design of the Labyrinth at Arras, which forms the illustration of this note, is taken from Mons. Terninck's *Essai historique et monographique sur l'ancienne Cathédral d'Arras* (Quarto, Paris and Arras) pp. 55-57, with an accompanying plate. The Labyrinth is also figured in *Arras et ses Monuments, sommaire historique, statistique, et chronologique* (8vo., Arras, 1853.)

Those who desire further information on this curious subject are referred to Dr. Trollope's paper, which, as will have been observed, has supplied the material for the present note.

[1] M. Wallet. *Description d'une Crypte et d'un Pavé mosaïque de l'ancienne église de S. Bertin à Saint-Omer.* Douai, 1843.

XI.

The Sainte Ampoule.

The word *Ampullae* frequently denotes "the flasks or cruets, generally of precious metal, which contain the wine and water used at the Altar." In some parts of Germany these vessels are known by the name of "pollen," which is probably derived from ampullae.

More commonly, however, the term ampulla denotes a vessel used for consecrated oil or chrism. In the Gregorian Sacramentary, in the directions for the benediction of Chrism, on Thursday in Holy Week, "Ampullae duo cum oleo" are to be prepared.

By far the most renowned ampulla of this kind is that which was said to have been brought by a dove from heaven at the Baptism of Clovis. "Hincmar, in the service which he drew up for the coronation of Charles the Bald, 840 A.D., speaks of the first Christian King of the Franks having been anointed and consecrated with the heaven-descended chrism, whence that which he himself used was derived (coelitus sumpto chrismate, unde nunc habemus, perunctus et in regem sacratus), as if of a thing well known."

"In Flodoard, who wrote in the first half of the tenth century, we find the legend fully developed. He tells us,[1] that at the Baptism of Clovis, the clerk who bore the chrism was prevented by the crowd from reaching his proper station; and that when the moment for unction arrived, S. Remi raised his eyes to heaven and prayed,

[1] *Historia Ecclesiae Remensis* i. 13, in Migne's *Patrologia*, vol. cxxxv. p. 52, c.

when 'ecce subito columba ceu nix advolat candida rostro deferens ampullam caelestis doni chrismate repletam.'"[1]

The Article *Ampulla* in the *Dictionary of Christian Antiquities*, from which the above paragraphs are taken, contains an illustration of an ampulla of the seventh century.

There does not appear to be any contemporary or even early mention of this curious and poetical legend.

The first mention of the story of the Sainte Ampoule is found in Hincmar (*Coronationes Regiae*: Migne, *Patrologia Latina*, vol. cxxv., p. 806), and is therefore of very late origin. In a note to Gibbon's *Decline and Fall of the Roman Empire* (edition of 1853-5, iv., 166) it is said that the Abbé de Vertot (*Mémoires de l'Académie des Inscriptions*, tom. ii., pp. 619-633) has undermined the foundations of the story with consummate dexterity. I have not seen this memoir.

In Baedeker's *Handbook to Northern France*[2] an account is given of the Treasures preserved in the Cathedral at Rheims. Amongst these is the

"Sainte Ampoule, the successor of the famous *Ampulla Remensis*, which a dove is said to have brought from heaven at the Baptism of Clovis. With the inexhaustible oil which this flask contained all the Kings of France were anointed down to Louis XVI. During the Revolution the sacred vessel was shattered, but a fragment was piously preserved in which some of the oil was said still to remain. This was carefully placed in a new Sainte Ampoule, and used at the Coronation of Charles X. in 1825."

Carlyle, in his inimitable style, gives a graphic account of the iconoclasts at Rheims.[3] "Last and grimmest of all, note old Ruhl, with his brown dusky face and long white hair; of Alsatian Lutheran breed; a man whom age and book-learning have not taught; who, haranguing the old men of Rheims, doth hold up the sacred

[1] See *supra*. p. 24.
[2] Edition of 1894, p. 127. Reims.
[3] *French Revolution*, Book v., Ch. ii., under date 1791.

Ampulla (Heaven-sent, wherefrom Clovis and all Kings have been anointed) as a mere worthless oil-bottle, and dash it to sherds on the pavement there; who alas, shall dash much to sherds, and finally his own wild head by pistol shot, and so end it."

And indeed that tragic end soon came: for "Old Ruhl shot a pistol through his old white head; dashed his life to pieces as he had done the sacred Phial of Rheims."[1]

A picture in the North Transept of the Cathedral of Rheims represents the Baptism of Clovis.

[1] Ibid, Book v., Ch. v., under date 1795.

XII.

Note on the Library at Arras.

In the second *Voyage Littéraire de deux Religieux Bénédictins de la Congrégation de Saint Maur*[1] is a very pleasant account of their visit to the Abbey of S. Vaast. The two fellow-travellers were Dom Edmund Martene and Dom Ursin Durand, and the object of their mission was historical research. They record, with evident gratification, the hospitality with which they were received; they relate their generous treatment by the Grand Prior, and their cordial welcome from the aged Bishop. They give some account of the Treasury of the Abbey, and note some ritual peculiarities in the service. But, of course, the chief interest for them centres in the Library. "La Bibliothèque est excellente, soit pour le nombre, soit pour la qualité des livres, et passe avec justice pour la meilleure et la plus nombreuse qui soit en province. . . Ce que nous venons de rapporter nous fait voir que les six incendies qui sont arrivées à S. VVast, n'ont pas tout consumé, et nous font aisément juger des trésors immenses que nous y trouverions, si nous avions tout ce que les flammes nous ont ravi; mais ce n'est pas seulement la bibliothèque et les archives qu'on doit admirer à S. VVast. Tout y est grand et magnifique. L'église est comparable aux plus belles du royaume, grande, large, élevée, delicate, et ornée: surtout le tour des chapelles et le choeur. Les chaires sont d'un travail immense. L'histoire de l'ancien et du nouveau testament y est representée. L'autel est simple

[1] Quarto. Paris. 1724. pp. 62, 65, 66.

STAMP FOR COVERS OF BOOKS IN THE LIBRARY OF ARRAS.

S. VEDAST, IN HEAVEN, DICTATING TO A SCRIBE.

Illumination from a Manuscript of the Eleventh Century at Arras.

To face page 113.

selon l'ancien usage, mais derrière l'autel on voit une pyramide de pierre soutenue par quatre colomnes de porphyre, au-dessus de laquelle sont les corps de S. VVast, de S. Adulfe et de S. Ranulfe, dans trois châsses d'argent."

They mention the magnificent Evangéliaire de S. Vaast: "Un très-beau texte des Evangiles écrit en lettre d'or, qui servit autrefois à la messe." It is indeed "un très-beau texte," written on purple vellum in alternate lines of gold and silver, and containing the Gospels for certain Holy Days.

This wonderful book has been made the subject of a monograph, entitled "L'Evangéliaire de Saint Vaast d'Arras et la calligraphie Franco-Saxonne du IXe siècle, par Léopold Delisle," published in Paris in 1888, and now out of print. It contains a series of five fine plates, illustrating the admirable illuminations of the manuscript.

The learned Benedictines also supply an illustration (not, it must be confessed, an accurate one) of the seated monk, so delicately traced in the original manuscript, an exact facsimile of which will be found in the present volume. The scribe, they say, represents the Rodulfus of the verses commencing "Hunc ego Rodulfus."[1] "Parmi les plus anciens manuscrits il y en a un de S. Augustin sur les Pseaumes, écrit dans le neuvième siècle; à la tête duquel le moine Rodulfe qui l'a copié est ainsi representé avec l'ancien habit monastique des religieux de S. Wast."

It is impossible to describe, in this place, the precious treasures of the Arras Library, with its eleven hundred manuscripts.[2] It is exceedingly rich in Liturgical manuscripts belonging to Arras itself. Of Arras Missals, there are two of the thirteenth century, Nos. 309, 334; five of the fourteenth, Nos. 297, 303, 391, 687, 886; two of the fifteenth, Nos. 275, 638. Of Arras Breviaries, one of the fourteenth century, No. 412; two of the fifteenth, Nos. 356, 768. Of Hymns, an extremely valuable collection,

[1] Printed in *Carmina Vedastina*, p. 47.

[2] See a few words upon the subject in *Carmina Vedastina*, p. viii.

compiled in the eleventh century, No. 734, laid under contribution in *Carmina Vedastina*.

These are but a few of the Liturgical treasures of the collection. The printed *Catalogue* of manuscripts in the Library, carefully compiled, is of great value to the student; and much interesting information will be found in Canon Van Drival's *L'Abbaye de Saint Vaast d'Arras*, printed at Arras in 1877. The Library itself is a noble building. A good view of it is given in the last-named work.

XIII.

Illustrations to the Present Volume.

Two of these illustrations are taken from windows in Suffolk churches, and were traced by Mr. Watling, who devoted much time to the examination of the painted glass remaining in the county.

1. From Blythburgh Church. The fragment of inscription beneath the figure supplies three letters only of the Saint's name, S. FOS . . . , a portion of the letter T can still be read. The whole name should be S. FOSTER, an alternative name for S. VEDAST. The Saint is vested in episcopal robes, holds his pastoral staff in his left hand, whilst his right is raised in benediction: at his feet are a fox or wolf, and a dead goose.

2. From Long Melford Church. Here also the Saint is episcopally vested, but the fox is at his feet with the goose hanging over his back, the head of the goose between the fox's jaws.

The two following illustrations are taken from manuscripts at Arras, both of the eleventh century. The admirable tracings were executed by Monsieur Lavoine.

3. This facsimile, which is exactly the size of the original, is part of a delicately-executed border which frames some verses composed by Rodulphus de Monchy, printed in *Carmina Vedastina*, p. 47. (The MS. itself, No. 860, is a commentary on the Psalms, by S. Jerome.) Here is seen S. Vedast seated on a throne in heaven, a long scroll before him, on which he is tracing characters with a pen: a kind of inverted rainbow hangs beneath him. The throne on which the Saint sits is coloured green, the background behind the figure glows with roseate

hues; the letters which he is tracing on the scroll are lightly indicated, but are not legible. The arc of the rainbow is tinted with various lines of gold colour, of red, and of green. Below him sits a scribe, his hood thrown back from his head, writing from the dictation of the Saint on the pages of an open book: the letters are black with a rubricated initial. The inkhorn on his right is placed in a cup-like stand, its stopper secured by a string. The whole composition is very delicately drawn.

4. This very curious illustration is taken from MS. No. 903 in the Arras Library, the Tractatus de Trinitate of S. Augustine. The original picture is drawn with a pen, and is of the same age as the manuscript, that is to say, of the eleventh century. Here the scribe, Evrardus by name, offers his book, this very treatise, to S. Vedast in heaven. The Saint wears no mitre, but he holds in his hand his pastoral staff, and a nimbus surrounds his head. Below his feet are the following verses:

Scire volens summam Deitatem cuncta creantem
Ter quinos hinc, lector, habes ex ordine libros,
Quos Augustinus, claro sermone retexens,
Edidit insignis rethor studio vehementi.
Ergo, Vedaste, favens scriptoris suscipe munus
Evrardi poscens regnum miserando polorum.

5. A Labyrinth formerly existing in the pavement of the ancient Cathedral of Arras. This has already been described in a preceding article, No. IX.

6. A stamp for the covers of books used in 1610 in the Library at Arras.

A figure of the Bishop standing, in benediction, holding his pastoral staff. At his feet the bear, his frequent companion. On either side two branches, perhaps intended for palms. Beneath his feet three shields:

Dexter. Or, a cross moline gules: for S. Vedast.
Centre. Argent, a chevron vert between three estoiles gules: for Abbot Philip de Caverel.
Sinister. A castle with three towers: for Arras.

Each of these shields is ensigned by a pastoral staff, and in the case of the centre shield, a mitre is added.

XIV.

List of a few Books Relating to S. Vedast and to Arras. *(In my own Collection).*

LITURGICAL.

Missale Parisiense cum Proprio Atrebatensi. 4to. Paris, 1841.

Breviarium Atrebatense. 8vo. Paris, 1834. 4 vols.

Rituale ad usum Dioecesis Atrebatensis. 4to. Arras, 1757.

Supplément aux Graduel et Antiphonaire Romains pour le Diocèse d'Arras. 8vo. Arras, 1889.

Eucologe (français-latin) du Diocèse d'Arras. 12mo. Lille, 1845.

Office Divin complet en Latin et en Français a l'usage du Diocèse d'Arras. 8vo. Arras, c. 1827.

HAGIOLOGY.

Acta Sanctorum. (Bollandist). Volume containing Feb. 6.

Les Petits Bollandistes. 8vo. Paris, 1880. (17 volumes).

Vie de Saint Vaast premier Evêque d'Arras. 8vo. Arras, 1877.

Mémoires de l'Académie des Sciences, Lettres, et Arts d'Arras.

Series ii. Tome xvii. 8vo. Arras, 1886.

p. 193. Polémique sur le Lieu de Naissance de Saint-Vaast, par M. le Chanoine Van Drival.

p. 204. Des diverses transformations du Nom de S. Vaast.

p. 209. Vita Sanctissimi ac Beatissimi Vedasti Episcopi et Confessoris. [See appendix i. pp. 47-58].

Mémoires. Series ii. Tome v.
p. 251. Le lieu de naissance de S. Vaast : dissertation historique, par M. l'Abbé Van Drival.

ARRAS : THE CITY AND THE ABBEY.

L'Abbaye de Saint-Vaast : Monographie Historique, Archéologique, et Littéraire de ce Monastère par MM. Adolphe de Cardevacque et Auguste Terninck. 4to. Arras, 1865-8. 3 vols.

Arras, Histoire de l'Architecture et des beaux-arts, par A. Terninck. 4to. Arras, 1879.

L'Abbaye de Saint-Vaast d'Arras : description et histoire des bâtiments, par M. le Chanoine E. Van Drival. 4to. Arras, 1877. (Statistique Monumentale du département du Pas-de-Calais).

Recherches sur les Monuments et les Objets d'Art relatifs à l'Abbaye de Saint-Vaast par Auguste Terninck, accompagnées d'une étude numismatique par L. Dancoisne. 4to. Arras, 1869.

Sigillographie de la Ville d'Arras et de la Cité . . . par A. Guesnon. 4to. Arras et Paris. 1865.

Essai Historique et Monographique sur l'ancienne Cathédrale d'Arras, par M. Terninck. 4to. Paris et Arras. N.D.

Le Trésor Sacré de la Cathédrale d'Arras . . . par M. l'Abbé E. Van Drival. 8vo. Arras, 1860.

Le Vieil Arras, ses Faubourgs, sa Banlieue, ses Environs, Souvenirs Archéologiques et Historiques par C. le Gentil. 8vo. Arras, 1887.

Catalogue des Manuscrits de la Bibliothèque de la Ville d'Arras. 8vo. Arras, 1860.

Notice sur l'ancienne Cathédral d'Arras et sur la nouvelle église Saint-Nicholas. 8vo. Arras, 1839.

Règlements Ecclésiastiques et Statuts pour le Diocèse d'Arras. 8vo. Arras, 1855, avec supplément.

La Place Saint-Vaast et la Croix dite de S. Bernard par Henri Loriquet. 8vo. Arras, 1884.

Arras et ses Monuments, sommaire historique, statistique, et chronologique. 8vo. Arras et Plancy. 1853.

Arras Gallo-Romain. Description d'objets de cette époque et topographie de la ville antique, par A. Terninck. 8vo. Arras, 1886.

Daily Life at Old S. Gregory's at Douai, with an Inventory of 1636. (*Downside Review.* Vol. xi., No. 1., 1892. pp. 29-49).

CHRONICLES AND CARTULARIES.

Cartulaire de l'Abbaye de Saint-Vaast d'Arras rédigé au XIIe siècle par Guimann, et publié pour la première fois, au nom de l'Académie d'Arras par M. le Chanoine Van Drival. 8vo. Arras. 1875.

Ambassade en Espagne et en Portugal (en 1582) de Dom Jean Sarrazin, Abbé de S. Vaast. . . par Philippe de Caverel. 8vo. Arras. 1860.

Nécrologe de l'Abbaye de S. Vaast d'Arras publié pour la première fois au nom de l'Académie d'Arras par M. le Chanoine Van Drival. 8vo. Arras. 1878.

Les Annales de Saint-Bertin et de Saint-Vaast, suivies de fragments d'une chronique inédite. . . par l'Abbé C. Dehaisnes. 8vo. Paris. 1871.

Le Collége de Saint-Vaast à Douai 1619-1789, par M. Adolphe de Cardevacque. (Mémoires de la Société d'Agriculture de Sciences et d'Arts séant à Douai. Deuxième Série. Tom. xv., pp. 89-208). 8vo. Douai. 1882.

Chronique d'Arras et de Cambrai par Balderic, Chantre de Térouane au XIe siècle. . . par le Docteur Le Glay. 8vo. Paris. 1834.

Chronique d'Arras et de Cambrai par Balderic . . . traduite en Français, d'après l'édition latine de M. Le Glay par M. Faverot. 8vo. Valenciennes. N.D.

XV.

List of Rectors of S. Vedast, Foster Lane, in the City of London, from 1291 to the Present Time.

For this list I am indebted to the courtesy of the Rev. George Hennessy, who is preparing for publication a work, entitled "Novum Repertorium Ecclesiasticum Parochiale Londinense," and who has favoured me with this important extract from his manuscript. It is by far the fullest and most accurate list which has ever been printed, and is the result of close and careful study of Episcopal Registers, Patent Rolls, Original Wills, and other authentic sources of information.

LIST OF RECTORS.

Name	Date
John de Ruberge	1291
John de Sevenoke	1299
Walter de Salerns, *alias* de London	1308 to 1350
John de Watford	1313
Richard Symon de Northwolde	1316/7
Walter called "le Fuster"	
John de Pryttlewell	1322 to 1327
William de Rothwell	1327
Robert de Stokes	1335
Hugh Aunfray	1335
Robert Luke	1350 to 1351
Thomas Vaghan	1351
William de Cranesley	1358/9 to 1363
John de Hermesthorp	1364/5
John de Lynton	1367 to 1391
Henry Brown	1396 ,, 1404
Richard Cawdray	1421 ,, 1421/2
Henry Penwortham	1421/2

Robert Felton	1425 to 1438
Richard Andrew, LL.D.	1438 " 1440
Adam Moleynes	1440 " 1440
William Skelton, LL.B.	1440 " 1448
Robert Smith	1448 " 1457
Haymund Haydock, S.T.B.	1457 " 1465/6
Thomas Rotheram, *alias* Scott, S.T.B.	1465/6 " 1467
Edmund Lichfield, A.M.	1467 " 1479
David Williams, D.D.	1479 " 1482
William Skyby, A.M.	1482 " 1488
John Argenteyn.	1488 " 1507/8
John Peers, LL.B.	1507/8 "
John Peers	1523 " 1536
Richard Champion, A.M.	1536 " 1542
Richard Ridge	1542 " 1550
Gilbert Laybourne, S.T.B.	1550
William Morsett	1564
Martin Clipsham	1571
Thomas Blage, B.A.	1571 to 1578
Joshua Gilpin, M.A.	1578 " 1603/4
Michael Rabbet, S.T.B.	1603/4 to 1617
James Batty, M.A.	1617 " 1645
Foulke Bellers, M.A.	1643

INTERREGNUM.

Christopher Shute, S.T.P.	1661 to 1663
—— Usher	1671
William Masters, M.A.	1671 to 1684
Marmaduke Hopkins	1684 " 1707
Benjamin Ibbot, M.A.	1707 " 1716
Nathaniel Marshall, LL.B.	1716 " 1729
Isaac Maddox, D.D.	1729/30 " 1736
John Thomas, D.D.	1736 " 1744
Theophilus Lewis Barbault, M.A.	1744 " 1779
Francis Wollaston, M.A., LL.D.	1779 " 1815
Tindal Thompson Walmsley, B.D.	1815 " 1847
Thomas Pelham Dale, B.A.	1847 " 1882
William Sparrow Simpson, D.D.	1882

NOTES ON A FEW OF THE RECTORS.[1]

Walter de London was Prebendary of Brownswood, in S. Paul's Cathedral, from about 1331 to 1336. In 1335 he became Dean of Wells. He was the King's confessor and almoner.

William de Rothwell was presented by the King to the prebendal stall of Isledon, in S. Paul's Cathedral, 22nd July, 1350. He became Archdeacon of Essex, 20th June, 1351.

John de Hermesthorp was Master of S. Katherine's Hospital, 26th December, 1368. On 13th May, 1363, the King, whose chaplain he was, made him Prebendary of S. Stephen's, Westminster; a preferment which he soon resigned, though he resumed it in 1366.

Richard Cawdray became Rector of S. Dunstan-in-the-East in 1439. He was Dean of the Collegiate Church of S. Martin-le-Grand in the same year.

Henry Penwortham became Rector of S. Mary-le-Bow, 21st December, 1420.

Robert Felton was Prebendary of Caddington Major, in S. Paul's Cathedral.

Adam Moleynes was Prebendary of Weldland, in S. Paul's Cathedral. In September, 1440, he became Archdeacon of Sarum, and in the following year, Dean of that Cathedral. He was also Dean of S. Burian, Cornwall. In 1445 he was consecrated Bishop of Chichester, and was made keeper of the Privy Seal. "He was slain at Portsmouth by the Mariners suborned thereunto by Richard, Duke of York, 9th June, 1449."

Haymund Haydock became Rector of S. Mary-le-Bow, 17th April, 1456.

Thomas Rotheram was a Fellow of King's College, Cambridge, then Master of Pembroke Hall, Chaplain to King Edward IV., Provost of Beverley, keeper of the King's Privy Seal, Bishop of Rochester, 1467; Bishop of Lincoln, 1471; Lord Chancellor, 1474; Archbishop of

[1] For Rectors prior to 1708, these notes are derived mainly from Newcourt and Le Neve: after that period, from various sources.

York in 1480. He died, it is said, of the plague, 29th May, 1500.

David Williams became Rector of S. Dunstan-in-the-East, 24th May, 1482, Master of the Rolls, 26th November, 1487; died 1492.

Richard Ridge was perhaps the last Abbot of Notley, near Long Crendon, in Buckinghamshire.

Martin Clipsham became Rector of Stanford-le-Hope, in the county of Essex, 14th May, 1584.

Thomas Blage became Rector of Braxted Magna, in the county of Essex, 9th September, 1570. On 1st February, 1591-2, being then Master of Clare Hall, Cambridge, he was made Dean of Rochester: he died in October, 1611.

Joshua Gilpin became Rector of S. Anne, Aldersgate, 2nd September, 1575.

James Batty "was for his loyalty in the late rebellion of 1642, sequestered, plundered, forced to flie, and died." (*Mercurius Rusticus*, p. 254).

Christopher Shute, Prebendary of Portpool, in S. Paul's Cathedral, was collated to the Archdeaconry of S. Albans, 30th June, 1664, and died 24th April, 1671.

William Masters became Prebendary of Caddington Major, in S. Paul's Cathedral, 14th February, 1666-7.

Benjamin Ibbot became Prebendary of Westminster, 26th November, 1724. He had previously been Treasurer of Wells Cathedral, 13th November, 1708; Boyle Lecturer in 1713 and 1714; Rector of S. Paul's, Shadwell. He died in April, 1725.

Nathaniel Marshall was made Canon of Windsor, 1st May, 1722, and died 5th February, 1729-30.

Isaac Maddox became Dean of Wells in 1773; Bishop of S. Asaph, 1736; translated to Worcester, 1743; died 27th September, 1759.

John Thomas was chaplain in ordinary to the King; Dean of Peterborough 1740; Prebendary of Westminster and Canon Residentiary of S. Paul's, 1742; Bishop of Lincoln, 1st April, 1744; translated to Salisbury in 1761. He died 20th July, 1766, aged 85, and was buried in Salisbury Cathedral. (It is very remarkable that there were three contemporary Bishops named John Thomas; and that two of these were Bishops of Salisbury, one from 25th May, 1757 to 4th May, 1761;[1] the other from 4th November, 1761, till his death in 1766. The last named was Rector of S. Vedast).

Thomas Pelham Dale, son of Thomas Dale, Canon Residentiary of S. Paul's, on leaving S. Vedast in 1881, became Rector of Sawsthorpe, Lincolnshire, and died 19th April, 1892.

In ancient times, till 1351, the living was in the gift of the Prior and Convent of Christ Church, Canterbury. King Edward III. presented John de Hermesthorp: from which period (1421), it remained in the gift of the Archbishop of Canterbury "to this time," says Newcourt, writing in 1708. After the Great Fire of 1666, the parish of S. Michael-le-Quern was united with that of S. Vedast, and the presentation to this united benefice was in the alternate patronage of the Archbishop and the Bishop of London. In 1882, the already united benefices of S. Matthew Friday Street with S. Peter Cheap (in the alternate patronage of the Bishop of London and the Duke of Buccleuch), were united to the benefices of S. Vedast with S. Michael-le-Quern. The presentation to these four united benefices is now vested in the Bishop of London (who presents twice in every three turns), and the Duke of Buccleuch (who presents once in every three turns).

[1] In the brief period between 2nd June, 1761 and 5th October, 1761, the see was occupied by Robert Hay Drummond, translated from S. Asaph to Salisbury, and from Salisbury to York.

NOTE TO PAGE 89.

In addition to Ralph d'Arras named at the above reference as having filled the office of Sheriff in 1276, one Robert d'Arras is also found as a resident in London at about the same period. His name occurs in the important *Calendar of Wills proved and enrolled in the Court of Husting, London*, A.D. 1258—A.D. 1688, edited by Dr. Sharpe for the Corporation of the City. The following entries relate to the family:

About 1281, Henry le Wimpler leaves to Thomas his son his chest in the seld (or shop) of Robert de Arraz. p. 56.

About 1283, Stephen de Scholaunde leaves to Roger his son two chests in the seld of Robert de Arras. p. 66.

About 1299, Hugh son of Robert de Arras bequeaths to Alice his mother his capital tenement in the parish of S. Antonin. p. 144.

About 1326-7, Robert de Worstede, mercer, bequeaths to Richard his son his entire aumbry (*armariolum*) and chest with two covers in the seld of Alice de Arras. p. 319.

About 1326-7, Alice late wife of Robert de Arras bequeaths certain property to persons named in her will. No part of the property, however, is in the parish of S. Vedast. p. 320.

In 1342, mention is made (in the will of Thomas atte Puwe) of a seld called "Arraces Selde"; which the editor suggests is probably the same as that which formerly belonged to Robert de Arras, referred to in previous entries. p. 472.

In a list of Aldermen, probably written *circa* 14 Edward I. (1285-6) occurs the name of Robertus de Arras as Alderman of the "Warda de Lodingeberi." p. 703.

Here then we have Robert d'Arras the Alderman, Alice his wife, and Hugh their son. Either the seld must have been of considerable importance, for it was known in 1342 as "Arraces Selde"; or else the family must have been still resident in London at that period.

sanCtVs VeDastVs epIsCopVs

atrebatensIs LIbera gratIa

saLVatorIs ChrIstI CateChIsta et

InstrVCtor regIs ChLoDoVaeI.

INDEX

S. VEDAST, IN HEAVEN, DICTATING TO A SCRIBE.

Illumination from a Manuscript of the Eleventh Century at Arras.

CARMINA VEDASTINA.

COLLECTED AND EDITED BY

W. SPARROW SIMPSON, D.D., F.S.A.,

Sub-Dean and Librarian of S. Paul's Cathedral,
One of the Honorary Librarians of His Grace the Archbishop of Canterbury,
Rector of S. Vedast, London.

LONDON:
ELLIOT STOCK, 62, PATERNOSTER ROW, E.C.
1895.

[This impression is limited to 250 copies, of which only a few will be offered for sale.]

To

SIDNEY YOUNG, Esq., F.S.A.,

Master of the Barber Surgeons' Company,

IN GRATEFUL ACKNOWLEDGMENT

OF HIS ENTHUSIASTIC INTEREST IN THE HISTORY OF

S. VEDAST,

AND OF HIS LABOURS ON MY BEHALF AT

ARRAS,

I DEDICATE THESE PAGES.

INTRODUCTION.

In all broad England there are, so far as I am able to ascertain, only two churches which bear the name of the Apostle of the Atrebates. These are the Church of S. Vedast, in Foster Lane, in the heart of the city of London, and the Church of Tathwell, in Lincolnshire, about three miles from Louth.

There was, indeed, a third church under the same invocation at Norwich, about midway between the Castle and the River Wenson, near the Cathedral precinct, and on the edge of the precinct of the Grey Friars; but the church was destroyed in 1564, and the parish united to that of S. Peter, Permountergate.

I was presented to the rectory of S. Vedast, in the city of London, in 1882, and, naturally enough, the history of the patron saint at once engaged my attention. Notwithstanding the dedication of the Church, which should have kept him in remembrance, it soon became apparent to me that S. Vedast and his apostolic labours were almost entirely forgotten; some even went so far as to doubt whether such a person had ever lived. To remedy this state of things, I gave a lecture in the parish on *The Life and Legend of S. Vedast*, which was printed in 1887.

I have devoted much of my all too scanty leisure to further researches on the same subject, and I hope to be able to print some of the results of my labours. The present publication is the first fasciculus. It is an attempt to gather together all the Vedastine hymns which I have been able to discover in ancient manuscripts or in printed ritual books, and to add to these a few verses from different sources in further illustration of the subject.

In the autumn of 1894 I was able to carry out a long-cherished wish, that, namely, of making a pilgrimage to Arras. The Bibliothèque de la Ville formed the principal attraction, scarcely second to which was the delight of visiting the scene of S. Vedast's labours, the heart of the diocese of which he was the first Bishop.

Of the 1,102 manuscripts which the town of Arras now possesses, no less than 857 were written in the monastery of S. Vaast, whose library was 'l'une des plus riches et des mieux composées du nord de la France.' The monks of Arras, as Messieurs Cardevacque and Terninck record (*L'Abbaye de Saint Vaast*, iii. 58), were diligent in writing and transcribing, not for their own house alone, but also for a great number of religious houses in their neighbourhood, and even for convents at some considerable distance. These precious manuscripts are carefully and minutely described in the excellent *Catalogue des Manuscrits de la Bibliothèque de la Ville d'Arras*, printed at Arras in 1860. The catalogue is enriched by two copious indices—the first, *Table alphabétique par nom d'auteurs et par titres;* the second, *Table par ordre de matières*—exceedingly well arranged. A careful preliminary study of the catalogue enabled me to obtain ready access to its treasures.

As regards the texts of the hymns and other poems here printed, I have in every case (with the exception mentioned below) transcribed from the most ancient manuscript at my disposal the text which is here exhibited. I have not endeavoured to construct a composite text from a comparison of several manuscripts, which is, to my mind, a most unsatisfactory work ; but I have preferred to exhibit the reading of the earliest manuscript, adding in the notes any variations which seemed worthy of preservation. I have seen with my own eyes the manuscripts cited, save in the case of the three proses numbered IX., X., and XI. These I have taken from Father Dreves' great work (of which it is difficult to speak in too high terms of commendation), the *Analecta Hymnica Medii Aevi.* The collections of Daniel, Mone, Kehrein, and that of Misset and Weale have been carefully consulted.

The numbering of the verses has been added for convenience of reference.

No doubt there are many Vedastine hymns, ancient and modern, which have not yet fallen under my notice. May I beg, as a special kindness, that any reader of these pages who meets with a hymn not included in them will be so good as to send me a transcript with a reference to the source from which it is derived?

The illustration facing the title-page is a facsimile, exactly the size of the original, of an illumination in a manuscript of the eleventh century in the library at Arras. The verses composed by Rodolphus de Monchy (No. IV. amongst the poems now printed) are framed in a delicately-executed border, the uppermost side of which is formed by the picture here exhibited. The copy very carefully made for me by M. Lavoine preserves with great nicety the character of the original.

The picture represents S. Vedast seated on a throne in heaven, a long scroll before him, on which he is tracing characters with a pen; a kind of inverted rainbow guards him. The throne on which the saint is sitting is coloured green, the background behind his figure glows with roseate hues; the letters which he is tracing on the scroll are lightly indicated, but are not legible. The arc of the rainbow is tinted with various lines of gold colour, of red, and of green. Below him sits a scribe, his hood thrown back from his head, writing from the dictation of the saint on the pages of an open book; the letters are black, with a rubricated initial. The ink-horn on his right is placed in a cup-like stand, its stopper secured by a string. The whole composition is very delicately drawn.

My cordial thanks are due to M. Wicquot, librarian of the Bibliothèque de la Ville d'Arras, for the facilities which he afforded for my researches; to the Rev. Canon Parent, of the Grand Séminaire at Arras, for his generous gift, the Missal and Breviary now in use in that diocese; to the Prior of the English Benedictines at Douai, for his kindness in sending me a transcript of a prose from the Arras Missal of 1491; to Sir John Stainer, Professor of Music in the University of Oxford, for the harmonization of the music of the Flemish hymn; and to his daughter, Miss Stainer, for the transcription of the Flemish words; to Dr. G. C. Martin, organist of S. Paul's Cathedral, for translating into modern notation, and for adding harmonies to the ancient melody of the hymn, 'Voce jucunda resonemus omnes'; and to my younger son, the Rev. Charles Sparrow Simpson, who accompanied me to Arras, and acted as my secretary during our labours in the library.

INDEX.

LATIN HYMNS.

FRENCH HYMNS.

PAGE

FLEMISH HYMN.

VERSES IN HONOUR OF S. VEDAST.

MUSIC.

CARMINA VEDASTINA.

THE hymns numbered I. to VIII. in the present collection are transcribed from a very important manuscript preserved at Arras, entitled *Liber Miraculorum et Officii beati Vedasti, Episcopi Atrebatensis*, written at S. Vaast at the commencement of the eleventh century. A full technical description of the volume from the *Catalogue des Manuscrits de la Bibliothèque de la Ville d'Arras* is given below.* It is written in a clear and beautiful hand, and the text is very pure. The hymns are here printed in alphabetical order.

I.

HYMNUS DE SANCTO VEDASTO, EDITUS AB HAIMINO METRO DACTILICO TETRAMETRO CATALECTICO.

(*Arras MS. No.* 734, *folio* 78*b*.)

1. Auctor supplicibus annue votis,
Sit haec Christi dies festa beatis;
Hac tristes releva, erumna† dele,
Vedasti meritis gaudeat omnis.

* 734. In folio parvo.—Vélin blanc, choisi, détérioré en quelques endroits par l'humidité; tracé à la pointe; longues lines; commencement du XIe siècle; exécution de luxe; têtes de livres sur feuillets de pourpre avec encadrements peints, écrits au vermillon; grandes lettres historiées et dorées; têtes de chapitres disposés en inscriptions, écrites en capitales et chargées de vert ou de jaune, ou bien alternées par lettres rouges et vertes; rubriques en petites capitales mêlées d'onciales (116 feuillets; manuscrit écrit à St. Vaast).

† 'Erumna' in MS.; probably for *aerumnas*.

2. Qui binis tribuit lumina caecis,
Multorum tenebras corde revulsit,
Claudorumque gradus compede solvit
Fecit perque viam ire beatam.

3. Cum Christi tenuit sanctus amorem,
Siccum vas dederat nectaris unda,*
Designatque fides quid pia possit
Quod natura negat illa meretur.

4. Gaude, pange choros, plebs veneranda,
Qua nunc renitent culmina templi,
Hic quondam fuerat dira spelunca
Psallentumque loca lustra ferarum.

5. Et terrae specimen et status alter,
Sic mores alii tum pia corda ;
Laus Christi resonat, error abesto,
Vedasti studiis culta refulgent.

6. Dux sicut populi Israhel olim
Praecessit species mira columnae,
Sic servum dominus igne vocavit
Ut verus peteret Israhel altum.

7. Urbs gaude proprio laeta patrono,
Atrebas reboa carminas† odas ;
Si terrent fragilis proelia mundi,
Ad muros refuge patris Amandi.

8. Sit Patri domino summa potestas,
Jesu Christe tibi gloria perpes,
Par culmen teneat Spiritus almus,
Virtus una Tribus sit honor unus. Amen.

II.

In Vigilia Sancti Vedasti ad Vesperas.

(*Arras MS. No.* 734, *folio* 81*b*. The music to which this hymn is to be sung is given in the manuscript.)

Ave presul gloriose,
Ave sidus jam coeleste,
Decorans, Vedaste, coelum ;
Nos guberna visens humum
Quo laetemur triumphantes,
Te patronum venerantes.

This hymn is found as the antiphon at vespers on the *Depositio S. Vedasti Episcopi et Confessoris*, in the Sloane MS., No. 2,637, in the British Museum.

* 'Unda' in MS. ; probably for *undas*.

† 'Carminas' in MS. ; probably for *carmina*.

III.

Hymnus Davini compositus metro iambico tetrametro.

(*Arras MS. No.* 734, *folio* 80.)

1. [Christe*] Rectorum gloria,
Vita, salus, clementia,
Fave precamur servulis
Agendo festum presulis.

2. Adesto nunc clementius
Sancti pulsatus precibus;
Exaudi voces supplicum
Donando nexus criminum.

3. Hic sacer fultus plurima
Vedastus, Christi gratia,
His redidit† digredium,
His visuale gaudium:

4. Quibus ut sibi urbica
Ultro pateret regia
Auspiciis nunc gemmos
Ope sanabit miseros.

5. [M]adore namque viteo
Vase carente ligneo,
Intus superna gratia
Amico dedit pocula.

6. Hujus decessu nobili
Chori gaudent angelici,
Tellus meret‡ justicio
Amaricata nimio.

7. Laus et aeterna gloria
Deo Patri et Filio,
Sit simul et Paraclyto,
In aevitate perpeti. Amen.

---

* The scribe has not inserted the first word of the hymn; most probably it should be 'Christe.'

† 'Redidit' in MS.; for *reddidit*.

‡ *I.e.*, moeret.

IV.

Hymnus de Sancto Vedasto editus metro dactilico saphico et pentametro.

(*Arras MS. No.* 734, *folio* 77*b.*)

1. Christe Salvator hominis ab ore
Hostis antiqui superantis Adam,
Nostra clementer, Domine, precamur,
Suscipe vota.

2. Multa fecisti meritis tuorum
Dona, Vedasto propria dedisti,
Nos tui servi tua larga, Christe,
Corde rogamus.

3. Terra Francorum tenebras habebat
Horridas; dempsit radio salutis
Viscera nostra pietate Patris
Christe refulge.

4. Vultibus caecis pietate motus,
Lumina clara dedit ipse sanctus,
Lucida fecit tenebrosa corda
Ignifer ille.

5. Mortifer ursus timidus recessit,
Voce Vedasti prohibentis, ultra
Terminum scriptum penetrare dirum
Omne per aevum.

6. Debiles turbas, solita salute,
Reddidit sanas populo vidente;
Multa praeclara, Domino favente.
Fortiter egit.

7. Pectore puro pia verba vera
Auribus fudit populi fidelis:
Auxerat inde numerum piorum
Sedibus altis.

8. Obvia venit radians columna,
Splendida cœli comitata plebe,
Spiritum purum Domino vocante,
Fine beato.

9. Zabulo victo fide cum labore
Belliger miles penetravit astra;
Praemia digna obtinet honore
Regis in aula.

10. Gloria laudis resonet in ore
Omnium Patris, genitaeque Prolis,
Spiritus sancti pariter resultet
Laude perenni. Amen.

This hymn is printed amongst the works of Alcuin in Migne's *Patrologiae cursus Completus*, vol. ci., p. 682, with the title 'Alcuini Hymnus de S. Vedasto' (Ex Lambecio, *Annal.*, tom. i., p. 413). The following various readings are to be noted:

Verse 2, line 2, 'Vedasti' for 'Vedasto.'

Verse 3, line 2, 'radios' for 'radio.'

Verse 6 is placed before verse 5.

Verse 9, line 3, 'praemia digno' for 'praemia digna,' and the following notes are added:

Verse 3, line 3. *Viscera nostra:* Ita quidem in codice, sed de genuina hujus loci lectione nondum mihi satis constat (Lambecius). Forte legendum: *Miserans nostri.*

Verse 9, line 1. *Zabulo:* Apud veteres pro diabolo (*vide* Lambecius).

V.

Hymnus ab Utmaro editus metro iambico tetrametro.

(*Arras MS.*, *No.* 734, *folio* 80*b.*)

1. Felix Vedastus pontifex,
Cujus coelum mens possidet,
In terris templum fieri
Corpori mandant angeli.

2. Te, pastor alme, petimus,
Nobis deposcas veniam,
Ut nos superna civitas
Perennes cives habeat.

3. Honor, virtus et gloria,
Potestas et imperium
Sit Trinitati unicae
In sempiterno saecula.

In the Arras MS., No. 734, this hymn does not form a complete work in itself, but is found as part of the hymn *Praeclara Christi carmina* (No. VII. in the present collection), following immediately after the fifth verse. Father Guido Maria Dreves, however, prints this hymn in his *Analecta Hymnica Medii Aevi* (8vo., Leipzig, 1891), Fascic. XI., from three Vedastine Breviaries at Arras, all of the fourteenth century, Nos. 639, 676, 716, and from the Breviarium Cameracense, printed at Paris in 1497. In the last line the Vedastine Breviaries read 'In sempiterno tempore,' and the Cambrai Breviary reads 'Constans aeterno tempore.' The hymn is No. 472 in M. Dreves' collection, and it bears the title 'De Sancto Vedasto. *Ad Laudes*' The manuscript used in the text is of much earlier date than those used by M. Dreves.

VI.

Hymnus Remigii metro quo supra [*i.e.*, metro iambico tetrametro].

(*Arras MS., No.* 734, *folio* 80.)

1. Gaudet chorus aecclesiae
Pollens triumphali die,
Votis resultant hymnicis
Astra simul et terrea.

2. Vedastus presul inclytus,
Aeterni regis nuntius,
Post acta vitae insignia
Scandit laetus ad supera.

3. Virtutis hic aemeritae
Declaratus stipendiis,
Caecis refudit lumina,
Claudorum gressus dirigens.

4. Implevit idem vacua
Dulci Falerno vascula,
Vas ipse sistens utile
Christi repletum gratia.

5. Haec inter illum fulgida
Coeli poscebat regia,
Cum mox iturum ad proemia
Inguis* columna proderet.

6. Jam nunc, pastor egregie,
Audi canentes supplices,
Et laudis nostrae victimas
Divinum fer ad solium.

7. Purga sordes peccaminum,
Reddens quietem temporum,
Nosque solutos saeculo
Apta perenni gaudio.

8. Laus, honor, virtus.

It is difficult, if not impossible, to identify the author of this hymn. It would be pleasant to think that it was the composition of S. Remi, by whom S. Vedast was ordained. Their close and intimate association is well known to every reader of the fascinating history of the baptism of Clovis. But it is impossible to arrive at such a conclusion if we accept the

* 'Inguis' in MS., for 'ignis.'

chronology of the Bollandists, for S. Remigius died in 530, S. Vedast about the year 540; ten years, that is, after the death of S. Remi.*

There were, indeed, others who bore the same name. The twenty-ninth Bishop of Rouen, who died about 772, and the twenty-third Bishop of Strasburg, who died in 803, were both named Remigius or Remedius. Either of these prelates, or any other person bearing this name, may have written the hymn. There is not sufficient evidence to permit of a decision.

VII.

Hymnus ab Utmaro editus metro iambico tetrametro.

(*Arras MS.*, *No.* 734, *folio* 80*b.*)

1. Praeclara Christi carmina
Digno pangentes jubilo
Vedasti summi praesulis
Festa devote colimus.

2. Cujus doctrina coelitus
Multis collata profuit,
Larvales fugans tenebras
Verbo fideque radians.

3. Signis virtutum plurimis
Pollens doctor egregius
Caecis videre praestitit
Et claudis gressum reddidit.

4. Dulcis in patre karitas,
Haustum vini nectareum
Enoforo sicco dedit,
Quo laetus hospes rediit.

5. Migrantem hinc ad patriam
Laus excepit angelica
Et viri sancti meritum
Ignis columna prodidit.

6. Honor, virtus, et gloria,
Potestas et imperium
Sit Trinitati unicae
In sempiterna saecula.

---

* *Acta Sanctorum*, February, VI., pp. 793, 794, 796.

After the fifth verse of this hymn in the Arras MS., No. 734, follow the three verses of the hymn *Felix Vedastus pontifex*, already printed (No. V. in this collection). I have divided the one hymn into two parts because it is so divided in later liturgical MSS. at Arras.

M. Dreves prints the hymn (*Analecta Hymnica Medii Aevi*, Fascic. XI., No. 471) with the title 'De Sancto Vedasto. Ad Nocturnum.' His text is formed from three Vedastine Breviaries of the fourteenth century, Nos. 639, 676, and 905, at Arras. There are no various readings of any importance. The words 'caritas' and 'enophoro' in verse 4 do not follow the ancient spelling; but this is scarcely worth notice. After verse 5, M. Dreves adds the following verse (not found in the text of MS. No. 734):

Honor, virtus, et gloria,
Potestas et imperium
Sit Trinitati unicae
In sempiterna saecula.

VIII.

HYMNUS CUJUS SUPRA [*i.e.*, HAIMINI] DE SANCTO VEDASTO METRO DACTILICO SAPHICO PENTAMETRO EDITUS.

(*Arras MS., No.* 734, *folio* 79.)

1. Voce jocunda resonemus omnes
Laudibus sacris studium ferentes
Atrebatensem modolando patrem
Laude Vedastum.

2. Hic pius pastor gregis atque jutor,
Lux fuit caecis baculusque claudis,
Signaque fecit paradysiaca
Plurima terris.

3. Obvio caeco comes ipse regis
Lumen ablatum citius rependit,
Unde cernentes meruere cordis
Sumere lumen.

4. Summa virtutum viguit per ipsum,
Caritas, cunctum superans carisma,
Vase nam sicco dederat amico
Gaudia vitis.

5. Lustra beluarum dedit angelorum
Esse concentum Dominique templum
Ac decachordo reboare psalmo
Nocte dieque.

6. Laus Deo Patri genitaeque Proli
Et tibi, compar utriusque semper
Spiritus alme, Deus unus omni
Tempore saecli. ✠ Amen.

Of Haiminus, the author of this hymn, some account is given by Valerius Andreas in the *Bibliotheca Belgica:*

'Hayminus, Ordinis S. Benedicti, monachus ad S. Vedastum in civitate Atrebatensi, reliquit librum de miraculis S. Vedasti, cujus initium: Sane quae super et oculis probavimus, etc. Legi is per Octavam in choro Basilicae cathedralis Atrebatensis solet. Item sermonem de virtutibus ejusdem Sancti; incipit: Excitentur, obsecro, filii lucis, corda vestra. Fuit Alcuini discipulus, Caroli Magni condiscipulus. Obiit anno Domini 834.'*

The Bollandist editors, however, subjoin to this passage: 'Ubi numeris transversis reponimus annum 843,' for very sufficient reasons then set forth.

The treatises above named, the *Miracula S. Vedasti auctore Haimino Presbytero* and the *Sermo Haimini in Natali S. Vedasti de ii parvulis meritis ejus sanatis*, are both printed by the Bollandists.†

This very pleasing hymn is found in the *Acta Sanctorum*,‡ with three variations from the text already given.

Verse 2, line 1, 'Hic pius pastor gregis atque tutor.'

Verse 2, line 3, 'Signa patravit, miserante Christo.'

Verse 5, line 3, 'psalmum' for 'psalmo.'

I do not notice variations in spelling.

In M. Dreves' *Analecta Hymnica Medii Aevi*, Fascic. XI., this hymn is No. 470, and has the title *De Sancto Vedasto. Ad Vesperas.* The text there printed is formed from five manuscripts: a Vedastine Breviary of the thirteenth century, Arras MS., No. 330; three Vedastine Breviaries of the fourteenth century, Arras MSS., Nos. 639, 676, 717; and a Cambrai Breviary printed at Paris in 1497. The various readings are:

* *Acta Sanctorum*, February, VI., p. 798, column 2.

† *Ibid.*, pp. 810, 811.

‡ *Ibid.*, p. 80[illegible].

Verse 1, 'jucunda, modulando.'
Verse 3. line 1, 'obvius.'
Verse 5, line 1, 'belluarum.'
Verse 5, line 3, 'roborare psalmum.'

The hymn occurs also in the Sloane MS., No. 2,637, with these variations:

Verse 2, line 1, 'atque tutor.'
Verse 3, line 1, 'Et bino ceco comes.'

The hymn was in use before the Revolution; afterwards a hymn in the *Office Divin* took its place; but now the hymn is once more in use, for it is found in the *Supplement aux Graduel et Antiphonaire Romains pour le Diocèse d'Arras*, printed at Arras in 1889. The melody to which it is sung is there given; it will be found in this collection, *infra*, p. 58.

IX.

Sequentia de Sancto Vedasto.

(*Arras MS.*, *No.* 888, *fourteenth century*, *etc.*)

1. Magnificantes,
pater optime,
tuam gloriam,

2. *a.* Dei judicia
commode ad nostra
adhibemus praeconia.

2. *b.* Quibus, dum vita
hac functus es, tua
clarificavit merita.

3. *a.* Ergo comitem
regis dignitas
adsciverat
te, pater, ut verba
praedicares coelestia
properanti ad baptisma.

3. *b.* Dum te implorat
caecus in via,
ut succurras,
tu Deum exoras,
Deus audit et annuit,
rex credit et plebs exultat.

4. *a.* Quendam refeceras
verbi Dei copia,

4. *b.* Quem corporaliter
cibare decreveras.

5. *a.* Sed tunc vinum defecerat,
Invocasti Deum * * * *
ut in hoc subveniat, * * * * *

5. *b.* Qui de sicco vase
larga mox dedit vina.
Honorans tua merita

6. *a.* Atrebata tua
dum te meruerat,
ingrediens portas

6. *b.* Caecum illuminas
et claudum restauras
virtute solita.

7. *a.* Relicturo arva,

7. *b.* Petituro astra

8. *a.* Columna ignea
fit tibi obvia,

8. *b.* Quae rexit ad coelum
beatam animam.

9. *a.* Nunc e coelis nos, Vedaste,
pater sancte, visita.

9. *b.* Ac securos ad aeterna
perduc tecum gaudia.

Edited by M. Dreves, S.J., in his *Analecta Hymnica Medii Aevi*, Fasc. x., Sequentiæ Ineditæ, from two fourteenth-century missals in the library at Arras, Nos. 888 A and 882 B, and from a fifteenth-century gradual in the same collection, No. 638 C. In 8. *b* it is suggested that *vexit* should take the place of *rexit.* Strophe 7. *et seqq.* is wanting in B, as is also line 1 of Strophe 5. *b.*

Mel., *Oramus te aeterna spes.*

X.

Sequentia de Sancto Vedasto.

In Octava.

(*Arras MS.* 888, *fourteenth century, etc.*)

1. Christo hodierna
sacrificemus solemnia.

2. *a.* Atque suas victimas
nostra immolent labia.

2. *b.* Intentio devota
sacrificii sit ara,

3. *a.* Cum magna
merita Vedasti
nostra celebrent carmina,

3. *b.* Quem coelo
terraque honorat
Deus noster et exaltat:

4. *a.* Miraculis in terra,
in coelo
beatorum gloria,

4. *b.* Hic servorum cultura,
in coelo
sanctorum frequentia.

5. *a.* Ergo Francorum regi
comes factus in via
caeco puris precibus
obtinet lucis bona
ostendens Dei magnalia.

5. *b.* Item de vase sicco
profert vini gaudia,
cujus ut cunctis magnae
pateat caritatis
atque sanctitatis copia.

6. *a.* Attrebatae
dum primum portas
feliciter intrat
divina facturus opera,

6. *b.* Caeco lumen
et claudo gressum
reddit ac populis
jecit fidei fundamenta.

7. *a.* Profanis sacris infecto
dum liquori
crucis signa
dedit dextra, fugit
pestis, dissolvuntur vasa
virgada.

7. *b.* Igneus splendor ab aethre
exporrectus
ad culmina
pontificis funus
observat sancti secumque
receptat.

8. *a.* Chorus lugubris
patrem pia
deflerit lacrima,

8. *b.* Chorus coelestis
sed auditus
transfert ad astra.

9. *a.* Sublimis praesul, servos
humiles visita

9. *b.* Et sordes peccatorum
lava et super astra

10. Leva et tuos
supplices salva.

Edited by M. Dreves, *loco citato*, from two fourteenth-century missals at Arras, Nos. 888 A, and 882 B; a missal of Tours of the fifteenth century, No. 194, C. Strophe 7. *a et seqq.* wanting in B; 7. *a* 2, A reads *liquoris*; 7. *a* 4, A reads *fugat*; 7. *b* 1, C reads, *Ingens splendor*; after Strophe 10, C reads, *Amen dicat concio nostra.*

Mel., *Christi hodierna pangimini.*

XI.

Sequentia de Sancto Vedasto.

(*MS. missal of Cambray, fourteenth century.*)

1. *a.* Lauda, cohors clericalis,
Cum devotae plebis alis
Vedastum pontificem.

1. *b.* Ludovicus rex Francorum
Bellis ut Allemannorum
Fastus fregit apicem,

2. *a.* Ad Vedastum properavit,
Quem Vedastus perornavit
Fidei cum chlamide.

2. *b.* Idolatra rex renatus
Est devotus Christo datus
Propulsa tyrannide.

3. *a.* Isti rege comitante
Caecus voce pertonante
Acclamat itinere:

3. *b.* Sancte Dei, confer lumen,
Quia potens es acumen
Visus restituere

4. *a.* Praesul orat, quod oravit,
Ut abdatur impetravit
Cordium duritia;

4. *b.* Caecus mox illuminatur,
Rex, plebs fide solidatur
Per signi mysteria.

5. *a* Antistes Atrebatensis
Cunctos signis cum immensis
Per regnum Picardiae

5. *b.* Reliquias Vandalorum
Sordidatos idolorum
Junxit Christi latriae.

6. *a.* Hic in porta civitatis
Caeco, claudo sanitatis
Contulit subsidia,

6. *b.* Templa Deo restauravit,
Verbum Dei praedicavit
Pulsa idolatria.

7. *a.* Urna meri venenati
A nefandis aulae dati
Per intrantis civitati
Patris cruce crepuit.

7. *b.* Petra bibunt ut Hebraei,
Prece sic dona Lyaei
Vasi sicco sanctus Dei
Suo caro tribuit.

8. *a.* Quo per virgam lucis merae
Ab hac vita te ciere,
Nosti nunc aeterno vere
Fruens Christo cohaerere
Gaudens coeli curia.

8. *b.* O Vedaste, praesul bone,
Nos consortes in agone
Prece, pastor et patrone,
Da nos caeli statione
Frui cum laetitia.

Edited by M. Dreves from Missale MS. Cameracense, sæc. 14, Cod. Cameracens. 123 add. sæc. 15.

XII.

De Sancto Vedasto.—Prosa.

(*Missale Atrebatense, Paris,* 1491.)

Unus Deus, amor una, [*sic*] concordia una et caritas.
Unus Deus, amor dilectio unica, singularis caritas.
Tantum ea, quae nectit unitas, servat caritas.
Que dissipant lis et discordia, fugat caritas.
Martyria et elemosinas, angelorum hominumque linguas, probat caritas.
Major horum et Deo coeterna caritas.
Ut Christus vellet carnem sumere, suasit caritas.
Ut aulam celi Vedastus intraret, fecit caritas.
O Domine, O quem fecit nostra petere ima, insita tibi caritas.
O Vedaste, O quem fecit celsam scandere ethram, impensa tibi caritas.
Credit cuncta, suffert universa, atque sustinet cuncta caritas.
Non est vana, non ambiciosa, non querit sua lucra caritas.
Est ipsa flama, et lampas, ignis, carbo, caritas.
Est Pater, et est Patris doxa, flamen sacrum caritas.
Monas trias caritas. Amen.

This prose is taken from the Arras Missal printed in 1491. There is no title-page. The first page has a large woodcut occupying two-thirds of the page; then follows 'Incipit Missale,' etc., and the Introit *Ad Te levavi.* The colophon:

'Ad laudē dei ōipotentis ejusq3 btissime matris v'ginis Marie et oim sctōr' et sāctar'. Ad usū eccl'ie attrebateñ. istar exemplaris emendatissimi ritus dicte eccl'ie poptime cōtinentes hoc īsigne sacri missalis opus. Anno īcarnationis dñice M° cccc° xci° Kalendis octobris parisii arte impressoria per Johannem de prato finem accepit.'

The proses are collected at the end of the Missal, after the Masses, and before the *Benedictiones*, which conclude the volume.

A version of this curious prose is found in Kehrein's *Lateinische Sequenzen des Mittelalters*, No. 717, for use *in festo S. Stephani*, printed from a Liége Missal of 1513. The principal variations are these:

1. Unus amor et una concordia, una est et charitas.
2. Unum Deum amat dilectio una, singularis charitas.
5. praestat charitas.
6. Manent tria: fides, spes, charitas; major horum extat coaeterna Deo charitas.
7. Ut Christus nostram vellet gestare formam, suasit charitas.
8. Ut coeli claram Stephanus intret aulam, facit charitas.
15. Monas trinas est charitas.

The prose appears in the same form in Daniel's *Thesaurus Hymnologicus*, v., p. 176, from which, indeed, Kehrein takes it.

XIII.

Sancto Vedasto Episcopo Attrebatensi.

VI. Februarii.

Cui Deus crescit, peritura vani
Cuncta decrescunt simulacra mundi,
More torrentis fugitivus illi
Praeterit Orbis.

Nil domus splendor, nec opes avitae,
Blanda nec flexit juvenem voluptas;
Quos Fides monstrat superos Vedastus
Ambit honores.

Ne quid in dulci Patriâ retardet,
Et suos inter, nimis Aula mentem
Blandiens frangat, fugit in remotas
Providus oras.

Quàm salutaris fuga! quàm profundo
Jussa decreto! reget ille Reges,
Et jugo Christi fera corda subdi
Nescia subdet.

Summa laus Patri, genitóque Verbo,
Et tibi compar, utriusque nexus,
Qui Sacerdotes Deus intùs ungis,
Spiritus alme.

XIV.

Qui fugit longè patriâ relictâ,
Sæculi pompam malè blandientem,
Hic sacris Reges monitis, et omnem
Imbuet aulam.

Ut redit victor spoliis superbus
Post triumphatas Clodovaeus Urbes :
Jam Deo victus, prope noster, ardet
Ritè doceri.

Primus occurris, tua fama prodit
Hoc pium munus tibi destinatur.
Jura qui nuper dabat Imperator
Ipse subibit.

Regium pectus tumidum triumpho
Gaudet irrisae Crucis in trophaeo
Arma deponit novus ille Christi
Miles ab hoste.

Quis tibi sensus fuit, ô Vedaste ?
Dum fugis Reges cupidus latere,
Te vocant Reges, cupiunt doceri
Teque Magistro.

Dum petit Rhemos, per iter docebas ;
A tuo Princeps pius ore pendet,
Instar Eunuchi docilis, fuisti
Tuque Philippus.

Signa non verbis manifesta desunt
Nam diem caeco dedit ut videret,
Principis caeci tenebras superno
Lumine pellit.

Rex novus velis penitùs remotis,
Solis aeterni jubar intuetur.
Atra nox cedit, procul obstinatus
Exulat error.

XV.

Quàm Deo gratus, procul à tumultu
Qui, sibi quando vacat, et saluti :
Pontifex curas, sibi raptus ipsi,
Sustinet omnes.

Intrat hanc Urbem tenebris sepultam
Belluas audit rabie frementes
Civitas omnis, velut alta sylva
Horrida dumis.

Prisca divini monumenta cultûs
Barbarae gentes tulerant; VEDASTUS
Vana subvertit simulacrâ, Divûm
Diruit aras.

Redditur caeco sua lux, et auris
Redditur surdo, sua lingua muto;
Impari qui vix pede claudus ibat,
Ambulat aequo.

Luce coelesti meliùs fugabat
Mentibus noctem, simul ora muta,
Et Deo surdas reserabat aures:
Omnia quanta!

Civium terror, ferus hospes Urbis,
Ursus immani latitabat antro,
Imperas Praesul, tremit imperantis
Bellua vocem.

E specu flecti docilis profundo
Exit oblitus feritatis ursus;
Gestiunt cives, sonat urbs recenti
Laeta triumpho.

Praesulis faustum fuit illud omen
Efferas mentes malus occuparat
Daemon, ut cedat jubet, efficaci
Voce fugatur.

Regis accumbens epulis VEDASTUS
Fregit impresso Crucis illa signo
Vasa Fanorum, quibus est litatum,
Impia vasa.

Tota Gens, Praesul, modò Christiana,
Se tibi debet; Fidei jacentis
Prisca coelesti rediviva rore
Semina surgant.

These three hymns, Nos. XIII., XIV., and XV., are taken from a volume entitled '*Hymni Sacri et Novi Autore Santolio Victorino.* Editio novissima. In quâ Hymni omnes, quos Autor usque ad mortem concinuerat, reperiuntur. Parisiis, Apud Dionysium Thierry, viâ Jacobeâ, sub signo Urbis Lutetiae. MDCXCVIII. Cum privilegio Regis.'

The first edition of these hymns seems to have been issued some nine years earlier than the *Editio Novissima* here employed, for after the *Privilege du Roy* occurs this sentence: 'Achevé d'imprimer pour la première fois le 30. Juin 1689.'

XVI.

Hymne de S. Vaast ou Saint Vedaste Evêque d'Arras.

VI. Fevrier.

Pour qui n'aime que Dieu de l'ardeur la plus vive,
Il n'est rien ici-bas dont son cœur soit tenté :
Le monde est un torrent, une ombre fugitive,
Dont il connoit la vanité.

Vedaste peu sensible à sa propre opulence,
Résiste constamment aux charmes des plaisirs ;
Les célestes grandeurs étoient, dès son enfonce,
L'unique objet de ses désirs.

Pour que rien ne s'oppose à sa vertu parfaite,
Il renonce aux attraits d'une brillante Cour ;
Il quitte son pays, et veut dans la retraite,
Prodiguer à Dieu son amour.

O prudente retraite ! où le Dieu qui l'appelle,
Pour le salut d'un Prince, y forme son esprit !
Sa voix doit triompher du cœur d'un Roi rebelle,
Et le soumettre à Jesus-Christ.

Gloire au Pere Eternel, au Fils dont la doctrine
Eclaire notre esprit, et console nos cœurs ;
Même gloire à l'Esprit, dont l'onction Divine,
Nous consacre de saints Pasteurs.

XVII.

Autre Hymne.

En quittant tous ses biens, ses parents, sa patrie,
Vedaste est à couvert du monde, et de ses traits ;
Mais on l'entend tonner contre l'idolâtrie
Et de Princes, et des sujets.

Tout couvert des lauriers qui brillent sur sa tête,
Clovis, aux ennemis, vient d'imposer la loi ;
Et déja ce héros, Seigneur, est ta conquéte,
Eclaire, et confirme sa foi.

Le ciel, à ta vertu, donne la préférence,
Vedaste, cet emploi dans tes mains est remis ;
Le Roi qui soumet tout à son obéissance,
A tes leçons sera soumis.

Ce Prince encor tout fier des fruits de sa victoire,
Vient mêler son triomphe à celui de la croix :
Nouveau soldat du Christ, il dépose sa gloire
Aux pieds de ce maître des Rois.

Saint Prêtre, quel dessein avoit pu le conduire
A quitter pour jamais la Cour, et ses plaisirs ?
Un Prince encor payen t'appelle pour l'instruire,
Vole seconder ses désirs.

Tel cet officier* d'un Reine payenne
Ecoutoit un Apôtre avec avidité :
Telle est, du grand Clovis, à ta leçon chrétienne,
L'admirable docilité.

Tu soutiens tes discours par l'eclat des miracles ;
Tu touches un aveugle, il voit dans le moment ;
Et le Prince éclairé, surmonte les obstacles,
Qui formoient son aveuglement.

Il ressent tout à coup l'effet de ta priere,
Du Soleil de justice, il fixe la splendeur ;
Les ombres de la nuit font place à la lumiere,
Qui vient dissiper son erreur.

Gloire au Pere Eternel, au Fils dont la doctrine
Eclaire notre esprit, et console nos cœurs ;
Même gloire à l'Esprit, dont l'onction Divine,
Nous consacre de saints Pasteurs.

XVIII.

Autre Hymne.

Si le Seigneur appreuve un pieux solitaire,
Qui n'a de son salut que l'unique fardeau,
Qu'il estime un Prélat, qui dans son ministere,
Se consacre aux soins d'un troupeau !

Vedaste, dans Arras, entend frémir la rage,
D'un peuple enseveli dans la nuit de l'erreur :
Quelle ville ! (grand Dieu) c'est un autre sauvage,
Où le Saint est saisi d'horreur.

* L'Eunuque de la Reine de Candale, instruit par l'Apôtre Saint Philippe.

Des temples, autrefois, consacrés à ta gloire,
Seigneur, ils ont détruits les restes précieux ;
Mais Vedaste, attentif à venger ta mémoire,
Brise les autels des faux Dieux.

Sur tous les affligés, ses dons vont se répandre ;
L'aveugle sent ses yeux s'éclaircir sous sa main ;
Le muet parle au sourd, étonné de l'entendre ;
Le boiteux va d'un pas certain.

Le Saint opere encore de plus grandes merveilles,
Le flambeau de la foi dissipe leur erreur.
Que de bouches alors ; que de chastes oreilles,
S'ouvrent à la loi du Seigneur.

Dans le sein de la ville, une bête cruelle,
Causoit aux habitants le plus terrible effroi ;
Mais cédant tout à coup à la voix qui l'appelle,
L'ours tremble, et rampe devant toi.

De son antre profond, sortant sans résistance
Cet ours n'exhale plus le feu de sa fureur ;
Et le peuple charmé de cette délivrance,
Exalte son libérateur.

Ce trait, pour notre Saint, fut d'un heureux présage,
Le démon les avoit captivés sous ses loix ;
Vedaste lui commande, et l'esprit plein de rage
Est forcé de fuir à sa voix.

Le Roi, dans un repas, fit placer sur sa table
Les vases destinés au culte des faux Dieux,
D'un seul signe de croix, le Prélat respectable,
Les mit en poudre sous ses yeux.

Ce peuple, saint Pasteur, doit à ta vigilance,
De sa naissante foi l'inestimable bien
Fais revivre à jamais cette sainte semence,
Que tu répandis dans son sein.

Gloire au Pere Eternel, au Fils dont la doctrine
Eclaire notre esprit, et console nos cœurs ;
Même gloire à l'Esprit, dont l'onction Divine,
Nous consacre de saints Pasteurs.

These three hymns, Nos. XVI., XVII., and XVIII., are translations of Hymns Nos. XIII., XIV., and XV., and are taken from a volume entitled '*Hymnes de Santeuil, traduites en vers François.* Par I. P. C. P. D. A Paris, chez J. Barbou, rue S. Jacques, proche la fontaine S. Benoît, aux Cigognes. MDCCLX.'

A MS. note on the front fly-leaf is as follows: 'Cette traduction supérieure à celle de Saurin est de J. Poupin curé Prieur d'Auxon, puis chanoine de la Cathédrale de Troyes.'

Élie Saurin's translation of Santeul's hymns is contained in a volume dedicated to Madame de Maintenon:

Traduction en vers François des Hymnes de Monsieur de Santeul, Chanoine regulier de Saint Victor. 12°, Paris, 1691.

Saurin describes Santeul's Latin hymns as worthy of the Augustan age; and M. Santeul expresses himself as being satisfied with Saurin's version, for he says:

'Je suis tres-obligé à l'Auteur de la Traduction de mes Hymnes; je la reconnois comme une copie parfaite de l'Original.'

De Santeul, de Saint Victor.

It may be added that M. Poupin (who dedicates his work to Madame la Dauphine) speaks of the version of the *late* 'M. l'Abbé Saurin de l'Académie Royal de Nîmes'; states that three editions of it were issued before 1699, but that it was now nearly forgotten; and adds, moreover, that it did not include thirty-three of Santeul's hymns. Amongst the omitted hymns are those to S. Vedast.

XIX.

Sequentia de Missa in Festis S. P. Vedasti Episcopi et Confessoris.

1. Frustra tuos, bona, cives
   Fugis, et Vedaste, lates,
      Terrâ procul hospite.

2. Comitatur fugientem,
   Fama sequax et latentem:
      Teque prodit ubique,

3. Hoste Victor triumphato,
   Se sibi rex ipse, Christo
      Victus, ultro subjicit.

4. Ambo Remos dum petitis,
   Fingis pectus institutis,
      Per te Christum induit.

5\. Pendet ab ore docentis,
Instar eunuchi fidelis,
Tu Philippus aderas.

6\. Illic caeco reddis lucem
Ac illico regis mentem,
Quo splendore recreas.

7\. Plebi nocte sub profunda,
Quam lux ipse tu, jucunda,
Praesul factus advenis.

8\. Urbs vastata dumis horret,
Fide vulsa pejor haeret,
Aspris error animis.

9\. Ut affulges, mox fugatur,
Prisca fides revocatur,
Domus Dei restauratur,
Quae nova fit civitas.

10\. Ex immani specu pulsus,
Te jubente cedit ursus,
Cum fera gentis, quod majus,
Exulat et feritas.

11\. Quis pastoris pandat curas,
Quis amoris artes miras?
Totum te das ovibus.

12\. Summis gratus imos foves,
Ut Christo lucreris omnes,
Omnia sis omnibus.

13\. Crescit amor, totus langues,
Jam vix capit pectus ignes,
Evolant cum anima.

14\. Migrat ecce, stupent cuncti,
Flagrans seu jubar, attolli
Sublimem in aethera.

15\. Cursu qui coelos flammeo
Petis: O dilecte Deo,
Tua duplex sit mens nobis:
En trahe nos post te votis,
Ad coelum quo raperis.

16\. Tu qui sidus praesulum,
Dei fulges ante thronum,
Lucem mitte, vibra faces,
Ure corda, lustra mentes,
Igne quo nunc ureris.
Amen. Alleluia.

For this hymn I am indebted to the great kindness of the Rev. Canon Parent, of the Grand Séminaire at Arras, who transcribed it for me with his own hand from a loose printed sheet of a mass of S. Vedast which he discovered in a *Missale ad usum Benedictinorum* printed at Douai in 1729. The mass differs from any now in use. Canon Parent, I am informed, does not know of any other copy.

XX.

Sequentia in Festo Depositionis S. Vedasti, Episcopi et hujus Diocoesis Patroni Secundarii.

(*From the Missale Parisiense cum Proprio Atrebatensi. Quarto. Paris,* 1841.)

1. Lethalis umbra pellitur
Lux redit: somno surgite:
Fatale vinclum solvitur;
Vos, O redempti, plaudite

2. Quas Vandali reduxerant,
Umbras Vedastus expulit;
Quae Vandali injecerant,
Vincla Vedastus abstulit.

3. Celsis natus honoribus,
Honores prudens despicit:
Amplis redundat opibus,
Opes invisas abjicit.

4. Exul latere voluit:
(Sibi timet humilitas.)
An virtus diu latuit?
An latet alta civitas?

5. En tua, disce, munia:
Reges ipsos erudies;
Et corda subdi nescia
Christi jugo subjicies.

6. Sat Chlodovaeus restitit:
A te doceri postulat.
Doces: (ut Deus astitit!)
Nox cedit; error exulat.

7. Sed quanta seges operum
Fidem Atrebas exuit;
In omne genus scelerum
Idololatra proruit.

8. Nil dura corda civium,
Horrens nil movet civitas.
Quo non, servatrix ovium,
Quo non impellit caritas!

9. Intus movente Numine
Christum Vedastus praedicat,
Sparso salutis semine,
Quam ampla messis emicat!

10. Verba quot signis astruit!
Caeco sua lux redditur;
Claudo pedem restituit;
Salus aequo refunditur.

11. Vos Atrebates, dicite
Ut fana, deos verteret;
Ut lingua potens divite
Deo rebelles subderet.

12. Quos dura gens induerat
Mores ferinos exuit;
Infida, quem exuerat,
Christum docilis induit.

13. Multis partam sudoribus
Prolem, Pater, ne deseras!
O Vedaste, clientibus
Opem e coelo conferas!

14. Piis aequa laboribus
Qui jam refulges gloria,
O Vedaste, clientibus
Coeli precare gaudia. Amen.

This hymn is also found in the *Office Divin complet, en Latin et en Français, à l'usage Diocèse d'Arras*, printed at Arras, but without a date. The *Approbation*, however, prefixed to the volume is dated May 30, 1827. It is signed by the Bishop of Arras, Hugues-Robert-Jean-Charles de la Tour d'Auvergne-Lauraguais.

It is also printed in the *Eucologe (français-latin) du Diocèse d'Arras, contenant l'Office du tous les Dimanches et Fêtes de l'Année, avec approbation*, printed at Lille, in 1845.

In both these books the hymn is entitled a *Prose.*

The four hymns which follow next in order, Nos. XXI. to XXIV., are taken from the *Breviarium Atrebatensè*, printed in Paris in 1834, in four volumes 8vo.*

XXI.

In I. Vesperis.

(*Breviarium Atrebatense*, 1834.)

1. Annuos, cives, renovemus hymnos ;
Orta jam splendet sacra lux Vedasto :
Praesulis tanti memores canamus
Corde triumphos.

2. Nil domus splendor, nec opes avitae,
Blanda nec flexit juvenem voluptas ;
Quos fides monstrat superos Vedastus
Ambit honores.

3. Ne quid in dulci patria retardet,
Et suos inter, nimis aula mentem
Blandiens frangat, fugit in remotas
Providus oras.

4. Quam salutaris fuga ! quam profundo
Jussa decreto ! reget ille reges ;
Et jugo Christi fera corda, subdi
Nescia, subdet.

5. Ut redit victor, spoliis superbus,
Post triumphatos Clodoveus hostes,
Jam Deo victus, prope noster, ardet
Rite doceri.

6. Primus occurris ; tua fama prodit :
Hoc pium munus tibi destinatur.
Jura qui nuper dabat Imperator,
Ipse subibit.

7. Dum petit Remos, per iter docebas ;
A tuo Princeps pius ore pendet,
Instar Eunuchi docilis, fuisti
Tuque Philippus.

8. Signa non verbis manifesta desunt :
Nam diem caeco dedit ut videret ;
Principis caeci tenebras et omnis
Depulit aulae.

* *Breviarium Atrebatense jussu illustrissimi ac reverendissimi in Christo Patris, D.D., Hugonis-Roberti-Joannis-Caroli de Latour-D'Auvergne-Lauraguais vulgatum.*

9. Praepotens regum moderator, unus
In tribus regnans, meritis Vedasti,
Supplicem coetum pius ad superna
Dirige regna. Amen.

This hymn is also found in the *Eucologe du Diocèse d'Arras* already referred to.

XXII.

Ad Officium Noct.

(*Breviarium Atrebatense*, 1834.)

1. Christe totius reparator orbis
Mitte quem nosti fidei ministrum.
Nostra quid mortis sedet urbs sepulta
Jugiter umbris?

2. En Deo tandem fideique plenus
Advolat Praesul; Deus ipse Dux est:
Orcus infrendet: resonant Olympi
Atria plausu.

3. Intrat hanc urbem nimis heu! dolendam,
Nulla jam veri monumenta cultus;
Efferas mentes vetus occupavit
Altius error.

4. Spiritu fervens hominem Deumque
Intonat Christum; simulacra vertit.
Fert diem; vulsis meliora spinis
Semina mandat.

5. Asserit magnis sua dicta factis.
Imperat: caecus jubar intuetur;
Exilit claudus, loquiturque mutus,
Surdus et audit.

6. Inde nostrorum pietas parentum
Prisca defluxit; maneat superstes,
Fracta nec longo minuentis aevi
Concidat actu.

7. Summa laus Patri, Genitoque summa,
Et tibi compar, utriusque vinclum:
Fac tuis vivat, Deus, in ministris
Pristina virtus. Amen.

XXIII.

Ad Laudes.

(*Breviarium Atrebatense*, 1834.)

1. Dexter huc nobis ades, O Vedaste!
Te tui rursus celebrare certant;
Quos, Pater, Christo fide parturisti,
Annue natis.

2. O pias dicat quis amoris artes!
Ut trahat Christo, subigatque corda,
Sponte demissa gravitate, sese
Omnibus aptat.

3. Fronte non asper facilis, benignus,
Voce non sola docet; ipsa vultus
Blanda majestas pietatis almum
Afflat amorem.

4. Erigit tristes, inopesque pascit,
Vestit ac nudum, miseretur aegri;
Divitum mensas, fidei futurus
Praeco nec horret.

5. Quos docet nondum stabiles alumnos,
Firmat exemplis, animatque factis;
Monstrat, accensa face, quae tenenda
Sit via coelo.

6. His fides tandem remeavit oris:
Templa ponuntur, reparantur arae;
Quas furor stravit, pietas vicissim
Excitat aedes.

7. Quae fuit vivo tibi cura, Praesul,
Hanc, licet vectus super astra, serves;
Et tuam, nostrae bone tutor urbis,
Respice gentem.

8. Laus sit aeternae Triadi per aevum,
Quae Patri nostro superos honores
Largiens, nobis tribuat perennis
Gaudia vitæ. Amen.

XXIV.

Ad II. Vesperas.

(*Breviarium Atrebatense*, 1834.)

1. Qui te beatis coetibus inseris,
Quos linquis orbos, respice coelitus,
Vedaste; clemens O tuorum
Sume preces, gemitus clientum.

2. Quiesce, duris functe laboribus ;
Vertuntur arae, numina corruunt ;
Victo rebelli corde, caecis
Vera dies rediviva lucet.

3. Jam cedit ultro, jam patiens jugi,
Ponit Sicamber colla ferocia ;
Sacras piandus, te docente,
Intrat ovans Clodoveus undas.

4. Quae te premebant, solvere vinculis,
Quem vanus error luserat, Atrebas ;
Gaudes reperta veritate,
Subdis amans fera corda Christo.

5. Vedaste, noster Pastor, Apostolus
Ames vocari ; sedibus e tuis
Tuere prolem ; te magistrum,
Teque patrem studet aemulari.

6. Sit summa Patri, summaque Filio,
Tibique compar gloria, Spiritus ;
Qui dura solvis, da perennes
Concipiant nova corda flammas. Amen.

This hymn is found in the *Office Divin* and in the *Eucologe*, of the diocese of Arras, both already referred to in these pages

XXV.

Flemish Hymn to S. Vedast.

VAN DEN HEYLIGEN VEDASTUS.

1. Wee, de woeste Nederlanden,
Wee de ryken daer ontrent ;
Nog gestelt in duyvels banden,
Nog van Christi kerk vervremt ;
Maer Vedastus is verschenen
Als een fakkel in den nacht,
En net heydendom verdwenen,
Heeft verlooren syne kragt.
Den franschen vorst,
Naer 't doopsel dorst,
En verwinner in den stryt,
Door Vedastus ook verwonnen,
Christi waere wet belydt.

2. 't Atregt, in een opperstede,
Heeft hy synen stoel gestelt ;
En syn leer met wonderheden
Was ook dikwils vergeselt.

Goden, beelden, helsche geesten,
Zyn gerloden op zyn woort.
Schim gedrojten, wilde beesten,
Hebben syne stemm' gehoort.
De Blinde lien,
Het ligt aensien ;
Kreupel krygen hunnen gank ;
En de stomme, die nu spreken,
Singen God den heere dank.

3. Maer 't geluk der ingeseten,
Een geluk van meer gewigt,
Was het waer geloop te weten
En naer siel te syn verligt ;
Was nu vry van alle afgoden
Op den regten weg te staen,
Om 't aenhooren Gods geboden
En naer 't hemelryk te gaen.
Ook naederhant
Heeft Vlaenderlant
Sig tot 't christendom bekeert ;
En den grooten man Vedastus
Wort als leeraer daer geeert.

4. Hontschoot, Renegels en Belle
Sveken nyt in dankbaerheyt ;
Hebben stadt en kerk gestellen
Synen naeme toegeseyt.
Overheden en gemeente
Sien met groot genoegen aen
Nu een deel van syn gebeente
op hun pronkantaeren staen.
Den yver groeyt ;
De kerke bloeyt ;
en door heel het belsch gebiet,
Den verheven man Vedastus
Vrugten van syn arbeyt siet.

5. En nu ook de sondagschoole,
Tot het onderwys der jeugt,
Is u vader toebevolen,
Is in uwen naem verheugt.
Hout den helschen beir gebonden,
Onder uwen bisschops voet ;
En bewaert ons van de wonden
Die syn felle bete doet.
Dit dankbaer liet,
De schole u biet,
En wysingen vol van vreugt :
Wilt met zegen onderstennen
Die ons stieren tot de deugdt.

The popular devotion to S. Vedast has found expression in this vernacular hymn in Flemish, consisting of five verses of thirteen lines each. It is printed by Mons. F. de Coussemaker in his *Chants Populaires des Flamands de France* (8vo., Gand., 1856). I do not understand the Flemish tongue, and as some of my readers may be equally unfortunate, I think it well to subjoin M. de Coussemaker's translation.

'Cantique en l'honneur de St. Vaast.

1.

'Qu'elle était malheureuse notre Néerlande, alors qu'avec toute la région d'alentour, elle était encore barbare, soumise au joug du démon et privée de temples chrétiens! Mais S^t. Vaast a paru comme un flambeau dans la nuit, et le paganisme a perdu son empire. Le monarque franc, victorieux dans les batailles, fut converti par S^t. Vaast; il reçut le baptême et confessa la foi du Christ.

2.

'Il fixa son siége dans la ville d'Arras; des miracles accompagnaient souvent ses prédications. A sa parole, on voyait tomber les faux dieux les idoles et les simulacres de l'enfer. Spectres, monstres, bêtes féroces obéirent à sa voix; les aveugles voient la lumière; les boiteux retrouvent leur marche; les muets recouvrent la voix, chantant la louange de Dieu.

3.

'Mais le bonheur, le véritable bonheur des habitants de la contrée fut d'avoir connu la vraie foi, cette consolation des âmes; ce fut d'être délivrés du culte des faux dieux et de se trouver sur le chemin des commandements de Dieu et du salut éternel. Aussi, bientôt la Flandre se convertit au christianisme, et S^t. Vaast fut honoré comme l'apôtre du pays.

4.

'Hondschoote, Renegelst et Bailleul, rivalisant de reconnaissance, ont mis leur ville et leur église sous le patronage de son nom. Les autorités et le peuple voient maintenant avec satisfaction une partie de ses ossements placés sur leurs plus beaux autels. Ce zèle s'accroit, l'église prospère et dans tous les états belges le grand S^t. Vaast voit le fruit de ses labeurs.

5.

'Et maintenant aussi l'école dominicale, cet asile de la jeunesse, vous est consacrée, ô saint patron, et est placée sous l'égide de votre nom. Enchaînez à vos pieds l'ours de l'enfer et sauvez-nous de ses cruelles morsures. L'école vous adresse ce cantique de reconnaissance, que nous chantons tous avec allégresse. Etendez vos bénédictions sur ceux qui nous conduisent dans le chemin de la vertu.'

The music to which the Flemish words are sung will be found at p. 59 *infra*.

M. de Coussemaker adds a valuable note :

'Nous avons trouvé ce cantique dans le manuscrit appartenant à l'école dominicale de Bailleul, dite de St. Vaast. Il y est chanté à diverses époques de l'année et notamment à la fête de ce saint, qui est le patron d'une des églises paroissiales de la même ville. Les noms d'Hondschoote, de Renegelst, et de Bailleul, mentionnés dans cette pièce, indiquent son origine locale et expliquent sa popularité. La mélodie que nous donnons ici, nous a été chantée par une des anciennes élèves de cette école. Elle ne paraît pas appartenir à une époque plus reculée que le commencement du XVIIIe siècle.'

Bailleul, according to the guide books, is some forty-nine miles from Calais, on the road to Lille: a curious and picturesque Flemish town, with 13,276 inhabitants, largely engaged in the production of hand-made lace.

Hondschoote is eight miles to the east of Bergues, which is five miles from Dunkirk. It is reached by diligence from Bergues, and is a small town of 3,464 inhabitants at the present time, though formerly it had a population of 20,000.

—

POEMS.

THE short series of Latin verses which follow are taken from ancient manuscripts in the library at Arras, mostly of the eleventh century, with one or two later compositions.

The first, second, and third are ascribed to our own Alcuin. Born of noble Northumbrian parents about the year 735, he was the hereditary representative of the noble house from which sprung S. Willibrord, the apostle of the Frisians. He was brought up from infancy in the school founded by Archbishop Egbert, in connection with the Church of York. Here he received instruction from the Archbishop, himself the disciple and friend of Bede, and from Ethelbehrt, the master of the school, who was made Archbishop in 767. He became proficient in secular as well as in ecclesiastical learning. He twice visited Rome, returning in 790 to Northumbria. Ethelred endeavoured in vain to retain him at his Court; but Alcuin hastened back to Tours, where he governed the monastery of S. Martin, although still a deacon, and here he died.* His Life of S. Vedast is printed in the *Acta Sanctorum*, Feb., VI., pp. 803-809.

The poems numbered I., II., and III. are found in the eleventh century manuscript, of which so much use has been already made. They form part of a series of verses (in which they are numbered XLI., XLII., and XLIII.) under the general heading:

IN ECCLESIA SANCTI VEDASTI IN PARIETE SCRIBENDUM.

Other inscriptions following these three are intended to be placed on or near the altars of the following Saints:

S. Martin, S. Dionysius and his companions, SS. Remigius and Audoinus, SS. Lantbertus and Richarius, SS. Gregory and Jerome, SS. Benedict and Scholastica, SS. Cosmas and Damian, the Holy Virgins, the Holy Cross, SS. Mary and Clement, SS. John and Matthew, SS. Piatus and George, SS. Laurence, John and Paul.

The inscriptions which belong to the Church of S. Vedast are numbered XLI.-LXV.

I.

DE ECCLESIA SANCTI VEDASTI A RADONE ABBATE RENOVATA.

(*Arras MS., No.* 734, *folio* 91.)

Haec domus alma Dei flammis crepitantibus olim
Arsit, et in cineres tota redacta fuit;
Sed miserante Deo, Rado venerabilis abba
Construxit melius, ac renovavit eam.

---

* These particulars are taken, often in the precise words of the writer, from the biographical notice of Alcuin, contributed to the *Dictionary of Christian Biography* by the Bishop of Oxford.

Plurima praesenti domui ornamenta ministrans,
  Exornans totam muneribusque sacris.
Cancellos aras voluit vestire metallis,
  Vedasti fabricans sarcophagumque Patris.
Pallia suspendit parietibus atque lucernas,
  Addidit, ut fieret lumen in aede sacrum.
Officiis Domini fecit quoque vasa sacrata
  Argento, nec non aurea tota quidem.
Induit altaris speciosa veste ministros,
  Ut foret egregium semper ubique decus.
Omnia mellifluo Christi devotus amore
  Restaurans opera, vir pius, in melius.
Pro quo quisque legas titulos, rogitare menento,
  Adjuvit utque illum gratia summa Dei.

Abbot Radon was the eleventh abbot of the Abbey of S. Vaast, at Arras, from 795 to 815. He was 'grand-référendaire de la couronne et chancelier de Charlemagne, avait été élu abbé en 795 par le suffrage unanime de la communauté. Aussi ce prélat, dont les chroniqueurs mentionnent la piété aussi profonde qu'éclairée, put réparer les dégats causés à l'église du monastère par l'incendie de 783 ; de plus il contribua à la solennité du culte rendu à Saint Vaast, en décorant son sanctuaire, en embellisant son autel de beaux ornements, et en rendant l'église plus vaste et plus grandiose, sans négliger l'administration intérieure.'

'Radon intimement lié avec le célèbre Alcuin, précepteur du monarque Français, l'engagea à rédiger une nouvelle vie de Saint Vaast, d'après les documents anciens et les biographies que l'on possédait déjà, mais que l'on regardait comme défectueuses.'*

These passages show the connection between Alcuin and Radon, and explain the circumstances under which the verses were written

The fire of 795 appears to have been exceedingly destructive, for the Abbot Radon 'fut obligé de la reconstruire de fond en comble.'† The writers just cited go on to say that

* *L'Abbaye de Saint-Vaast*, par MM. Adolphe de Cardevacque et Auguste Terninck. 4to., Arras, 1865. I., p. 55.

† *Ibid.*, III., pp. 90, 91.

the chronicles and writings of Alcuin 'poete et religieux du monastere,' testify to the greatness and beauty of his work. 'Les autels étaient enrichis de métaux, le tombeau de Saint Vaast était orné de lames d'or et d'argent, et les murs étaient recouverts d'élégantes tapisserie. Radon suspendit des lampes dans les nefs et dans le sanctuaire, il fit confectionner des vases sacrés en or et en argent, et acheta de riches ornements pour les officiants.' As a note to this passage our poem is printed, as, indeed, it was also at the place first cited.

In the *Acta Sanctorum* (February, VI., p. 809, column 2) are found these verses:

'*Versus Alcuini ad Radonem Abbatem.*
Noli, quaeso, Pater, munuscula spernere nostra.
Parvula si videas, magna haec dilectio mittit.'

They are printed at the end of Alcuin's *Adhortatio ad imitandas virtutes S. Vedasti in Actis descriptis.**

II.

Ad Corpus Sancti Vedasti.

(*Arras MS.*, *No.* 734, *folio* 91.)

Hic Pater egregius Vedastus corpore pausat,
  Cujus honore sacro haec domus alma micat.
Fulcitur tanti meritis per saecla patroni,
  Per quem multa Deus signa salutis agit.
Qui sacra celsitroni vivens vestigia Christi,
  Lingua, mente, manu namque secutus erat.
Multiplicavit opes bis quinis forte talentis,
  Nec data marsupiis lucra ligavit iners.
Audiet idcirco vocem mox judicis almi :
  Intra nunc Domini gaudia sancta tui.

In the *Acta Sanctorum* (p. 809, column 2) these verses are entitled *Epitaphium S. Vedasti.*

In the Abbé Destombes' *Les Vies des Saints et des Personnes d'une éminente piété des Diocèses de Cambrai et d'Arras* (4 vols., 12mo., Douai, 1868, i. 212) is a translation of this Epitaph into French :

* See also the *Acta Sanctorum*, p. 797.

Ici repose le corps de Saint Vaast, notre illustre père,
Dont la gloire immortelle embellit cette demeure.
Elle est fondée pour des siècles, sous l'auguste patronage
De celui par qui Dieu opéra beaucoup d'œuvres de salut.
Toute sa vie il marcha sur les traces sacrées de Jésus-Christ ;
Sa bouche, son cœur, sa main, tout lui fut consacré :
Il multiplia les dix talents que Dieu lui donna,
Et ne les enfouit point après les avoir reçus.
C'est pourquoi il entendra cette parole du juge miséricordieux :
Entrez maintenant dans les joies de votre Seigneur.

III.

Ad aram Sancti Vedasti.

(*Arras MS., No.* 734, *folio* 91.)

Pontificalis apex, meritis vivacibus, aram
  Vedastus sanctus hanc regit ipse Pater.
Hanc abbas humilis vestivit Rado metallis,
  In Domini laudem ductus amore Patris.

These three poems, Nos. I., II. and III., are printed amongst Alcuin's works in the Abbé Migne's *Patrologiae cursus completus* (tom. ci., p. 741), with the heading, 'Carmina. Inscriptiones variae in Ecclesia S. Vedasti.' The learned editor does not appear to have seen the Arras MS. cited above, for he writes: 'Cur carmina sequentia ad Ecclesiam Sancti Vedasti pertinere censeamus, causa est, quod non initio solum, sed et in medio occurrat mentio de Radone Abbate illius monasterii.' The Arras MS. determines the question.

To the first of the poems the Abbé Migne appends the following note, which is equally decisive :

'Hoc carmen emendavimus ex editione celeberrimi Lambecii (tom. ii., *Comment. Bibl. Caesar.*, p. 414 ; novae editionis, tom. i., p. 643). In *Cod. Vindobonensi* his versibus praefigitur titulus : In Ecclesia Sancti Vedasti in pariete scribendum. Ubi notari vult idem Lambecius, non hic legi scriptum, sed scribendum ; nempe quod pervetustus ille Codex Caesareus prius est exaratus quam epigramma hoc parieti ecclesiae Sancti Vedasti inscriptum est.'

A careful collation of the Arras text here printed with the Abbé Migne's version gives the following various readings. In Poem I. :

Line 1, *Alma:* Henschen leg. alta.
Line 2, *Fuit:* Lambecius, ruit.

Line 3, *Rado:* Radon.
Venerabilis: Quercet, miserabilis.
Line 7, *Cancellis:* Lambecius, cancellos; but cancellis is printed.
Line 16, *Opera:* Quercet, opere.
Line 17, *Rogitare:* Quercet, cogitare.

In Poem II.:
Line 5, Celsithroni for celsitroni.
Line 8, Marsupii for marsupiis.
And to line 8 the following note is appended:

Ligavit iners: vera haec est, ait Lambecius *loc. cit.* et genuina hujus loci lectio; non autem ut in editione Quercetani: *lucra ligavit opes;* vel in codicibus MSS. quibus RR. PP. Bollandus et Henschenius usi sunt: *lucri migravit opes.*

IV.

Verses composed by Rodulphus de Monchy.

(*Arras MS., No.* 860, *folio* 1.)

Hunc ego Rodulphus Monachus tantum modo dictus,
Nomine, non merito, sed fretus praesule Christo,
Conscripsi librum coelesti dogmate plenum.
Nec grave sit cuiquam libri si lucra capescam.
Magnum pro libro certe quia pignus habebo.
Quod pignus, sodes? Quod pignus? Jam modo nosces.
Cum librum scribo, Vedastus ab ethere summo
Respicit e coelis, notat et quot grammata nostris.
Depingam calamis, quot aretur pagina sulcis,
Quot folium punctis, hinc hinc laceretur acutis;
Tuncque favens operi nostro, nostroque labori,
Grammata quot, sulci quot sunt, quot denique puncti,
Inquit, in hoc libro, tot crimina jam tibi dono
Hancque potestatem dat Christus habere perhennem.
Nec labor iste tibi, frater, jam proderit uni,
Sed pro quibuscumque velis detur pars magna laboris,
Hec merces operis, quam dat scriptoribus ipsis
Sanctus Vedastus, pater optimus, atque benignus.
Hac mercede librum perscripsi sedulus istum.
Quem si quis tollat, tellus huic ima dehiscat,
Vivus ut infernum petat amplis ignibus atrum.
Fiat. Fiat.

This poem is inscribed on the *recto* of the first leaf of the Arras MS., No. 860:

'Sur le recto folio primo, un frontispice encadré, dessine a la plume, et dans l'encadrement des vers latins assez curieux composes par Rodulphus de Monchy. Audessus de cette pièce de vers est répresenté saint Vaast, parlant du haut de ciel au scribe placé sous lui.'

It is a finely-executed manuscript, and the figures both of S. Vaast and of the scribe are very carefully drawn. An accurate copy of this interesting drawing will be found in the frontispiece. The description of the manuscript (from the *Catalogue*) is given in the note.*

V.

Verses composed by Alard.

(*Arras MS.*, *No.* 616, *folio* 2.)

Junctus in aethereo, Vedaste, pater pie, regno,
His licet aeterno regi trans omnia pulchro,
Cernis servorum tamen hic pia vota tuorum,
Nec tanti donum quantum scis pendere votum ;
Tu memor ergo tui non dedigneris Alardi
Esse. Sed hunc modicum cum voto suscipe librum.
Cum capis librum, cum libro mox cape servum
Omnibus ut vitiis purges, des munera lucis.
Cum mors ingruerit et cum clamata jacebit
Materies, misero mihi tunc, pie Presul, adesto.

These verses are taken from the Arras MS., No. 616 ; a fine manuscript of S. Augustine's *Confessions*, and of his *Liber de vera religione.*

'Au recto folio deux, on lit dix vers, par un nommé Alard, qui a écrit ce manuscrit, addressés à St. Vaast.'

It is a manuscript of the commencement of the eleventh century.†

* No. 860. S. Hieronymi Commentarius in Libro Psalmorum. In folio quadrato ; velin fort et blanc ; tracé à la pointe ; deux colonnes ; XIe siècle ; grandes lettres ornées dans le style roman ; rubriques en onciales et capitales romaines ; initiales en vert minéral et en rouge de plomb ; 135 feuillets ; manuscrit écrit à St. Vaast.

† In folio quadrato ; vélin gratté, très beau et très fort ; tracé à la pointe ; deux colonnes ; têtes de livres en capitales romaines ; rubriques au rouge de plomb ; grandes lettres à la plume, ornées de vert, dans le style roman ; 75 feuillets.

The verses are printed in the official *Catalogue*, where the first word of the second line appears as *Sis*. The initial letter of the line was not inserted by the original scribe: a later, but still ancient, hand has written the letter H. On this account, to present an exact transcript of the earliest text which I could procure, I have printed *His* in the text, though *Sis* gives the better sense.

Over the word *materies*, in the last line, an ancient, probably contemporary, hand has written, 'S. [*i.e.*, scilicet] mei corporis.'

VI.

A Short Poem on S. Vedast.

(*Arras MS., No.* 380, *last leaf.*)

Arthesiis summo splendore Vedastus in oris
  Fulget, et eterni nomen honoris habet,
Dogmate celesti Christi exornavit ovile.
  Plebs, cole tam sanctum, relligiosa, patrem

VII.

French Verses by 'le mesme Autheur.'

(*Arras MS., No.* 380, *last leaf.*)

Le peaple doux, humain & très courtois,
Siège tenant ès limites d'Arthois,
De tel honeur tousieurs sainct Vadz vénère
Comme s'il fut son patron et vrai père;
Car il donna de charitable main
Du ciel luisant le salutaire pain.

These short compositions, Nos. VI. and VII., are found on the last leaf of the Arras MS., No. 380.*

The manuscript contains the life and miracles of S. Vedast, of which the editor of the *Catalogue* observes:

'Sur les derniers feuillets sont quelques miracles ajoutés à

* In folio mediocri; vélin blanc, sali par l'usage; tracé à l'encre pourpre; XIVe siècle; grande écriture gothique; initiales festonnées rouges et bleues; 25 feuillets.

une époque postérieure, et qui ne sont pas imprimés dans les Bollandistes, le dernier est daté de 1339.'

Immediately after the French verses is written: 'Beatus Vedastus Episcopus Atrebatensis per Grimaul Pont 1584.'

VIII.

Prayer to S. Vedast.

(*Arras MS., No. 903, last leaf. Eleventh century.*)

Scire volens summam deitatem cuncta excreantem
Ter quinos hinc, lector, habes ex ordine libros
Quos Augustinus, claro sermone retexens,
Edidit insignis rethor studio vehementi.
Ergo, Vedaste, favens scriptoris, suscipe munus
Evrardi, poscens regnum miserando polorum.

The manuscript from which these verses are taken contains the *Tractatus Sancti Augustini de Trinitate*, to which the writer alludes. On the last leaf is a design representing S. Vedast, executed contemporaneously with the volume itself, and beneath this representation are the verses now printed.

IX.

Extrait du Manuscrit No. 58 de la Bibliothèque d'Arras.

(*Vedastiados libri, Panagii Salii Audomarensis.*)

Liber Primus.

Sacra cano, regemque pium qui Francica primus
Sceptra Deo addixit, Christoque in regna vocato
Impia purgatis exclusit numina terris.
Multum illi valuere preces lacrymaeque decorae
Conjugis auditae caelo: multum ipse Vedastus.
Profuit, aeterne pandens mysteria vitae,
Errorem evolvens, et vulgus inane Deorum.
Spiritus O patris natique aeterna voluntas
Sancte veni, felixque animis illabere nostris.
Da memorare quibus Regem rationibus olim
Vir gratus superis, a relligione nefanda
Ad veros ritus traduxerit: et quibus inde
Auspiciis actus, varias penetrarit ad urbes
Artesiaeque solum; quanto recidiva, labore

Moenia condiderit sparsis Atrebatibus utque
Rexerit hunc populum et parvi Critienis ad amnem
Fundarit cellam, que nunc se mole minaci
Extulit ad coelum, caput inter nubila condit,
Atque Vedastinum servat per secula nomen.
Clodoveus ovans jam sub sua jura fluentem
Quinquebat* Rhenum, profligatasque potentes
Germanorum acies, Christo duce et auspice Christo
Signaque Teutonicis Victor referebat ab oris.
Multa movens animo diversus ab agmine princeps
Ibat, et ingentes agitabat pectore curas.
Eventus omnes, pugnataque in ordine secum
Bella recensebat reputans : sic comminus hostem
Aggredimur : sic pugna fuit, sic terruit hostes
Acer agens victos multo cum sanguine Francos.
Sic perii oppressus miser, aut periisse putavi.
Sic vovi, sic me certo mea vota Deusque
Eripuit letho, medioque ex hoste recepit
Ad socios, victis sic in precordia virtus
Atque animus rediit melior : sic vicimus ipsi
Aspirante Deo, voti reus insuper angor.
Nam Deus ille Deus mea quem Clotildis adorat,
Cujus opem expertus vivo, victorque triumpho,
Nescio quod numen, qua religione colendum
Adveniat? que sacra sibi, quos poscat honores.

* * * * *

Urbs antiqua fuit Leucorum in vallibus imis,
Quam fama est regem Hostilium dum occurrere tentat
Viribus atque armis Belgarum, ubi castra locabat
Instituisse, suo finxisse que nomine Tullum.
Exiguis illic tectis et paupere cella
Vivebat casta sub religione Vedastus,
Cui studium execrari Aras Phebique Jovisque
Et quecumque Deum larve, et simulata vigebant.

* * * * *

Sed postquam summosque duces, primosque suorum
Dimisit, fandique aptissima tempora vidit,
Et vacuam sine teste domum, qua parte sedebat
Aureus exurgit gradiens, dextraque Vedastum
Protinus apprensum verbis compellat amicis :
Huc ades, o felix, nec enim mihi jurgia tecum
Aut rixe, aut lesa de majestate Deorum
Ipse reum questor te sub mea tecta vocari.

There is in the British Museum a printed copy of the *Vedastiados* of some special interest, for on the title-page is a

* Quinquebat. Quinquare = lustrare, purgare. To expiate, to purify by religious rites.

written dedication of this copy in the author's own very legible hand:

> 'Panagius Salius Stephano Clavo dedit Autor
> ejus et hac propria sunt monimenta manu.'

On the back of the title* is a quaint portrait of the author; below it are four lines 'In Imaginem Auctoris' by A. Meier; and on one of the leaves is the curious anagram:

PANAGIUS SALIUS.
AGNUS, APIS SILVA.

The poem seems to have been a good deal revised and altered from the Arras MS., if that is indeed the earliest form, as seems very probable. I proceed to note a few variations between the MS. and the printed text:

After verse 19 occur nine lines of dedication to Abbot Sarrazin.

Verse 21.—The unusual word 'Quinquebat' disappears, and 'Linquebat' takes its place.

Verse 22.—The Virgilian, 'Christo duce et auspice Christo,' gives place to 'Voto non viribus usus.'

And in the second selected passage verses 2-4 run thus:

> 'Quam fert fama Ducem Hostilia de gente profectum
> Adversum Belgas posuisse, ubi castra locabat,
> Et proavi Tulli finxisse a nomine Tullum.'

The whole poem is an important contribution to Vedastine literature, and it seems worth while to give the author's own summary of the contents of his work.

Argumentum libri primi.—Clodoveus rex Francorum victoria de Germanis reportata in Galliam redit. Et primum Tullum Austrasiae urbem venit, illic que votum est solicitus (venerat autem Germanico proelio, si victor esset, se relicta deorum vana superstitione Christianam religionem amplexurum) consulit Vedastum sacerdotem illique solum et voti causas exponit, narrat a principio quibus conditionibus et pactis Clotildin uxorem duxerit, nempe si ipse Christianismum profiteretur. Tum uxoris pietatem commemorat, unius filii mortem alterius periculum, bellum Germanorum, et quo discrimine in illo sit versatus, victoriam demum suam post Christum vocatum. Tandem petit de diis sententiam. Vedastus Dei naturam explicat, docet Deum esse

* The title is: 'Panagii Salii Audomarensis Vedastiados seu Galliae Christianae libri quinque. Duaci. Ex Officina Ioannis Bogardi, 1591.' Quarto, 146 numbered pages + 4 unnumbered leaves. (Press mark, 11403. *k.* 46.)

unum, aeternum, immortalem, sub sensum non cadentem omnipotentem, optimus maximus ideamque boni et pulcri. Rejecit Deos antiquae impietatis Saturnum, Jovem, Neptunum, Plutonem, etc. Causas affert Idololatriæ, illius inconstantiam, constantiam autem verae religionis quae in paucis mansit ab Adamo, Noe, Abraham, per totum populum Israël, usque ad Christum qui ipsam adimplevit. His auditis Rex Christianae doctrinae adhaeret, et Remos adire instituit ut a Remigio expiari possit. Interea id consilii dissimulat paratque convivium.

Argumentum libri secundi.—Regi in somnis apparet Christi imago miserandum in modum cruenta et lacera, et qualis in cruce fuit, cumque illa Angelus bellicum signum ferens, quod Rex acceptum a Christo munus Auriflammam vocat. Vedastus de crucis admirabili virtute disserit, historiamque Constantini commemorat. Rex Crucem albam sibi Francisque pro discrimine militari assumit. Aurelius ad Clotildin Reginam mittitur. Bellum paratur in Virdunenses, sed rex illis parcit victus precibus Euspicii sacerdotis et Vedasti. Clotildis ad Remos venit, et illic cum Remigio Regem expectat. Vedastus in ponte Axonae in finibus Remorum coram Rege, et regio exercitu caeco homini oculos restituit. Vaticinatur futurum ut reges Christiani Franci gutturalem morbum* alias incurabilem, sola manus appositione curent. Venitur ad Remos. Occurrunt Regi Clotildis et Remigius. Rex ad suam nobilitatem orationem habet, illamque hortatur ut secum Christianam religionem amplecti velit. Cui postquam persuasit, magna pompa templum petit, et a Remigio, virtute Baptismi, expiatur. Ungitur chrismate divinitus oblato.

Argumentum libri tertii.— Regi jam per Baptismum expiato occurrit Eremita ferens scutum in quo picta erant lilia aurea. Illud Regi tradit, et a Christo missum exponit. Rex statim bufonibus rejectis (quae sua erant prima insignia) lilia assumit. Remigius Regem admonet officii, afflatus furore divino vaticinatur et canit fata Franciae. Hinc Rex discedens Vedastum Remigio commendat: Vedastus agit cum Remigio. Deus Raphaelem ad Remigium mittit, cui imperat ut Vedastum ad Atrebates mittat Episcopum. Vedastus Atrebates petit. Ad portas urbis caecum et claudum sanat. Describitur urbs vetus, et pene diruta, barbaries gentis et feritas. Ursus Vedasti imperio paret, et sylvas mansuetus repetit. Comius senior narrat calamitatem et eversionem urbis per tempora Hunorum, et de nece Diogenis. Vedastus plebem dispersam ferarum more convocat. In concione eos hortatur ut civiliorem vitae cultum sequantur, ad urbem sibi instaurandam excitet, persuadet. Templum D. Virgini dedicatur. Urbs nova excitatur.

Argumentum libri quarti.—Instaurata urbe Vedastus curat leges et jura antiquata restitui, senatum legi, Magistratusque creari, cellas Mercurio et Dianae positas destrui, cellam suburbanam sibi per data otia contemplationi secessum aedificari. In illa somno divino corripitur. In somnis Angelum videt, auditque ventura sibi praedicentem, honoresque futuros illius cellae, quae autoribus Autberto primum Episcopo, deinde Theodorico Rege, et Vindiciano Pontifice summum incrementum sit acceptura. Eodem Angelo monstrante videt seriem omnium Abbatum Vedastinorum ab Hatta usque

* Probably the King's Evil is intended.

ad Joannem Saracenum, corumque res gerendas cognoscit. Tandem, Oratoribus Bellovacis interpellantibus, a somno excitatur.

Argumentum libri quinti.—Corbides unus ex oratoribus Bellovacorum suae legationis causas exponit. Vedastus Bellovacorum urbem aditurum se pollicetur. Revertuntur Deprecatores. Ipse cellam suburbanam, insomniorum memor locum sepulturae sibi decernit. Ad Bellovacos tendit per Ambianos et Velocasses. In Velocassibus occurrit Paternus veteranus eques, Clodovaci quondam Regis domesticus, qui illum hospitio excipit. Petit consilium a Vedasto, quo facto maxime beatam vitam consequi possit. Vedastus suadet, ut Xenodochium extruat: nihil enim liberalitate et misericordia in pauperes Deo gratius esse. Aegre assentitur Paternus, quippe nimis attentus ad rem. Vedastus virgam tiliae, quo scipione utebatur, jam aridam humi figit, et hoc facto Xenodochii extructionem firmat, si virga illa tracto humore revirescat et succrescat in arborem. Pactionem subito fides secuta est, virga reviruit, arbor enata est, et ex arbore ingens silva. Vedastus Bratuspantium ad Bellovacus venit, populum in Christiana religione confirmat, Pontificemque illis Dominicum attribuit. A Clotilde ad Parisios advocatur. Lutetiam petit, ubi Genovefam mortuam lugeri intelligit. Clotildis curas illi suas exponit. Eam consolatur Vedastus. Genovefam sepelit. A rege Clotario ad coenam invitatur. Prodigium facit, tandemque domum se recipit.

It is impossible to resist the temptation of adding one other specimen of the poem, the very graphic description of the gift of the *Sainte Ampulle* at the baptism of Clovis.

Liber II., p. 64.

Jamque uncturus erat sacrato Chrismate Regem
(Pontifices hoc Chrisma vocant quod vulgus olivum),
Sed dum vas aperit quo promere Chrisma volebat,
Horret, nil olei in sicco jam vase repertum,
Quod tamen ante sacro plenum pinguebat olivo.
Prodigio stupet, et turbari sacra veretur.

* * * * *

Dumque haec judicia inter se contraria mussant,
Ecce alis subito geminis librata Columba
Visa per exiguam se Templo inferre fenestram.
Vas fictum in cymbam rostro portabat in unco.
Illa ubi ter circum populum volitavit et ora,
Remigio illapsa est, ejus dextraque resedit,
Et pronum praetendit onus, quo lenitur illic
Deposito, in coelum pennis ablata refugit,
Attonitum populum linquens, monstroque silentem.
Remigius vase, et divino munere laetus
(Namque Dei agnovit famulum, qui venerat ales,
Et vas attulerat coelo delapsus ab alto),
Inde oleum sumit, peragitque ex ordine sacra;
Inque caput lympham, conceptaque verba profundit:

Qui postquam perfectus honos, et sacra quierunt,
Jam lituique tubaeque canunt, jam gaudia totis
Accendit populus studiis, plausumque frequentat,
Concitaque ingentem resonant delubra per urbem.

Messieurs de Cardevacque and Terninck, in their important monograph upon the Abbey of S. Vaast,* observe that 'Saint Vaast n'a pas eu seulement ses biographes et ses panégyristes, il a eu aussi ses poètes. Il existe une épopée latine peu connue, mais assez remarquable, intitulée *la Védastiade*. Antoine Meyer, l'un de nos écrivains les plus distingués du xvie siècle, publia en 1580 un poëme en trois chants sous ce titre singulier : *L'ours ou la vie de saint Vaast*.'

In the Arras Library there is a manuscript copy of the former poem.† I am indebted to Monsieur A. Lavoine for the transcript of a portion of the work (sufficient to give a general idea of its merits), which forms the present section of the *Poemata*. I have not seen the original manuscript.

I have not been so fortunate as to see a copy of Meier's *Ursus*. It is not to be found in the library at Arras. Messieurs de Cardevacque and Terninck give its title-page thus :

'Antonii Meyeri Ursus, sive de rebus divi Vedasti, episcopi Atrebatensis, libri iii., in 8[vo.] Lutetiæ apud Carolum Roger, 1580. L'ouvrage est dédié à Jean Sarrazin, abbé de Saint-Vaast.'

In the list of the men of letters who were contemporary with Jean Sarrazin, seventy-sixth Abbot of S. Vaast, 1578-1598, are enumerated Toussaint de la Salle and Antoine Meyer ; and here it is said that the former, 'Panagius Salius de Saint Omer, lui envoya avec une dédicace, un poème intitulé :

'Vedastiados, Calliopesacka ad amplissimum virum Joannem Sarracenum, abbatem Vedastinum pieridum Mecenatem renatum. Vol. in 4[to.] 27 pages. Arras. G. de la Rivière, 1595.'‡

* *L'Abbaye de Saint-Vaast*, I. 21.

† MS. No. 58. *Panagii Salii Audomarensis Vedastiados libri quinque.* In folio ; papier ; écriture bâtarde du XVIe siècle ; 42 feuillets.

‡ *L'Abbaye de Saint-Vaast*, I. 286.

I am not able to determine, from the materials before me, whether this work is a second edition of that printed in Douai in 1591.

It will have been observed that A. Meier, no doubt the author of the *Ursus*, wrote the quatrain below the portrait of Toussaint de la Salle, or, to use the Latinised form of his name, Panagius Salius.

X.

Versus in laudem S. Vedasti.

(*Arras MS., No.* 493.)

Amor, timorque, spes, metus, infirmitas,
Ardorque mentis, quo trasitis? Huc me rapit
Fervens voluntas, at metus flammam avocat:
Illuc amor ducit, sed impotens meos
Supplantat ausus musa. Spirant intimae
Fibrae Vedastum, Galliae lumen, Deus,
Famemque mundi: vix tamen lactam ratem
Mari aestuoso credere audiam. Sed i
Exprome musa quamquam in primoribus
Labris sedebat, exeat fausta alite
Leves in auras: si modo faves meis,
Vedaste, caeptis. Sed faves, vide, faves.

The Arras MS. No. 493, is entitled 'Aliquot versus in laudem S. Vedasti'; a quarto volume, on paper, 'écriture bâtarde du XVIIe siècle; 16 feuillets. Pour dédicace:

> 'Ad Reverendissimum D. Abbatem sancti Vedasti Maecenatem suum, Philippum Kavrel, Gaugericus hispanus.'

The volume contains a series of thirteen poems, of which the specimen above printed will probably suffice; it is the first of the series. Here follows a list of the subjects of the verses:

1. Ad Sanctum Vedastum.
2. Nativitas S. Vedasti.
3. Vedasto jam nato.
4. Vedasti quaerimonia de Galliae infidelitate.
5. A lecto quaeritur quod Gallia S. Vedasti labore ad fidem sit conversa.

6. De caeco illuminato a S. Vedasto in ponte Axome.*
7. De Sancto Vedasto Atrebatum obligente.
8. De Templo Beatae Mariae Atrebati a S. Vedasto constructo.
9. De Sella Mercurii et Dianae a S. Vedasto excisa.
10. De prodigio in mensis a S. Vedasto functo.
11. De columna ignis quae mortem S. Vedasti praecurrebat.
12. Ad P. Hubum se satis meruisse.
13. Ad reverendissimum S. Vedasti abbatem Philippum Kaurelle Maecenatem suum.

Philippe de Caverel was the seventy-seventh abbot of S. Vaast, 1598-1636, and was one of the most distinguished of the dignified ecclesiastics who have occupied the abbatial throne. A full account of him will be found in *L'Abbaye de Saint Vaast*, par MM. Adolphe de Cardevacque et Auguste Terninck.† It is to him that Gaugericus, the Spaniard, dedicates his verses.‡

XI.

Verses by Petrus Justus Sautel.

(*Printed in his 'Annus Sacer Poeticus,' Vol. I., p.* 63.)

VI. Februarii.

S. Vedastus Episcopus Atrebatensis, cuius obitum insistens tecto columna ignea praenuntiauit.

Dvm premit affectos morbus tibi lethifer artûs,
  Insedit Laribus pendula flamma tuis.
Solemnes succendit faces in funera, Praesul,
  Ignis enim cineres nuntiat iste tuos.

Sautel's work is well known. It will suffice to say that the *Annus Sacer Poeticus* was printed in two duodecimo volumes, in Paris, in 1665.

* In the short life of S. Vedast printed in the *Mémoires de l'Académie d'Arras*, 1886, the river is called Axona (p. 211), that is, the Aisne.

† Vol. II., pp. 5-18.

‡ The fourth Bishop of Cambrai, Gaugericus, or S. Gery, a native of Yvoy, in Luxembourg, bore the same somewhat unusual name (*Gallia Christiana*, III. 4).

THE MUSIC OF TWO OF THE HYMNS.

By the great kindness of two friends, learned in the heaven-sent art, I am able to add the music to which two of the hymns should be sung.

Taking these hymns in chronological order the first will be No. VIII. in the present collection:

'Voce jucunda resonemus omnes.'

Here will be found, in the ancient notation, the melody to which the hymn is set in the *Supplement aux Graduel et Antiphonaire Romains pour le Diocèse d'Arras*, printed at Arras in 1889, and then a transcription of this melody into modern notation with delightful harmonies added by Dr. Martin, the Organist of S. Paul's Cathedral, who is always ready, with generous kindness, to help the searcher after that musical lore in which he is so great a proficient.

Here follows the same melody harmonised:

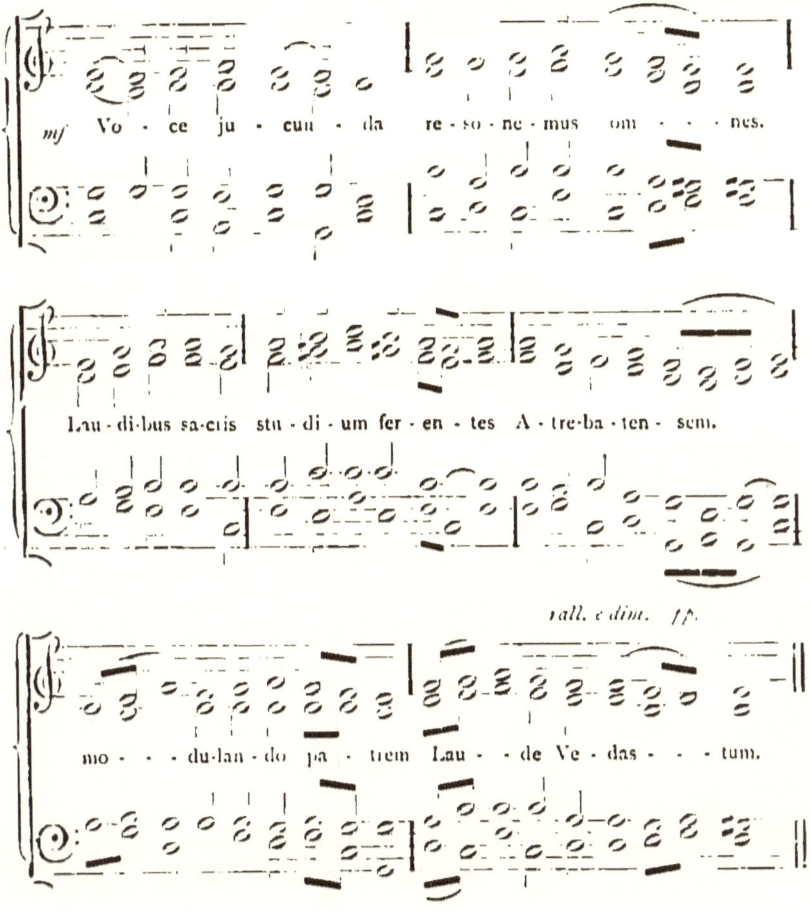
mf Vo - ce ju - cun - da re - so - ne - mus om - - - nes.
Lau - di-bus sa-cris stu - di - um fer - en - tes A - tre-ba - ten - sem.
rall. e dim. ff.
mo - - - du-lan - do pa - trem Lau - - de Ve - das - - - tum.

Then follows the music of the Flemish hymn, No. XXV. :

VAN DEN HEYLIGEN VEDASTUS.

Andantino maestoso.
mf
cres.

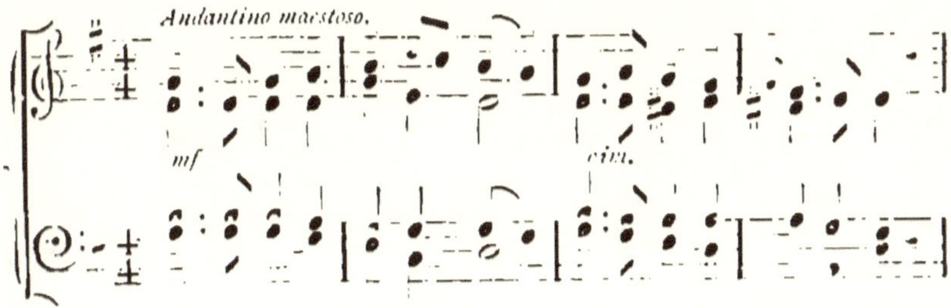

mf
dim.
cres.
cres.
f
dim.
cres.
f
ff

As has been already said (page 42), the melody of the hymn was taken by M. de Coussemaker from the lips of an old pupil of the Ecole dominicale at Bailleul. He considers it to belong to the beginning of the eighteenth century, and this is probably the earliest date that can be assigned to it.

Sir John Stainer, the Professor of Music in the University of Oxford, and formerly Organist of S. Paul's Cathedral, has harmonised the melody for me, catching exactly the spirit of the original, and producing a hymn tune which might well serve for a Processional.

With the usual generosity of their profession, these eminent musicians present me with the result of their labours to brighten the pages of this tractate.

SUPPLEMENTUM AD CARMINA VEDASTINA.

XXVI.

Hymn in the Irish Language.

(*Martyrology of Gorman*, 1166—1174 A.D.)

Uedaist amra, Amaint,*
  Fustais ni chel charaim,
  epscop Mel† nos-molaimm,
Anatholian, Teophil,
feil Dura‡ bhain bladhuill,
  Branduibh chaid is Cholaim[m],§
dom breith don flaith léa
  Dorothéa thogaimm,
Finnian|| abb na hinnse
  'sin¶ rindse mo roraind.

TRANSLATION.

Wonderful Vedastus, (bishop) Amandus, Fausta (?), I will not conceal whom I love: Bishop Mel,** I praise him, Anatholianus, Theophilus, the festival of fair, great-famed Dura,†† of Brandub the chaste and Colomb.‡‡ 'Tis Dorothea I choose to take me with her to the Kingdom (of heaven). Findián,§§ abbot of the island, in this end of the stanza (is) my great portion.

This hymn is taken from the *Martyrology of Gorman*, edited by Dr. Whitley Stokes, for the *Henry Bradshaw Society*, in 1895. Pp. 30, 31.

Gorman was Abbot of Cnoc na n-Apstol (otherwise called Cnoc na Sengán, 'The Hill of the Pismires'), and he appears to have composed his *Martyrology* while Ruaidre hua Conchobair was King of Ireland, between 1166 and 1174. P. xix.

* Seems altered from 'Amaitt,' in marg. man. rec. 'Amait—Amaind.' i. 'Amandus qui hodie ponitur.'

† epscop Ard-achaid i Tethba, descipal Patraicc eside.

‡ epscop mac Coluim ó Dhruim chremha.

§ Bran 7 colum ó Loch Munremhuir.

|| Maelfindiáin abb Insi Patraic.

¶ MS. 'san.'

** Bishop of Ard-Achad in Tethba, a disciple of Patrick he.

†† Bishop, son of Colomb, of Druim Crema.

‡‡ Bran and Colomb, from Loch Munremuir.

§§ Mael-Findiáin, Abbot of Inis-Pátraic.

XXVII.*

Prosa de Sancto Vedasto. *Feb. 6.*

(*Collégiale de la Ferté-Milon : au Diocèse de Soissons*, 1683.)

A la Messe. Prose.

1. Christo laudes attollamus,
Qui praeclara celebramus
Vedasti solemnia ;
Corde puro, mente munda,
Moduletur vox jucunda,
Lucis hujus gaudia.

2. Lux est grata, lux insignis,
In quo digna Deo dignis
Conferuntur praemia.
Hymnos ergo concinentes,
Corda novemus et voces
. Novemus et opera.

3. Ille pater et patronus,
Quem pastorem summe bonus
Pastor nobis tribuit.
Zelo plenus, christianae
Arcana sacra doctrinae
Leucis ille detegit.

4. Mox Jesum evangelizat,
Clodovaeo quem confirmat
In fide miraculis.
Remos petit, ubi clarus
Sanctitate, dat benignus
Sanitatem languidis.

5. Inde praesul Atrebatum
Missus, genti Christum Jesum
Infideli praedicat.
Fidus ubi dispensator,
Non avarus fenerator,
Talentum multiplicat.

---

* I desire to express my most grateful thanks to the venerable Abbé Tousonde for his great courtesy in transcribing for me, in his own fair handwriting, Hymns Nos. XXVII., XXVIII., XXIX., XXX., and XXXI. in this Supplement.

6. Consolator afflictorum,
Propugnator miserorum,
Infirmorum medicus.
Idolorum vanitatem
Et Christi Divinitatem
Suis probat civibus.

7. Lumen caecis, gressum claudis,
Surdis auditum et mutis
Reddit vocem, Salvatoris
Adjuvante gratia.
O quam felix, quam ornata,
Fuit urbs et honorata,
Tanto viro desponsata
Soli sine macula.

8. Morum et vitae radios
Dum dispensat in filios
Cultus relinquit varios
Adhaerens Ecclesiae.
Convertuntur, baptizantur,
Ecclesiae reparantur,
Fugit ursus, perfringuntur
Ocini fideliae.*

9. Tandem vitam consummavit,
Qui daemones effugavit,
Fidem Gallis praedicavit,
In Christo tanta patravit,
Donante miracula.
Ante thronum Trinitatis
Ora, Vedaste, pro nobis
Ut mundemur a peccatis
Et supernae caritatis
Habeamus gaudia. Amen.

XXVIII.

Hymnus de Sancto Vedasto. *Feb. 6.*

(*Proprium Ecclesiae Collegiatae S. Vedasti. La Ferté-Milon,* 1683.)

Aux Vêpres.

1. Voce jucunda resonemus omnes,
Laudibus sanctam Triadem colentes;
Quae dedit nobis sacra conferentem
Dona Vedastum.

---

* *Fidelia:* an earthen vessel.

2. Illius castum pietatis ardor,
Pectus accendit teneris ab annis
Et sacris, Christo miserante, dignum
Admovet aris.

3. Jussu divinae veneranda legis
Explicat Tulli : Clodovix docentem
Audit et sanctae fidei peroptat
Subdere collum.

4. Mox renascendo Comes ille regis
Advenit Remos, ubi languidorum
Annuens votis, febrium molestos
Temperat ignes.

5. Vana commissae simulacra plebis
Diruit cura vigili, creatus
Praesul et sanctis regit infidelem
Legibus urbem.

6. Ampla regalis monimenta cultus
Erigit Christo nova templa : jussis
Obsequens ursus fugit et propinquum
Transnatat amnem.

7. Laus Deo Patri, genitaeque Proli,
Et tibi cómpar utriusque virtus
Spiritus, semper Deus unus, omni
Tempore saecli. Amen.

XXIX.

(*From the same source as No. XXVIII.*)

A Matines.

1. Pange, lingua, gloriosi
Vedasti praeconium,
Posce votis adjuvari
Detur ut caelestium
Fortunatus intueri
Mansiones civium.

2. Remenses coadjutorem
Regalis ecclesiae,
Atrebatenses doctorem
Praedicant Artesiae :
Cameracenses pastorem
Gaudent suum dicere.

3. Amatorem paupertatis
Laudant cum pauperes,
Assertorem veritatis
Admirantur principes,
Defensorem castitatis
Intuentur virgines.

4. Magne doctor Clodovei
Preces nostras suscipe,
Et gregem tuum perenni
Pacis uno foedere,
Atque nostro Conditori
Nos transferre satage.

5. Summa summo laus Parenti,
Summa laus et Filio,
Ab utroque procedenti
Par decus Paracleto,
Qui beati nos Vedasti
Conjungat consortio.

XXX.

(From the same source as No. XXVIII.)

A Laudes.

1. Felix Vedastus pontifex
Terrena spernens gaudia,
Saevosque vincens daemones
Fatur Dei magnalia.

2. Christum volens sequi ducem
Prodesse cunctis appetit,
Apostolis haud imparem
Miraculis se detegit.

3. Obfirmat artus languidos,
Aegris refundit spiritum,
Linguas ligatas expedit,
Caecisque lumen impetrat.

4. O sancte Francorum parens
Auge fidem credentium,
Et caritatis intimis
Succende flammas cordibus.

5. Sit laus tibi, sit gloria
Perennis auctor omnium,
Qui trinus ante saecula
Unusque subsistis Deus. Amen.

XXXI.

Hymnus de Sancto Vedasto. *Feb. 6.*

(*Proprium Ecclesiae Collegiatae S. Vedasti Suessionensis, Anno* 1747.)

Soissons, Bibliothèque du Grand Séminaire.

Ad Missam : Sequentia.

1. Omnes Deo jubilemus,
Corde toto celebremus,
Vedasti solemnia.

2. A cognatis hic remotus,
Et praediis spoliatus,
Discessit a patria.

3. Solus ipse Tullum fugit,
Inibique Deo servit,
Seque mundo submovet.

4. Illum pietas jam prodit,
Factus sacerdos obedit,
Coeli vias edocet.

5. Vicos pagosque percurrit,
Jesum indoctis edicit,
Fidem cunctis praedicat.

6. Ut Clodovix Germanos subdidit,
Statim votum ardenter reddidit,
Rex Vedastum postulat.

7. Uterque dum Remos petit,
Illum sacerdos erudit
Sacris Dei legibus.

8. Quem in fide confirmavit
Et in Christo solidavit
Signis et virtutibus.

9. Praesul Atrebatum factus,
Infidam gentem docturus,
Deo parat segetem.

10. Terror idolorum factus ;
Jam fana ruunt et saltus
Spirat daemon rabiem.

11. Pagani mox convertuntur,
Aedes sacrae construuntur,
Solus Deus colitur.

12. Caeci luce perfunduntur,
Claudi pedes eriguntur,
Ursus ferox pellitur.

13. Instituit sacerdotes,
Et levitas et pastores ;
Totum gentem renovat.

14. Nutrit et fovet egentes,
Et edit apud magnates,
Hos ut Christo pariat.

15. Jam cunctis omnia factus,
Lucratur omnes Vedastus,
Movet illum sanctitas.

16. Pro suis ut pastor bonus,
Sua seque tradit totus,
Urget illum caritas,

17. Facto potens et sermone,
Corda suorum ardere,
Igne Dei compulit.

18. Consumptus demum labore,
Confractusque senectute,
Vitam Deo reddidit.

19. O qui tuo nos cruore
Redemisti, Pastor bone,
Jesu, nostri miserere
Vedasti suffragiis.

20. Da nobis semper tenere,
Quod nos edocuit ipse
Per aeternae verbum vitae
Ope tui luminis.

21. Christe, Deus et Salvator,
Pastorum caput et honor,
Tu nostrae salutis auctor
Sit pro nobis intercessor,
Cujus laudes gerimus.

22. O Vedaste, memor esto
Tui gregis qui se voto
Tibi dicavit Patrono.
Praesta, tecum ut in caelo
Laetemur perennius. Amen.

XXXII.

Hymnus in Festo Translationis S. Vedasti. *Oct.* 1.*

(*Proprium Atrebatense*, 1806.)

In I. Vesperis et ad Officium Nocturnum.

1. Dum mens Pontificis numine pascitur,
Siccis en suis est hic honor ossibus :
Istis quanta fluant, quot bona fontibus,
Experti toties canant.

2. Dilectos cineres, pignora Praesulis,
O cives, memori visite pectore ;
Exornate novis fercula floribus ;
Laudes thuraque fundite.

3. Sed marmor Parium, vasa nec aurea,
Dulces nec moduli Pontificem juvant,
Ni sit vita piis consona vocibus :
Lauda, quisquis es aemulus.

4. His quae spirat adhuc pignoribus fides,
Accendat gelidis pectoribus fidem ;
Et quos in tumulo servat adhuc cinis,
Ignes mentibus excitet.

5. Hunc portu placido certa licet quies
Securum teneat, fluctibus obrutos
Cum spectat mediis, sollicitum facit
Nunc et patria caritas.

6. A quo cuncta fluunt, sit Tibi laus, Deus ;
Sacros qua decuit dum reverentia
Artus nos colimus, tota refunditur
Summo gloria vertici. Amen.

---

* This hymn appears to have been in use till 1834.

XXXIII.

Hymnus in Festo Translationis S. Vedasti. *Oct.* 1.*

(*Proprium Atrebatense*, 1806.)

Ad Laudes et ad II. Vesperas.

1. Heroum tumulos bustaque vidimus
Regum magnanimum : tot meritis viri,
Tot factis celebres, heu ! sterili jacent,
Pulvis degener, otio.

2. Terris sic residem non patitur Deus
Sanctorum cinerem turpe quiescere :
Claros prodigiis ac venerabiles
Ipsos vel tumulos facit.

3. Urnam depositi corporis hospitam,
Cives, perpetuis cingite floribus :
Dulces exuvias quas colitis, sacra
Tot sunt pignora Praesulis.

4. Illic prisca Patris spirat adhuc fides ;
Ardens fervet adhuc et sua caritas :
Si nos fida parum pectora vivimus,
Vivos mortuus arguet.

5. Talis depositi nos sumus et simul
Custodes fidei ; nos super excubat
Ex illa specula ; de cathedra docet
Plenus numine Pontifex.

6. Hinc nos assiduus praeco redarguit :
Quam sudore sibi totque laboribus
Palmam quaesierit, scilicet otio
Nos speremus inutili ?

7. Natos, alme Pater, sedibus e tuis,
Si te nostra movent, nos bonus aspice ;
Flammis ure tuis frigida pectora,
Et mentes dubias rege.

8. Ut cum nostra novis splendida dotibus
Surget juncta choris spirituum caro,
Indivisa Trias sit Deus omnia
Nobis semper in omnibus. Amen.

---

* This hymn appears to have been in use till 1834.

This hymn is also found in the Noyon Breviary of 1764, where it is adapted to S. Eligius of Noyon, June 25. *In Festo Translationis Corporis Sancti Eligii.* Here verses 1 to 4, 7, 8, are identical with the hymn as printed above, save in verse 3, line 3, where *exuviae* is printed instead of *exuvias*; and in place of verses 5 and 6, is found:

Dum nos assiduus praeco redarguit
Quam sudore sibi, totque laboribus
Palmam quaesierit, scilicet otio
Nos speremus inutili?

XXXIV.

Hymnus in Festo Relationis S. Vedasti. *Jul.* 15.*

(*Proprium Atrebatense*, 1806.)

Hymnus in utrisque Vesperis.

1. Magni fama volat nuntia gaudii;
Portis ecce ruit turba patentibus:
Urbem nempe Vedastus
Sublimi feretro redit.

2. Aspexere simul. Quis venerabilis
Non optavit onus tollere corporis?
Quis non oscula ferre.
Sacris ambiit artubus?

3. Neutrum si liceat, quod licet omnibus,
Grato corde fovent, laudibus efferunt:
Pulsus cantibus aether
Hymnis accinit aemulis.

4. Cujus parta venit munere sanctitas,
Haec laus, Christe, Tibi tota refunditur:
Dum nos membra veremur,
Supremum coleris caput. Amen.

---

* This hymn appears to have been in use till 1834.

XXXV.

Hymnus ad Completorium. *Feb. 6.**

(*Arras Breviary*, 1834.)

1. Grates, peracto jam die,
Deus, tibi persolvimus;
Pronoque, dum nox incipit
Prosternimus vultu preces.

2. Quod longa peccavit dies,
Amarus expiet dolor;
Somno gravatis ne nova
Infligat hostis vulnera.

3. Infestus usque circuit
Quaerens leo quem devoret:
Umbra sub alarum tuos
Defende filios, Pater.

4. O quando lucesset tuus
Qui nescit occasum dies!
O quando sancta se dabit
Quae nescit hostem patria!

5. Uni sit et trino Deo
Suprema laus, summum decus,
De nocte qui nos ad suae
Lumen vocavit gloriae.

There is no reference to S. Vedast in the hymn, yet it is included here as being the compline hymn for the Feast of S. Vedast, and because it is made in some sort special, by having a doxology attached to it, differing from that used when it is sung at other times.

* In the Arras Breviary, printed at Paris in 1834, the following rubric is found on February 6, p. 537: 'Ad Completorium. *Hymnus* Grates *cum Doxologia* Uni sit, *ut supra ad Horas.*' The hymn GRATES is the common hymn for the season, 'a crastino Praesentationis Domini, ad Feriam III. Hebdomadae Quinquagesimae,' to be sung at Compline; see p. 144. But the doxology there given is 'Deo patri sit gloria.' The hymn, with the special doxology, is printed above. In the Proprium Atrebatense, 1806, p. 52, the Rubric is somewhat more full: '*Hymnus* Grates, *cum Doxologia seq. quae etiam dicitur ad omnes Horas in Hymnis ejusdem metri per totam Octavam, quoties de ea fit Officium.*'

INDEX TO SUPPLEMENT.

NOTES.

Page 14, verse 7, line 2. A friendly critic has suggested *carminis* for text.

Page 15, verse 4, line 3. The same friend suggests *geminos* (*i.e.*, the blind and lame).

Page 16, verse 3, line 4. *Refulgens.* (Ernestus Duemmler prints the hymn, No. 4, in his *Poetae Latinae Aevi Carolini*, 4to., Berolini, 1881, p. 313, exactly as it stands in the text, but reverses the order of verses 5 and 6.)

Page 25. In the Arras Missal of 1508 (in British Museum), in Hymn No. XII., after line 5 follows:

'Manent tria, fides, spes, caritas.'

Page 28. The three hymns, XIII., XIV., XV., do not appear in the first edition of Santeul; they were added in the second edition.

Page 36. The four hymns, XXI.—XXIV., are also in the *Proprium Atrebatense*, 1806, where No. XXI. has the heading *Santol. Vict.*, and with good reason, as verses 2, 3, 4 are identical with No. XIII., 2, 3, 4; and verses 5, 6, 7, 8 with No. XIV., 2, 3, 6, 7.

Page 44, line 16. Professor Duemmler prints *adjuvet.*

Page 45, No. II., line 8. Professor Duemmler reads *marsupii* in his text, but gives *marsupiis* as a various reading.

Page 57, No. XI., line 3. Perhaps *succende.*

ERRATA.

Page 30, No. XVIII., line 7, for *autre* read *antre;* and in note, for *Candale* read *Candace.*

Page 32, line 5, for *Elie* read *Abbé.*

Page 44, line 15, for *menento* read *memento.*

Page 47, line 5, for *Quærct* read *Quercet.*

Page 48, line 3 from bottom of text, for *addressés* read *adressés.*

Page 52, note on verse 22, for *Virgilian* read *Horatian* (Odes, I., 7, 27).

Page 55, last sentence, read *Calliope Sacra* and *Pieridum.*

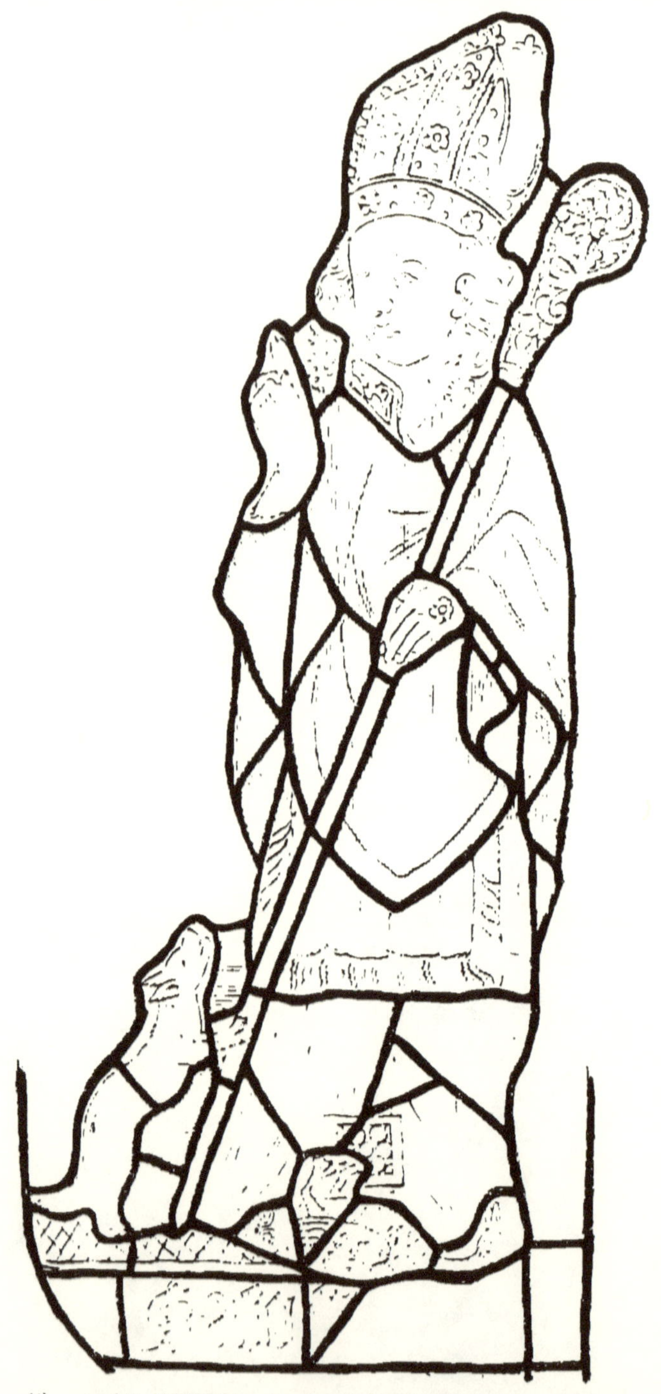

Figure of S. FOSTER, that is, S. VEDAST, Bishop of Arras, from a window in Blythborough Church, Norfolk.

TRAGICO-COMOEDIA

DE

SANCTO VEDASTO:

EDITED FROM MANUSCRIPTS AT ARRAS

BY

W. SPARROW SIMPSON, D.D., F.S.A.,
Sub-Dean and Librarian of S. Paul's Cathedral,
One of the Honorary Librarians of His Grace the Archbishop of Canterbury,
Rector of S. Vedast, London.

LONDON:
ELLIOT STOCK, 62, PATERNOSTER ROW.
1895.

[*The impression is limited to* 250 *copies, of which only a few will be offered for sale.*]

PREFACE.

The *Tragico-Comoedia de Sancto Vedasto* is here printed from two manuscripts in the Bibliothèque de la Ville at Arras, of which the following description is given in the printed catalogue:

'No. 678. *Tragicomedia de Sancto Vedasto.* In folio, papier, écriture cursive du XVIe [XVIIe ?] siècle, 52 feuillets. Prov St Vaast.' On the title-page is written, 'Bibliothecae monasterii S. Vedasti Atrebat. 1618, K.'

'No. 936. *Tragico-Comoedia de Sto. Vedasto*, data a studiosa juventute Collegii S. J. Atrebati, 13° Septembris, 1611. Papier, écriture bâtarde du temps, 136 feuillets. Prov. St. Vaast. Le Poème est en vers trochaïques et iambiques, avec choeurs dans les règles de la tragédie antique.'

Then follows the author's dedication:

'Amplissimo et admodum reverendo domino D. Philippo de Caverel, Abbati D. Vedasti, tantillam hanc actiunculam, paucorum dierum opus, gratitudinis erga Collegium Societatis Jesu Atrebatense, D. C. Q. *Tragico-Comoedia de Sancto Vedasto*, primo parente religiosorum Coenobii Vedastini, necnon Atrebatium patrono, data a studiosa juventute Collegii Societatis Jesu Atrebati, 13° Septembris, 1611.'

The text now given is that of MS. No. 678, with which the MS. No. 936 has been carefully collated. Any variations found in the latter manuscript are placed as footnotes. The text of MS. No. 678 was preferred to that of the other manuscript, because the character of the handwriting appeared to indicate that it was of somewhat earlier date, although there can be but a few years' difference of age between them. Each MS. is carefully written and well preserved.

For the transcript and collation the editor is indebted to Monsieur A. Lavoine, of Arras, Chef de Bureau aux Archives Départementales, to whom he desires to express his acknowledgments.

In the correction of the press, and in the minute comparison of the printed text with Monsieur Lavoine's transcript, the editor has had the very valuable assistance of Mr. W. De Gray Birch, F.S.A., of the Department of Manuscripts in the British Museum, whose careful study of the transcript and whose acute criticisms have cleared up many intricacies and solved many perplexities.

The text, although the two manuscripts have been minutely collated, is still very obscure in many places. Some of the obscurities may be due to the pedantry of the author; others to his employment of unusual words, which may have perplexed the scribes who wrote the two nearly contemporary manuscripts at Arras. The minute collation to which Monsieur Lavoine has submitted these copies of the play, and the consideration which he has given to any cases of special difficulty which have been referred to him, have not succeeded in removing all the obscurities: and the editor has thought it best to exhibit the text as it stands in the Arras manuscripts, correcting only flagrant and obvious errors, and avoiding merely conjectural emendations.

The representation of S. Vedast which faces the title-page is taken from a fifteenth-century stained glass window on the north side of Blythborough Church, Norfolk, where it stood in close proximity to figures of S. Amandus and S. Remigius.

This collocation is easily explained, for in the Calendar of the Sarum Breviary these saints are associated together :

> Feb : 6. Vedasti et Amandi Episcoporum et Confessorum.
> Oct : 1. Remigii sociorumque ejus [Germani, Vedasti et Bavonis] Episcoporum et Confessorum.

Mr. H. Watling, a well-known Norfolk antiquary, made a tracing of this subject in 1836, and has favoured me with a copy, from which this illustration is taken. The glass adjacent to the figure of S. Vedast was at the period in question in a very bad condition. Some pieces of the beautiful glass had been taken out, and 'a piece of brick with mortar inserted to fill up the space, and no care whatever taken to preserve' these precious relics. Mr. Watling says that a restoration of the church has since taken place, but he adds : 'I am afraid most of interest is now gone.' In a southern window were to be seen S. Anthony of Padua preaching to the fishes, S. Etheldreda, S. Helen with a large cross upon her shoulder, S. Mary Magdalene robed in her rich and abundant tresses, and many bishops and other saints.

The fragment of inscription below the figure of S. Vedast reads, 'S. FOS . . .' the remainder is lost, though part of the letter T is still legible ; it is clear that the name should be read 'S. FOSTER,' the alternative name of S. Vedast. The London church under this dedication is still called S. VEDAST *alias* FOSTER. There is a popular tradition, says Mr. Baring-Gould, that the Saint 'saved a goose belonging to some poor people from a wolf that was running away with it,' and, accordingly, a wolf and goose (or, perhaps, a fox and goose) form part of the design.

His more usual symbol is a bear : the 'mortifer ursus' of the fourth hymn in *Carmina Vedastina* ; the 'rabidus ursus' of the *Tragico-Comœdia* (Act IV., Scene 3) :

> 'Deformem unguibus fert huc pedem
> Armatus ursus.'

The story of the bear will be told in detail in the *Life and Legend of S. Vedast.* Suffice it now to say that when the saint visited the ruins of the ancient cathedral at Arras, a savage bear, which had long been the terror of the neighbourhood, came forth from the dense thickets to assail him. Obedient to the voice of the holy Bishop, the ferocious creature fled from its gloomy haunts and did not again return: or, as a more poetic legend relates, attached itself to his person as a defence against all enemies.

The very dignified figure from Blythborough has supplied the design from which a clerestory window in the City church just named was erected in 1886. The wolf and goose were, however, omitted.

INTRODUCTION.

Of the religious drama in general it is not necessary to speak in this place. The subject is very large and very full of interest, and has already been dealt with by many able hands, experts in dramatic literature, on whose special domain the editor has no desire to intrude. Much has been done in the way of printing and editing early English Mysteries, and there are even now many curious religious plays still waiting for an editor. In due time, when the available material has become more accessible than it is at present, the historian will arise who will gather together and condense into convenient form the great mass of information now lying scattered in the transactions of learned societies, in county histories, and in local publications.

It is only necessary to refer to the Chester *Mysteries*, the Coventry *Mysteries*, the York *Mysteries*, the Towneley *Mysteries* (Surtees Society, 1836); the Digby *Mysteries* (Abbotsford Club, 1835); the *Christmas Mummer Plays at Lincoln*; Marriott's *Collection of English Miracle Plays and Mysteries* (8vo., Basel, 1838); Sharpe, *The Presentation in the Temple* (Abbotsford Club, 1836), to indicate the rich mine of material in England alone. Whilst for France, Coussemaker's *Drames Liturgiques*, 1860, the *Dictionnaire des Mystères* of M. le Comte de Douhet (in the Abbé Migne's series of Dictionaries, 1854), and the separate issues of the miracle-plays of Strasburg and of Beauvais, constitute a very important contribution to the history of religious dramatic literature.

The Vedastine drama, now printed, it is believed, for the first time, was written with a special view to its performance by the students of the great College of the Jesuits at Arras. As the dedication of the play states clearly, it was 'data a studiosa juventute Collegii Societatis Jesu Atrebati, 13° Septembris, 1611.' Is it possible to determine the name of

The Author of the Piece and its Date?

The two manuscripts from which the play is printed do not contain the author's name. MS. No. 936 contains, however, the author's dedication of the piece to Abbot Caverel[1] (printed at p. v *supra*), but it seems scarcely probable that D. C. Q. can be the initial letters of his name. It is more likely that D. may stand for *dedicat*, and C. Q. for *consecratque*, or for some other similar words. A list is given by Messieurs de Cardevacque and Terninck of the principal *religious* of the monastery of S. Vaast during the administration of Abbot Caverel, but it supplies no apparent clue to the name of the author of the drama.

The period at which the piece was written can be more easily determined, for in Act V., Scene 8, will be found a chronogram,

'eVeCta In aera CeLLa sVCCresCet Mage,'

which gives 1611, no doubt the exact year of the composition, corresponding precisely with the date given in the dedication.

Philip de Caverel, to whom this Tragico-Comoedia is dedicated, was seventy-seventh abbot of the monastery of S. Vaast, over which he presided with great dignity and acceptance from 1598 to 1636. Born at Maizières, near Saint-Pol, in 1555, he entered the monastery of S. Vaast when only thirteen and a half years old. He was ordained priest in 1579. He soon attracted the notice of the famous Abbot Sarrazin, to whom he

[1] The Abbot's arms are on the cover of the MS.

became chaplain and secretary, accompanying him on an important mission to Spain. In 1585 Sarrazin was raised to the dignity of Archbishop of Cambrai, an office which he held till his death in 1598, at the age of fifty-eight. A stately monument, surmounted by a dignified effigy of the prelate, marks his resting-place in the cathedral at Arras.[1]

The Archduke Albert and his wife Isabella appointed Philip de Caverel as Sarrazin's successor in 1598, though the Papal Bull confirming him in that dignity was not received till two years later. He filled many important offices with honour: enriched the monastic library with many precious gifts; decorated the apsidal chapels of the cathedral; caused the choir-stalls (unhappily destroyed in the days of the French Revolution) to be carved with subjects taken from the Old and New Testaments; and carried out important works in connection with the cloisters of the monastery. He wrote a Life of Abbot Sarrazin, a Treatise on the miracles of S. Vaast, a Commentary on the Rule of S. Benedict, and a History of the Monasteries of that Order in the Province of Flanders of which he was visitor. His life is said to have illustrated his motto:

'SOULAGER, ÉCLAIRER.'

He died December 1, 1636, in the eighty-second year of his age. His monument is to be seen, in close proximity to that of his eminent predecessor, in the Chapel of S. Vaast, on the north side of the choir of the cathedral. The effigy is figured by Monsieur Terninck on the same plate with that of Abbot Sarrazin.

An extract from his biography in *L'Abbaye de Saint-Vaast*[2] will complete all that need here be said of him:

'Philippe de Caverel fut sans contredit le plus grand Abbé de Saint Vaast. Il fut grand par ses vertus, grand par son

[1] It is figured in Mons. Terninck's *Arras: Histoire de l'Architecture et des Beaux-Arts dans cette Ville. Planche* 67.

[2] MM. Adolphe de Cardevacque et A. Terninck. II. 15.

intelligence, grand par ses œuvres et par son zèle à soulager les pauvres et à propager l'enseignement. Il brilla, comme le dit avec vérité son épitaphe, plus par ses exemples que par l'éclat et les perles de sa mitre, qu'il avait enrichie de beaucoup de pierres précieuses. Il était charitable envers les pauvres, sobre pour lui-même, doux envers ses frères, zélé pour faire étudier les pauvres écoliers. Au milieu de toutes ces œuvres accomplies avec une libéralité qui tient du prodige, Philippe de Caverel n'oubliait point son amour pour les sciences.'

The Dramatis Personae.

The Dramatis Personae are exceedingly numerous, and the author seems never tired of introducing fresh persons ; even in the last scene but one a new character appears. Probably he desired to give an opportunity to as many students of the college as could possibly be employed to play their little part upon the stage. As it is hoped that the present publication may be followed by a Life of S. Vedast, in which some account will be given of the really historical persons whose names occur in the piece, these, important as they are, will receive but the briefest notice now—just sufficient, it is hoped, to set the main lines of the story before the reader.

First are S. VEDAST, his father and mother, his paternal uncle, his brothers Anonimus and Imus (see page 15), and the Famuli.

Next in importance are CLOVIS and his family :

Clovis, or Chlodoveus, King of the Franks.

Clotilde, or Clotildis, his queen.

Lantieldis, or Landehildis, his sister.

Theodoricus, or Thierry, Clodamirus, Childebertus, Clotarius, his sons.

Orelianus, a noble Gallo-Roman, son of a senator, an officer of the army of Clovis.

Sigibertus, dux Sicambrorum, and his son, Filius Sigiberti.

Rex Alemannorum, slain at the battle of Tolbiac.

FAMOUS ECCLESIASTICS:

S. Remigius, Archbishop of Rheims.
S. Amandus, Bishop of Maestricht.
S. Audomarus, or S. Omer.

GLORIFIED SAINTS:

S. Diogenes, Bishop of Arras.
S. Eleutherius, Bishop of Tournai.
S. Piatus, Apostle of Tournai.
S. Medardus, Bishop of Noyon.

ARCHANGELS AND ANGELS:

Michael, Raphael, Gabriel, Uriel: and inferior members of the heavenly hierarchy.

VIRTUES AND GRACES:

Castitas, Paupertas, Humilitas, Latria, Fides; perhaps Misericors, Prudens, Clemens, Beatus, Integer and Pius may be added.

ALLEGORICAL PERSONS:

Caritius, Themius, Philedonus, Plutius, Megalegorus.

EVIL POWERS AND VICES:

Concupiscentia Carnis, Concupiscentia Oculorum, Superbia Vitae.
Idololatria, Haeresis, Invidia, Calumnia, Satyri, Varia Monstra.

OBJECTS OF SOME OF S. VEDAST'S MIRACLES:

Typhlus, or Cecus, Paraliticus, Demoniacus, Aphonus, Loquitus, Pauper, et cæteri.

MISCELLANEOUS PERSONS:

Armies of Clovis, and of the King of the Alemanni, Equites, Nobiles Tullenses, the CHORUS, and a crowd of people whom it seems scarcely worth while to enumerate.

Amongst the multitude, Mego, and perhaps Hortubal, or Hortulbal, may be singled out. Mego especially speaks an eccentric kind of language (see p. 24), pretends that he is able to cure a blind man (p. 34), and is, in some sort, the comic actor of the piece. Hortulbal, Raganarius, and Harpagarius are chiefly remarkable for their names.

It may perhaps be necessary to remind the general reader that 'the Franks and the Alemanni met in battle at Tolbiac, not far from Cologne. The Franks were worsted, when Clovis bethought him of Clotilda's God. He cast off his own inefficient divinities. He prayed to Christ, and made a solemn vow, that if he were succoured, he would be baptized as a Christian. The tide of battle turned; the King of the Alemanni was slain; and the Alemanni, in danger of total destruction, hailed Clovis as their sovereign.' So writes Milman, in his *History of Latin Christianity*.[1]

Four glorified saints receive the soul of S. Vedast: SS. Diogenes, Eleutherius, Piatus, Medardus.

S. DIOGENES, of Greek origin, was sent to the country of the Atrebates by Pope Siricius about the year 390 A.D. Consecrated Bishop of Arras by S. Nicaise of Rheims, he laboured with zeal and with success for the conversion of the people. It was he who built the first cathedral at Arras, in the ruins of which in later years S. Vedast found an altar. The Vandals strangled him in his church at Arras at the same time that S. Nicaise was murdered at Rheims. December 14 is observed at Arras as the day of his martyrdom. On the beautiful shrine which encloses relics of S. Vaast a figure of S. Diogenes appears, in the costume of a Greek bishop, in the attitude of benediction according to the Oriental rite; his name, written in Greek letters arranged vertically, serves to identify the saint.[2]

S. ELEUTHERIUS, born at Tournai in 456, was educated with S. Medard, who predicted, whilst he was still young, that

[1] Fourth edition, vol. i., p. 352. [2] *Les Petits Bollandistes*, March 22.

his pupil should be Bishop of Tournai. To this see he was consecrated in 486, when thirty years of age. He is said to have converted eleven thousand heathens; whom he baptized on December 26, 496. He died February 20, 531, of wounds which he received at the hands of heretics.[1]

S. PIATUS (Piato, Piatonus), the Apostle of Tournai, born at Beneventum, priest and martyr, came from Rome to Gaul with S. Quentin and his companions to preach the Gospel. He was martyred about the year 287 at Tournai, during the persecution of Maximianus, by the soldiers of Rictiovarus, President and Governor of Gaul.[2]

S. MÉDARD, Bishop of Noyon, was born in Picardy in the beginning of the reign of Childeric, the father of Clovis. He was associated with S. Vedast and S. Remi in the conversion of Clovis, and, when dying, Clotaire came to him to receive his benediction. The date of his death is given by some authors as June 8, *circa* 545 ; Père Giry says 560. In art he is usually represented with an eagle hovering above his head, its outspread wings protecting the saint from rain.[3]

In addition to these, brief mention must be made of:

S. AMANDUS, who was consecrated a missionary bishop, at the command of Clotaire, about the year 630. He laboured in the neighbourhood of Ghent and Antwerp, exhorting the Frisian tribes to forsake the worship of trees and groves, and to embrace the faith of Christ. After an unsuccessful attempt to establish a mission amongst the savage Sclaves of the Danube, he became Bishop of Maestricht about the year 646, and died about 679.[4]

S. REMIGIUS, Remedius, or Remi, needs no detailed notice here, as he plays an important part in the conversion of Clovis, and will appear again and again in the *Life of S. Vedast*.

It is hoped that the reader will not be too critical in the matter of chronology. If the dates given in that valuable book,

[1] *Les Petits Bollandistes*, Feb. 20. [2] *Ibid.*, Oct. 1. [3] *Ibid.*, June 8.

[4] *Dictionary of Ecclesiastical Biography*: on the authority of Mabillon, *Acta Benedictina*, II. 681.

the *Dictionary of Christian Biography*, be accepted, the following short notes will represent the generally received periods of the leading events in the play :

Clovis. Born, 466. Baptized, 496. Died, 511.

Clotilda. Married about 492 or 493.

S. Vedast. Bishop of Arras and Cambray, from about 500 to 540. Died, 540.

S. Remi, Archbishop of Rheims, *circa* 457-530.

The first Sigibert who occurs in the *Dictionary of Christian Biography* is Sigibert I., King of the Austrasian Franks, 561-575, son of Clotaire I. Amandus was not consecrated Bishop till 630, and died about 679. If the Sigibert and Amandus of the drama are intended for these two persons, it is to be feared that an anachronism will be discovered. Nor is it quite easy to understand how S. Médard, if he died in 545, could, as a glorified saint, receive the soul of S. Vedast, who died five years earlier. S. Omer, too, died about 667. But these are trifles with which the reader must not trouble himself. Minute historical accuracy does not always characterize a novel or a play.

The Action of the Play

is greatly complicated by the number of different persons introduced upon the stage, many of whom hinder rather than help the progress of the piece. Some of these are so little worthy of notice that they have not been included even in the list of names given in the previous section.

It has been thought well to supply a rapid analysis of each act and scene, in order that the reader may be able to select for himself those portions of the play which seem likely to be most interesting. Here follows what the writers of a past age would have called the

Argument of the Play:

Act I.

Scene 1. The father and mother of Vedast congratulate themselves on the admirable character of their son, but they deplore his unwillingness to marry. Vedast conjures his father to permit him to retire to the solitude of the woods, and to devote himself to the service of God. The father is greatly angered.

Scene 2. The King of the Alemanni and Maurus discuss the triumphs of Clovis, to whom Maurus and Prosper are sent on an ambassage.

Scene 3. Vedast, with Chastity and Humility on his side, has a controversy with the Lust of the Flesh, the Lust of the Eyes, and the Pride of Life. The latter intimate their intention of attacking Vedast again and again, and they predict his fall. The former give him sage counsel.

Scene 4. The father and mother of Vedast again endeavour to persuade him to renounce his intention of leading a celibate life, but without avail.

Scene 5. Sigibert, leader of the Sicambrians, threatens vengeance against the King of the Alemanni. His son endeavours to appease him.

Scene 6. The mother of Vedast, Philedonus (the Pleasure-lover), Plutius (the Man of Wealth), and Megalegorus (the Boaster) endeavour to dissuade him from his religious intention. Vedast yields in some degree to his mother's appeal not to forsake her now that she has become a widow.

Scene 7. King Clovis is enraged with the King of the Alemanni. His sons discuss with him the situation of affairs, and declare their intention of following him to the battle.

Scene 8. Vedast endeavours to mollify his mother; his uncle gives him encouragement. Vedast renounces his inheritance of his father's property. In a discussion with the

Lust of the Flesh, the Lust of the Eyes, and the Pride of Life, he shows the superiority of heavenly over earthly riches. He takes leave of his brother Anonimus. The uncle is converted to Vedast's opinion, and speeds him on his heaven-sent way.

Chorus 1. Poverty, Humility, and Chastity on the one side, and the Lust of the Flesh, the Lust of the Eyes, and the Pride of Life on the other, strive to show their power, and the advantages which they respectively offer to their votaries.

Chorus 2. A musical chorus celebrates the victory of Clovis over the Saxons.

Act II.

Scene 1. The King of the Alemanni proudly vaunts his power as likely to defeat Clovis.

Scene 2. Soliloquy of Vedast in the woods. He rejoices that he has attained his desire of a life of solitude and calm, and that he has rejected the riches of the world, which are but dross.

Scene 3. Idolatry, Satyrs, and divers Monsters assail Vedast, who vanquishes them with the sign of the Cross. Vedast apostrophizes the Supreme.

Scene 4. Clovis animates the Frankish soldiers. Sigibert appeals to the King for assistance.

Scene 5. Vedast persuades the men of Toul to destroy their idols.

Scene 6. Battle between Clovis and the King of the Alemanni.

Scene 7. Clovis bewails his discomfiture, and vows that he will become a Christian if he can gain the victory.

Chorus. Michael, Gabriel, and Raphael on the one side; Heresy, Envy, and Calumny on the other.

Act III.

Scene 1. Clotildis, with her sons Clodomirus and Theodoricus, inquire of Remigius, the Bishop of Rheims, as to the future successes of Clovis against the Alemanni. The sons exult over the recent victory.

Scene 2. Vedast instructs Clovis in the principles of the Christian faith, which Clovis willingly accepts.

Scene 3. Lantieldis, sister of Clovis, with the help of Idolatry and Heresy, Envy and Calumny, endeavours to disseminate the errors of Arianism.

Scene 4. Typhlus, the blind man, seeks restoration of his sight. He is mocked and deceived by Mego. He goes to the bridge over the Aisne to find Vedast.

Scene 5. Vedast gives sight to Typhlus in the presence of Clovis, who, witnessing the miracle, is converted.

Scene 6. Rejoicings at the safe return of Clovis. Remigius rebukes Lantieldis for her errors. Clovis desires baptism at the hands of Remigius.

Scene 7. Vedast converts Lantieldis, notwithstanding the efforts of Heresy, Envy, and Calumny to hinder her conversion.

Scene 8. Various opinions about the baptism of Clovis are expressed by Mego, Hortulbal, Tuccius, and a party of Knights.

Scene 9. Remigius encourages Vedast to continue in the good work of the conversion of the heathen, and Vedast signifies his willingness so to do.

Scene 10. Contention between Idolatry and Religion.

Scene 11. Vedast performs the miracle of causing wine to flow from empty vessels.

Scene 12. Remigius consecrates Vedast to be Bishop of the Atrebati.

Chorus. Religion rejoices at, Idolatry laments over, the efforts of Vedast against the powers of evil.

Act IV.

Scene 1. Vedast restores sight to Tilcanus, and bestows the power of walking upon Codrus. He is welcomed to the city of Arras by Victor.

Scene 2. Aurelian declares his fidelity to the new King, Clotaire. Clotaire rejoices at the coming of Vedast, which is announced by Ocinus.

Scene 3. Vedast arrives at Arras, and is shocked at the desolation of the city wrought by the Alemanni. Caligon warns Vedast against a wild bear haunting the ruins. The bear retires at the saint's command. Vedast comforts the timid Felix and Caligon, who receive his words with pleasure.

Scene 4. Contest between Idololatria and Latria, in which the former is worsted. Latria rejoices at the advance of the true faith.

Scene 5. Vedast is encouraged by various persons to persevere in his missionary labours.

Scene 6. Mego makes sport of Hortulbal. Magus, Envy, and Calumny prepare a cup of poison for Clotaire.

Scene 7. The poison is detected by Vedast, who makes the sign of the cross in the Name of the Holy Trinity. The King rejoices, and declares his intention of uniting himself with Vedast.

Scene 8. Conversion of Magus.

Scene 9. Vedast encourages and consoles Clotildis, who is now a widow. Clotildis, on her part, animates Vedast to persevere in his work of evangelizing her subjects, and declares her readiness to co-operate with him in their conversion.

Scene 10. Dietus, Bribax, Pericles, and Sepho, all suffering from prolonged hunger, determine to appeal for succour to Vedast, who is already regarded by the people as the father of the city.

Scene 11. The poor and hungry approach Vedast, who succours them. Gabriel and Raphael announce the heavenly reward reserved for Vedast. The beggars Dietus, Bribax, and others quarrel about a cloak given to Sepho by Antonius.

Scene 12. Castus and Felix, encouraged by Vedast, declare their submission to the faith.

Scene 13. Metanor and others converse about a fiery column which has appeared over the house in which Vedast dwells.

Scene 14. Vedast is aware that his end is approaching. He comforts his sorrowing friends, and dies, as he had lived, for Jesus. Latria announces his happy decease.

Chorus. Vedast sings of his blissful state. He is welcomed to the heavenly regions by S. Diogenes, S. Eleutherius, S. Piatus, and S. Medard. Angels sing the anthem 'Euge, serve, bone et fidelis'—'Well done, good and faithful servant.'

Act V.

Scene 1. Universal joy that S. Vedast has become the patron of Arras.

Scene 2. Attempt to destroy the city of Arras by fire. The archangels Gabriel, Raphael, Michael, and Uriel intervene. The city is preserved.

Scene 3. Autbertus, at the command of the archangel Michael, sets about the erection of a church. Its measurements are to be one hundred feet in height, two hundred feet in length.

Scene 4. Progress of the building.

Scene 5. Contest between the archangel Michael and Envy concerning the construction of the church.

Scene 6. A paralytic, a demoniac, and a dumb man bewail their sad condition. Latria assures them of relief upon their invocation of S. Vedast.

Scene 7. General delight at the beatification of S. Vedast, and at the discomfiture of Idolatry.

Scene 8. Glorification of S. Vedast by Fides, the paralytic, the demoniac, the dumb man, and others. An angel concludes by calling on the audience for applause.

TRAGICOMEDIA

DE

SANCTO VEDASTO.

PROLOGUS.

Audite procerum turma decora Atrebatium
Audite, seu queis infula accingit comas,
Astrea seu quos nobiles ditat toga.
Novi theatri syrmate haud plebes stupe.
Novos cothurno vincta tibi ludos redit
Positura pubes: dextera, age votis veni:
Ludos Vedastus revehet actutum pugil.
Clarus, parente Athleta nemoribus Dei
Tullum requirit: celica incensus face,
Merita coruscat infula, Atrebeum gregem
Miseratur, incestam stygis rabiem pugil
Valide retundit, mentibus densas tuis
Fugat tenebras, Celicum et pandit[1] jubar.
Sacrum Vedasti presule Autberto magis
Pignus nitescit, cui domum terra hac facie
Metatur alea, pugilis ut primum tua
Luctam juventus dederit, hec laurum dabit,
Adsit benignus scenice pubi favor.

---

[1] Monstrat.

ACTUS I[us].—SCENA I[a].

PATER VEDASTI, MATER, VEDASTUS.[1]

Pater Vedasti. Ter me beatum, cujus opulentat sinus
Agmen bonorum cujus in tecta impluit
Felicitatum glomera Leucorum solum.
Aureis ministrat quidquid excurrens aquis
Rutilans Hidaspes, quique gemmarum nitor
Coruscat auro, sufficit tectis humus
Natalis aure, plus satis ditat domos.
Mage ter beatum me facit senio gravem,
Quem prole tanta donat ethereus favor.
Fuso senilis non mihi febricitat color
Candore vultus, prole revirescit nove
Ætatis evum, prole numerosa seni
Animus resultat, corque compulsum salit.

Mater Vedasti. Unanime conjux gaudio nostrum pari
Pectus redundat generi ut expendo datos
Celo favores ; una me versat tamen
Angitque mentem cura solicitam diu,
Quonam subivit limina ex studiis redux,
Firmamen evi natus, etate, indole
Princeps Vedastus, varius ancipiti coquit
Consilia mente, refugit oblatas faces
Dubius maritas, coelibem vitam gemens
Molitur animis,[2] mente nec sana ferus
Monitis rebellat. Cernis ut vultus tegit,
Avertit ora, cocta consilia occulit !

Pater Vedasti. Quid spes parentis generis et robur domus,
Quid nate mentis nubila in vultus agunt ?

Vedastus. Pater !

---

[1] Interlocutores : Patruus, Anonymus, Imus. [2] Animus.

Pater Vedasti. Loquere, quid ora singultu sonant?
Quid advolutus genibus illacrymas patris.
Patruus. Assurge, letos junge complexus patri,
Letitia juvenem, moeror annosum decet.
Anonymus. Ainimos[1] serenet purpura vestis nitens.
Imus. Quanta parentem clade funestes vide.
Mater Vedasti. Effare aperte, pande quae mente occulis
Arcana tacitus, nec timor mentem gravet.
Vedastus. Venerande genitor, nemora si lubeat procul
Leucis cappessam, ubi animus exsultans polo
Spei, metusque liber eternet dies,
Tutè relictis moenibus sylvas colam.
Pater Vedasti. Longo excitatas consequi cursu feras
Mens estuat, ut opinor; id dabitur tuis
Vedaste flammis, mitte solicitos metus.
Vedastus. Non illa genitor flamma depascit diu
Noctuque fibras, sed Deus crede intime
Sorbet medullas, orbe nil toto meos
Sedabit estus, vestis auro non rigens,
Non quae tumultu[2] tecta famulari[3] strepunt
Qui cor perurit solus etherea face
Fovebit ignes solus: Arduenne precor,
Hunc ustulantem da sequar sylvis pater.
Oro per[4] Jesu latere profusum mare,
Cruenta per flumina, piis nati pater
Subscribe votis.
Pater Vedasti. Regere non posse impetum
Juvenilis animi: missa fac crepundia
Hec non adultum mage sed infantem decent.
Animos aviti generis excita inclytas
Laudes sequi, te facta genitoris decet.
Accingat ensis nobile hoc pignus patris
Tua latera, facessant tot infans nova
Concilia mentis.
Vedastus. Gladius accinget latus?
Egon' Olympo terga poscenti dabo?
Pater Vedasti. Facesse nostra imperia, sic mandat parens.
Vedastus. Facesso superum imperia, sic mandat Deus.

---

[1] Animos. [2] Beato. [3] Famulatu. [4] Per precor.

Pater Vedasti. Gerere parenti filium morem Deus
Imperat.
Vedastus. Et illi si imperat genitor prius
Obtemperandum est.
Pater Vedasti. Nectis imperiis patris
Remoras inanes: huc pedes mecum domum.
Nox atra lucem, sol prius tenebras feret,
Quam te per omne dedecus nostre sinam
Turpare gentis nomen, ac titulos domus.

SCENA SECUNDA.

REX ALEMANORUM, DUO LEGATI, QUATUOR NOBILES.[1]

Rex Alemanorum. Quid anime torpes? segnis irarum jubas
Tollit Sicamber, foedera Alemannis negat
Francum reposcit, sponte queis subdit manus;
Tua sceptra ridet tumidus et pace insolens.
Has lentus iras percipis? lentus vides?
Siccine secundis efferus de te canet
Turpem triumphum? sorbeam infamis sales?
Infame tantum dedecus? turpem notam?
Hec astra celi testor, eternum Jovem,
Non sic abibunt odia; vel ponet jocos,
Vel ille Francis, quam dedit, solvet fidem.
Maurus. Quid nisi feroci militis fidit manu
Imbellis hostis, deses, ignavus!
Prosper. Ferus
Ille est secundis, facilis invertat rotam
Fortuna, segnis languida torpet manu.
Dexter. Alta vagetur fronte Sigiberti impetus?
Gravesque patrie tumidus intentet minas?
Rex Alemanorum. Generose miles vester igniculat magis
Motos calores, ultro ne peccet tamen
Tepida quiescat mixtus et estus domet:
Regnare nescit, cui furor nimium imperat.
I Maure, Prosper, ad ducem celeri pede
Properate, mentis pandite arcana intime,
Bilisque rabiem: noster erasus furor

[1] Maurus, Serus, Amandus, Prosper, Dexter.

Animis in auras ibit ut pones suos
Animi tumores, ut datam paucis fidem
Foedusque solvet: pertinax si fors negat
Celeri referte ad regiam gressus pede.

Maurus. Rex magne solita, quod jubes, facimus fide.

Serus. Si renuat acuere miles auspiciis tuis
Martem reposcit.

Amandus. Quo rapit pectus ducis
Generosus ardor, sequimur unanimes citi.

Rex Alemanorum. Miles, laboris amplate merces manent,
Virtute macte: copie regno mihi
Toto legantur, pila queis hostem opprimam.

SCÆNA TERTIA.

VEDASTUS, CONCUPISCENTIA CARNIS, CONCUPISCENTIA OCULORUM, SUPERBIA VITE, CASTITAS, HUMILITAS.[1]

Vedastus. O dulce mentis delicium Jesu! undique
Insultet ut sanguis vide; undique impetat
Telis inermem; carnis ut fœde, aspice,
Inhamet illecebris! mihi suffice Deus robur.

Castitas. Vedaste lilium palmam feret
Hoc castitatis; nixus age vive etheri.

Concupiscentia carnis. Vedaste facili mentis utere indole,
Animos serena, conspice ut roseo nitet
Colore vultus, quanta consurgat toris.
Juvenilis etas mox virum spirantibus:
Aureo liquores vasculo roseos paro.

Vedastus. Mendax cicutam melle sub dulci tegis,
Philtris furores jungis, infestum malum!

Castitas. Sapis, Vedaste, mitte pestiferam luem.

Humilitas. Ecce alia pestis graditur, hec paribus tibi
Superanda miles artibus: cernis manu
Quas tracto frondes; queis Olympi viribus
Niteare pandent: hedera stat firmis virens
Stabilita muris stet magis celsis[2] polis

---

[1] Paupertas. [2] Celsus.

Suffultus animus; viribus nimium suis
Qui tribuit audax, decidit facili impete.

Superbia. Siccine Vedaste glorie falsem iniicis
Ætatis evo? que (malum!) cecam rapit
Nox atra mentem? honoribus mox ut sinum
Subripere libeat?[1] quid fugis titulos patrum?
Tibi vela jam pregnantur et celeri ad decus
Fereris quadriga: sequere quo nactus ducem,
Ducam per altum nomen et clarum genus.

Humilitas. Cave, cave miles, mentis obtura forem,
Ne te superba sceptra que dextra tenet
Technis, doloris artibus captum clepat.

Vedastus. Nihil hic timendum splendidos umbras scio
Titulos honorum. Excede pestis, hinc pedes.
Minitare tandem cassibus cogam meis
Premaris ultro.

Paupertas. Perge nunc lauro immines
Animose miles: tertius restat tibi
Calcandus hostis, tumida marsupia exspue,
Inane pondus.

Concupiscentia oculorum. Nunquid argenti decus
Titillat oculos? nunquid hic auri nitor
Jubar coruscans pellicit rutilo novam
Fulgore mentem? pondus hoc ditet dies,
Beetque primam quam legis vite rosam.
Quid ora moestus evehas, rectam indolens?
His fruere letus; perdere est dignus bona
Qui nescit uti.

Paupertas. Spondet eternas tibi
Sublimis astris clara pauperies opes.
Ad hec protervos insolens ludos ciat
Fortuna, nihil est stabile quod non impetat,
Quod non furenti turbine excutiat gradu.
Dum mane nitida Cynthius rutilat die
Christas superbus opibus attollit, sue
Et sortis immemor et mali instantis sibi.
Sed fessus ubi dum Lucifer feras videt

---

[1] Lubeat.

Occiduus undas rebus ejectus suis,
Cogere perenni cogitur stipem stugo.[1]
I fide sorti, quamlibet blando tibi
Vultu renidens cuncta pro voto ingerat.

Vedastus. Abite pestes, procul abite, jam meum
Æther vibrata pectus obsedit face.
Tolerare stabili mente pauperiem placet,
Legere virentis lilii florem, casa;
Vili morari corpus et lacerum rudi
Velare sacco.

Castitas. Fugite mendaces opes.
Bulle voluptatum fugite, et elatus tumor.
Nostrum suave noster amplexus jugum.
Bulle voluptatum fugite et hinc altus tumor.

Superbia. Nova bella coquimus requerimus et fraudes novas.

Concupiscentia carnis. Quocumque gressus tuleris amentes cite
Properamus ultro.

Concupiscentia oculorum. Veniet in nostras manus
Et sero quamvis veniet. Hac mecum pedes.

SCÆNA QUARTA.

PATER VEDASTI CUM FAMULIS, PATRUUS, VEDASTUS.

Pater Vedasti. Vedaste, patris gaudium et telum simul!
Diu efferatus lege concessas fugis.
Tœdas jugales? sicne legitimis thoris
Asper? rebellis? nate, quo patrem rapis?
Nominis inustum dedecus tantum meis
Annis relinquam? Vilis abjectis plagis
Vitam remote toleret ignavam procul?
Haud patiar. Huc accerse quo latitat loco
Famule rebellem resciat certe probe
Que censa mentis ultimam et mentem hauriat.

Faustus. Ni pervicaci pectore exuto tuos
Monitus facesset territa verbis, minis,

---

[1] Jugo.

Verberibus acquiescet e domibus malo
Sic facile monitis.

Pater Vedasti. Hec coquit mens estuans
Intus furore.

Margus. Rogatus affatus patris
Supplex reposcit.

Pater Vedasti. Cingat hic solus latus
Proprius parentis, mentis occulte abdita
Scrutabor, et animi eruam latebram intimam.

Vedastus. O Christe mentis robur impactum adiice.

Pater Vedasti. Age nunc rebellis patris imperiis, mei
Oblitus sui, patrie, juris Dei:
Que sic furorem diuomit serpens fera.
Compressa pedibus bellua hircana opprimit
Partus ferocem, nacta raptorem unguibus,
Ut tu parentem impete insano furens
Ætate fessum rabidus addictas neci!

Vedastus. Fulmen coruscum potius immittat manu
Mox fulminanti numen ex alto ethere,
Cyclops cruentus Lestrigon, trux et Charibs
Lacerata rumpant membra, quam in patrem mali
Ingratus aliquid machiner, avorum genus
Foedare tentem, labe conspergam domum?
Haurire jussa patris est semper ratum
Animoque fixum penitus, hoc dignum puto
Munus benigni jussa genitoris sequi
Parere didici, debeo, exopto, scio,
Et liceat oro genitor.

Pater Vedasti. Hanc nosco indolem
Sic equa juris ratio, sic pietas jubet.
Minaris ergo quid fugam toties lare!
Toties quid anxia suggerit de te parens
Te velle sylvis agere religatum Deo
Vitam perennem.

Vedastus. Candidam mentem accipe;
Me velle fateor, si meus volet pater,
Sed velle patrem spero, si velit Deus.

Pater Vedasti. Deus parentem temnere imperet, o scelus!

Vedastus. Compesce fluctus turbide mentis, precor.

Pater Vedasti. Ab ire gestis perfide ignava fuga.
Vedastus. Ab ire genitor gestio insonti fuga.
Pater Vedasti. Insons rebellis patriæ, matri, patri?
Sic casta conubia eiicis?
Vedastus. Genitor mihi
Connubia credo casta?
Pater Vedasti. Que?
Vedastus. Christi.
Pater Vedasti. Putas
Connubia Christo dissona?
Vedastus. Admittunt viros
Nunquam duos connubia sacrata etheris
Consortem in unam nec sibi anima fert Deus.
Pater Vedasti. Damnabis ergo tot virum thalamos? cave!
Vedastus. Damnabo nunquam; virginum thalamos tamen
Prestare quid infiteor?
Pater Vedasti. Has remoras trahis
Perfide parentis contumax jussa aburis?
Arcete famuli perfidum,[1] morte effera
Ictus furore concidat ne mox fero.
Patruus. Compesce fluctus anime, quid odia excoquis?
Est natus.
Pater Vedasti. Est rebellis.
Patruus. Hunc calor rapit
Juvenilis animi.
Pater Vedasti. Stygius hunc rapit furor
Nocentis animi.
Patruus. Cui levis flamme vapor
Fugit per Eurum, mentis accense impetus
Sic fugiet ultro. Mox patri dabit manus.
Pater Vedasti. Serum est dabit, dedisse debuit, nimis,
Scelestus ille frontis effrontis caput.
Fabula nepotum dicar ob turpem hanc fugam?
Nunquam ira perge, comprime juvenis impetus.

---

[1] Hunc procul.

SCÆNA QUINTA.

SIGIBERTUS DUX SICAMBRORUM CUM FILIO, NOBILIBUS, LEGATIS, MAURO ET PROSPERO.

Sigibertus. Francus Sicambrum pace tutatus ducem
Tranquilla reddit sceptra, nunc tantum efferus
Alemannus audet foedus inversum dare.
Stat ire contra, stat feros ausus fero
Domare Marte, viribus fero datam
Pacem tueri; symbola hec regi mei
Deferte nutus.

Maurus. Dabimus has regi notas
Indicia mentis certa, sed grate parum.

Prosper. Mox contumaces fortis Alemannus suis
Retundet armis spiritus.

Sigibertus. Quid, improbe?
Ducem lacessis? Saxones pernix pete
Vel te!

Filius Sigiberti. Recessit hostis accensus truci,
Rabie furoris. Tu parens cohibe impetus
Nimium cruentos.

Diranus. Deleat turpem notam
Patrie coruscans mucro.

Mitius. Bellona intonet
Passim per agros, lithuus et multus strepat,
Clangor tubarum personet.

Sigibertus. Vili jugo
Premetur hostis mox dabit victas manus.

SCÆNA SEXTA.

PHILEDONUS, MEGALEGORUS, PLUTIUS, VEDASTUS, MATER VEDASTI.

Philedonus. Huc cara socii gaudia effundat modos
Dulces canora tibia.

Megalegorus. Hanc primam decet
Rosam juvente, florida roseos via
Vernare odores.

Plutius. Pascere aspectum juvat
Vario colore, degere etatem in bonis.

Philedonus. Ferire Megalegore, placet rursum mihi
Plectro suaves tumulo cordas.

Megalegorus. Decent
Hec nostra jubila tempora, etatem decent.

Plutius. O leta mentis gaudia! o festos[1] dies!

Vedastus. O quantus animos abripit cecos furor,
En victa luxu marcet, atque animum jugo
Premit cupido turpis, et rectam indolem
Animumque summi compotem coeli necat.
Nec que sequantur claustra letalis lacus
Æterna tendit![2] fata ventura exspuit!
Da rector orbis fortis infringo[3] pugil,
Laqueos dolosus queis suos mundus premit
Orbus parente libera terris cano
Te voce patrem, Christe nunc vivo etheri!

Mater Vedasti. Miserere nate matris et vidue precor,
Exstingue quondam cordis accensi faces
Novosque mores indue orbatus patre.

Vedastus. Absit vocanti mater obvertam moras.

Mater Vedasti. Viduam relinques?

Vedastus. Aderit e coelo Deus.

Mater Vedasti. Per has parentis squalidas supplex comas
Fessumque senio pectus et cara ubera
Miserere matris, unicum fessis meis
Solamen annis.

Vedastus. Misereor et annum parens,
Sed ustulantes pectus internis faces
Calcata matris per ubera sequi me addecet.

Mater Vedasti. Crudelis in me nate, sic rupem induis?

Vedastus. Ubi numen animo meditor in chalybem omnibus
Abeo medullis, et fibra rupem induo.

Mater Vedasti. Largire vidue temporis saltem moram
Aliquam parentis donec afflicte dolor
Mitescat animis.

Vedastus. Quod petis dabimus parens
Tempus moramque, sed brevem votis moram.

---

[1] Lætos. [2] Pendit. [3] Infringam.

SCÆNA SEPTIMA.

Rex Clodoueus, Childebertus, Clodouillus, Clodamirus, Theodoricus, pueri cum insignibus.

Clodoueus. Quisquis Sabeus dives eois plagis
Iberus armis, quisquis occasu potens,
Terore sceptri, regia quatitur manu
Placata tellus undique exsultat bonis
Et pace plaudit ; unus adversos mihi
Attollit animos, audet atque unus, truces
Lacessere iras rabidus Alemanni furor.
O sanguis audax et meo invisum genus,
Alemanne generi ; tu trucem nostrum in caput
Armare rabiem ; foedus et regis datum
Frangere Sicambris ? testor ethereum Jovem ?
Per regna juro, juro penetrales Deos
Non sic inultus odia defugies mea :
Quid concitatus valeat hic mentis calor
Cogam fateri, vel reluctantem malo.

Clodamirus. Passim per agros fervet incensus ducis
Calor Sicambri, jungere armatus manus
Ferro tueri foedere adjunctos avet
Animus.

Theodoricus. Rebelles Marte Sigibertus potens
Ut frenet ausus flagitat regis manum.

Clodareus. Premunt superbos principes, humiles tegunt,
Sigiberto adero, mox Francicas jungam duci
Armatus acies, queis jugo infami premam
Hostis superbos impetus domem probe.

Childebertus. Rex magne quo te manibus expansis vocat
Fortuna, euntem passibus sequimur citis.

Clodouillus. Certum est sequi quocumque tua signa inferes,
Seu sub maligno sidere informes gelu,
Seu vasta Lybie nemora que calidi vapor
Solis perurit, fidus accedam comes.

Clodoueus. Age miles animos redde quos tantos facis
Congredere, mecum classicum primus cane.
Regis furores discat imbellis pati.

SCÆNA OCTAVA.

VEDASTUS, MATER VEDASTI, PATRUUS, ANONIMUS, IMUS.[1]

Vedastus. O quam potenti pectus incensum ustulat
Superis amoris ignibus, numen polis :
Non tantus acri rupis Ethnee jugo
Exundat ignis, cum vapor patulo furit
Missus camino quantus in fibris calor
Imis resultat: estuat venis jecur
Tenerque totus animus in flammas abit.
Satis est Olympe, quo rapis velox sequor.
Comitata mater patruo prodit gemens :
Adibo, fortis nuncium pugil bonis,
Matrique mittam Christe postremum. Parens
Quid ora toties fletus ubertim rigat?

Mater Vedasti. Vedaste tantis lacrymis matrem opprimis,
Patruum, tuosque, quod gemo cuncti gemunt?

Vedastus. Sepone lacrymas, sepius superos parens
Sequor vocantes.

Patruus. Qui nepos tantos feres
Nemorum labores, qui sitim, famem, notos
Agris minantes, frigus et brume impetus,
Leonis estus, belluas sylvis truces :
Inverte mentem haud sana consilia eiice.

Vedastus. Mihi robur addet, qui dedit animos Deus :
Est, fateor, aliquis qui manet sylvis labor,
Sed iste non exterret, igniculat magis
Sublime pectus et animum innixum polo.

Patruus. Divine vicisti nepos, callem inchoa :
O pessulatam trade lamentis tue
Aurem parenti, lacrymis ponet modum.

Imus. Heres paternis opibus et dives solo
Quo fugiet exsul?

Vedastus. Nuncium cunctis lubens
Bonis remitto, me abdico, ut Christum sequar!

Concupiscentia oculorum. Egenus?

---

[1] Concupiscentia carnis, Concupiscentia oculorum, Superbia vitæ.

Vedastus. Astris dives.
Superbia. Ignobilis?
Vedastus. Et hic
Celoque nobilis.
Concupiscentia carnis. Lacer?
Vedastus. Nunquam lacer
Est castus animus.
Concupiscentia oculorum. Aderit at mors mox atrox
Vedastus. Metus malorum.
Superbia. Te impetet.
Vedastus. Celum ut petam.
Induta cautem mens; fugite pestes procul.
Radice egenus arborum pascam famem,
Solabor estus frigida sylvis aqua.
Non gladius ultra vesciat nostrum latus
Non pectore ultra pendeat torques meo.
Tu matris unum pignus afflicte vale.
Anonimus. Frater per omnes sanguinis nexus precor
Per defluentes lacrymas matris sinu
Fratrumque gemitus, da breves annis moras
Adulta donec creverit nobis mage
Juvenilis etas.
Vedastus. Verbera ne cassa insere.
Satis est morarum, jam etherem sequi addecet
Toties vocantem.
Patruus. Junge complexus breves
Nepos parenti, patribus, mihi, omnibus.
Vedastus. Jungam ultimos, mi patrue!
Imus. Mi frater vale.
Anonimus. Mi frater! animi magna pars, frater! vale.
Vedastus. Tandem recedo.
Imus. Rursus amplexus meos,
Iterumque frater repete!
Patruus. Quo celum vocat
Citato gressus.
Mater Vedasti. Ergo prosequere impetum
Flamme vocantis.
Vedastus. Ibo cum liceat pie

Venia parentis, sed prius natum parens
Asperge dextra rore celesti et vale.

Mater Vedasti. Te fili Olympus augeat charitum imbribus,
Moestam fluentes lacryme vocem obstruunt.

Imus. Procul recessit columen afflicti laris.
Discessus (heu me!) lancinat morsu jecur.

Anonimus. Abiit parentis gaudium, fratrum decus,
Spes una annorum generis et lampas domus!
Splendor recedat purpure, luctus placet.

Mater Vedasti. Lamenta, gemitus, tristis accedat dolor.

Patruus. Subite tecta, nullus est lacrymis modus.

CHORUS.

Castitas, Paupertas, Humilitas, Concupiscentia carnis, Concupiscentia oculorum, Superbia vitæ.

Humilitas.

Celi tramite nobili
Victor progreditur pugil.
Altos mittite spiritus
Vultus mittite turgidos.
Celi tramite nobili
Victor progreditur pugil.

Superbia.

Erro siccine me ferox
Tullanus rabie domet.
Meos scelestus ausus
Premat? ferus triumphet?
Ter vilior fimoque,
Ter vilior lutoque?
Victus cadet rebelli
Nostro ferus furore.

Castitas.

Frustra vomis furores,
Fallace virus ore.
Frustra tuum sagittas
Vedastus impotenti

Quidquid paras furore
Fortis pugil retundet.
Procul venena mitte.
Quotquot latent pharetra
Vedastus hic supremo
Nixus pugil Tonanti
Franget tuas sagittas.
Frustra vomis furores,
Fallace virus ore
Frustra tuum sagittas.

Concupiscentia carnis.

Dire manent inermi
Hosti fere timores.
Manent cruenta monstra
Quotquot latent cavernis
Satyri manent bicornes.
Redux timore tutam
Crassus petet coronam.
Dire manent inermi
Hosti fere timores.

Paupertas.

Nihil feras cruentas
Satyros nihil pavescit.
Nil possidet nec optat
Nil auream favillam
Nil aureasque bullas
Solutus expavescit.

Concupiscentia oculorum.

Pavescat haud pavescat
Siti, fame, peribit ;
Peribo cum cadente
Si sic potes perire.
Meo meo cruore
Hostilem emo cruorem.
Pavescat haud pavescat
Siti, fame, peribit.
Egenus ero sylvis.

Concupiscentia carnis.

Infamis erro.

Superbia.

Vilis.

Paupertas.

Vives[1] Deo.

Castitas.

Serenis

Astris.

Humilitas.

Nitens beatus.

Superbia.

Nil jacta terrent verba mox facta exsequor.

Humilitas.

Nil dira rabies terret ut coelum favet.

CHORUS MUSICUS.

Jam tubae passim sonitus resultet.
Jam sonet[2] clangor litui sonorus,
Et phalanx toto fremat arma campo,
Saxones armis superet Sicamber,
Tympanum don don resonet don don don,
concidat hostis.

ACTUS SECUNDUS.—SCENA I^a^.

REX ALEMANORUM, MAURUS, PROSPER, DEXTER, SERUS, AMANDUS, ETC.

Rex Alemanorum. Tantas Gradivus intus incendit faces
Nesciat ut iras coquere flammatus calor.
Alto Sicamber tumidus imperio meos
Rejectat animos, renuet et Francis datum
Pacis perennis foedus exstinctum dare.
Nostro superbos[3] Marte feriendus cadet.[4]

---

[1] Dives. [2] Tonet. [3] Superbes. [4] Cades.

Maurus. Invicte Cesar foedere adjunctus duci
Clodoveus aderit milite instructo efferus.
Rex Alemanorum. Gestare pila ignarus et pugne inscius!
Rex languida cui torpet ad bellum manus.
Prosper. Fretus Sicamber rege Sigibertus[1] furit,
Aderit coactis copiis, jugo ut premat
Nos insolenti.
Rex Alemanorum. Turgidum prius opprimam,
Animis timorem ejice, ignavos metus
Generosus ardor nescit hostem sed premit.
Quid miles ante terreat lituum pavor?
Dexter. Ferum reposcit Martie mentis calor
Magnanime princeps, nec timor mentem opprimit.
Serus. Nobis cicatrix sanguis et mors adlubet
Modo inter arma.
Amandus. Lambit hanc dextram calor
Lambetque donec sanguinem inimicum hauriat.
Serus. Hostile ferrum nescit ulterius moras.
Amandus. Armis triumphet, regnet Alemannus potens.
Omnes simul. Armis triumphet, regnet Alemannus potens.
Rex Alemanorum. Quam grata mentis jubila auribus intonas,
Generose miles: macte patria, insolens
Jugandus hostis milite est tanto tibi.
Jamjam era crepitent, obvias hosti placet
Acuere dextras: crastinus sol ut feret
Radiata terris lumina, addensis frequens
Acies maniplis urbe properato irruat.

SCENA SECUNDA.

Vedastus solus.

Tandem quietus animus emensi maris
Fugit Charybdas salvas[2] et tutum tenet
Portum salutis, ancoram fondat nemus
Toties rogatum (ast heu!) quot in scopulos ruit
Qui transfretare pelagus immensum hoc parat:
Perfert labores non tot Alcides mare

[1] Sigiberto. [2] Salvus.

Vastum pererrans, quot subit fortis pugil
Vitare syrtes avidus ancipitis maris :
Vicisse tantos turbines juvat tamen
Fluente ubi Deus dextra[1] celi imbribus
Animos serenat, candido et recreat die.
Ignis perennis pectus allambit meum
Ingensque flamme vis meam mentem obruit.
O quod mihi sagum Christe quod lacerum, rude
Favos rependit, quam juvat opes sordibus
Mutasse dum sic mutor : assolitas tibi
Nemore recumbens, Christe, persolvo preces,
Dein fortis ethere tecta contendo pede
Tullana celeri, diriges gressum Deus.

SCENA TERTIA.

IDOLOLATRIA, SATYRI, VARIA MONSTRA, VEDASTUS.

Idololatria. Pro summe divum Lucifer Tullum meus
Invadet hostis? quod mei juris fuit
Virtute domitum sub suas leges trahet?
Canetur orbe Christus ejecto Jove
Simulacra Divum funditus quassa occident?
Ego Dearum maxima et cujus jugo
Strate tot urbes unius subdar jugo
Vedasti inermis? dedecus tantum hauriam?
Terram ante, celum, Tartarum invertam truces
Limphata in iras volvar et vertam omnia.
Furibunda perge, suscita rabiem tuis
Dignam triumphis, pergito, aude, nunc age
Quidquid potes truculenta, quidquid et haud potes.
Huc huc cruenta monstra, satyri quot feris
Nemorum cavernis, preda vos ingens manet.
Terrete, tundite, faucibus premite efferis
Telis inermem, nemora qui vestra incolit,
Nullum palato pinguius risit pecus
Cibusque terris gratior nullus datus.

Satyrus 1us. Ab antri nos sonu devocavit quispiam?

---

[1] Dextera.

Idololatria. Agedum inventus prona satyrorum[1] dolos
Nemorumque numen, ducite alterno pede
Late choreas, nemore terrete medio
Vestri Vedastum et orbis instantem luem.

Satyrus 1us. Horribilitudine terrificulemur pessumum
Pessumi homini caput querquera ut febri tremat.

Satyrus 2us. Saltemus. Grata gratiam nobis ampliter
Redamtruabis.

Satyrus 3us. Pyrricham primus[2] amptrus.

Satyrus 4us. En sonitu extemplo aurium tangit foris.

Satyrus 5us. Amphracta quam belle ebriulat aurium lyra.

Satyrus 6us. Meum et per aures pectus irrigarier
Dulcitudine[3] sentisco: Pyrricham[4] letus amptrua

Idololatria. Saltatum abunde ne moribus abactus cadat.
O Machinator criminum quo te via?

Vedastus. O summe celi, summe dominator poli,
Adsit secundus numinis vestri favor.
Suprema celi sydera in sylvis peto.

Idololatria. Nil tela metius?

Vedastus. Sint vel inferni feris
Decocta flammis.

Idololatria. Nil vagi sylvis movent
Satyri biformes?

Vedastus. Monstra puerorum metus
Satyri biformes, non visum. Credite loco
Lasciva monstra, credite hec Jesus jubet.

Idololatria. Quis iste furor est?

Vedastus. Quem suos Christus docet.

Idololatria. Animosne fixus stipiti Christus facit?

Vedastus. Animos Averni domitor invictus facit.

Idololatria. Hec tenta deses patiar, o nostri leves
Furoris ire! nemore portenta ruite.
Impetite inermem funditus preceps cadat.
In te cruenti (ne qua pars sceleris vacet)
Surgent tyranni.

Vedastus. Surgat Hesperiis metus

---

[1] Ad. [2] Pyrrucham primus. [3] Dulcetudine. [4] Pyrrucham.

Terris Geryon, surgat Ismiaca scinis
Pinu verendus, aut sub eterna nive
Inhospitalem Caucasi rupis domum.
Heniochus habitans, nulla me rabies fere
Virumque teret. O trifauci Cerberi
Ignava soboles, mene percelli tuo
Speras furore? Antra agite sylvarum cite
Repetite larve, mandat id signum crucis.

Idololatria. Tutabor alta regna, tua vertam impie.

Vedastus. Quocumque gressus tuleris, hac fortis sequor
Tullana celeri tecta contendo pede.
Dirige favente tramitem dextra Deus.

SCENA QUARTA.

REX CLODOVEUS,[1] SIGIBERTUS CUM SUIS.

Clodoveus. Alto superbas vertice elatis domos
Amplas columnis Regis infidi intuor.
Macti este Franci milites, socios ducis
Vobis Sicambri viribus tutamini.
Quecumque tellus dives, inimica afferet
Vicina spoliis referet hoc vester labor.

Omnes simul. Arma arma lentas animus haud patitur moras.

Clodovillus. Dum pendet alea ancipite victoria
Athram aspice memor conjugis monitum tue.
Solicita princeps, sepius tibi fidem
Nesciri Olympi numen ethereum gemit.

Clodoveus. Hec alia poscunt tempora meis Juppiter
Votis, Gradivus aderit et Deum favor.
Quis buccinator intonat repens meas
Et clangor aures perculit.

Clodamirus. Prodit citus
Comitatus acie foedere adjunctus tuis
Signis Sicamber.

Sigibertus. Magne Francorum parens
Nostris petitus sepius votis ades.

Clodoveus. Quo fare paucis ferveat bellum loco.

Sigibertus. Vallatus[2] hostis militum ingenti manu

[1] Cum suis. [2] Bellatus.

Alemannus instat, tota quem raptis cohors
Agglomerat armis, finibus pedes agit,
Sicambriam alto spiritu totam impetit,
Populatur agros, diruit diro impete
Sternitque passim, quidquid adversum obviat
Ira moratur regis adventum ferus
Nimiumque tumidus viribus tribuit suis.

Clodoveus. Qui sepe nimium viribus tribuit, cadit,
Cadet et rebellis perpeti indocilis jugum,
Mox stratus armis discet imperia pati.
Animose miles, quidquid est animi ocyus
Expande. Per fas et nefas legum inscius
Raptare predas, et lacessere audeat
Socios duello? Nec sui poenas luat
Ausus rebellis? Æra jam litui strepant,
Et tympanorum mugiat toto ethere
Raucus resultans sonitus excitum sono
Ni prodit agmen, regiam invado domum.

SCENA QUINTA.

VEDASTUS, NOBILIS[1] TULLENSES, TILMANUS, MEGARUS, HENRICUS, FAMULI MEGO, HORTULBAL, EUXIUS.

Vedastus. Quid turba segnes queris imperiis moras
Facesse jussa, idola, decuit te diu
Prophana pedibus terere, inanes ignibus
Cremare truncos.

Megarus. Agedum Mego truncos feri
Demonas et ense turgidos macta ocyus.

Henricus. Huc huc penates quot tegunt famuli Deum
Simulacra ferte.

Tilmanus. Frangite.

Mego. In rogum date,
Comminuo membrum.

Euxius. Turgidas aures seco.

Hortulbal. Heus Mego nasum disseca.

Mego. Naso caret.
Inane trunci pondus.

[1] Nobiles.

Hortulbal. O lepidum caput.
Euxius. Hec tundo pugnis monstra ferio, hay, hay, hay.
Mego. An mordet? Age cedo, ervam dentes probe
Cervice ab ima. Dentibus monstrum caret,
Quid ergo quereris?
Euxius. Non queror mastigia,
Tua quero latera tundere baculo probe
Mego. Hay, hay, hay, hay, hay, hay.
Euxius. An mordet? hec joca tibi refero verbero.
Henricus. Mittite sales citique Vulcano date.
Manu politos Dedala artificum Deos.
Hortulbal. Haurimus (heu mihi!) quam jussa o here,
Euxius. Huc ferte[1] stramen salice discutiam rogum.
Parata belle cuncta Vulcanum myxe.
Mego. Vulcanum? at ille finibus dudum procul
Exsul pererrat claudicans alios lares.
Euxius. Iterum jocari furcifer tibi mens avet
Ut video, ferto ignem jocos alias feres.
Megarus. Properate totus fumet ether ignibus.
Hortulbal. Quis credat incenso rogo exuri Deos?
Euxius. Mutire nesciunt inania pondera.
Mego. Quam flamma belle frigus egelidum fugat!
Tilmanus. Assata trunci membra deferte alite
Gressu penatibus procul, rogum procul.
Mego. Prunæ remordent dexteram Tucci manum?
Euxius. Honiche[2] gratiose crede jam[3] prunæ afforent.
Tilmanus. Queis me tenebris nuper errorum chaos
Quam viperina compede impietas meum
Implicuit animum!
Megarus. Quantus ha! furor sequi!
Calcanda trunci pondera aut e marmore,
Aut e metalli numina eliquabili
Compacta massa, quantus ah! furor sequi.
Vedastus. Bene est, cremata numina in Tullo jacent,
Ve quos nefanda cecitas ultra obsidet
Quosque furor arcta compede insanus ligat,
Tu vero generis prima Tulliaci phalanx

---

[1] Ferto. [2] Honiche, *sic* in MSS. [3] Mihi.

Letare rutilum permeans sinus jubar,
Affulget animis lumen etherie facis.

Henricus. Vedaste fervens animus ad Christum evolat.

Megarus. Christus perurit, solus est fibras rapit
Vedaste solus: imus in jussus tuos.

Vedastus. Delecta coelo turba, qui molem Deus
Totius orbis librat immensam manu,
Tantos benigna porrigit dextra sui
Favos amoris, arce coelesti dapes
Ævo perenni preparat lautas magis,
Pauca hec docebo, flecte quo gradior pedem.

SCENA SEXTA.

CLODOVEUS CUM EXERCITU, REX ALEMANORUM CUM EXERCITU, SIGIBERTUS CUM EXERCITU.

Clodoveus. Bene habet nefandus frendet et pugnum vocat.
Hic viribus opus miles, hic quisquis cadit
Cadat ore in hostem. Constet hoc acies loco
Peditumque oberrans agmen equitatus tegat.
Ego te sceleste.

Rex Alemanorum. Miles hic animos cie
Regnis nefandus inhiat et Martem ciet
Francus feroci premere nos jugo parans.
Nunc vile pondus serviti, et jugum excute
Eia agite, dextra tela nunc fortes manu
Arripite, primos dirigite in hostem impetus.

Clodoveus. Armate dextras equitis et primum manus
Vibret sagittas.

Eques 1us. Saucius telo occides.

Eques 2us. Vix frena mandit audit ut litui sonos
Equus rebellis.

Eques 3us. Quere properato fugam.

Eques 4us Cave tela.

Eques 5us Fugito, fugito.

Eques 6us. Te jaculo impeto.

Omnes simul. Telo hoc peremptus sanguinem inimicum dabis.

Rex Alemanorum. Eques remotum tutus obvallet latus.

Clodoveus. Secedat equitum turma. Vos premite ensibus
Superate primum hoc agmen.
Rex Alemanorum. Arcedo[1] impetus
Primi caloris.
Maurus. Fervet ad primum impetum
Francus furore percitus, victas manus
Nobis rebellis mox dabit.
Milites Clodovei. Ad arma, occidant.
Clodoveus. Nunc premite, scutis scuta conjungite, pedem
Pede. Exeat in hostes secunda ala. Premite.
Rex Alemanorum. Subdite fessis protinus.
Sigibertus. Facto agmine
Hostem petamus. Primus hanc paro viam.
Rex Alemanorum. Instate. Sequere. Premite fugientes procul.
Prosper. Huc huc superbe tende veloci gradu.
Filius Sigiberti. Raperet parentem manibus avulsum meis
Elatus hostis, torpor ignavus fedet
Quis miles animis? Euge nunc mecum advola
Huc siste gressum perfide, aut sica cades
Quem sauciatum credito, captum tenes.
Prosper. Insequere, predam miles e manibus tulit.
Rex Alemanorum. Premite fugaces.
Dexter. Morere.
Miles. Da veniam obsecro.
Alius Miles. Vitam salutem posco.
Rex Alemanorum. Abunde est. Milites
Peracta strages cessit aversus fugam
Petiit Sicamber. Tuba receptui canat,
Artusque sapidum massicum fessos levet.

SCENA SEPTIMA.

FIDEM CUM ANGELO.

Clodoveus. Pro sortem acerbam! pro diem, infandum diem!
Quo sociatum Martiâ plagâ ducem
Infesta raptas? fata quo fallax trahis?

[1] Arcete.

Clodovillus. Magnanime princeps conjugis numen memor
Agnosce Christum, Victor et palmam feres.
Clodoveus. Mihi reddis animos, robur et vitam facies.
O Christe, numen Christe Clotildis, tuas
Leges facessam, victor ut palmam fero
Tibi sceptra voveo: conjugis jussa exsequor,
Si palma maneat militem Francum ethere.
Angelus. Clodovei mentis turbidos estus preme
Palmam suprema arce ales ethereus tibi
Summi supremam numinis jussu paro
Ingredere callem conjugis, palmam feres.
Clodoveus. Agnosco divinum ethera, agnosco fidem.
Equestris acies, quodque robur est super,
Reliquum furore Martio fractum mihi
Revocate mentem, dedecus partum ocyus.
Diluere ferro nominis labem adjuvat.
Childebertus. Lubet inter arma cadere.
Omnes milites.[1] Arma, arma.
Filius Sigiberti. Turgidi
Hostis cruorem mucro sitibundus petit.
Mactabit ille purpura medius rubena.[2]
Clodoveus. Generose juvenis, patris acceptum tuos
Oberret animos, vultus et patrie decus
Tutare fortis.
Filius Sigiberti. Patris ulcisci data
Vita inter arma animo ratum est, cedam aut cadam.
Rex Alemanorum. Rursus rebellat hostis in fugam datus?
Generose miles, quidquid est animi ocyus
Exsere, tumore turgidum Francum doma.
Clodoveus. Equites paventes premite, clypeis jungite
Clypeos.
Primus eques. Reposcis arma, cave. 2us. Cave.
3us. Cave.
Eques 4us. Rursum rape fugam vel cades telo obrutus.
Eques 5us. Fuge, fuge. 6us. ferro hoc furcifer cades, fuge.
Clodoveus. Eques remotas agminis partes tegat.
Juvenis in astantem irrue miles pedes.

---

[1] Simul. [2] Rubena, *sic* in MSS.

Filius Sigibertus. Virum vir urgeat, instet, et cunctos brevi
Premat fugaces.

Rex Alemanorum. Quid rapis segnis fugam?
Petiste, morior, occidi. Pacem obsecro.[1]

Filius Sigibertus. Instate, fugientem premite. Telo occidat.

Clodoveus. Peracta cuncta victus aversus fugam
Petiit superbus strage miseranda obrutus.
Fossus per agros saxo devictus jacet.

Theodoricus. Io triumphe miles Alemannus jacet.

Omnes simul. Io triumphe miles Alemannus jacet.

Clodoveus. Miles triumphum nobilem Christo refer
Ille insolentem pressit Alemanni impetum
Fortique palmam dextera victis dedit.
Clotildis illud numen est toto Deus
Canendus orbe. Miles huic palmam refer.

Childebertus. Comitatus euge milite ad Tullum cito
Properato gressu dabitur et votis frui.

Clodoveus. Quis monstret ignotum mihi callem vie,
Numcumque pandet?

Clodovillus. Mista Leucorum sacer
Tulli moratur, pandet ignotum tibi
Numen Tonantis.

Childebertus. Fortis in Tullo pugil
Vedastus ille est, inclytus fama undique
Virtute rutilus, clarus et patrio lare.

Clodoveus. Ibo rudimenta hauriam avidis auribus
Miste Vedasti vota persolvam etheri.
Comitare miles ubi jubar croceo nitens
Subibit ortu premia viritim dabo.

CHORUS SECUNDUS.

MICHAEL, GABRIEL, RAPHAEL, INVIDIA, HERESIS, CALUMNIA.

Michael.

Seni rabies ferri cecidit,
Rapidum Martis sileat murmur
Sat lucit fortuna per orbem

---

[1] Miles: alius miles: alius miles.

Dubio incedens temulenta pede,
Sat lucit : pax clara per astra
Meliore nitens sidere redeat.

Invidia.

Colubro quidquid terra inficiam.
Redeat ? subvertet[1] prius astra
Terram, Oceanus sidera, quatiet,
Umbre facient[2] cum luce fidem
Cum fluctu flamma, nece vita.

Gabriel.

Unica celi tenuisque manus
Pugilis validi, ducente Deo
Stygiam rabiem franget et umbram.

Heresis.

Adversum ibit rutilans ferrum
Nil valida licet dextra nocebit
Erebi germen regisque soror
Mox data terris foedera solvet.

Raphael.

Foedera melior sancita polis
Meliora colet, patris sacram
Meliore fidem mente sequetur.

Calumnia.

Furor obstabit rabiesque Stygis
Hanc manibus nec predam rapiet
Nostris dudum nostram, predo
Quicumque, cadet vel mox ira.

Invidia.

Nostra serpente cadet.

Heresis.

Ferro.

Michael.

Bene tutantur pugilem celi

---

[1] Subvertent. [2] Faciem.

Gabriel.

Constans animus, cruciatur amor.

Heresis.

Nil tela contra scuta celituum nocent.

Michael.

Nil scuta contra tela et inferum nocent.

ACTUS TERTIUS.—SCÆNA PRIMA.

REMIGIUS, CLOTILDIS CUM SUIS.

Remigius. Rotator orbis summe qui nutu regis
Cohibesque fluctus dextera dubios maris,
Quanti procella ferveat luctus vide,
Nec ullus estus gaudii portum paret,
Hinc sevit alto turbine impietas suum
Lambens cruorem, scelera sceleribus diu
Cumulata nexans. Inde tenebrose Stygis
Cecus prophanum ritus idolum quatit,
Sorbetque Christi naufragum[1] sponse ratum.[2]
Periculoso fluctuantibus salo.
Da Christe dextram, da dies rutilo mage
Coelo serenos, arce stridentes notos,
Et sevientes turbidi nimium impetus
Maris retunde.

Clotildis. Mysta venerande etheris
Agitat procella major et mentem ferit,
Noctu diuque me simul variam rapit
Vario dolorum turbine et pene obruit.

Remigius. Regina tantus fare quis turbo impetat?

Clotildis. Clodoveus atra nocte per tenebras ruit
Sine lumine errorum, aleam dubiam subit
Martis cruenti. consilia nostra aburit
Christique legis inscius truncos manu
Fabricata monstra ritibus fictis colit.

Remigius. Dilecta coelo precibus et votis Deus
Excitus aderit, statuet et lacrymis favens

---

[1] Naufragam. [2] Ratem.

Toties obortis exitum, fide optimum.
Nec enim perire lacrymis quisquam potest.
Toties ademptus fletibus statue modum.

Clodamirus. Io triumphe Francicum exulta solum.

Theodoricus. Io triumphe domitus Alemannus jacet.

Remigius. Quid hi quadrigis jubilo letis ferunt?

Clodamirus. Venerande Presul, tuque Clodovei potens
Regina conjux tolle victrices manus,
Clodoveus aderit Victor, incolumis sua
Et gloria et fama inclytus diros jugo
Compressit hostes, has breves leti lege
Reditus tabellas.

Theodoricus. Volve quam dubio stetit
Bello tropheum nactus ut vires polis.

Clotildis. O magne coeli rector et mundi arbiter,
Quanto immerentem celitus foves bono?
Aderit subactis victor[1] Alemannis mihi
Redux maritus? aderit? et Christum fibris
Avidus vocantem consequi? o letos dies!

Remigius. Regina plausus obvios regi addecet
Conferre reduci, tota glomeretur phalanx
Collecta, Remis tota turmatim ruat,
Obvia juventus principi applaudat suo,
Cui plaudit ether rutilus aspectu favens.

SCÆNA SECUNDA.

VEDASTUS, CLODOVEUS.

Vedastus. Passim triumphis nobilem plebes refert
Regem subire tecta et affatus meos
Avidum morari: non dabit rumor jocos.
Ecce ille parva militis cinctus manu
Sollicitus heret, moestus huc confer gradum.

Clodoveus. Vir magne[2] regis gratus aspectu venis
Longo petitus tramite, et longo datus.

Vedastus. Quis summe Regum territat mentem pavor,
Dubiumque versat, fervidis supplex tuis
Alemanus hostis viribus pressus jacet.

---

[1] Victis. [2] Regis.

Clodoveus. Jacet subactus viribus credo etheris
Non regis hanc palmam Deus quisquis timet
Merito reposcit quem sequi fixum omnibus
Voto medullis, pelle tu densas prius
Animis tenebras, numen et sanctum doce.

Vedastus. Sermone quidquid poscis expediam brevi,
Deus potenti cuncta fabricatus manu
Qui torquet astra, sceptra qui Regum quatit
Orbemque totum solus imperio premit
Condiderat hominem principem terre, maris
Orbisque dominum, sedibus superis simul
Bearat, at mox celica patria excidit
Errore ductus. Nobili aula corruit.
Fatale ducens funus humanum genus!
Misertum ab alto numen illapsi ethere
Pietate Christus decoris oblitus tui
Mortale corpus induit, miseros Deus
Circumdat artus, dira supplicia subit,
Mortemque dira pendulus perfert trabe.

Clodoveus. Infame lignum dedecus tantum probrum
Tolerare potuit astra qui nutu quatit?

Vedastus. Tolerare potuit, turpe superavit probrum
Invictus ardor, funera horride necis
Tulit homo Christus, non tulit lethum Deus.

Clodoveus. Oculis nigrantes sentio obtendi meis
Nubes et angorem a quibus cecus Deum
Cernere retardor. Usque mihi mens nubila
Errore coecos ducta per gyros ruet
In damna preceps! Usque curarem diu
Ruptura pacem placidam, in adversum mihi
Spineta surgent! Variis implicitor miser
Pedicis voluptatum, tenebris opprimor,
Nec usque cecis numinis sacrum jubar
Illuxit animis, junge te facilem vie
Vedaste comitem, pelle condensum chaos,
Lucemque pande.

Vedastus. Magne Francorum parens
Quocumque gressus tuleris, hac letus sequar.
Pandam supreme lucis auroram tibi
Verumque numen etheris votis Deum.

SCÆNA TERTIA.

Idololatria, Heresis, Lantieldis, Invidia, Calumnia.

Idololatria. Va misera, vecors, pectore incenso, novis
Lymphata furiis laceror, invertet ferox
Vedastus hostis regna, Regem mox suis
Parere coget legibus? date fulmina,
Tela date, telis occidant hostes meis.
Nil monstra terrent? terreant pestes lacu
Excite ab imo Tartari. Huc pestes gradus
Adeste adeste facinorum artifices Dee
Huc se novo furore precipitem ferat.
Ad asma, ad artus, heresis cito advolet,
Invidia et oris putidi mendax sonus
Adeste vestras hic dies poscit manus.

Heresis. Quid hec furoris signa lymphati ferunt?

Invidia. Quid est quod imo Tartaro invidiam cias?

Calumnia. Quem fare lingue spiculo et fraude impetam?

Idololatria. Vedastus Erebi vulnus et mundi lues
Inimicus hostis generis et nostris scelus
Petendus ultro fraudibus, facibus, dolis.

Invidia. Vivit superstes.

Idololatria. Vivit ut plagis hydra
Damnis superstes major evadit malis
Regem dolosis retibus laqueat suis,
Rapitque predam manibus evulsam meis.

Heresis. Scrutabor ense viscera, et victrix fero
Ludam cruore, Vacchicam rabiem tene,
Hic Lantieldis aderit infesto Stygis
Ferale germen, obvios fratri dabit
Scelerata gressus, exsequar munus probe.
En tumida graditur, frendet et spirat scelus,
Adeste furie ferte sociatas manus.

Lantieldis. Quid anime langues obvios dudum pedes
Fratri tulisse decuit, et Christi novo[1]
Votis clienti[2] dogma Arianum dare.

Heresis. Nondum dedisti languida? Actum est, dabis
Nunquam hostis obstat regio lateri assidens.

[1] Novam. [2] Imbuere legem.

Lantieldis. Quis Lantieldis tardet inimicus feros
Ausus rebellis?

Invidia. Turma numerosa ausibus
Adversa Tullo properat, et regem suis
Escare tecnis querit. Invisum genus!

Calumnia. Arcete pestes, occupa properans latus
Reducis ad urbem, pande Arianam luem.

Heresis. Accerbo[1] regis latere pestiferum mei
Generis Vedastum virus. I propera gradum.

Lantieldis. Nihil morarum curro properanti obvia
Semine que Arii reducis aspergo domos.

Heresis. Bene est, abivit Bacchico mulier furens
Philtro, tenebit retibus captum meis.

SCÆNA QUARTA.

TYPHLUS, MEGO, TUCCIUS, HORTULBAL.

Typhlus. Miserrimo misereor orbatus die
Stipem plateis cogere et maciem pati
Sufferre plebis sepius cogor jocus[2]
Cecutienti quis feret solatium?
Nullusne? nullus. Nullus? o luctus graves!

Mego. Tibi adero Typhle, ne metue, solatium
Tibi adero, pharmacum optimo melius mihi est.
Huc ergo celeres huc cita gressus.

Typhlus. Mego
O Mego celeris sis vie fidus comes,
Lucisque clarum redde luminibus jubar.

Mego. Ne metue, faciem huc admove, unguentariam
Nigrantis olei capsulam mecum tuli.
Restituet oculos, admove.

Typhlus. Quid furcifer
Sordibus inungis palpebras, apage procul,

Mego. Hinc abeo, baculo latera mox edentulus
Ne nostra tundat.

Typhlus. In malam propera crucem.
Sic risus omnibus, sic jocus (malum!) ferar!

[1] Arceto. [2] Jocos.

Claram tueri lampada astrorum mihi
Heu! quando dabitur?
Tuccius. Dabitur, animi tot procul
Lamenta mitte, dabitur, accelera pedes.
Hortulbal. Summi Tonantis mista Clodovei latus
Cingit Vedastus, reddet hic oculos tibi.
Typhlus. Ubi ille terror demonum et Tulli salus?
Tuccius. Ad Axonam congredere nunc pontem petat.
Typhlus. Congredior, at vos pandite ignotam viam.

SCÆNA QUINTA.

VEDASTUS, REX CUM SUIS, CECUS.

Clodoveus. Caligo sensim mentis in nihilum cadit,
Rutilumque lumen vibrat ethereum jubar,
Simulacra coluisse pudet artificum manu
Excisa saxa demonas, Martem Jovem.
Vedastus. Quo magius[1] animis lumen irradiat polis,
Portenta memori citius e mente excident.
Typhlus. Vedaste mista numinis magni, etheris
Sacrate mista da salutarem manum,
Convexa celi cernere et rutilum diem.
Vedastus. O Christe egeno redde subreptum jubar,
Miserere Christe, sic tuas laudet[2] canet
Ignara veri numinis[3] plebes rudis
Teneraque regis major accrescet fides.
Rutilum age cerne lucidi solis jubar.
Typhlus. Quid istud? oculis quantus irrepit nitor
O quantus auri splendor et celi decus.
Meritis rependo magne vir grates lubens.
Vedastus. Fletus[4] ethere, quas mihi grates refer
Date salutis numen agnosce unicum.
Clodoveus. Que signa cernis anime? que rerum nova
Prodigia.
Childebertus. Ad hec stupet animus.
Clodovillus. Martis dedit
Aut quis sacerdos simile prodigium Jovis?
Clodoveus. Abjuro honores impiis larvis dare.

---

[1] Majus. [2] Laudes. [3] Luminis. [4] l fletus.

Vedastus. Hoc calle perge turma supremi etheris.
Childebertus. Agnosco numen, celicam agnosco manum.
Vedastus. Majora potis est, qui potest omnia Deus
Invicto princeps: luce defunctis dedit
Rursum potiri strumaque sanie fluit
Arctaque fauces, corpus et leto opprimit
Medela nulla cui male peste[1] datur.
Dabis medelam fonte dum lotus sacro
Signo hoc beabit regis et prolem Deus
Propriumque fuerit regium hoc solum decus
Gloriaque Francis.
Clodoveus. Mista quid vates refers
Ventura Francis signa dum sacris ovans
Lymphis piabor. Ergo complector sacre
Decreta legis, numen et Christum sequor.
Filius Sigibertus. Rex magne tota ex urbe letitia strepens
Agmen resultat.
Clodoveus. Obvios gressus damus.

SCÆNA SEXTA.

IIDEM, REMIGIUS, CLOTILDIS, LANTIELDIS, HERESIS.

Remigius. Huc huc adeste turma conferto agmine
Effusa portis: tota letitiam intonet
Novata facies urbis, et regem novo
Plausu receptet, flore purpureo via
Barbarica tota niteat, et totis tube
Remis resultent.
Puer Honorarius. Victor incolumis redit,
Remis festa dies eat,
Lucent sidera purius.
Puer 2us. Plausus ingeminent tube
Lucet sidereus favor.
Puer 3us. Princeps incolumis redit,
Remis festa dies eat.
Clotildis. Adesne tandem, adesne post tantos mihi
Remisne luctus, rursus, ut multis tuo
Votis poposci, dabitur aspectu[2] frui?

---

[1] Pesti. [2] Amplexu.

Clodoveus. Dilecta conjux incolumis adsum tibi
Periculis labore defunctus gravi.
Remigius. Rex magne salvum grator et reditum novo
Celum favore cumulet incolumen precor.
Heresis. Progredere pestis tardas quid remoras trahis?
Lantieldis. Germane totum vulgus applaudit, tube
Sonantis alta signa letitie strepunt.
Cives Remenses. Rex vive, regna victor incolumis diu.
Alii cives. Regnet, triumphet Francie gentis decus.
Clodoveus. Christus triumphet victore coelo Deus
Tulit ille palmam, referat et laudem addecet.
Lantieldis. Frater cave, cave dogma Christiadum nova
Strictet catena, laqueet et mentem novo
Errore falsam, ne utiquam Christum parem
Fateare patri dogma quod gentis docet.
Vedastus. Equalis ille est dogma quod sanctum docet.
Clodoveus. Dilectis stirpis regie sanguis soror.
Quam pandit arce numen etherea fidem
Clotildis aveo, pandit hanc regis latus.
Pressans Vedastus.
Lantieldis. Ille quis lurco comes?
Invisus error.
Clodoveus. Mista sacratus Dei est
Qui me catechistam fide ignarum imbuit
Moderare mentem, huic celice acceptum fero
Spiramen aure, sociat hic reducis latus.
Clotildis. Sacrate presul unda baptismi eluat
Animum salubris.
Clodoveus. Unicum id votis peto:
Jam vincla cui erroris excutio volens
Partesque melior transfuga accedo etheris.
Remigius. Vix animus intus gaudia augustus capit.
Tenebris fugatis corde sic Christum induis?
Sacramque legem doctus ad coelum advolas?
Age ergo lymphis tingier propera sacris.
Tota aulicorum turma conglomeret latus,
Societque reducem, tota baptismo novos
Indutet animos, jubilo plaudat novo.
Filius Sigibertus. Sequimur ovantes presulis gressus citi.

---

[1] Baptismi.

SCÆNA SEPTIMA.

LANTIELDIS, VEDASTUS, HERESIS, INVIDIA, CALUMNIA.

Lantieldis. Quo ceca preceps turma properato ruis?
Quo mentis amentis pellicit cecum chaos?
Infestat adeo virus effusum malo
Phyltro furorem, cecus ut sane aburas
Concilia mentis? cecus o regis furor?
Levis ille nimium corde qui credit cito.

Clodovillus. Ratione princeps pulsus et signo ethere
Edoctus alto, legibus summi dedit
Manus Tonantis.

Lantieldis. Fraudibus falsus dedit.

Vedastus. Queis queso regem fraudibus falsum tenet?

Lantieldis. Quicumque terris fraudibus captus manet.

Vedastus. Virilis animus Regis est constans bene.

Lantieldis. Ignavus animus Regis inconstans male.

Vedastus. Ignavus hostis terror et palme decus.

Lantieldis. Ignavus ille terga qui vertit Deo.

Vedastus. Generosus ille qui polo doctus sapit.

Lantieldis. Sapit ille solus?

Vedastus. Sapere se vellet simul.

Lantieldis. Non sensa alia requiro, sat sola sapio.
Bene sapit ille qui Deo primum sapit.

Vedastus. Me mente cecam reris?

Lantieldis. Et cecam gemo

Vedastus. Orbamque vera luce.

Lantieldis. Tum solus vides?

Vedastus. Mecum orbis unus.

Lantieldis. Lucis est mihi plus satis.

Vedastus. Si mente tenebras pellis est lucis satis,
Fove polorum lampada, ubi lampas micat,
Micat corusca mente, quam exstinctat jecur
Nimio furore fervidum, totam voca
Mentem in senatum, mente pensicula Dei
Strictam[1] tonantis; trutinam,[2] queis mox dabis
Æterna penas preda tenaris cani

[1] Trutinam. [2] Pertinax.

Edocta ni mox lucis auroram tenes,
Fatearis ultro quod ratio, quod jus volunt
Sacrum, catena codicum firmat probe,
Quam doctus alto ethere sacram lubens fidem
Germanus ultro amplectitur, fovet, colit
Novisque tota Francia exsultat bonis.

Heresis. Cave Lantieldis, cave, cavat saxum diu
Cadendo gutta, creber et durum domat
Ictus metallum.

Lantieldis. Dubia quo preceps agor?
Quid fluctuaris anime, quod credit tibi
Age frenum Olympus mande, non redit male.
Elusus ether menti age exortum nove
Jubar fove, ne lumen alio tibi polus
Vibret paratum. Pristinam mentem exuam?
Heu dubia titubo rursus et rursus cado!

Heresis. Revertere, quid ancipitibus credis ratum
Vagam notis? Revertere.

Vedastus. O cave, cave
Oppessulatas ingeni prebe fores.
Larvata monstra sternito et callem pede[1]
Sancto[2] inchoatum sequere.

Lantieldis. Satis est, jam sequor.
Abite pestes artibus dudum malis
Elusa, vobis nuncio repudium omnibus.
Vedaste toties lumen ostensum sequor.
Sequor vocantem ethera, tue incudi lubens
Me trado, forma, finge, ne parce ictibus.

Vedastus. Docebo sacram sequere mox paucis fidem.

Heresis. Siccine repudium mulier inconstans paras?
Fugitiva? nimium o mentis ancipitis malum
Muliebre Stygio Tartaro invisum genus.

Invidia. Tua castra repetet leta mox constans magis.

Heresis. Repetet?

Invidia. Vel angue presso succumbet meo.

Calumnia. Instabilem animum penitet facilis fuge
Redibit amens transfuga in laqueos brevi.

Heresis. Redibit? arctat funibus predam nimis
Infestus hostis, preda sit nostra hic prior.

[1] Fide. [2] Sancta.

SCÆNA OCTAVA.

MEGO, HORTULBAL, TUCCIUS, EQUITES 10.

Mego. Ay, hay, hay, hay, hay, hay.
Irata totam lacerat hanc dextram.
Hortulbal. Trabi
Figenda nobis ilico jam aderit, ovans
Juvenum caterva que jocos novos dabit,
Lepidosque multum.
Mego. Tu pedem Tucci rape.
Tuccius. Pendere nolo.
Mego. Credo, tu vis pendere.
Tuccius. Tectivaga aduncis unguibus dextram tenet.
Hay, hay, hay, hay, hay, hay.
Hortulbal. Thecam indue, pavor si malus mentem tenet.
Mego. Refige ligno fune densato.
Hortulbal. Cito
En turba juvenum properat, equitatus ruit
Tota urbe lusus hoc loco spiciam probe.
Tuccius. Ut mox suaves voce condita sonos
Eliciet.
Mego. Ore virus irarum vomet.
Phy lectulorum turpis imbricitor.
Tuccius. Bene est.
Jam pulchre adheret fixus elate trabi.
Clodamiris. Audite juvenum turma, letitie seges
Tota recrescit urbe, Clodoveus sacris
Piatus undis tradidit supplex manus
Æthre vocanti, signa letitie strepant ;
Geminate plausus, leti et in lusum novas
Afflate dextras.
A. Eques 1us. Sequere, [1]properato sequor
Quicumque princeps dextera excutet manu
Predam rebellem victor hic palmam feret.
Sortita quisque teneat, ordiri placet.
B. Eques 2us. [2]Sequor, secundas fors favens tribuit mihi.
D. Eques 3us. Mea est futura palma.
E. Eques 4us. Aberratum fuit.

[1] 2us Eques. [2] 3us Eques.

F. Eques 5us.	Mox dente felis stridulo vocem dabit.
G. Eques 6us.	Armata membrum forte comminuet manus.
Mego.	Moras trahite, jam funis e ligno excidit.
	Nunc pergite, heret firmus ut clavus trabi.
Eques 1us. Ale.	Tentanda fors est, septimus palmam feram.
Eques 2us.	Mihi mox sequendum, paululum mane, meum est.
	Ita namque sors addixit.
Eques 3us.	Ipse mox sequor.
Eques 4us.	Clangore litui excitus in palmam involo.
Eques 5us.	Faleratus animos vix tenet fortes equus.
Sextus.	Pars aliqua palme me manet.
Primus A.	Recte ruit
	Prout ergo, meritus jure tu palmam cape.
Tertius C.	Repetenda lusus alea ut victis cadat
	Favens tropeum.
Quartus D.	Perplacet. Primas feram.
Eques 1us.	Quisque inchoatos ordinis ductet bene,
	Excurso primus, sequere.
Eques 2us.	Te, Victor, sequor,
Clodamirus.	Adeptus ultro quisquis est palmam ferat.

SCÆNA NONA.

VEDASTUS, CLODOVEUS, CLOTILDIS CUM[1] SUIS.

Clotildis.	Miranda quae Rex magne prodigia refers.
Clodoveus.	Ita gesta, liliata, nunc Francus feret
	Bufone presso signa donata ethere,
	Tu mysta pandito ita quid portent polis.
Vedastus.	Hec aurea notant signa, candorem nove
	Rex summe mentis. Turpis ablatus color
	Bufonis atri putidam mentem notat,
	Animumque turpi labe conspersum diu :
	Missos favores celico agnosce ethere.
Clodoveus.	Nosco favoris indices Christi notas
	Qui supero ab orbe perditum miserans facem
	Mihi coruscam prebuit, mentem novam
	Aureis beavit liliis, et hec ubi

[1] Omnibus.

Jam prona fidei colla subjeci jugo,
Animumque labe lympha baptismi clui.

Theodoricus. Nos ter beatos dia quorum fax polo
Alluxit oculis, pepulit errorum chaos.

Clotildis. Quater o beatos, jussa queis Christi sequi
Concorde voto placuit, altitonam quibus
Post fata sedes reserat ethereas Deus.

Vedastus. Nunc perge princeps regna quo lentum vocant.
Favore perge dives ethereo, manus
Feret faventes, ante qui tulit Deus.

Clodoveus. Pergo, supremum antistiti sacro decet
Vale precari : At ecce nobis obvio
Gressu propinquat : Ultimum affatum peto.
Sacrate presul me procul regnum vocat,
Milesque victor remeat, ad proprios lares.

Remigius. Si regna poscunt, ire si menti sedet
Nihil hinc retracto: tutus accelera viam,
Memorque nostri vive sed Christi magis.

Clodoveus. Vivam per evum muneris tanti memor,
Christusque solus vivet eternum fibris,
Quod restat unum, societ ut comitem sibi
Rogo Vedastum, vinculum nectat duos
Amoris unum, quidquid huic presul favens
Regi dedisti, mentis hoc votum cape.

Remigius. Rex magne gratum munus acceptum fero
Dium morari sedibus mystam meis :
Mecum unus erit, incumbet et mecum arduis
Generosus ausis, aureis binos habet
Amor catenis, gradere quo regnum trahit.

Clodoveus. Nos nulla tanti presul immemores dies
Videbit unquam muneris, grates feret
Pares Olympiis solus, extremum vale.

Remigius. Vedaste tandem fortis ad pugnam pugil
Armato dextras, ardue est terris tibi,
Subeunda messis alea, at Christo duce.

Vedastus. Nil me labores terreant Christo duce
Divine presul impera jussa exequor.
Jubente ego te summa non timeo aggredi.
Non ima tanti presulis jussa aburo.

Remigius. Certas tuere mentis etheree notas :

Opulenta meritis[1] premia, et virtus feret,
Superis et astris ipse virtutum parens
Beabit ultro luce decoratum nova.

Vedastus. Hanc nulla nobis auferet mentem dies.

Remigius. Sic perge : celum donec ad messem vocet
Alio colendam vive Remensi lare.

SCÆNA DECIMA.

IDOLOLATRIA, RAGANARIUS, LITANAS,[2] BARBARUS, DOCILIS,[3] CALIGONUS.

Raganarius. Aurora roseis vecta lucescit rotis
Clarumque Phoebi devehit terris jubar
Solita sacratas hostias Divis prece
Litemus aris.

Litanas. Vestiant diuum prius
Capita corolle flore vernantes novo.

Agaud. Sacris parata contuli serta usibus.

Raganarius. Ergo citati numinum altaria, licet
Onerate sertis splendor hic divis placet

Idololatria. O quanta cultrix celitum tellus meis
Votis serena surgis : orbis tu plagis
Refers tropheum, solatu laudem refers.
Per te potentis sceptra tutor imperi
Celebro triumphos, vulgus in totum mee
Dominantur artes. Agite sacrati diis
Myste litate munus assueta prece
Divis ad aras. Agite mactate hostias.

Raganarius. Fundamus una poplite inflexo preces
A, ba, ca, da, fa, ga, la, ma, na, pa,
Ra, sa, ta, va, xa.[4]

Ragan. Placata thure numina effuso deum
Preces secundent.

Litan. Vota sint divis rata.

Agaud. Hanc dies volucrem consecro Titaniam.

Latria. Risiaca tellus, quot mihi luctus facis.
O quot querellis cogor infelix tuam

---

[1] Mentis. [2] Agaud. [3] Victor.

[4] Omnes : A, ba, ca, da, fa, ga, la, ma, na, pa, ra, sa, ta, va, xa.

Deflere sortem, cogor et cecum queri
Chaos malorum: Quot mihi luctus facis!

Idololatria. Tellure nobili exsulet Christi fides:
Neglecta virtus exsulet, nihil impium,
Nihil scelestum, non agit noster furor:
Erasa prisca mente Diogenis fides
Qui pervicacem pabulum mentem induens
Fero peremptus prebuit dudum feris.

Latria. Novus resurget qui dolum invertet pugil.

Idololatria. Telo premendus pariter hostili meo.

Latria. Umbone Christi tectus insurget meus.

Idololatria. Feriendus astu, fraudibus, diris[1] dolis.

Latria. Innixus ethre franget astutos dolos.

Idololatria. Armare contra mente stat totum ethera.

Latria. Meliore contra mente stat totum ethera.

Idololatria. Novas profundo Tartaro pestes ciam.

Latria. Novos supremis arcibus[2] pugiles ciam.
Larvata pestis.

Idololatria. Semina amandas mari
I curre superos supplici voto invoca,
Stygias cohortes inferum adversas cio.
Vos petite leti sacra dum divum favent
Una penates, dapibus et lautis pari
Litate genio.

Raganarius. Collatrans intus mihi
Dudum reposcit venter exactor dapes.
Properemus avide gratus[3] orexi cibus.

SCÆNA 11ª.

VEDASTUS, INTEGER, PIUS,[4] MARIUS.

Vedastus. Jam fessus undis Phoebus Hesperiis cadens
Lassas in alto mersat Oceano rotas.
I prome velox famule, quo fessas levent
Vires Lyeum.

Marius. Que decet jussa exsequor.

Pius. Istis Vedaste nil opus, letam tua
Virtus serenat plus bonis mentem satis.

---

[1] Nostris. [2] Sedibus. [3] Ut. [4] Castus.

Vedastus. Una serenet tenuis et Bacchi liquor.
Hoc equa amoris ratio quod justum est, petit.
Levate vires sedibus fessas meis.
Marius. Nil vase reliquum massici exhausto super.
Vedastus. Ergone multis estibus fessos domum
Multaque pressos hospites mittam fame?
O Christe coelo depluat rorem novum,
Que larga egenos pascit et potat manus,
Audis precantem. Vota sunt superis rata,
Properato rursum vasculum largos dabit
Foetum liquores.
Marius. Curro.
Vedastus. Si mecum libet.
Aliquid morarum dabitis, huc referet pedem
Celerem citatus.
Integer. Cura sollicitat nimis
Te mysta nostri, multa te forsan brevi
Gerenda rerum pondera, amandant procul.
Vedastus. Negotiorum pondus haud ullum gravat,
Gratari amicis ferere vobiscum mihi
Colloquia mente ridet id solum diu.
Marius. Que prodigia! jam Massici exundat liquor
Exante vacuo vase: liquor hic optimus.
Uve Falerne est.
Vedastus. Mente quid tacita tenes
Immissa celo munera, et grates refer
Stupore misso, jure cui debes Deo.
Infunde: dulce nectar, ambrosiam simul
Fovet[1] Falernum.
Pius. Munerum acceptum tibi
Ego propino, pace cum lubeat tua.
Vedastus. Bibat salutem.
Integer. Quam juvat tecum moras
Sermone facili trahere, ni nox pallio
Lurida nigranti mox vocatque nos domum
Umbraret orbem.
Vedastus. Quo vocat preceps fugam
Lucem Hesperugo, mora ire nos nulla addecet
Valete ovantes, vivite eternos dies.

---

[1] Credo.

Pius. Vedaste vive Nestoris terris dies,
Letus perennes fata post vives vale.

SCÆNA 12a.

VEDASTUS, CASTUS, REMIGIUS, FELIX, ANGELUS, LATRIA.

Remigius. Quousque diris flatibus nassam Petri
Stygia procella sorbet? Usquequo impete
[1]Larvata toto seviet pestis mari:
Vixdum quietem nactus ut surgit repens
Ignotus ante turbo qui mentem obruit
Christi per oras Belgicas exul fides
Dominata quondam pressa sub pedibus jacet.
Fumant Deorum templa, vitiorum seges
Scelerum libido, turpe dominantur nefas.

Angelus. Non ultra ovile Remigi in preceps ruat
Que tincta quondam Rigiaci Atrebatium
Tellus cruore Diogenis alium sibi
Meritis[2] Vedastum presulem clarum ciet.
Cave ire contra sic jubet coelo Deus.

Remigius. Que vox in aures involat nosco ethera
Nutum potentis, celicum nosco Dei
Huc mox Vedastus propius acceleret pedem.

Castus. Venerande presul munus hoc superi decet
Mystam tonantis, cujus expertus fuit
Mammertus olim mentis eximium decus,
Cujus Vienna tota virtutes canit
Virumque meritis nobilem paucus stupet.

Felix. Nulla mora sacrum Pontifex subeat decus.

Remigius. Nunc[3] agedum [4]athleta fortis etheree domus
Te quando messis ampla Rigiacum vocat
Celumque, robur mentis invictum indue
Caput tyara nobilis frontis decus
Radiata cingat, infulamque te decet
Assume honoris candidam vestem indue
Agmenque Christi pasce per sylvas vagum.

Vedastus. Est impar humeris pondus hoc tantum meis
Venerande presul: onera si subeo lubens

---

[1] Furens rebelli taurus adversum ruet? [2] Mentis. [3] Pugil. [4] Qui.

Non tamen honoris avidus adjunctum decus.
Sat ferre constans animus.

Remigius. Imperium polo
Missum facesse qui jubet aderit Deus.

Vedastus. Haud dignor equidem honore me tanto Dei
Sacrate Presul.

Remigius. Te polus dignum facit.
Quod jure mandat culmen ascende infule
Veles rebellis.

Vedastus. Numini victas manus
Trado lubentes, gratus est coelo labor
Tormenta mille perpeti, gratum meis
Lubescit animis.

Remigius. Age bonam [1]mentem indue.[2]
Humeros honestet candide vestis nitor.
Aureis smaragdis pendeant collo cruces.

Latria. Atrebas tenebras mentis excute, en venit
Jam meta prede Tartari, rursum Atrebas.
Ter flende, ter miserabilis Stygias datur
Vitare syrtes. Canite io superum chori,
Io ter io canite nascitur Baratro dolor
Vobis novantur jubila, io superum chori
Io ter, io canite.

Remigius. Viridanti manus
Gemma hac nitescat : pignus hoc sume ultimum.

Vedastus. Accipio amica Presulis donum manu.

Remigius. I perge properus Belgice messor plage.

Vedastus. Jam pergo, caro presul amplexu vale,
Ibo, ibo tenebrarum eruam obscurum chaos,
Dirige faventem tramitem coelo Deus.

CHORUS TERTIUS.

Latria, Idololatria.

Latria.

I pugil tutus celeri quadriga,
Ad novum gressus celerato ovile :
I pugil terris jubar Atrebeis

[1] Debitam. [2] Induis.

Mentibus fortis tenebras fugato.
Prima sic[1] solis radio coruscat
Lux novo : Presul novus ut renides.
Mente flammatos jacularis ignes.
I pugil tutus celeri quadriga
Ad novum gressus celerato ovile.

Idololatria.

Obvium contra celerabo ferrum.
Quos alunt mortem rabide minantes
Armode sylvis rigidos et ursos
Bellue victus rabie feroci
Mox truci victus cadet et furore.

Latria.

Ut jacet cantes mediis in undis
Et maris fluctus rapidos retundit,
Sic sacrati mens pugilis tonantis[2]
Omne fulgebit rutilans per evum
Flatibus multis licet impetatur
Ut stat et stabit mediis procelle
fortis in undis.

Idololatria.

Hanc parte fortis regna tutabor mea.

Latria.

Te te insequor, congredere vel victa occides.

ACTUS QUARTUS.—SCÆNA PRIMA.

TILCANUS, CODRUS, VEDASTUS, CASTUS, FELIX, BARBARUS, DOCILIS, VICTOR.

Tilcanus. Miser ille quisquis luminis carpit viam
Orbus sereni, cogitur semper novam
Sine luce lucem ducere, et fati dies
Baculo senili trahere compressus malis.

Codrus. Tilcane fateor lumine orbari grave est
Carere longe gravius est membris malum.

---

[1] Non. [2] Vedasti.

Mihi membra ruptis artubus sensim labant,
Corpusque pessum sepius terris datus.

Vilcanus. Mutare sortem liceat o utinam mihi,
Letum colore pascerem aspectum novo.

Codrus. Nunc desine queri, properus et mecum pedes.
Irradiat (hei mihi!) quantus ad portam nitor
Virne ille? divorum an aliquis?

Vedastus. Satis est vie
Monumenta vastatae urbis antique intuor.
Optata salve terra, quam tanti est mihi
Umbone fidei tegere, tutari meo
Nobile cruore funditus rupto decus.

Codrus. Miseris egenis porrige benigna stipem
Vir magne dextra.

Vilcanus. Lumine orbatum vides
Miserere, miserere.

Vedastus. Misereor, auri nihil
Mihi bursa condit, quod tamen solum licet,
Precabor ethera opemque suprema feret
Ab arce numen : O Deus cecum aspice
Novamque cecis mentibus vultu facem
Meliore pande, videat et cecus jubar
Æthre micantis videat ut lumen novum
Fidei perennis, ambulet claudus pede
Recto pererrans letus ut calle ambulet
Sereniore semitas sacri etheris.

Vilcanus. Quis fulgor oculos reddit? insuetum jubar
Vix patior : amore decus quantum est polis!
Jam video, video.

Codrus. Pedibus equalis meis
Mensura, nunc recte ambulo : constant loco
Firmi pedes : abjicio manibus lignea
Hec fulcra.

Docilis. Quaenam signa, quae rerum tuor
Prodigia.

Barbarus. Mysta magne dic quo te pedes?

Victor. Subire nostras causa quae patrias domos?

Vedastus. Subire cogit flammeus vestre calor
Avidus salutis.

Docilis. Fare quod numen doces?

Vedastus. Quod docuit olim clarus antistes solo
Hoc nobili, qui morte, testatum sua
Sanxit perenne foedus et numen sacrum.
Hoc pando numen atra quod mentis male
Caligo nescit, quod dedit ceco diem
Cernere coruscum, membra restituit loco
Disrupta claudi. Pastor advenio gregem
Miseratus. Atrebas advenio semen tuis
Sparsurus agris : subruas verum cave
Immissa superis semina, hec melior fove.
Victor. Quamcumque pandis gradimur antistes viam.
Barbarus. Nullum deorum numen hoc signum dedit
Quodcumque numen pandis hoc letus sequor.
Docilis. Ades beatum celitus missum decus
Cecisque lumen tolle condensum chaos
Christumque numen pande quem solum doces.
Vedastus. Hec leta menti exordia insurgunt mee
Pandam serene lucis auroram novam,
Prius citato ducite per urbem pede.
Victor. Divine Presul ingredere leto sacris
Urbem paratam nutibus totam pede.

SCÆNA SECUNDA.

REX CLOTARIUS, AURELIANUS, OCINUS, THEODORICUS, ETC.

Clotarius. Postquam supreme fata Clodoveus parens
Mortis subivit, jamque divis additus
Coelos oberrat, ponderi ratus parem
Sceptri ferendo jure me heredem patri
Populus reposcit, flagitat turma aulicum.
Quod si animus alta mole suppressus labet,
Vel regna verset mentis insolitus pavor
Vos fida sceptri pectora innixus bene
Queis tutus animus robur ac animos datis.
Aurelianus. Invicte princeps seviat quantum libet
Fortuna preceps, blanda seu rebus favet,
Pro te quibusvis pectus objicio malis
Childebertus. Ad cuncta nos imperia proclives habe.
Theodoricus. Regis salutem capitis oppositu tegam.

Clotarius. Hoc robur animi, pectoris laudo fibras.
Vos certa vestrum premia laborum manent.

Ocinus. Rex magne tempus dum otio letus teris
Lubeat profari pauca pro votis mihi,
Clara clientis luce vicinum solum
Subire lubeat regis accessum diu
Avidi moramur, lubeat et tectis dapes
Libare nostris, aura radiantis poli
Hec leta poscit.

Clotarius. Animo votis favens.

Ocinus. Subibit una Francie quondam decus
Nunc Belgie Vedastus hos tecum lares.

Clotarius. O quanta menti gaudii exoritur seges
Dum recolo munera presulis coelo patri
Collata quondam. Presul hic totus meis
Heret medullis pectus et totum rapit,
Hac cito Dium antistitem pernix precor.[1]

Ocinus. Nulla mora princeps referet ut Titanidem
Vectus quadrigis aderit actutum lare.

SCÆNA TERTIA.

VEDASTUS, CASTUS, FELIX,[2] PHILIPARCUS, METANOR, ETC.

Vedastus. Ut volvo mecum mente vestibula immitus
Summi Tonantis templa, vix teneo impetus
Gementis animi, hocne urbis antiquum decus?
Hecne facies? hec clara que quondam Dei
Æquata coelo templa? Barbariem nefas
Potuisse tantum! rapere, predari, solo
Vertere sacratas numini eterno domos!
Quid lustra signant bellue? quid rudera
Saxorum acerti? num Attila immanem tuam
Rabiem? verendum quem dedit quondam Deus
Orbi flagellum? Scelera consignant Deus.
Hec tanta promeruit nocens populus Deus?
Ha parce, lacrymis mitior parce o Deus!

---

[1] Sequar. [2] Caligonus.

Felix. Quid surgit altis vepribus monstrum? fugam
Vedaste celera.

Vedastus. Quis pavor mentem quatit?
Cohibete gressus.

Felix. Effugio.

Castus. Mecum fuge.

Vedastus. Tutatur alto sidere impavidum Deus.

Caligon. Quis clamor[1] aures tantus increpitat repens?
Quid specto? deformem unguibus fert huc pedem
Armatus ursus, quisquis es gressum eripe
Vel mox cruentus[2] corpus in preceps dabit.

Vedastus. Horrore quatitur nixa mens nullo etheri
Truculenta bellua procul hinc sylvis vaga
Latebras pererrans devias refert pedem.
Exiguus amnis limitet gressus feros.
Non hic ferarum lustra, Christiadas locus
Poscit colonos: apage, sic Christus jubet.

Caligon. Quid hoc! facessit jussa properato alveo!
Quo rabidus ursus mitis arripuit fugam.

Philiparcus. Posito furore!

Vedastus. Bellue jussa hauriunt
Natura nullum, queis dedit mentis jubar.
At tu rebellis Atrebas clare facem
Qui mentis ether indidit jussa exsequi
Renuis jubentis? lumen exoritur novi
Surgentis astri, cecus et tenebras[3] Stygis
Foede vagaris? Abjicis fidei facem
Trunquosque spreto squallidos Christicolis!

Caligon. O parce quisquis territas mentem impete
Albus sereno amplectimur jussa etheris.

Philiparcus. Conflata canis monstra letales deos
Dudum caminis mille per partes damus.

Metanor. Imus perennes Presul in jussus tuos,
Cremanda dabimus muta simulacra ignibus.
Fove benigno perditas oves sinu.

Vedastus. Amplector ulnis perditum pastor gregem.
O sola nostri gaudia delecti o meo

---

[1] Tantus. [2] Cruente. [3] Tenebris.

Pendete collo, vive nunc tandem redux
Ovile Christo, vive sed letus sinu.
Caligon. Arcebo domibus quotquot obsertat chaos
Simulacra muta, concremo et inanes trabes.
Vedastus. I perge coelo lumen immittet Deus.
Caligon. Nulla mora sede numina abripimus[1] Stygis.
Vedastus. Hic nos beatos condat exiguus locus
Si quando munus subeo quod sacrum moras
Otiaque tradat aptus hic menti manet,
Feret[2] quietem : ferte qua subeo pedem.
Castus. Quocumque ducis sequimur haud tarda mora.
Felix. Gratum recessus referet Arduenne nemus.

SCÆNA QUARTA.

IDOLOLATRIA, LATRIA, CALIGONUS, PHILIPARCUS, METANOR.

Idololatria. Vah misera perii! concidi! hostilis furor
Huc foeda ructat phyltra. Rigiacum suis
Artibus inhamat, fervet insuetum dolor,
Nec frena patitur, nota si mihi sum satis
Non ibo inulta, tam ferum atque atrox gero
Genumque[3] in iras pectus et furiis agor.
Caligonus. Calcabo pedibus monstra, larvatos Deos
Dilacero.
Metanor. Monstrosum meto gladio caput.
Philiparcus. Coluisse larvas pudeat horrende Stygis,
Idololatria. Quo cecus, amens Atrebas facilem furor
Mentem resorbet : devias quo tramite
Divorum aberrans? siste furibundum impetum.
Latria. Fortis pavescit turma non celi impetus
Sevos minarum perge, lania, disseca,
Idola muta contere, incertam luem
Phlegetontis atri, germen inferne Stygis.
Metanor. Portenta ferro demones fossi occidant.
Caligonus. Famuli cremandas ferte relliquias domum.
Idololatria. Maligna Stygii turba convici ; tua

[1] Fede lumina abripimus. [2] Ferens. [3] Senumque.

Sic regna solvi languida pateris? Atrebas
Sic post deorum munus (ingratum caput)
Odio retorques? ludis insontes Deos.

Latria. Age pestis alio perge properanti pede.
Non te quieta tecta, non fidi lares,
Non hospitalis exsulem excipiat domus.

Idololatria. Ignava fugiam.

Latria. Nulla mora.

Idololatria. Caveo fugam.

Latria. Et jamne segni restitas effrons gradu
Furiale monstrum? pestis execrabilis?
Larvata bellua? Tartaro sacrum caput?
Age imperantis jussa properato ocyus.
Profugere dubitas? curre veloci pede.

Idololatria. Disrumpor.

Latria. I flammam excoque irarum procul.
Cruce hac subacta cede.

Idololatria. Latronis cruce.

Latria. Cruce hac Tonantis,[1] putidum leti genus
Hoc ferre cogar. Atrebas miseram fugas.

Philipar. I larva ditis repete letales domos.

Latria. Scelesta profuge, profuge sic Jesus jubet
Recessit impia, vicit infandi lacus
Manum minacem dextra, minitandis Dei
Letare fortis Atrebas, palmas ovans
Attolle superis, rursus antiquum tibi
Resurgit evum, prisca Diogenis fides
Peritura nunquam presule insurgit novo.
Versabit arctos quamdiu siccas polus
Noctem sequentur astra Titanem dies
Semper nitescet major assurgens fides.
En jacta fidei semina exurgunt sacra
Lustrata coeli rore. Coenobii inclytum
Avidus requiris nosse venturi decus.
Umbram vide: ecce presulis sauciam manum.

[1] *Idololatria.*

SCÆNA QUINTA.

VEDASTUS, SCOPILIO, INTEGER, PIUS, ANTONIUS, BEATUS, PAUPER, RAGANARIUS, LITANAS.

Vedastus.
Magnum Vedaste munus est et magnum onus
Aliis preesse, sanguine redemptas suo
Tibi regendas tradidit Jesus oves.
O quam timendum est ne qua depereat tua
Subrepta culpa, semper invidias lupi
Tendent ovili, semper invidias agent.

Scopilio.
Divine Presul mitte quos animus coquit
Luctus inanes, masculas vires dabit
Qui pastor agmen dirigit tecum Deus.

Integer.
Ne metue rapido totus in terras ruat
Æther fluento, cana jus terre incubet
Et omne coelum ceca tempestas agat.
Tibi militabit pectus assuetum malis.

Pius.
Ex quo Lyei nectar augustum Deo
Ovans litavit animus ac Cererem sacram
Amoris omne numinis divis tulit
Pignus sacratum: fervet insolitus calor
Imisque latitat pectus exurens fibris.

Clemens.
Armetur in me quidquid infausto tulit
Nox atra foetu, quidquid infernus creat
Unctus sacrato chrismate adversus Styga,
Audax rebellem Tartari superem dolos.

Antonius.
Per latus agatur ensis aut flamme leves
Hoc vile tristi corpus absumant rogo,
Nec parte vitam redimo, membratim Deo
Juvat perire.

Beatus.
Lenta supplicio gravi
Mors protrahatur, viva visceribus meis
Rapientur exsta, pectus erumne gravent,
Quemcumque dederint exitum divi feram.

Pauper.
Eadem voluntas celitus mentem fovet.
Eadem, nec ullus nocte discussa dies
Votum hoc notabit sede dejectum sua.

Vedastus.
Flammis resultat animus accensus novis,
Dum forte vobis pectus et leto obvium
Tacitus revolvo, leta sic tenero parens

Crescente nato vota vix capit sua.
Quo mente properat turbida infensum Deum
Divus sacerdos? Ore quid tacito insonat?

Raganarius. Bene habet, jacent nunc putide terris Stygis
Superata monstra pudet: pudet inermes male
Coluisse larvas! Semen infandum! lacus
Stygii cloacam! ha pudet.

Litanas. Amor melior rapit
Christi medullas cana quem docuit fides
Larvata toto pestis ex orbe exsulet.

Scopilio. Viden' Vedaste quanta mature seges
Messis virescat, quantus insurgat nitor
Jubaris suborti.

Integer. Vinculo junctus tibi
Christus perenni pascit Atrebeas oves.
I letus agris vive maturis satis.
Ecce huc prophanus mysta conglomerat pedem.

Raganarius. Celis sacratum proximum Christo caput.[1]

Litanas. Miserare sacro dilue errorum notas
Turpes lavacro.

Vedastus. Poplites fixos solo
Levate leti, miseror id rectum decet.
Ovile tuti petite tranquillum gregis.

Raganarius. Vix patitur animus rebus in sacris moras.

Vedastus. Ite, ite leti pandet ad sacras viam
Lymphas petitam mysta qui multus vitet.
Fatus reposcit prepotens Clotarius,
Audete turma, nulla vos moneat mali
Facies laboris, quidquid est durum pati,
Tolerasse dulce est, hac patet coelum via
Tu junge Clemens presuli socium latus.

SCÆNA SEXTA.

MEGO, HORTULBAL, TUCCIUS, MAGUS, CALUMNIA, INVIDIA, ETC.

Mego. Parata mensae fercula Hortulbal?

Hortulbal. Mego

[1] Miserare eccum tramite ignoto gregem.

Dudum paratissima, sed hoc qui nescio
Mantile mensae quadret.

Mego. O sanum parum
Cerebrum! Docebo expande.

Hortulbal. Sic?

Mego. Non sic, phy phy.

Hortulbal. Sic ergo.

Mego. Phy phy pudeat.

Hortulbal. Ergo sic.

Mego. Adhuc
Erras. Latere mantile propendet nimis.

Hortulbal. Rem temere mentis video per vestigium
Mantile jaceat penitus inversum solo
Æquetur hinc, inde, undique. Æqualissimam
Suppono mensam. Recta stat, mecum huc manus.
Ha, ha, ha, ha, ha, ha, nihil cerebri reor
Hoc capite, caula fare vel qua de grege
Podium oriundus.

Hortulbal. Verba ne frustra sere.
Nobis propinquat Tuccius cito da manus.

Mego. Lepidissimum caput! quis hic Tucci comes?

Tuccius. Properato opus Mego aderit actutum cohors
Comitata regem: bene sacrum hic socius mihi
Magus liquorem Massicum sacret magis.

Mego. Illud moramur, vasa mox mensae sacret
Domini locanda Juppiter jubet id Deus.
Parate cuncta vasculum mensam operiat.

Magus. Solitam profundo Tartaro furiam cio.
Latebris adesto turma desertis Stygis,
Alcidis hydra scisaque serpens manu
Huc redeat.

Invidia. Adsumus.

Calumnia. Adsumus, quid rei est?

Magus. Adhibite solitas artibus fictis manus.

Invidia. Hunc calleo probe quem modum nutu doces.

Calumnia. Accedo, Lybica quas creat fervens plaga
Has contuli herbas. Vasculis lateant bene.

Invidia. His gelida pigri frigoris glacies inest.

Calumnia. Serpentium saniem exprimunt hec gramina,

Bubonis hoc cor putidum lance Stygis
Hec secta foede viscera hec capiat latex.

Magus. Vulgus silentum rector umbrosae domus
Chaosque cecum ditis Eumenides feras
Conferte dextras, denegat quisquis Deos
Mensasque tangit concidat dira manu.

Mego. Secedite citi regius cardo strepit
Ictu insolenti, Presul huc gressum movet.

Magus. Scelerate pestes.

Invidia. Curro per notas lacus.

Calumnia. Belle omnia excurro.

Magus. Ite prestolor latens
Quidquid futurus exitus pandet brevis.

SCÆNA SEPTIMA.

REX CLOTARIUS, OCINUS, VEDASTUS, CLODOMIRUS, CHILDEBERTUS, AURELIANUS.

Clotarius. Phalanx nitescat syrmate aurato licet
Seresque leta vellera extremi legant
Gratoque ducant pollice, atque altum caput
Levans in ostro letus etatis dies
Traham serenos, indigus forem tamen
Parumque letus, ni novos frequens nova
Animos bearet subditum favens manus.
En stirpe nobis Ocinus clara nitens
Accivit ultro Presulem auditum mihi
Toties Vedastum cujus affatus mage
Pertentat animum gaudio quovis meum.

Vedastus. Rex magne, ridet sermo si noster brevis
Memor parentis vive cui numen dedit
Fluente dextra nectar, eternas domos.

Clotarius. Divine Presul patris immemorem dies
Nullus per evum muneris nullus dati
Aspiciet unquam. Regius sanguis tibi
Litatur ultro, Francia cui suam refert
Merito salutem, cujus empyreus parens
Indutus orbes legibus tutus tenet.

Vedastus. Quascumque nobis, numini grates refer,
Magnanime princeps, si quod exiguum tuli

Munus parenti, gratia fretus tuli
Supera Tonantis, munus hoc totum Dei est.

Ocinus. Verborum abunde; Cynthius mediam cito
Lucem rotatum properat, aptatas simul
Dudum subite principes tectis dapes.

Clotarius. Subimus ultro: more quo solitus bona
Precare Presul verba.

Vedastus. Faxo quod jubes,
Lubens id ante postulant signum dapes
In nomine Patris et Fili et Spiritus Sancti.

Aurelianus. Terrore quatior.

Theodoricus. Membra vix constant loco
Totus stupesco pavidus.

Childebertus. Effuso natat
Asser cruore madidus.

Clotarius. Attonitus stupet animus
Malumque nescit ignote luis.

Vedastus. Proceres moveri sinite fraus nota est doli.
Hic magus aliquis magicis vasa artibus
Succis malignis Thessala aut saga induit
Leto periret ut quis associans comes
Conviva regem: nota fraus, notus dolus.

Clotarius. Atqui latentes demonis tantas potis
Rescire fraudes?

Vedastus. Detegit signum crucis
Artes cytaeas demonis technas notat
Nocturna spectra profugat sortes malas
Cantata verba pandit, hac cruce subruit
Cruor malignis sortibus fusus solo.

Ocinus. Grates Tonanti numini meritas damus
Epulasque princeps magne properato pete.

Clotarius. Tremore rigeo totus inconstans mihi.

Vedastus. Arceto Principis pectore impavido metus.

Clotarius. Arcere nequeo, corda qui feriunt metus.

Vedastus. Æquum timere Principem quidnam addecet?

Clotarius. Æquum timere Principem cuncta addecet.

Vedastus. Malus satelles semper heroum timor.

Clotarius. Malus satelles? sepius in auro bibunt
Reges venenum.

Vedastus. Clara securos facit
Virtus.

Clotarius. Beatos presules!
Vedastus. Reges simul.
Clotarius. Virtus nitescit rara Regum mentibus.
Vedastus. Frequens nitescit clara celsis mentibus.
Animose Princeps turbido statue modum
Brevem timori tempus actutum vocat.
Clotarius. Quocumque Presul comitor acceleras pedem.
Ocinus. Deferte mensas turma famulorum procul.

SCÆNA OCTAVA.

MAGUS, MEGO, HORTULBAL, TUCCIUS, CALUMNIA, INVIDIA, LATRIA.

Magus. Devota raperis preda tenarco cani!
Age redi, aberrasne satis, age pernix redi!
Lucisque Averni fraudibus Christum indue.
Ast heu quid angues turba furiarum nigros
Scelerața versat!
Mego. Quem trabe infesta petunt
Furiata monstra?
Magus. Viperis tortis secent
Humeros patentes, verberent lanient sequor
Christum per enses, effugio densum chaos.
Mego. Arripite socii rudera et sordes solo
Lectas in ora jacite furiarum.
Hortulbal. Stygis
Ad perduelles currite citate domos.
Tuccius. Pestes lacus repetite veloci impete.
Invidia. Etiamne diras sordibus lurco pedes?
Calumnia. Erebo rebellas tumide? Mox poenas dabis.
Invidia. Ad Styga rebellis.
Calumnia. Numen exturba ocyus
Fidem, pudorem vile mancipium mei.
Magus. Feri retunde, nulla vis Christum auferet.
O Christe larvas abige.
Hortulbal. Qua fugiam miser?
Invidia. Ad Styga cruenti.
Latria. Turma que Christum ciet.
Magus. Succurre miseris.
Latria. Germen inferni lacus

	Vivit superstes? cedito predam imperat
	Jesus, profunde domitor et vindex Stygis.
	Vitate pestes, rursus astutis dolis.
	Ne vos cruentus hostis incautos clepat.
Hortulbal.	Quam Mego letus profugis Stygias manus.
Mego.	Hac letiorem non tulit Titan diem.
Magus.	Detestor insanos dolos, queis actenus
	Insanus usus, Presuli grates fero
	Cujus salutem signa testantur meam.
	Agnosce felix Atrebas clarum tui
	Sidus Vedastum.
Tuccius.	Vos manus mecum date.

SCÆNA NONA.

CLOTILDIS CUM SUIS, VEDASTUS, CLEMENS, ETC.

Clotildis.	O quantus udis imber emanat genus
	Mentemque varius versat ancipitem dolor :
	Eurus notusque tempore hyberno impetunt
	Non tot procellis naufrago ponto ratem
	Quantis dolorum quassa curarum estibus
	Mens fluctuatur, cure et erumne opprimunt.
Vedastus.	Regina mentis robur antiquum voca
	Viresque forti masculas corde indue,
	Nec ulla terris terreat facies mali
	Quin rumpe fortis quidquid adversum obviat.
Clotildis.	Orbata conjuge sola quid vitam traho?
Vedastus.	Quidquid ferendum est numen ætherеum parat
	Quod cuique metam terminat vite brevem
	Pauperi, opulento, principi, sero, cito.
Clotildis.	Casum ferendo Presul evici ferum.
	Solamen aderat unicum constans meis
	Genovefa lacrymis, hanc quoque eripuit mihi
	Libithina preceps: moesta queis lacrymas ciam!
	Genovefa! sic heu! corpus examinum jacet!
Clemens.	Moderare lacrymas, illa stellatas poli
	Domos pererrat, fundit eternum tibi
	Beata supplex vota.

Vedastus. Mage regum parens
Regina, prole, quam polus multam dedit
Queo pace, functi sceptra moderatur patris
Letare melius.

Clotildis. Tangis en alios metus
Aliasque lacrymas inscius prolis moves.

Vedastus. Proles parentis illa virtutem refert.

Clotildis. Illa Clodomiri patris insignem sui
Sobolem nepotes, sanguine (invisum scelus!)
Fuso cruentat, Lybicus haud tantum gerit
Panther furorem, corde non ursus ferox,
Nemeæque monstrum gaudet incestus furor
Foedare quantum sanguine insontum manus.

Vedastus. Adeone patrum degener sanguis furit?

Clotildis. Raptat scelestus sanguis avulsos sinu
Per vim puellos, perdit et fratris nece
Prolem cruentus vix potuit unus sinu
Profugere salvus. En tibi sanguis meus.
Multa illa soboles, flere quid matrem vetas?
Tantisque pressam pondere erumnis pium
Oculis liquorem.

Vedastus. Lacrymis nunc plus satis
Princeps datum est. Age Regiam mentem indue
Animosa Regis vidua, nam majoribus
Est digna palma te manens, coelo malis.

Clotildis. Hec una presul animat et moestam levat
Merces perennis: dege si lubeat lare
Longasque mecum temporis moras trahe.

Vedastus. Ovile revocat pace dum liceat procul
Nec longiores trahere dat tempus moras.

Clotildis. I Presul, i pasce tibi delectum gregem
I Presul, i licet usibus, credo, tuis
Quod Augicourtense annuum reddit solum.

Vedastus. Regina tantis referet eternam Deus
Meritis salutem: hoc usibus trado sacris.
Solum perenne.

Clotildis. Me abdico terra lubens
Utere solumque trade si lubeat sacris
Dum Presul hora convocat gradere, sequor.

SCÆNA DECIMA.

DIETUS, BRIBAX, PERICLES, SEPHO.

Dietus. Oi mi! dolore stomachus insano gemit.
Nec panem in alvum mittere insanum datur.
Bribax. Pro summe divorum Deus semper famem
Tolerabo egenus?
Pericles. Allatrat venter mihi
Siti fame.
Sepho. Mihi totus insanit quoque,
Obgannit usque nec famem quisquam levat.
Dietus. Mihi quarta nullo cum cibo exigitur dies,
Punica velut laterna sum pellucidus.
Bribax. Chameleontem jure me voca, mihi
Quippe cibus aer.
Pericles. Moriar an vivam haud satis
Scio, mihi dudum ferias dentes agunt.
Sepho. Heus boni aliquid ventura presagit dies.
Pericles. Quid fare?
Sepho. Presul omnibus toties redit.
Votis petitus solitos hic nobis cibos
Suggere semper affatim.
Dietus. Recte mones
Benignus adeo prodigus rerum fuit
Opumque largus, ut patrem hunc urbis[1] indigae
Plebs nuncuparet.
Bribax. Jam redit salvus scio.
Ut ante socii nullus optatam stipem
Preripiat ejus obsidere fores placet.
Pericles. Sequimur euntem, tu gradum primus move
Sed ecce sociorum agmen egreditur foras.

SCÆNA 11ª.

FIDEM, VEDASTUS, SCOPILIO, CLEMENS, ANGELI, ETC.

Vedastus. Quando Tonantis munere eximio Dei
Dilecta turma, numina et vani Jovis
Erasa plebis mentibus, fidei faces

[1] Turbe.

Lustrant corusce quidquid obtectum fuit,
Grates supremo numini immensas agi
Fas esse credo.

Scopilio. Jam ipse quins foeta Deum
Veneror acerra, celites cogam meis
Servire votis.

Vedastus. Dabitur alternis quies:
Vicina nobis cellula adjunctos habet
Socios laborum, hos adeo votivas Deo
Preces laturus, cella quae condet meum
Aliquando major corpus exanimum brevi.

Integer. Sacrate presul pauperum coetus domus
Pro foribus agitat.

Vedastus. Ut auguror meam sibi
Opem reposcit.

Bribax. Nos egestas opprimit,
Miserere. Modica refice nos Presul stipe.

Omnes pauperes. Egena turba marcet in foribus fame.

Vedastus. Et vix lacerna corpus exigua tegit:
Ferre hec Vedasto duros aspectus potes?
Properate famuli penulas ferte huc leves
Tostamque Cererem.

Marius. Quod jubes factum puta.

Vedastus. Egena membra pascite ad cellam, dies
Vocat precatus.

Pius. Quo vocat mens enthea
Properato gressus.

Anton. Nullus infestat lupus
Ovile, leta gradere securus via.

Pauper. Nos una egenum mente pascamus gregem.

Clemens. Sic nos decet perenne jussis obsequi.

Scopilio. Quis non stupescat ista nobilium pia
Documenta morum? laude quis merita efferat
Hec tanta velut exempla preeuntis ducis?

Marius. En postulata Presulis presto manent.

Scopilio. Hec cocta Cereris dona vobis sumite.

Integer. Sedate vestram fruge collata famem.

Pauper. Vestram agite pariter potus expleat sitim.

Gabriel.

Larga quam virtus animique candor
In sui impellit superos amorem :
Jam tibi Presul superis paratur
Arcibus merces, tibi totus una
Annuit ether.

Raphael.

Quisquis ingentem capiti ruinam
Et Stygis semper metuenda fata
Post rogi flammas removere tentat,
Is sibi tentet superos favore
Jungere gratus.

Anton. Onerate vestrum penula corpus rudi.
Sepho. Vestram beabit Presulem merces polis,
Et vestra vitae tempora eternet Deus.
Scopilio. Hoc Presulem unum recreat, hec cordi mihi
Est una pietas vivite beatos dies.
Dietus. Quid harpagare penulam tentas manu?
Mea est.
Bribax. Tua erras verbero, cedo, tuos
Vel baculus ulmos tundet.
Dietus. Hanc per vim rapis?
Furem scelestum rapite, totam penulam
Vobis lubens tradidero.
Sapho. Cedito furcifer.
Pericles. Profugiet amens? insequor, cedet brevi.

SCÆNARIO 12ª.

VEDASTUS, CASTUS, FELIX.

Vedastus. Hic mesta mentis nubila arcebit locus,
Celique dulces proprius affatus dabit,
Age sociorum turma pateant mihi fores
Toties petitae, rursus Arduenne nemus
Curis levamen cellula ex voto dabit.
Castus. Dilecte Presul pasce qua solitus dape
Celi serena mentis eximium decus.
Felix. Subibo cellam et obviis celestibus

Levato mentem, deferet charites locus
Pluetque rores celica numen manu.
Vedastus. Subibo letus gratus arridet locus.

SCÆNA 13a.

METANOR, VICTOR, PHILIPARCUS, INTEGER, SCOPILIO, ETC.

Metanor. Quis nocte media vertice elato domos
Fulgor coruscat?
Philiparcus. Animus attonitus stupet.
Victor. Ignea columna tollit ardentes globos
Flammasque ructat, lucidum monstrat jubar
Novum aliquid.
Philiparcus. Ut monstra reor interitum parant
Cedes minantur.
Scopilio. Leva presagit mali
Mens aliquid animis insolens fatum manet.
Integer. Prodigia dubii attonitus eventus nequit
Animus referre crescit ostentum magis!
Metanor. Docete paucis quidquid hoc monstrum petit?
Clarasque sursum flammulas dudum trahit.
Scopilio. Ignarus animus heret incerti mali
Acerso properus presulem, pandet polo
Hic doctus alto nos quod incertum fugit.
Philiparcus. Hec signa nondum rescit?
Scopilio. Actutum sciet.
Integer. Solitos recessus petiit amotos lare,
Queis letus animum pascit etherea dape.
Imbres sacratos fortior factus bibit.
Metanor. Qui dapibus animos letus astriferis fovet,
Totiesque sacros numinis rores bibit,
Hic facile pandet signa quid portent male.
Philiparcus. Ecce ille, pallor quantus insidet genis?
Gressusque lentus promovet letos tamen.

SCÆNA 14^{a}.

FIDEM, VEDASTUS CUM SUIS, LOQUETUS, CHAVETUS, CARBONARIUS, HARPAGARIUS, MICHAEL, GABRIEL, RAPHAEL, URIEL.

Vedastus. Actum est, migrandum est, funis extremum mihi
Nexere Parcae, celicam id monstrat jubar,
Febrisque fervens fata protendunt mea.

Scopilio. Sacrate Presul, subleva sede hac caput
Morbo asperatum.

Vedastus. Tempus est vitae breve
Citate socios hauriant monitus senis
Breves parentis.

Scopilio. Turma sociorum gemit
Presto Vedaste, lacrymas pubes ciet
Lugetque toto nobilis phalanx solo.

Vedastus. Adeste lucta melius hac leti ultima.

Integer. Mors instat animos letus et cunctis facis
Divine Presul?

Vedastus. Apparat, letam scio
Fatum quietem letus et letas domos
Superum requiro.

Castus. Filii orbati patre,
Pastore ovile quo ruent passim vagum?

Vedastus. Numerosus aderit pastor equalis mihi
Nec fallit ether vivet Atrebatum novo
Perenne patre, cura te Castum manet
Cellae perennis vive tu fratrum memor,
Hec vilis alta surget eternum domus.

Castus. Vilis columnis nobilis surget casa?

Vedastus. Sic arce supera numen ethereum refert.
Sed heu! labascit pectus oppressum febri
Jesu, Jesu!

Scopilio. O Presul ultima signam manu
Stratos clientes rore sidereo bea.

Vedastus. Filioli amoris vinculum cunctos liget.
Filioli egenos larga sustentet manus,
Vos ditet ether, cumulet et charitum imbribus.

Loquetus. Instate Stygia stringite arma concili.
Chavetus. Proserpinam ditisque perjuro caput,
Instabo, predam rabio dejectam loco.
Carbonarius. Insequere.
Harpagarius. Curro.
Michael. Spiculis rupem petis
Averna bilis cede, cede.
Loquetus. Va miser.
Vedastus. Tibi vixi Jesu, morior et Jesu tibi.
Latria. Egredere fortis anime celituum choris
Agglutinare, egredere tibi celum patet.
Quid turma lacrymas preliis finem dedit
Tulitque laurum : flammea in sede excubat
Manus Tonantis muneraria hec suis
Fato triumphum dicit, hec statuit polus
Quicumque certat fortis hic felix diem
Triumphat, afferat arma qui palmam petit.

CHORUS 4us.

ANGELI 4 CANENTES, EUGE SERVE BONE ET FIDELIS, ETC. ; ANIMA VEDASTI, S. DIOGENES, S. ELEUTHERIUS, S. PIATUS, S. MEDARDUS.

Anima Vedasti.

O que gaudia sidere
Mulcent pectus et entheas
Fibras ethereus calor,
Et totum mihi me rapit!
Quam sudasse juvat solo
Celi gaudia dum manent
Æternum et satiant fibras.
O que gaudia sidere
Mulcent pectus entheas
Fibras ethereus calor
Et totum mihi me rapit.

Diogenes.

Fortes tanto nectare Christus
Pugiles supero potat Olympo.
Ipse Diogenes ferro quondam

Oris confossus Rigiacis.
Clarus supera palmam fede
Hanc victor certamine retuli.
Agedum mihi Vedaste secundus
Miserumque gregem miserans pastor.
En palma eadem te manet, agedum
Letus superas arces scande.
Fortes dio nectare Christus
Pugiles supero potat olympo.

Eleutherius.

Iterata meam potis est nulla
Frangere mentem virga tyrannum :
Non exsulium me perdomuit
Non strictum perdomuit ferrum :
Arcibus altis quidquid rutilat
Alto positus perlustro loco.
His fruere pugil letus in astris
Divorum epulis nectare fruere.

Anima Vedasti.

O que gaudia sidere
Mulcent pectus et entheas
Fibras ethereus calor
Et totum mihi me rapit.

S. Piatus.

Feret ambrosiam stellante domo
Nectarque Deus congredere pugil.
Meritis laurus casta paratur,
Congredere, quies saturet coeli
Æterna animum Belgia tellus
Tibi cervicem sanguine, rupto
Corpore, fudi, vive Vedasto
Preside felix Belgia vive.
Feret ambrosiam stellante domo
Nectarque Deus congredere pugil.

S. Medardus.

Aureis fultas mille columnis
Arces penetra, tuus est Christus,

Totus tuus est celicus orbis,
Aligerum ergo, coetu superos
Comitatus adi mille columnis
Aureis fultas arces penetra.

Angeli canent.

Euge serve bone et fidelis, etc.

Anima Vedasti.

O que gaudia sidere
Mulcent pectus et entheas
Fibras ethereus calor
Et totum mihi me rapit!

ACTUS QUINTUS.—SCÆNA 1a.

Caligonus, Philiparcus, Metanor, Victor, Docilis, Barbarus, Prudens, Constans, Themius, Latria, Autbertus, Aurelianus, Marius, etc.

Caligonus. Quam misera varie vita mortales rotat
Fugiensque preceps casus incertos agit,
Presuli trahebat nuper Emeberto dies
Ovans serenos nobile Atrebatium solum:
Nunc ecce vultum flebilem indutum ingemit.

Prudens. Ambigua properans Presuli letum tulit
Sua fila Clotho.

Constans. Parca crudelis nimis
Adversa votis, ferrata quamdiu manu
Caduca vite stamina erumpes brevis.

Philiparcus. Nunquam timoris vita solicito vacat,
Que fluxa semper casibus mille objacet.

Themius. Bis sol quater deno annuos cursu polis
Vixdum rotatus egit, et terris jubar
Retulit coruscum, tempore et properans brevi
Libitina rapuit Presules septem sibi.

Latria. Ne querere, totus Atrebas albus tibi
Blanditur ether, lumen exstinctum refert
Primum Vedastum sidus Autbertus novum,
Quem multa virtus laude numerosa extulit
Sacraque decorari infula donat caput:

Gratare letus Presuli et missos cole
Animo benigna celitum grates manu.

Caligonus. Tantumne nostris coelitum dono jubar
Clarescet oris? Nimius o superum favor.

Latria. Dilecte superis vincam rebus meis
Fulcimen age, nunc pasce dilectum gregem
Fortisque ahenum pectus accinge, impetum
Cohibe malorum, murus es dudum Deo
Electus istis, fortis Atrebato veni.

Autbertus. Quid diva ad ista me levem pupum vocas?
Adque vel Athlas fortis incurvat caput.

Latria. Autberte, numen aliquod hunc frenat globum,
Hoc tibi sagittas tibi manus presto feret,
Cave longiores etheri obvertas moras.

Autbertus. Meus iste animus est assequi semper polos
Et te imperantem, nunc age Autberto utere,
Monitis et armis instrue, actutum sequor.

Latria. I letus, astri munient, tuto viam.

Aurelianus. Age te moratur avida nobilium phalanx
Congredere Presul.

Metanor. Sartor Atrebeo grege
Letare, grex en gaudii expandit sinus.

Barbarus. Vivat beatos Presul eternum dies.

Caligonus. Pascat beatum pastor eternum gregem.

Omnes simul. Pastor beatum pascat eternum gregem.

Autbertus. Procul esto plausus non levem vocem ambio
Popularis aurae: Numinis crescens honos,
Mihique dudum cara vestrorum salus
Primus laboris ultimus finis mei.

Prudens. Divine Presul impera vel nutibus,
Quodcumque mandas sequimur.

Constans. Impera citi.
Tua jussa facimus.

Themius. Morte devotum tibi
Animum litabo.

Autbertus. Ista placet acclamatio.
Animos serenae mentis agnosco notas.
Ovile vestra nullus infestet lupus
Hac mente proceres: nullus irarum furor
Dejectet apice, cui vocat superum favor.
Subeamus urbem, domus et grates polis.

SCÆNA 2ª.

Loquetus, Chavetus, Carbonarius, Harpagarius, Michael, Gabriel, Raphael, Uriel.

Loquetus. Quid Stygia stertis turma torpenti lacu
Arcisse flammis debuit dudum domus
Infesta prede Tartari, ac nostri lues.
Chavetus. Mox tecta quassa trucidant flammis meis.
Loquetus. Tu sequere Carbonarie Harpagarium
Jamjam favillis tecta fumabunt meis.
Carbonarius. Non imperatum pectus ad noxam fero
Iniicio flammas, sulphur, et tecta ustulo.
Harpagarius. Inversus alto corruat apex funditus
Et alta toto jaceat haec moles solo.
Loquetus. Agite ruina perdite infestos lares.
Chavetus. Vulcanus omni parte succensus furit,
Delecta penitus mox domus tota occidet.
Michael. Quid larva tentas? posse te credis domum
Furiata divum vertere crematum solo.
Hinc ad cloacas Tartari gressus move.
Gabriel. Cui scutum Olympus militat vinci nequit.
Raphael. Cui sunt columne celites fortes manet.
Uriel. Frustra secessu mersa tenareo phalanx,
Superos lacessis.
Raphael.[1] Ceca nox jubari male
Impar duellas.
Loquetus.[2] Tartarum solus domat
Coelo Vedastus.
[3]Tartarum solus domet?
Pro caveo! adeste turma: quo rapitis fugam?
Constate fortes, jacite flammatas faces
Totumque tectum vertite.
Michael. Hinc, hinc vos rogi
Epule perennes noctis obscuros specus
Subite celeres: vos manet Stygis rota.
Loquetus. Nil noster in divos labor Stygius potest.
Chavetus. Heu vincor.
Carbonarius. Uror, undaque flammam opprimet?

---

[1] Gabriel. [2] Raphael. [3] Loquetus.

Michael. Sic, sic labascat[1] Stygius incassum labor
Gabriel. Nunquam labascat, quem favor divum tegit,
Vivat sacrato nobilis mysta domus.

SCÆNA 3ª.

AUTBERTUS, MICHAEL.

Autbertus. Aurora roseum propera Titanem refert
Solitas sacrata vota, celitibus preces
De more fundo. Verte quo supplex manus
Clarescit oriens versus eras domos.
Michael. Tandem Vedasti nobile absconsum solo
Pignus nitescat: metor orienti polo
Cui missus ales nobilem terris domum.
Levata sursum fabrica, elatos pedes
Centum reposcit, longa ducentos pedes,
Et lata centum: numerus hic constat loco.
Que jam ruinis arcta diuturnis labat
Lipsana fovebit cella, sic mandant poli.
Autbertus. Quid audio? quid insolens numen tonat?
Nunquid sacratum precipit pignus casa
Vili morari? Qui Deus tantum decus
Ignobilis, qui vilis acceptet domus?
Michael. Autberte, summo jussa demissa ethere
Velox facesse, major assurgens tholis
Clarescet edes numinis mentem accipe.
Autbertus. Agnosco rector fabricae ac mundi parens
Agnosco meritis indices nutu sacrae,
Nihil morabor, quod jubes mox assequor.

SCÆNA 4ª.

AURELIANUS, INTEGER, PIUS, CLEMENS, MARIUS, BARBARUS, AUTBERTUS, ETC.

Aurelianus. Quonam abiit! aut queis presul in latebris agit?
Integer. Mora tanta pectus versat ancipiti metu.
Pius. Indagine sagace mihi querendus.

[1] Labascit.

Clemens.	Metus
	Mittite, propinquat incolumis redux.
Aurelianus.	Sacrate Presul mente quid solus coquis
	Dubiusque versas?
Autbertus.	Visa quae numen docet
	Dubius revolvit animus attonitus[1] stupens.
Clemens.	Animose mysta dubius abscedat stupor,
	Supremaque rei capita lustrate refer.[2]
Autbertus.	Majora veris visa vix capiunt fidem.
Aurelianus.	Ordire paucis.
Autbertus.	Summa vix Titan juga
	Stringebat, astraque victa fedebant poli[3]
	Dum jam benigno numen impello prece,
	Aciemque mentis jaculos in superum plagas.
	Summi Tonantis ales insolitus meos
	Oculos oberrat, nitida radiabat coma
	Solare vultus luce superabat jubar
	Candore rutilus alta metatur loca
	Aurea futuris edibus virga sacris
	Hunc quem Crientio amnis exiguus notat.
Integer.	Cui templa mandat sacra divorum strui.
Autbertus.	Quondam Vedasto antistiti, hec ales tonat.
	Autberte summo jussa demissa ethere
	Velox facesse, major assurgens tholis
	Clarescet edes numinis mentem accipe.
Clemens.	Quis supera demens monita perficere aburat?
Aurelianus.	Autberte id ipsum scilicet noctis quies
	Augur futuri, placidus hoc in somniis
	Sera monebat nocte presagus sopor.
	Id retulit in votis Scopilio Presuli
	Dudum fuisse, cellula abjecta tegi
	A morte corpus. Muneri hinc te Deus
	Presul reservat, nimius hoc sacrum subi.
Autbertus.	Subibo preceps, vota respiciat Deus.
	Hanc Audomarum Presulem ad pompam cita
	Lambertus una presul acceleret pedem.
	Totam per urbem personet clangor tube
	Plebesque passim tota letitiam sonet.

[1] Attonitum. [2] At ora ceptis transitum verbis negant. [3] Polo.

Marius. Mox presul aderit, Morinus optatus lare.
Autbertus. Onerate sertis cellulam, majoribus
Adaucta trabibus aureis niteat casa.

SCÆNA 5ª.

INVIDIA, MICHAEL.

Invidia. Ego mox in hostes dira collecto ferar
Preceps furore flammeas livoribus
Faces et arma suggeram atque uno omnia
Quatiam tumultu.
Michael. Larva molitur Stygis
Hic aliquid Erebi sanguis et noctis vagae
Stat ire contra.
Invidia. Patiar hunc superis dari
Terris honorem? Corpus ingenti palam
Patiar corona Presulum facta avehi?
Assurgere et in altum urbe suppressa domos
Ignobilem amnem sidera et coelum tulit
Sepultus hostis rursus a fatis sibi
Terram reposcit? Ante turbabo Styga,
Celumque vertam, armabo contra et inferos.
Michael. Molitur aliquid germen infandi lacus.
Invidia. Quam vallat ingens montis adversi specus
Ultra nocentum exsulia discordem Deam,
Revocabo[1] in auras, verbera incutient manus
Viperia nostrae.
Michael. Mentis hinc alio procul
Virus sagittes? regnet in terris honos
Divum, triumphet.
Invidia. Regnet hic coelis satis.
Michael. Terrisque.
Invidia. Divos terra non vilis decet.
Michael. Celumque.
Invidia. Potius viperis corpus meis
Arcebo rabida vile prostratum solo.
Michael. Frustra furores evomis, cede aut cades.
Invidia. Avernus aderit, franget inceptum male.

[1] Remeabo.

Michael. Olympus aderit, faciet inceptum bene.
Invidia. Frustra tegetur ille quem inferi petunt.
Michael. Frustra petetur ille quem superi tegunt.

SCÆNA 6a.

PARALITICUS, APHONOS, DEMONIACUS, MISERICORS, CARITIUS, LATRIA.

Paraliticus. Heu quantus agitat corpus infirmum tremor
Vix rupta adherent membra dilacero cuti
Dieque nocteque queror, insanum caput.
Demoniacus. Vah furere furere, quere fluctivagam nigri
Cymbam Charontis, furere quere Tartarum.
[1]Nunquamne miseris lucis usura frui
Meliore dabitur? Vita, non vita.
Aphonos. Au, be, hau.
Demoniacus. Vah, vah.
Paraliticus. Caduca vita premitur erumna undique.
Tutusque nullus oritur e coelo dies.
Latria. Molire gressus moesta properato phalanx
Exueque pulle frontis exorto novo
Nubila nitore, surgit erumnis novae
Portus salutis, mox sacrum Presul frequens
Nobile Vedasti pignus ad cellam refert.
Huc vos citate pariter acceleres pedes
Instate calidis precibus afflictis malis
Aderit levamen Presul hic astris potens.
Caritius. Celerate gressus, lenta quid retinet mora?
Demoniacus. Quo trahitis?
Caritius. Ad cymbam Stygis ad Orcum celer
Accurre.
Demoniacus. Curro, curro precipitem date.
Caritius. Sede hac quietus comprime actutum pedes.
Paraliticus. Satis est viarum corpus hic sacrum moror.
Barbarus. Adhibete ramos liliis niteat via,
Rosis, ligustris undique parietes novo
Decorentur ostro Presulum instant agmina.
Mego. Tuto quadrabit ramus affixus loco.

---

1 Misericors.

Tuccius. Gratos odores thure succenso paro.
Barbarus. Properate en ecce tota ruit obvia cohors.

SCÆNA 7ª.

OMNES ACTORES: LATRIA, AUDOMARUS, LAMBERTUS,[1] THEMIUS, PRUDENS, ETC.

Latria. Spargite rubentes flore purpureo rosas
Passim plateis serta collecta undique
Arbosque niteat, resonet et festum melos
Modosque cantor ore predulces sciat.

Primus Puer.

Terris, polis beatum
Perenne vive nomen.

Puer 2us.

Cadat, cadat caduca
Mortale quidquid aura
Vultu tegit sereno.

Puer 3us.

Vivat pugil beatus,
Vivat choris beatus,
Superis omnis[2] perennet.

Omnes simul.

Terris, polis beatum
Perenne vive nomen.

Latria. Levate fessas Presulis vires dia
Et sede pignus colite depositum brevi.[3]
Audomarus. O Christe coelo lucis exiguum jubar
Oculis refunde, cernere sacratum decus
Solamen illud ultimum canis meis.
Ecce novus oculis splendor irradiat meis.
Prudens. Stupescit animus: Morinus en Presul sibi
Oculis tuetur redditis solis jubar.
Constans. Attonitus heres lumina inflectit procul!
Themius. Perlustrat oculis Lipsana arca condita.

---

[1] Caligonus, Constans. [2] Ovans. [3] Sacra.

Caligonus. Stupenda video cernit Audomarus diem.
Audomarus. Christe age, priores redde nebulosas meis
Oculis tenebras, plus satis votis datum est.
Lambertus. Age luce melius fruere donata ethere
Aliaque funde vota.
Audomarus. Quis frui tenebris vetat?
Placent tenebrae.
Lambertus. Luce quid frui vetat?
Audomarus. Nimium est periclum lucis.
Lambertus. Hi juvenem gravent
Levem timores, non senes.
Audomarus. Senes simul.
Lambertus. Non coeli[1] Athletas.
Audomarus. Arce fi coeli manent
Supera beati : semper hac vita gravent.
Beatus ille, quisquis alieno sapit
Doctus malo, olim luce liberior sua
Athleta fortis David illapsus ruit.
Autbertus. Documenta pandis posteris Presul nova.
He cerne quisquis pascis aspectum vagus
Aciemque turpi luminum spectro foves.
Audomarus. Signo hoc Vedasti clarior virtus micat,
Hinc ferte grates rursus et lituus strepat,
Ovansque subeat ordinem primum phalanx.
Latria. Agite nigrantis germina baratri cites
Celerate gressus.
Idololatria. Mihi tumet totum jecur
Biliquе rabida tota per furias agor.

SCÆNA 8ª ET ULTIMA.

FIDEM, PARALITICUS, DEMONIACUS ET APHONOS,[2] ETC.

Paraliticus. Gravibus sacratae reliquiae auxilium malis
Aliquod citate.
Caritius. Gravibus erumnis modum
Facilem Vedaste statue, terrebunt tuae
Hostem vel umbrae.

---

[1] Nobilem. [2] Loquetus.

Latria. Instate calidioribus,
Votis Vedastus facilis optatis favent.

Paraliticus. Adesto presul, adesto succurre ethere
Morbis serenus, fulcra precoci impete
Dilapsa terram verberant, artus suo
Constant loco.

Aphonus. Soluta lingua nexibus
Potis est profari quid libet.

Demonia. Cessit loco
Infensus hostis predo truculentus meis
Abiere diri turbines fibris procul.
Quanam rependam Presuli grates prece?
Superoque divum numini quantas feram!

Latria. Tu vero tantum nobilis pheretrum phalanx
Urbisque sacra Lipsana eternum fove.

Caligonus. Vivet perenni Presulis pignus fibra.

Philiparcus. Totum Vedasto funditus sparsum solo
Fundam cruorem.

Metanor. Nobile per enses decus
Medios tuebor, Presuli et totam lubens
Animam litabo.

Latria. Gratus est procerum favor.
Sic agite ferrum militet vestrum etheri,
Ætasque votum nulla subripiat ratum.

Prudens. Hunc animum et urbis consules clari toga
Referent patrone.

Constans. Mente perpetua manet
Merito clientum jura qui sanxit fidem
Legesque superis statuit edoctus polis.

Themius. Urbis patronum tota posteritas cliens
Colet Vedastum, signa quem dia ethere
Donata terris nobilem et clarum beant.

Victor. Regnet, perennet, gloria mysta inclytus.

Omnes simul. Regnet, perennet, gloria mysta inclytus.

Latria. Hoc calle proceres pergite et vocem ciat
Plebes sonoram, jubilum superis date.
Vos ordo quos ad ardua sacratus vocat
Mactate pugiles mentis excelsa indoles
Factis nitescat arduis : surgent casa
Olim columne posteris clara magis.

Hac purpurata veste clarescent patres,
Apexque honorum varius aptatus nitet
Septena terris nobili Presul dabit
Unus tiara lumina : hec quando tholis
eVeCta In aera CeLLa sVCCresCet Mage.
Agite futurae lampades olim novae[1]
Induite mentes Presuli unanimes sacrum
Deferte honorem, Presulis callem simul
Fovete fortes ampla vos merces manet.

Autbertus. Tantos favores celitum plebes canit,
Iteraque plausus tota nobilium phalanx.

Lambertus. Regnet Vedastus celicis regnet choris.

Caligonus. Regnet, triumphet, celicis junctus choris.

Omnes simul. Regnet, triumphet, celicis junctus choris.

Latria. Bene est, profunde monstra per syrtes Stygis
Celerate, terris foedus eternum manet
Ortumque lucet clarius coelis jubar.

Angelus. Geminate plausus buccinae rursum strepant.

EPILOGUS.

Occiduus undis Cinthius mergit caput
Et scena versa fronte depositis abit
Sero cothurnis : sacra tu procerum phalanx
Coetusque nobilis virum applaude et vale.

Ad maiorem Dei gloriam et sancti Vedasti.

---

[1] Novas.

www.ingramcontent.com/pod-product-compliance
Lightning Source LLC
Chambersburg PA
CBHW020938030726
47496CB00005B/1252

* 9 7 8 3 3 3 7 3 9 3 5 3 3 *